MAKING YOU MINE

MAKING YOU MINE

(The Moreno Brothers series #5)

Elizabeth Reyes

MAKING YOU MINE

Elizabeth Reyes
Copyright © 2011
All Rights Reserved.

AUTHOR'S NOTE

Cover art © Dundanim
http://www.dreamstime.com/Dundanim_info

Layout provided by Everything Indie
http://www.everything-indie.com

Dedicated to three people. My parents who without your wisdom, support and unconditional love I would not be the person I am today. And to Tia Mague. You will forever be in my heart. Amor eterno, e inolvidable.

Prologue
The Hangover

It took a few minutes for the blurry room to come into focus. That's when Salvador Moreno realized he wasn't dreaming. The agonizing throbbing in his head was real. He turned his body slowly and very cautiously so as to not further the strength of the pounding. Something jerked in his stomach and his mouth began to water. "Oh, shit."

He froze, willing the nausea to go away. After a few moments it did. He glanced around, assessing his predicament. Two things were clear: he was buck-naked and he wasn't home. Then it dawned on him—the bachelor party. No, he wasn't home. He wasn't even in California. He was in none other than sin city. Las Vegas.

Sal sat up, inching his way to the side of the bed, careful not to stir up trouble in his stomach. He blinked hard when he saw them. As if it would make them go away, he blinked again—still there—a pair of panties— a very sexy pair of black panties. They adorned the floor just off the side of the bed.

Panicked, he tried to remember what happened the night before, but everything was a blur. One thing he *did* remember was that he and his buddies weren't supposed to leave the casino. Not with the amount of bars and clubs readily available here at the Hard Rock Café, where they were staying. They could party their asses off without ever having to step foot outside the casino doors.

The only thing he recalled were the first few hours of drinking at the bar, then at a nightclub. After that, things got choppy. The round of shots kept coming. But he didn't remember any girls. Hooking up was the last thing on his mind.

Glancing around the room for any other clues, he noticed the folded note on the nightstand. His name was hand-written on the outside. He stared at it for a second, before reaching for it. Almost afraid to open it, he held it and squeezed his eyes shut. The thrumming of the blood pumping through his veins continued in his ears.

Opening only one eye, he glanced at the note and flipped it open.

Went to get us some real coffee. Be back in a few! XOXO.

His stomach did a flip and he thought he was going to be sick. Who the hell had he brought back to the r-oom with him? He stood up and began to pace, running his fingers through his hair. Fuck the headache — what the hell had he done? But he couldn't forget the nausea that easily. It was brutal and it came without warning.

He rushed to the restroom and threw up. With the water running while he rinsed his face he hadn't heard the door open.

"How you feeling?"

Sal spun around, and the room spun with him, causing him to nearly lose his balance. It was a good thing he held on to the vanity for support, because his legs almost gave out on him when he saw her. This was e-ven worse than what he'd imagined.

CHAPTER 1
Three Months EARLIER

As usual, Grace barely made it to class on time. Her morning interview had gone on longer than she expected. And for what? *Sorry but we're looking for someone more experienced.* With her years of cooking in Mexico, she had more than enough experience. Who cared if she was still in culinary school? Some of the required classes she took were such a joke. Her cooking skills were far beyond them.

Joey leaned over as she took her seat. "Miss the bus again?"

She frowned while pulling her notebook out of her backpack. "No. The stupid interview went on too long."

"Not good?"

She shook her head.

Joey reached over and squeezed her hand. "Well, don't give up. It'll happen. You'll see."

Grace didn't even bother trying to smile. She was so frustrated. Joey was the only friend she'd made in culinary school in all three years she'd attended. She met him when she first started and he was now one of the most loyal and loving friends she'd ever had. At first, she had a huge crush on him, until she found out he was living with his long-time boyfriend.

When she met his boyfriend Taylor, she fell in love with him, too. Joey and Taylor were perfect for each other. Now they were her two best friends. Finally, she'd found friends her age to talk to and hang out with since she'd moved here from El Paso. Just two years after she graduated high school, her mom met a trucker from California. Within a month, they were married and Grace and her younger sister Rose were hauled out to live in California. Neither had been happy about it, especially Rose, who was just about to finish middle school at the time. Since then her mom had divorced and remarried. She was on a roll with the truckers. Grace was now determined to make a name for herself and get her and her sister out of her step-father's clutches.

She put on the reading glasses she'd bought at the drugstore on her way to class and turned to Joey. "What do think?"

"Since when do you need glasses?"

"I don't, but I'm hoping they'll make me look older. I have another interview after class."

He gave her a look. "They'll know how old you are as soon as they read it on your application."

She tried not to smile, but she didn't respond. Joey knew her too well. "Grace?"

"Hmm?"

"You didn't lie about your age did you?"

She pretended to be completely absorbed in what she was reading, but the truth was that the glasses made her dizzy. Blinking hard, she continued to stare at the blurry notebook in front of her.

Joey nudged her. "I can't believe you. You don't think they'll find out when you have to show them your I.D.?"

She pulled off the glasses that had begun to give her a headache and rubbed her eyes. "I don't have to show them. It's already filled in on the application. I just changed the year so they'll think I'm twenty-three."

"Oh, please!" He waved a hand at her. "Honey, you don't even look your age, much less two years older."

She turned to him disheartened. "Really?"

"That's a good thing. Why would you wanna look older?"

"Because so far every stupid restaurant I've applied to, has taken one look at me and dismissed me, like there's no way I could know what I'm doing. If I could just get my foot in the door and show them what I can do, I know they'll give me a chance." She pulled her long hair up in a bun and put the glasses back on. "How's this?"

He smiled. "Adorable—but twenty-three—no way."

Her shoulders dropped. "Well, I don't care. I think I can do this." She lifted her chin. "I'll walk in there with confidence. All I need is one chance to prove myself. Then I can tell them the truth about my age and it won't matter."

Joey shook his head and started writing in his notebook. "Where are you applying now?"

She leaned over and whispered, "Moreno's, in La Jolla."

"Why are you whispering?" he whispered back without even looking at her.

Grace glanced at the girls in the front row of the class and continued to whisper, "Because," she gestured to the girls with her pen. "they're always going on and on about the guys that run the place." She rolled her eyes. "The three *dreamy* brothers. I don't want them to hear, and think that's the reason I'm applying there."

Joey turned to her. "Why *are* you applying there?

That's like thirty minutes away by a car. Even longer for you, since you'll be taking the bus."

"Are you kidding me? Do you know what working at a restaurant like that would do for my résumé? It's totally worth the time it'll take me to get there."

Joey smirked. "Are you sure the *dreamy* Moreno brothers are not why you're going all the way out there?"

She rolled her eyes again and immediately regretted it. With the glasses on it gave her a headache. She pulled them off, squeezing the bridge of her nose. "Trust me, I'm not looking to get swept up by some *Mr. Suave*. The way they talk about them, that's what they sound like. With only one left on the market I'm sure he's quite full of himself, probably loving all the attention, too. No thanks."

"Sounds like you've been doing a lot of listening."

"No," she said, too quickly, then smiled at him and admitted, "Well, yeah, but only since I heard them mention how young the brothers are and how they run the show now—not their parents. I figured maybe they'll be more open-minded than some of these older, unbending jerks I've interviewed with."

Joey raised his eyebrows. "Good point."

Grace smiled. Maybe she actually had a chance this time. She could only pray. Time was running out. She needed a job *now*, but she refused to settle for the only ones she could get.

After class, Joey insisted on taking her backpack home so she wouldn't have to walk into her interview with it. He said he'd drop it off at her apartment later. He felt bad about not being able to offer her a ride but he had another class he just couldn't miss. He squeezed her tight as he always did, wishing her good luck and she made her way to the bus stop.

*

Sal sat in the back room of the restaurant, skimming through the applications from the past week. All of the interviews had been such a waste of time. Alex walked in and dropped a file on the desk.

"Stop being such a hard ass and hire someone already. We need the help."

Sal picked up the file and pulled out the papers. "I'm not hiring just anyone, Alex. They don't have to be the best, but we do have standards."

Ever since they made extensive renovations to their family's Mexican restaurant, including adding a second floor and expanding the bar area, business had been booming. They could barely keep up. In the restaurant business, customer service was crucial. It could make or break you. Sal knew this but everyone he'd interviewed that week was grossly unqualified.

Word was already getting out that the second generation was taking over the restaurant. They had a reputation to keep up.

"I thought you had school today?"

"I do." Alex rushed by him, digging through one of the drawers in the desk. "I left a book I need here last night."

Technically, his younger brother Alex had taken over the restaurant. But ever since Alex had gone back to school, Sal had offered to help out. Sal had plans of opening up a few more restaurants. His youngest brother Angel and his wife ran the second restaurant over on the marina. Sal was more of an overseer of both. He'd finally gotten his master's in business management and had big plans for the family restaurant. For now, those plans were temporarily on hold. That was just until Alex could finish school. In the meantime, he was meeting with potential investors and looking into any and all possible options.

As big and threatening as Alex looked on the outside, he was soft when it came to his employees. Sal knew better. They had to hire quality. In a way, he was glad Alex was too busy to do the interviewing himself.

Alex grabbed the book and rushed out of the office. "I'm out, Sal. I'm late. Hire some cooks already. You're killing me."

Sal nodded, waving him away. His next interview was probably out front waiting for him. He stood up and walked out the office. He read her application and frowned when he saw the age. Graciela Zendejas, twenty-three. *Great*. And she was applying for the head chef position. Yeah, that was going to happen.

There were only customers out front. Sal glanced at his watch. It was ten after two. Her interview was set for two. Strike two. Punctuality was a must. If this girl couldn't even make the interview on time, how was he supposed to take her seriously? Everyone else he'd interviewed had either been on time or early.

Sal stopped at the refrigerator behind the bar and pulled out an energy drink. He'd just taken his first sip, when he saw the young girl walk in the front door. He could only assume this was his next interviewee. Her application said twenty-three, but she hardly looked it. Maybe this was someone else.

She *had* to be here for an interview because she held some kind of paperwork in her arm and seemed a bit lost. She wasn't as professionally dressed as some of the other interviewees but at least she'd worn a dress.

A loose, unflattering one but it would do. Her hair was in a tight bun and she wore glasses. The dark rimmed kind, that only teachers and older women wore. He jotted three words down: *trying too hard.* Even though she was late, she didn't seem to be in much of a hurry. She strutted in like she owned the place. The hostess at the front turned to Sal after the girl stopped to ask her something. Sal nodded and waved her over to a corner booth. He walked over already expecting another frustrating interview. Alex wouldn't be happy.

Julie, one of the waitresses, stopped him on his way to meet with Graciela. "Real quick. Can you make sure I'm off next Friday? I forgot to put in my request."

"I'm pretty sure Alex already made that schedule."

She squeezed her hands together in front of her. "Please! I need that day off. My best friend is gonna kill me. I was supposed to request the day off a long time ago."

Sal frowned but nodded. "If he scheduled you, I'll change it but next time don't forget."

Julie squealed and hugged him. Someone behind them cleared their throat loudly.

Sal turned around. Seeing her this close made her young age even more noticeable. He glanced back down at her résumé. No way was she twenty-three.

She took the initiative. "Hello." She held her hand out. "I'm Graciela Zendejas."

She was average height, and average looking all around except for the big brown perfectly almond shaped eyes. He smirked at her attempt to mask her accent. Though she rolled her r's, she did a good job of toning down the accent, but it wasn't entirely gone.

"I'm Sal Moreno." He reached his hand out and

took her firm handshake. "My parents own this restaurant, Graciela." He rolled his r's pretty well, if he did say so himself. "Is it okay if I call you Grace?"

"No. I prefer Graciela."

Her immediate and curt response took him by surprise. "Okay... Graciela. Have a seat."

He couldn't help notice what perfect posture she had and how she held her shoulders so high even when she sat. Her chin was up a bit as well. Sal glanced down at the paperwork and read the experience she had. She'd written paragraphs about her experience cooking with her grandmother but valid restaurant experience — not much.

"Okay," he smiled. "So it says here you'd like to be considered for the head cook."

"Yes." She nodded.

"But you don't have a lot of experience and you're still in culinary school."

"I have a lifetime of experience, Mr. Moreno." She pronounced his last name just as his parents did, rolling the r and short e as in *end* rather than the long e as in *eat* like *he* pronounced it and had grown accustomed hearing it. "My grandmother owned a restaurant in Juarez and I worked there since I was a child." She held her chin up a little higher. "As a cook."

Sal had to glance away from the big dark eyes that peered at him accusingly as if he just insulted her. "I see." He examined the rest of her résumé. "I was talking about professional experience."

"Mr. Moreno — "

"Call me Sal," he said, without looking up from her résumé. Her icy demeanor was beginning to annoy him.

"Mr. Moreno," she continued, ignoring his request.

"My grandmother's restaurant in Juarez was one of the most renowned restaurants for years and she trusted me in the kitchen even when I was ten, because she taught me everything she knew."

Sal glanced up at her, noticing how her eyes seemed to have darkened even more. "That's great, *Ms.* Zendejas."

Knowing it would be inappropriate, not to mention illegal, to ask he emphasized the *Ms.* and waited for her to correct him. Her expression remained rigid. Though he was certain because of her age, that she was a Ms. and not a Mrs., for some reason he was relieved that she didn't correct him. Maybe it was because he found her obvious contempt for him somewhat amusing. He wasn't used to women being put off by him. "It's just that for head chef, we're looking for a little more experience than—"

"Than a lifetime?"

"Well, Grace—"

"Graciela."

Sal pressed his lips together breathing in through his nostrils and nodded. "I'm sorry, Graciela. Our restaurant is quite renowned in San Diego County—"

"I've heard plenty about your restaurant. I only apply where I'd be proud to work. Moreno's has an impeccable reputation for serving only the most authentic dishes. I think I would bring my experience as a lifetime chef—"

"Graciela, you're only twenty-three. As much as I would love to accept your experience in cooking at your grandmother's restaurant, as a *lifetime* of experience, I just can't justify hiring a culinary student as a head chef."

"Give me a chance. I promise I won't disappoint

you, Mr. Moreno."

Sal frowned, flipping over to the next page in her résumé. "You have a bartender's certification?"

"Yes." She sat up again with a sharp arch of her brow. "But that's not what I'm applying for."

Sal glanced up at her. She looked so determined — and angry. "Well, I have openings for bartenders. We need them immediately." He went back to reading her résumé because her dark piercing eyes were beginning to distract him. "You have a lot more experience in that area. I could consider you as a bartender and maybe when things got slow, I could get you in the kitchen to help out."

"I could cook something for you; so you can see for yourself." The detail of her eyes was becoming increasingly distracting. She wore no makeup. He was just beginning to take in the mesmerizing way her lashes draped over them, when her eyes suddenly crossed completely, as if to stare at her nose. She took her glasses off and squeezed her eyes shut.

"You okay?"

Her eyebrow lifted again, and she put her glasses back on. "Yes, I'm fine."

He shook off the distraction. "Ms. Zendejas, I have no doubt by your passion that you're a good cook. Unfortunately, we need cooks with working experience in a fast paced environment like —"

"Have you ever been to Juarez, Mr. Moreno?" She spoke almost through her teeth. Sal wondered if she'd ever looked into interview etiquette. Did she really think her constant interruptions were going to buy her points?

"Yes, I have, actually."

"It doesn't get more fast paced than that, when it

comes to preparing Mexican cuisine, Mr. Moreno."

"Can you stop calling me that?" Unlike his brothers, Sal had never been short on patience, but something about her refusing to call him by his first name had begun to get to him.

Graciela slid out of the booth. Sal hurried to slide out of his side and stood up ready to face off with her.

"Will you be considering me for the position?"

"As a head chef? No. But I do need a bartender."

If looks could kill, he'd be a stinking corpse. "When can I expect an answer?"

"Well, I'll have to discuss it with my brother but I'll get back to you."

"Thank you." With that, she spun around and walked away.

Sal tried not to, but he couldn't help take in her long legs and the behind that swayed just under the soft fabric of her dress. As annoying as she was, he had to admit she'd managed to intrigue him. Aside from her eyes, nothing else really stood out about her looks; in fact he probably wouldn't have looked twice if he passed her on the street, but in a weird way her spunk had amused him. He sat down to examine her résumé a little further. It didn't take long to find a small, but significant, inconsistency about her age. He knew it. The disappointment came as a surprise. Strike three.

CHAPTER 2

The bus rolled through the picturesque streets of downtown La Jolla and out into the beat up neighborhood of Chula Vista. Grace stared out the window, mentally going over her last interview. She'd thrown the stupid glasses away as soon as she walked out. Wearing them that whole time had been torture. Her headache had just begun to subside.

She exited the bus two streets before her usual stop. She had to swing by the meat market and pick up a few drumsticks. Chicken soup was on the menu for tonight's dinner.

She hurried into the small mom-and-pop market, trying to snap out of the mood she'd fallen into during the interview.

"*Buenas tardes Señorita Zendejas.*" Armando, one of the butchers behind the counter, smiled brightly.

"*Buenas tardes.*" She didn't even try to match the smile.

She pointed at what she wanted and let him know how much. Taking deep frustrated breaths, she grabbed an onion and a few carrots while Armando bagged up her drumsticks.

The disappointment weighed heavily—another interview gone south before it even started. Grace had seen the way he looked at her before he even knew anything about her. Only that she was way too young, which meant inexperienced. She was so sick of the assumptions.

So much for *younger* meaning *open minded*. The brother she spoke with dismissed her experience as unprofessional. It was infuriating. For him to deem her experience as unprofessional just because it was in her grandmother's restaurant in Mexico was reprehensible. Where did he think all of his authentic dishes originated anyway? The more she thought about it, the angrier it made her.

The only thing the girls in her class had been right about was his looks. He certainly wasn't hard on the eyes. But even his heavy lashes and perfectly dimpled smile didn't erase the fact that he'd been just like all the other presumptuous hiring managers. That unattractive quality alone was enough to ugly any man in her head, no matter how good-looking he was on the outside.

She purchased her items and walked out into the declining sunlight. The damned buses were so undependable. She didn't bother waiting for one. Instead she hurried along the few blocks to her apartment.

Ruben, her stepfather, was passed out on the sofa when she walked in. She winced, closing the door as quietly as possible. The keys in her hand jingled as she made her way past him. *Damn.*

Ruben shifted on the sofa, grunting. One lazy eyelid lifted. When he saw her, he sat up. "Did you get the job?"

Grace set her bag of groceries on the small kitchen table and began to pull things out. "I don't know yet." She focused on the bag, not wanting to face him. "They're supposed to get back to me."

She wouldn't mention that morning's flat out *no*, in her first interview. The sofa rattled and squeaked, and she knew he was getting up. "Well the rent's not gonna pay itself. Your mom's piddly check, from the few hours she puts in at that cafeteria, ain't cutting it anymore."

He came up from behind her and she walked around the table. He had a habit of standing too close to her and it repulsed her. "Well, maybe you should start looking for a job."

He cackled. "No way, and give up my unemployment check? Don't be stupid."

"You're not gonna be able to collect that forever. It's been almost a year."

"Yeah, well when the checks stop coming I'll start looking." He walked around the table in the small kitchen. "In the mean time... " He paused when he saw her make her way around the table again. She didn't care if he noticed her obvious disgust for him.

"What the hell's your problem?" The smirk on his unshaven swollen face was teasing. "I ain't gonna bite you."

Grace said nothing. She grabbed her purse and headed to her room down the hall. She could still hear his cackles even as she closed the door behind her. The small room she shared with her sister was a complete contrast to the rest of the apartment. While the front room and kitchen were always a cluttered mess, her room was immaculate.

She couldn't stand clutter. Though she did her best to try to keep the rest of the apartment as tidy as her room, it was impossible with both Ruben and her mom being slobs.

A few stray rays of paling sunlight seeped in through the blinds as she walked to the closet. Lately, she'd been checking and double-checking the wooded box tucked up behind her sister's stuffed animals. In it was all the money she had. Money she'd worked long and hard to earn. She'd sooner trust a stranger than her own step-dad. He'd be out of money soon and just like before he started collecting unemployment, he'd come sniffing around her room.

Ruben knew she'd been saving up for years to move out. She was *this close* to moving in with Joey and Taylor. They had an extra room in their apartment and could use the help with the rent. She was more than anxious to, especially since her younger sister Rosie confessed to her that their step-dad had been giving her the creeps. The depraved animal had been sizing up a fifteen-year girl. It was disgusting. Joey had actually offered to let her sister stay with them as well for only Grace's share of the rent. Then of course, she lost her job.

Knowing she had no choice but to stick around, Grace had decided they'd tell her mom about her step-dad. She took a deep breath, trying to shake off the pain of her mother's reaction when they'd told her. She dismissed them immediately, calling them both liars and accusing them of hating Ruben to the point they'd make up outlandish accusations. When they tried to argue their case, she tried to make them feel guilty by crying and saying they were ganging up on her.

This was months ago and both she and Rosie had agreed not to bring it up again. It was pointless. Their mother was intent on keeping Ruben around. At least for now anyway. Her mother hated work of any kind. The only reason she'd taken the job at the school cafeteria was because it was only two hours a day. But Grace knew the minute her mother was able to, she'd quit. Her only chance of that, was if Ruben, or any man would be there to support her. So until she found a replacement for Ruben, he wasn't going anywhere.

Grace had already threatened to move out just before she lost her job. Now she was forced to suck up her pride and hang around at least until she could afford to not only get her own place but to take Rosie with her. Her mother wouldn't object to Rosie leaving. She'd never made it a secret that both Grace and Rosie were nothing but a burden to her, especially after their dad died.

She'd just tucked the box back behind the stuffed animals, when the bedroom door opened. She flung her hands behind her, not wanting whoever it was to see where they had been.

"What happened with the job?"

Her mom was done up again. Grace knew she was making every effort to find a replacement for Ruben already. Ruben was husband number four since her dad died. But since Ruben was laid off and showing no promise in finding another job anytime soon, her mother had gone on the lurk. Grace recognized the signs immediately. The sexier clothes, heavier makeup and perfume. Yep, Ruben had one foot out the door already.

"They said they'll get back to me."

Her mom stepped all the way in and closed the door behind her. "Have you applied as a bartender anywhere?"

Grace looked away without answering.

"Graciela, I asked you a question."

"Not really." She pulling a bag out of the closet. "But it's on my résumé, that I'm certified... "

"It damn well better be. I didn't pay for that bartending course for nothing. Why haven't you applied? I thought you said as soon as you turned twenty-one, you would?" Her mother crossed her arms. "Your birthday was over a month ago."

Grace sat down on her bed and pulled her notebook out of the bag. "The restaurant I applied to today has openings for bartenders. They said they'd call me."

Ruben yelled out from the front room. "What's for dinner?"

Her mother peered at her. "C'mon, Ms. Chef. Show us what you got."

Grace closed her notebook and stood up. Just before opening the door her mother stopped and turned to her. "Just so you know. I quit my job today. I couldn't stand that damn manager. Things are gonna get really tight around here, so I'd stop being so picky about where you apply if I were you."

*

Friday nights were especially busy lately. The TGIF specials that Moreno's offered for happy hour brought in enough business to carry over into the late hours. The newly remodeled sports bar area with the state-of-the-art flat screens also helped. Sal had hoped to get another bartender hired by this weekend. Unfortunately, the only person he'd interviewed that was even remotely qualified was the Zendejas girl.

Of course, Alex thought Sal was overreacting about her lying on her application. He actually laughed when Sal told him about the other two strikes against her. No matter how trivial Alex thought it was, Sal wasn't having it. If she was bold enough to lie about her age, no telling what else she'd be willing to lie about. The last thing he needed was to bring someone into the family business with integrity issues.

Truth was, he'd wasted way too much time already thinking about Ms. Zendejas. He'd actually gone back to read her résumé several more times. He'd even considered calling her and asking straight out why she lied. But something told him not to. It was probably better that he just let it go. At twenty-one, she couldn't have much experience anyway so what difference would it make?

Sal sat back and chewed the end of his pen. With that cute little accent and those hypnotic eyes, she'd be more of a distraction than any help. Nope. He threw her résumé back in the desk file. He was done thinking about her.

"I hope you have some more interviews lined up for today, Sal." Alex stalked into the back office. "I'm staying tonight to help out at the bar. Luis called in sick again and we were already short."

Sal winced. The one day he had to leave early, their best bartender calls in sick. "I got a few interviews lined up today." He turned to Alex, who was busy tying an apron around his waist. "Two of them are for the cook positions. One actually has some experience."

Alex looked up at him with a frown. "What about the other one?"

Sal shook his head. "Not much, but we'll see."

Oscar, one of their newer waiters, flew in the back and stopped when he saw Sal. "Suit and tie again, Sal?" he smirked. "What are you all dolled up for this time?"

Sal had gone against his own rules and hired a friend. Oscar had attended college with Sal for a while, until he got a girl pregnant and had to drop out to work full-time. Sal always knew women would be Oscar's failing. He went through them like the restaurant went through beans and rice.

There was no way Oscar and this girl would last, e-ven with a baby. Oscar always thought with the wrong head. So, of course, things ended badly between him and the girl. Oscar's parents said they'd help him out financially, if he went back to school. Having a baby wasn't cheap, though. He still needed to bring in some more money. That's when Sal stepped up and offered to let him work at the restaurant part-time.

"I got a meeting with some investors today."

Oscar continued to gawk, amused. "Ah, so that's what's up with the power suits these days."

"Nah," Alex added with a smirk. "I think he just likes intimidating potential new hires."

Oscar started putting on his apron. "Yep, I was to-tally intimidated when he interviewed me."

Alex chuckled. Sal rolled his eyes. "Shouldn't you two comedians be out there already? I thought we were busy."

Oscar pretended to crack a whip. "See what I mean?" He grinned at Sal. "I'm getting all intimidated again."

Oscar and Alex walked out of the back office but not before adding a few more wisecracks at Sal's ex-pense.

By that afternoon, Sal had finally hired a new cook but he wasn't entirely sure about it. There was one po-tential bartender but the idiot had forgotten to bring in his certification; otherwise Sal might have had another one ready to hire. He knew Alex was getting desperate for help. The guy's résumé looked great, but then so had Graciela's. Sal frowned before dropping the files on the desk in the back.

He grabbed his cell off the desk and rushed out.

"Did you hire anyone?" Alex asked, as he rushed by him.

"We got a cook." Sal winked, walking backwards. "And maybe a bartender, but he needs to bring in his credentials. I'll get back as soon as this meeting is over to help out."

Alex didn't exactly look thrilled but the relentless scowl softened. Any business owner would feel giddy about the amount of cars Sal saw waiting to make a left turn into their parking lot. But Sal was beginning to worry about being able to handle the kind of business they were generating.

The investors he was meeting with today had mentioned the possibility of opening several more restaurants. He was having a hard enough time getting qualified employees for one restaurant; how in the world would he staff several more?

*

Three days had gone by since her interview at Moreno's and still no call. Grace could kick herself for not jumping at the offer of the bartending position. She was too wound up to appreciate the opportunity Sal had offered. This was the closest she'd been to possibly getting her feet into a kitchen at a restaurant of that caliber.

She thought about calling but decided it was best if she spoke with him face to face. Maybe even apologize for her attitude that day. She'd been so frustrated from all the rejections everywhere else that she let it out on him.

The restaurant was not surprisingly busy when she arrived. She'd heard so much about it over the years but she'd never had the pleasure of eating there herself. The hostess, who obviously didn't recognize her from the day of the interview motioned for her to give her a second. She was busy getting a large group to their table.

Grace glanced around, looking for Sal. The restaurant was amazing. She was so riled up the day of the interview, she'd hardly had time to take it all in. The dramatic arches and all the artwork that adorned the walls reminded her so much of Mexico. It was genuinely true to the culture, unlike some of the cheesier restaurants she'd been to. The decoration was tasteful and not overdone.

As she wandered through one of the archways into the main dining area, she was drawn to one of the painted murals on the brick wall—an older Mexican woman making handmade tortillas. Immediately it brought a lump to her throat. She missed her grandmother terribly. Grace tried to shake off the overwhelming emotion. She hadn't allowed herself to become emotional over her grandmother's or her father's deaths in years, and this was definitely not the time or place.

The sudden dread of not being able to hold it together, made her spin around and head back to the door. In her haste, she didn't even see the waiter behind her and collided with him.

"Whoa, sorry are you okay?" He pulled the tray he was holding away from her, so he wouldn't spill anything on her.

"I'm so sorry." She felt like a fool. "I didn't—"

"It's okay. Don't worry about it." The waiter looked over her shoulder and smirked. "You just *had* to be watching didn't you?"

Grace turned to see who he was talking to. A guy

who looked just like Sal, only with twice the brawn, was trying not to smile. The undeniable Moreno dimples she'd heard so much about gave him away. He had to be one of the other brothers. Well, the girls had certainly been right about the looks running in this family. So far, the first two brothers she'd met had fit the gushing descriptions right on.

Maybe she'd have better luck with this brother. As big and daunting as he looked, seeing him have a good time with the waiter, already gave her hope that he wouldn't be as uptight as Sal.

"You sure you're okay, sweetheart?" he asked as he approached her.

"I'm fine," she smiled, even though she wasn't sure she liked the term of endearment. "It was my fault actually."

"Nope." He shook his head. "Here at Moreno's, the customer is always right. I apologize for my klutzy waiter."

The waiter rolled his eyes. "I already apologized."

"It's okay, really. I'm not even a customer."

With an eyebrow raised, he held out his hand. "Okay, I'm Alex." She shook his hand. "I run the restaurant. What can I do for you?"

The waiter she'd nearly knocked over nodded at her before walking away in a hurry. She glanced at him, then back at Alex. "I uh, was here the other day for an interview." Her stomach churned. "Sal, I believe he's your brother?"

Alex nodded but said nothing.

"He said there were immediate openings for bartenders. I'm certified and have a few years experience. He said he'd call me after he talked to you. I was just wondering if... "

Alex's lips curved into a slow smile. "Yeah, he mentioned something like that. Is it okay if we talk over here?" He motioned toward the bar area.

She nodded and followed him through the busy restaurant. Alex turned back as he walked. "What was your name again?"

"Graciela," she said quickly then added, "Zendejas. Graciela Zendejas."

He smiled even bigger. "Yeah, you're the one."

"What does that mean?" She tried not to sound as defensive as she felt.

"You're the one he mentioned," he said taking a seat at the bar.

Humor danced in Alex's eyes, making Grace wonder just what the hell Sal had *mentioned*. She crossed her arms in front of her, feeling her cheeks warm.

Alex didn't seem fazed at all by her glaring eyes. Instead he smirked leaning an elbow on the bar. "Tell me something. How does someone who just turned twenty-one, have any experience in bartending?"

Grace didn't flinch. With her arms still tightly wound in front of her, she shifted her weight and responded. "I used to live in El Paso. The bartending age in Texas is eighteen." She lifted her chin, trying not to think about the fact that they caught the age difference. "I've also done a lot of bartending over the border in Mexico."

For once, he stopped smirking and she seemed to have his attention. "So you really know how to bartend?"

"Yes." Grace felt an ounce of hope creep in.

"Can you make Mojitos?"

She almost laughed. "I've been making them since I was a kid."

He stood up off the stool. "You're kidding?"

"No." Her eyes followed him as he walked around the bar. "I can make anything you want me to."

"C'mere." He pulled out a few glasses out from the cabinet.

She did as he asked and walked around the bar.

Alex reached into the small fridge under the counter and pulled out a peach. "Make me a peach Mojito, a Cadillac Margarita, and a Piña Colada." He stepped back eyeing her. This time *he* crossed his big arms.

Grace glanced at the large tray at the bar with everything else she'd need for garnish and smiled. "Coming right up."

Within a few minutes, the drinks were ready and she waved her hands over them. "There you go."

Alex tasted them one by one without a change in his unreadable expression. When he finished tasting the last and most important one — the Mojito — he smiled. She'd heard about the peach Mojitos from Moreno's. They were supposedly the best in town.

"When can you start?"

Her mouth fell open, but she regained her composure as quickly as she could. She couldn't however help the silly smile. "Are you serious?"

"Hell, yeah." He took another sip of the Mojito. "This is damn good." After another sip of the margarita, he eyed her. "But first you have to explain why you lied about your age on your application or my brother is gonna have a cow."

She took a deep breath. "Mr. Moreno—"

"What?" He scoffed. "Call me Alex will you?"

He must've seen the apprehension in her eyes because he added with a smile, revealing those deep dimples again. "It *is* my name."

"Okay, *Alex*... if you're impressed by the drinks I just made, I promise you my cooking will impress you even more." She leaned against the counter. "The problem is no one ever takes me seriously because of my age." She glanced down at her feet not wanting to make eye contact. "I was going to come clean about my age. I swear. I just wanted to have the chance to prove myself first." She crossed her arms again. "Since I wasn't applying for the bartending position, I totally forgot about my birthday on the bartending certificate."

When she glanced up at Alex, she was expecting to see disapproval. Instead, he smiled. "Well, if your cooking is anywhere near as good as your bartending skills, I'd be willing to give you a chance."

Her hands flew to her face and she stood up straight. "Really?"

"I can't hire you as a cook, sweetheart," he added quickly. "My brother's gonna have a hard enough time with me hiring you as a bartender. But once you're in, I'll give you a shot in the kitchen. I'm actually curious now."

Grace fought the inappropriate urge to hug him. "Thank you so much!"

"Any chance you can start today?"

"Yes!" She didn't even know what the pay was, but she felt ecstatic. "I can start now."

After giving her a shirt with the restaurant's logo and an apron Alex excused himself to call his wife. He handed her off to Melanie, one of the other bartenders, to show her around. This was completely unexpected, but Grace was determined to make him proud. She had to. Finally, she had a chance to get in the kitchen of a worthwhile restaurant and her only hope of ever getting her own restaurant someday.

CHAPTER 3

The meeting didn't go at all as Sal hoped. It seemed the investors were interested in only one thing — using the Moreno name — and the reputation that came with it, to open up more restaurants. The second restaurant, which was run by his youngest brother Angel, had been an instant hit. There was no doubt in the investors' minds that all other restaurants with the name would follow suit; as long as they picked out the perfect locations.

However, they weren't interested at all in talking about the management of the restaurants or staying true to the menu. There were already talks of changing food suppliers to cut down on some of the costs in the food. Sal had nearly called the meeting to an end right there. As far as he was concerned, the food and the service were the main ingredients in running a successful restaurant. Anything else was a distant third. This was one of the reasons why he'd decided against going with a big franchising deal. The investors wanted to change a lot of things, including the menu, mostly to cut corners. They called it good business. Sal called it selling out.

He rushed to get back to the restaurant as soon as the meeting was over. He was feeling a little irritated about how the meeting had gone and wondered if maybe he was thinking too big. Maybe instead of opening up several restaurants all at once, like the investors wanted, one at a time would be best. Getting Angel's restaurant going had been quite a challenge. In the end, things worked out fine, but they never would've been able to give it the attention they had, if there were several other restaurants opening at the same time.

The back door to the restaurant swung open just as Sal pulled up and parked. Oscar waved at him as he threw a bag of trash in the back bin. Sal got out in a hurry.

"How'd it go?"

"Eh." Sal said loosening his tie. "Not too good." He hurried into the restaurant behind Oscar. "How's it going in here? Real busy?"

"Yeah, as usual, but the new bartender is really kicking ass."

"New bartender?"

Oscar turned back to look at him. "Yeah, Alex hired her today. The girl knows her drinks." Then he added with a grin, "not to mention, she's got a real nice rack."

As soon as they came around the corner and into view of the bar, Sal saw her. Ms. Zendejas was handling herself just fine behind the bar. A long, thick ponytail replaced the tight bun in her hair and the glasses were gone. Unlike the day of the interview, she smiled brightly as she made several drinks at one time. Alex said something to her as he walked behind her and she laughed.

Sal's irritation hit another level, as he stood glued to the spot. As soon as her eyes met his, the smile disappeared. Finally, he took a few steps toward the bar. Alex smirked when he saw him.

"Can I see you in the office?" Sal said, as he walked by them.

Graciela seemed ready to address him when he glanced at her, but Sal turned his attention back to Alex without so much as a nod. The last thing he wanted was for her to notice that her presence alone had somehow affected him. The worst part was it had nothing to do with her lying on her application. Seeing the way she'd carried on with Alex, then her obvious distaste when she saw him, annoyed him in a way he couldn't even begin to understand.

As soon as Alex walked in the back office, Sal closed the door. "Do you wanna explain that?" He pointed in the direction of the bar.

"Relax." Alex sat down on the chair in front of the desk. "Yeah, she lied about her age but only because she wanted a chance to prove herself before we dismissed her based on her age alone. "Which," Alex raised an eyebrow. "you have to admit, you did."

Sal couldn't believe this. Alex had always been too damn nonchalant when it came to this stuff. "Alex, what kind of experience can she have if she just turned twenty-one?"

Alex raised his palm up in an attempt to calm Sal. "She lived in Texas. You only have to be eighteen over there."

Unbelievable. "And you confirmed this with...?"

"I did better. I had her make me some drinks and she made one of the best Mojitos I've ever had. She's a natural, Sal. And she's fast."

"Alex you can't hire someone just like that. We gotta do a background check, a drug screen—"

"Dude." Alex chuckled. "Can you chill for a second? I can almost guarantee you that little girl has no criminal record; she's a sweetheart. We can still get all that stuff done later. But I needed someone tonight and Gracie was nice enough to start right away."

Sal felt every hair on his body stand at once. "Gracie?"

"Yeah." Alex stood up. "Listen, now that you're here, and with Gracie on duty I think I'm gonna head out. Valerie wasn't feeling too hot this morning when I left. I wanna make sure she's okay."

For a second Sal stopped thinking about Graciela and was immediately concerned. Alex and his wife were expecting twins. She was in her eighth month. The doctors had warned that as petite as she was the babies could come early. They'd already had one scare a few weeks ago. "Something wrong?"

"I don't know. She was just feeling extra tired in the morning. I made her stay in bed but you know how she is." Alex frowned. "Her dad and step-mom are over at the house now. I'd just feel better if I was there with her."

"Go ahead. I can handle things for the rest of the night. Take care of her and those babies."

After Alex left, Sal kept himself busy in the office for a while. A half hour later, he forced himself to do the inevitable: go out into the restaurant and face Graciela.

He walked out just in time to catch Oscar laughing it up with her. She finished a drink and set it on the tray Oscar held. "I'm serious!" Oscar said, as Graciela shook her head. He glanced at Sal. "Uh oh, here's the boss. Back to work."

Graciela turned to Sal and again, just like earlier, the smile dissolved. She wiped her hand on her apron. "Mr. Moreno." She nodded.

"Look," he said more annoyed than ever. "If you're gonna work here I'm gonna have to insist that you call me Sal. Is that alright?"

She nodded again then looked away. "Okay."

"Okay what?" He felt like a jerk acting so bossy but damn it he wanted to hear her say it.

She glanced at him and lifted a perfectly arched eyebrow. "Okay... *Sal.*"

Julie was already at the bar. Graciela turned her attention to her and listened for the next order. Sal stood there for a moment and watched her work. She *was* fast. And she certainly knew what she was doing. While Melanie, one of the other bartenders on duty seemed to take a little more time measuring her drinks and making sure of accuracy, Graciela flipped bottles over without hesitation and put drinks together like a pro. It reminded him of some of the older cooks they had who never used any measurements or read any of the recipes Sal printed up for them. They just put everything together by memory and it was always perfect.

When she was done with that round of drinks, she glanced at Sal. Her eyes were bigger than he remembered, and that dress she'd worn the day of the interview had done the curves she now revealed absolutely no justice.

"I'll need a few minutes with you when you get a chance," he said.

"Alex gave me the paperwork I need to fill out. I can fill it out for you on my lunch."

"When is that?" Sal needed to get a few things straight with Ms. Zendejas *now.*

She shrugged. "Alex said I could take a half hour whenever I felt like it. I'm not really hungry yet."

Sal took a deep breath. Alex and his managerial leniency would be the end of him. He glanced over at Melanie and Luis the other bartender. "You two think you can handle it out here for a few minutes while I have a word with Graciela?"

They both nodded and continued working. He turned to Graciela. "Follow me."

He didn't wait for a response. He simply turned and headed for the office. She may've impressed Alex with her drinks and that damn smile, but the fact remained she lied on her application. They hadn't had very many incidents with employees getting out of line, or being irresponsible, but from experience he knew the younger ones usually were more trouble than not. She *had* been late to the interview and at twenty-one, Graciela was now their youngest employee. He highly doubted Alex had explained any of the rules to her. As usual, he probably welcomed her on like family, just like he treated the rest of the staff.

He waited until she was in the office before closing the door behind her. "Have a seat."

She sat on the edge of the seat by the door as he sat back on the office chair. "I understand my brother was so impressed he hired you on the spot."

Her posture was perfectly erect and tense like he remembered the day of the interview. So unlike how she'd been behind the bar when he first walked in. "Yes, and I explained to him about my age. I only wanted to get a chance to prove myself and I was going to tell you the truth after."

"Yeah, well whatever the reason, lying on your application is pretty bad." He crossed his arms in front of him and leaned back. "First impressions go a long way. Not the smartest thing to do is start off lying."

With a slight lift of her chin she began, "I've already apologized to Alex and now I'll apologize to you. I'm sorry. I was only trying to make a point. But you're right. A liar is not how I'd like to be perceived. I'm only grateful that Alex was kind enough to give me the opportunity to prove myself."

He stared at her for a moment and she didn't look away. Instead stared right back. She didn't seem at all intimidated by him. In fact, he'd bet she added that last remark as a jab.

"There are still a few things we need to get taken care of." He sat up and spun the chair around so he faced the computer. "We'll need to run a background on you and do a drug screening." He turned to face her. The dry expression hadn't changed. In fact it seemed even more severe. "I'll also need to verify your past employment. You know, the bartending experience."

"You don't believe I have experience—"

Sal held up his hand. "This is standard procedure, Grace. It has nothing to do with believing you, but to be fair you did already lie about one thing and—"

"First of all." She stood up. "It's Graciela. And second, I just apologized for that. Alex didn't seem to mind. If you just give me a chance I can—"

"Have a seat, Graciela. Please."

"I'd rather stand."

What the hell happened to the smiley Graciela at the bar? The one that didn't have a problem with Alex referring to her as *Gracie*. Here, Sal wasn't even allowed to call her Grace?

He turned back to the computer trying to shake off the annoyance he felt. "You do realize my brother is married, right?"

"What does that have to do with anything?"

He lifted his shoulder. "Just thought I'd mention. That's all."

He felt like an ass now for even saying it. It was unprofessional and completely out of line. But it just came out. The fact that she didn't say more about his comment did *not* go unnoticed. Maybe it *had* come as an unpleasant surprise — one that rendered her speechless. He was suddenly grinding his teeth.

"Are we done here, Mr. Moreno?"

Sal turned around. "No, we're not. And I thought I asked you to call me Sal."

For the life of him, he couldn't understand why his words came out so harsh. The expression on her face was that of obvious aversion — aversion to him. And he couldn't say he blamed her. He was being a total dick. This was so out of character for him.

In a tone completely opposite to his, she asked, "What else do you need from me... *Sal*?" It was almost condescending.

"I'll need references." No he didn't. *What the hell was he doing?* They'd never once asked for references from any of the other employees.

"References? Like from past employers?"

"Yeah." Sal glanced at her. She chewed the corner of her lip. The disdainful expression was now replaced with a look of concern.

"If you can get them," he added, feeling guilty. "It's not a big a deal."

"Because the restaurant I worked at last, went out of business and the manager there moved back to Mexico. My other jobs were all in El Paso but —"

"That's fine, don't worry about it."

Sal gave her all the information on where to go to get the drug screening and she went back to work. Even after sitting in the back mulling over why the hell he'd behaved as he did, he still couldn't figure it out. He finally chalked it up to his already dire mood from the meeting with the investors, and then the surprise of finding out Alex had gone ahead and hired her, even though he knew Sal's apprehension about her — hired her on the spot no less.

He sulked in the back for hours getting the inventory sheets ready for that weekend. By closing time he couldn't stand it anymore, he needed to talk to Graciela. The more he thought about it the worse he felt about his behavior. His comment about Alex had been completely uncalled for.

The restaurant was closed now and everyone was cleaning up when he walked out into the bar area. Melanie and Graciela were laughing about something as Melanie wiped down the bar and Graciela filled the dishwasher.

"That time again, ladies. We're almost out of here." Both girls turned to look at him. Melanie smiled while Graciela's lips flat lined.

Graciela continued to put glasses in the dishwasher. Melanie's attention was taken by Oscar, who brought her more receipts to put in the closing drawer. Sal took advantage of Melanie's distraction and walked past her coming to a stop next to the dishwasher. Graciela glanced at him but said nothing.

"Look, I wanted to apologize for how I acted earlier. That's not me."

She stopped what she was doing but only for a moment and nodded her head. "No need to apologize. I know lying on my application was wrong and I get it. You don't trust me. But I'm okay with it. I know I can prove myself to you and Alex and I will."

"You don't need to prove anything Grace — uh, Graciela,"

Her perpetual glare finally eased up a bit. "You can call me Grace."

Feeling he'd made a small but significant bit of progress, he smiled. "Thank you, Grace. You don't need to prove anything, just show up and do your job. That's good enough for me."

She chewed the corner of her lip like she had earlier in his office. This time he noticed how perfect her lips were. Like the kind you see in drawings. The top one perfectly arched, the bottom soft and round. Not wanting her to notice him staring at her lips, he brought his eyes back to hers. Just like the day of the interview, she wore no makeup and now that she was finally not glaring or crossing her eyes at him, he could appreciate how pretty they were.

"Alex said he'd give me a shot in the kitchen... " She glanced away.

"I said that, too. Remember?"

She looked back at him, the corners of her lips lifting. It wasn't the same as the smile he'd seen on her face earlier when she'd actually laughed at whatever Alex said to her, but it was a start.

Something behind him suddenly got her attention and talk about a smile. Her eyes brightened in an instant. She almost seemed excited. Sal turned to see what it was. A guy with his hands against the window of the locked front door peered in. He smiled also when he saw her and he waved a hand holding keys.

"I'm all done here. Can I go now?"

Sal turned back to Grace who was already undoing her apron. "Sure."

She rushed to the back room. Within minutes she walked out, purse in hand. Sal followed her to the door to unlock it. The second he opened the door she was in his arms. "Thank you so much for coming, Joey."

Joey squeezed her tight. "Of course, sweetie. Anything for my Gracie."

The guy was clean cut and bit too generous with the cologne. It wasn't until he let go of Grace and she turned to say goodnight that Sal noticed how tight he was gripping the door handle. His knuckles had nearly gone white.

The guy glanced at him and smiled. Sal managed a smile before closing the door and locking it. He walked back to the office trying desperately to shake off the ridiculous unsettling tension he suddenly felt.

This entire day had been a roller coaster of emotions. From his frustration about the less than qualified applicants that morning, to the meeting gone wrong, to finding out Alex had gone against his wishes and hired Grace. Everything he felt when he saw Grace again was understandable. But what he felt now was infuriating because it made no sense — no sense at all.

CHAPTER 4

"Holy cow, Gracie is that one of the married ones or the single one?" Joey clicked the button on his keychain, causing his car to chirp and headlights to blink.

Grace walked around the car and opened the door. "He's the single one but he's kind of a jerk."

"What do you mean?" Joey said, climbing in the driver's seat. "Those bitches weren't lying when they said the Moreno brothers were hot. That is one hot *papi*, girl. How bad can he be?"

Grace wouldn't admit how breathless she'd been when he first walked in and stared her down, looking amazingly sexy in his suit. "Bad." She frowned as she put her seatbelt on. "He obviously wasn't happy about Alex hiring me. Apparently, he'd made up his mind about me already. Even went as far as to insinuate that I flirted with Alex to get the job."

"No! He said that?"

"Well, not exactly but he made a stupid comment— *'you do realize Alex is married right?'* That says a lot about his brother if he really thinks the only reason he hired me was because I flirted or something." Gracie crossed her arms in front of her. The more she thought about it the madder it made her. "You have no idea how hard it was for me to hold back what I really wanted to say. If I didn't need this job so bad…"

Joey rubbed her knee. "Let's focus on the positive. You got a job at one of the most upscale restaurants in La Jolla, of all places. And you said they're gonna give you a shot in the kitchen right? This is what you've been waiting for."

Grace smiled. Joey always had a way of making her see things in a different light. "You're right. This is my opportunity."

Joey wanted her to come over and hang out with him and Taylor and a few other friends. But Grace knew Rose was home alone with her stepdad. Her mom let her know earlier, that she was going to meet a few friends for dinner and might be home late. Grace knew what that meant—she was on the prowl. Dinner equaled drinks at a bar, looking for potential sucker number five.

To her surprise, not only was her mom home, they had company. Rose gave her a look as soon as she walked in. A man in a suit who looked thirtyish, sat on the sofa, holding a beer. The place had actually been cleaned up. Ruben stood behind the sofa. He was showered and shaved for a change. Her mom rushed over to her. "Oh, here she is now."

Grace smiled, glancing at the man who smiled as he stood then back at her mom. "Grace, this is Mr. Fuentes."

"Call me Frank," he said reaching his hand out.

Grace shook his hand and smiled. "I'm Grace."

"Mr. Fuentes—" Her mother caught herself and smiled, nodding at Mr. Fuentes. "Uh, Frank is a friend of Ruben's, from his days of doing long hauls to Nevada. He owns a casino in Laughlin."

"It's a work in progress," Frank said, smiling. "More of a hotel making the crossover to casino."

"Oh, but you said you got your gambling license and that's the biggest hurdle isn't it?" her mother said, with an over-sized smile.

Frank nodded in agreement. Grace glanced back and forth between them, wondering what, if anything, this had to do with her. "Anyway Grace, Frank stopped by while he was in town. He might have a job for Ruben in Laughlin."

Grace's heart sunk. "We're moving?"

Her mother did her fake laugh and placed her hand on her chest. "No, no. It's a driving job. You see Frank will need someone to drive fresh seafood to his *restaurant* in his casino every day." Her mother squeezed her hand at the mention of restaurant. "We're going out to discuss the details and I thought it'd be nice if you could join us."

No way. Her mother had had some crazy ideas in the past but there was no way she'd go along with where she thought this was going. "I... I have to study."

With another squeeze of her hand, her mother smiled at her then glanced at Frank. "She's very responsible when it come to her studies." Frank smiled and her mother turned back to her. "But I'm sure you can get it done tomorrow. We'll only be out a few hours."

She pulled Grace by the hand. "C'mon, I'll help you pick something out." She turned back to Frank. "We'll only be a few minutes. Make yourself at home. Ruben, offer him another beer."

Rose followed them into her bedroom. As soon as the door closed, Grace turned to her. "What are you doing? I don't want to go out with that man."

"Yeah," Rose said. "That's gross. He's old."

Her mother ignored Rose. "You're not going out with him. We're all going out together. He mentioned being a little lonely these days so I thought maybe if you came along he might sweeten his offer."

"No!"

Rose plopped onto the bed and crossed her legs, watching them both.

"Graciela, for Christ's sake, it's only dinner and you won't even be alone with him. Is that too much to ask? You're doing your family a favor." Her mother opened Grace's closet. "Where is that dress you wore for your cousin's *quinciniera*?"

"I thought you said this was just dinner? That dress is way too fancy."

Her mother was unbelievable. Of all the stunts she'd pulled this one took the cake. Even though she said it was just dinner, Grace had a feeling there was more up her mother's sleeve. Judging by the way she squeezed her hand at the mention of Frank owning a restaurant, she knew her mom was already scheming.

"Well, he's taking us somewhere fancy. So you have to look nice. Did you not notice the man is wearing a suit?"

Exasperated, but aware she wasn't going to win this battle, she walked over to the closet and pulled out the dress. "Isn't it a little late for dinner?"

"Dinner, cocktails, dancing, whatever, it's all the same thing. Just hurry up and get ready."

Her mom walked out the room but not before mouthing "*te apuras.*"

Yeah, she was in a real hurry to go out with this guy. Grace turned to Rose who looked at her sympathetically. "At least you won't be alone."

Suddenly Grace remembered and smiled. "I got a job today."

"You did?" Her sister's smile matched her own excitement. "Yeah, at Moreno's in La Jolla."

Rose's blank stare didn't surprise her. Unlike Grace, her sister wasn't up on all the area's best restaurants. She didn't read "Fine Cuisine" magazine and follow the reviews religiously like Grace did. "It's one of the best Mexican restaurants in the San Diego area — in all of Southern California if you ask me." That was saying a lot, especially since Los Angeles was only two hours north of them.

"Really? So you're their chef now?"

Grace chewed the corner of her lip. "No, I'm bartending. But they said they'd give me a chance and let me cook sometime."

For a second, Rose seemed disappointed but quickly snapped out of it. She knew how much Grace had been going on and on about trying to get hired at a good restaurant. She only had a couple more months of school before she graduated with her Culinary Arts degree. With her foot already in the door and with the opportunity to prove herself she was sure she'd make head chef in no time.

"I knew you'd find a job eventually, Grace. You're an awesome cook. *Abuelita* taught you well."

Grace felt a dull pang in her heart at the mention of her grandmother. Rose's cell phone beeped and she looked down at her hands. That phone may as well have been surgically attached to her hands the way Rose kept it by her at all times.

"Mom says to tell you to hurry."

With a roll of her eyes, Grace began changing. Her own phone was in her bag in the front room. No doubt her mother had already tried her phone. "Can you believe her?"

"Of course. This is so typical of her," Rose said, lying down, putting her hands behind her head.

She had a point. Her mother would stop at nothing short of prostitution and drug dealing to make an easy buck. Even then, Grace didn't completely rule those two out. She'd seen how her mom dressed on a few occasions when she was just going to *dinner* with a few friends. She was surprised Ruben let her walk out looking like that.

Grace didn't bother with makeup. Aside from some lip gloss and a little mascara sometimes she never wore the stuff. She wasn't starting now. The dress she wore was one her mother had picked out. Grace didn't mind the length, but it was tighter than she was used to and a bit low in the front.

Frank didn't even attempt to hide what he thought of her in the dress. The bulging eyes and goofy smile said it all. Her mother smiled in delight. "You look lovely, Grace. Don't you think, Frank?"

He stood up from the sofa. "Stunning," he said.

Ruben took advantage of the invitation to ogle and eyed her up and down with his own perverted smile. Grace had never felt like such a piece of meat. It was degrading and she glared at her mom. Her mother ignored the glare and gathered her things.

After her mother played the concerned mom in front of Frank, telling Rose not to answer the door for anyone and giving her instructions on what to do in case of an emergency, as if this were the first time Rose had been left alone, they were out the door.

Frank drove them in his brand new Cadillac to a jazz bar on the marina. He said the last time he'd been out here he went there and the music was fabulous. Maybe it was that Grace had had such a long day but the slow music was making her sleepy. Add to a glass of wine to that—forget about it. She caught herself nodding off twice. Thankfully, no one noticed.

When the song ended, the musicians excused themselves for a break. "Your mother tells me you're a culinary student. How's that going?"

Grace nodded. "I'll be done in a few months."

He leaned over to her. The music that played on the sound system was almost as loud as the live music. He paused to take a drink and Grace took the moment to scrutinize him. He wasn't unattractive by any means. He was tall, thin and dressed well. But he was at least ten years older than her. That, however, wasn't reason enough to dismiss him. She knew better than anyone not to judge people by their age. The fact that he was a friend of Ruben's was what made her question him. Anyone who considered Ruben a friend was suspect as far as she was concerned.

He noticed her scrutiny and smiled. "What are your plans once you finish?"

"I'm already working at a restaurant." She glanced at her mom who eyed her, almost as if she was hoping Grace wouldn't say anything wrong. "My hope is to move up once I've completed my courses. Then eventually open up my own restaurant."

She didn't feel the need to go into any more specifics. Luckily, she didn't have to. Her mother immediately started in asking Frank about his casino. Grace endured two and a half hours of Frank telling them about how his uncle had left him the hotel he was now running and every detail about his journey in turning it into a casino. Her mother cackled at anything that even remotely sounded like a joke or quick wit.

By the end of the night, Grace was both physically and mentally exhausted. She could hardly believe her mother invited Frank in at the end of the evening for another drink. Thankfully, he said he had a long drive home in the morning and declined but he did say he'd be back to visit again soon. *Wonderful.*

Her mother had another think coming if she thought Grace would go through another night like tonight. She plopped in bed with her already snoring sister. With a day like the one she'd had, she was out within minutes.

*

Sal didn't go into the restaurant on Saturday. Since Alex was hardly there during the week he'd go in on the weekends. Typically, Sal would drop by to check things out even if he wasn't scheduled to be there. Today however, he didn't want to. He checked first with Alex to make sure Valerie was feeling well enough to be left alone. She was. So after the day he had yesterday, Sal thought it better if he took the day off.

In college, Jason had become one of Sal's best buddies. They roomed for four years until Jason got engaged and moved in with his fiancé. Even then, they stayed close and often met up for a round of golf or just to throw a few beers back and shoot the breeze.

"So did you meet with the investors yet?"

Sal frowned as they rode in the cart to their next hole. "Yeah,"

"How'd it go?"

"Not good. I'm beginning to think this whole branching out thing may not be such a great idea."

"What?" Jason pulled over as they reached their next hole. "That's all you talked about in school. You can't let one bump derail all your plans."

Sal got out of the cart. There were still a few players

MAKING YOU MINE   47

finishing up on their next hole so Jason and Sal pulled beers out of the ice chest.

"It's just not what I was expecting." Sal took a swig of his ice-cold beer.

"If you want I can talk to my dad. He knows a bunch of investors always looking to get in on a good deal."

"It's not that," Sal took another drink. "I've got plenty of interested investors, it's just all they're thinking about is the money."

Jason laughed. "Sorry to break it to you bud, but that's usually all investors think about."

Sal flicked his bottle cap at Jason. "I know that, ass. I'm trying to be flexible but if I leave it up to them Moreno's will be the next El Torito or Acapulco's. That's not what I want."

"Hey, that doesn't sound too bad."

The hole opened up and Sal gave up trying to explain why he wasn't about to sell out his family name. Halfway through their last hole, Jason brought up an entirely new subject. "I need a favor."

"I knew it." When Jason called him out of the blue Sal had a feeling. The last time he'd asked for a favor things got pretty sour.

"What? You don't even know what I'm gonna ask."

Ten to one Sal knew exactly what it was. Almost a year ago, he'd gone out with Jason's fiancée's cousin Melissa. She was nice enough, in fact she seemed perfect at first. Beautiful, classy, just passed the bar exam, sexy as hell. But she turned into a clinger. Calling and texting him at all hours. Showing up at the restaurant until she finally somehow got in his apartment when he wasn't there. Made dinner and greeted him in her birthday suit. That actually wouldn't have been so bad if his date hadn't been with him when he walked in.

After that, Sal made it clear he wanted nothing to do with her. He couldn't believe someone so smart could stoop to that level. Before that happened, he'd done nothing to encourage that kind of behavior. In fact, he'd been so turned off by her pushiness he stopped taking her calls and returning her texts.

She called and texted him for months after he completely cut her off. The last time he bothered to read one of her texts, was when one woke him in the middle of the night. Apparently, in her inebriated state she decided she'd profess her love for him. They'd only gone out a few times and he slept with her twice before she started to annoy the hell out of him. Love? He remembered laughing, before rolling back to sleep.

"I'm afraid to ask," Sal said, taking a practice swing.

"Hear me out okay?"

Sal peered at him, bracing himself.

"Melissa—"

"Hell, no."

"C'mon, can you at least listen to what it is first?"

Sal shook his head. "No, no, no, no, no." He positioned himself to take a swing at his ball then turned back to Jason. "No."

"Dude, Kat's driving me fucking crazy. All Melissa wants is a chance to apologize to you in person. We'll be there. You won't be alone with her for a minute."

Sal continued to shake his head then stopped only long enough to take a swing. He turned back to Jason and shook his head again. "The girl is a whack job. It took me long enough to get rid of her. You think I wanna start that shit all over again?"

"I told Kat you'd say that, but she says Melissa understands you're not interested and she's okay with that. All she wants is a chance to apologize. This has been going on for months, Sal. Melissa's mom has even started calling Kat's mom about it. Then Kat's mom calls her, then who do you think has to hear the crap? I'm begging you, man, just a couple of hours. I'd do it for you."

For a moment, Sal considered it. He took a deep breath and looked up at the sky. The next thing he heard was Jason on the phone. "He said okay."

Sal jerked his attention back to Jason, eyes wide open. "What?"

Jason put his finger over his lips and smirked. Then he put his hand over the receiver. "Is tonight okay?"

"I didn't say I would!" Sal took off his glove and threw it at Jason.

"Tonight's fine," Jason said, laughing.

Sal put his hand on forehead. "Fuck me."

"Alright, honey. You're welcome. Yeah, I'll tell him."

Sal glared at him when he hung up.

"Kat said she loves you," he grinned. "She's my fiancée and you know what? I'm okay with that. Because right now I love you, too."

When Sal didn't say anything Jason added, "I'll buy you lunch." Sal still didn't answer. "C'mon how bad can it be? We'll go to DJ's, play a little pool, have a few beers, she apologizes and everyone's happy. Done. Just like that. You're my hero and my fiancée loves you. Beautiful."

"I want steak and lobster for lunch."

"Steak and lobster it is." Jason patted him on the shoulder as he walked over to take his shot with a grin.

Somehow, Sal was hoping for a less enthusiastic response.

CHAPTER 5

Sunday morning they were doing their weekly inventory. Somehow, for years his parents had managed everything on paper. Incredibly, they were very accurate but now that there was software for everything, it should've made things easier. Though, times like today things could get really screwed up.

He was already in a bad mood before he even got to the restaurant. The night before with Melissa had gone well. Her behavior was very impressive, but he'd been fooled by that before. She apologized while Jason and Kat played pool. They even had a somewhat intriguing conversation. She was the epitome of the perfect girl he once thought her to be. That is until that morning when he got a call from Jason.

"You're gonna be mad."

"What?"

"She has your sunglasses."

Sal knew what that meant. "Tell her she can have them."

"That's the first thing I said when Kat heard the message she left, but she already said she's going to drop them off today at the restaurant. Kat tried calling her but she's not answering. So I'm just giving you a heads up."

Here we go again. Melissa was notorious for leaving things in Sal's car or his house—her way of forcing another meeting. He should've known. He hadn't even noticed his sunglasses were missing. All he could hope now is that she'd drop them off and he'd be done with her. But Melissa didn't work that way.

Grace arrived at noon, adding to his already growing aggravated mood. He didn't understand why he felt the way he did around her. He was over her lying about her age and she'd passed the drug screening and background with flying colors. Yet, being around her made him feel anxious.

Tired of going over numbers, Sal decided to walk out and check on things in the dining room. He saw Grace peeking into the kitchen. He smiled when he realized she appeared to be trying to be sneaky. He took slow, quiet footsteps so she wouldn't hear him. She turned and saw him when he was only a few feet away and flinched. Sal had to stifle a laugh.

"I was just uh..."

"Checking out the kitchen?"

"Well, yeah, I wanted to..."

"C'mon I'll show you." He settled for a big smile instead of laughing. She was already blushing. "You haven't had a chance to acquaint yourself with the restaurant. There's a lot you haven't seen."

She followed him through the busy kitchen. Her caught-with-a-hand-in-the-cookie-jar expression, was now replaced with a look of pure awe. Her eyes opened wider with everything he showed her. Seeing how excited she got over something as simple as a kitchen was more than amusing. Sal couldn't wipe the smile off his own face.

The new stockroom had been added the previous year when they bought the place next door and expanded the restaurant. When they got to it, he stopped and his eyes met hers. "You ready for this?"

She nodded, reminding him of his younger brothers

when they were kids and he showed them a new card trick or new stunt on his bike. They were always so easily impressed. He slid the door open and motioned for her to go in first.

Sal had a lot to do with the design. The old stock room was all over the place. To Sal, organization was key, but it also had to look good. Like the rest of the restaurant, it was designed to feel old like the Mexican homes in the old country. The wood used for the shelves was new but painted so that it gave them a weathered look, as were the containers of spices. They had every spice in there needed for Mexican cuisine. Even the floors had been painted with a texture that made if feel as if they were standing on dirt.

He also made sure there were sitting areas and an old collapsible wooden cot like the ones he and his brothers would sleep in when they visited their grandfather's ranch in Mexico as kids. It was really meant to give the room an even more authentic look but Pablo, one of the older cooks that still came in a few times a week, was known to nap on it.

Grace walked around taking it all in — those eyes of hers practically twinkled. Her fingers caressed the antique looking barrels that contained rice, and beans as if she were touching a work of art. She turned back to him. "This is amazing."

It was the strangest thing. Every time he looked at her, he noticed something new he hadn't noticed about her before, like her perfectly manicured nails when she caressed the barrels. Instinctively, his eyes were on her ring finger. No engagement ring, but that didn't mean anything. She could just take it off for fear of it falling off while she worked.

He frowned annoyed at himself that his thoughts

would even go there. She caught him frowning which only irritated him further. "This is relatively new. We added this whole side of the restaurant last year.

"The whole restaurant is nice but this…" she glanced around, "this is special because it's like a treat for the employees."

"Everyone was real excited about it when it was unveiled. I wasn't really expecting that. I just wanted something more organized than the one we had before and I don't like employees feeling like this is just a place of work. My parents always made it a point to make the employees feel at home, like they were family. So I wanted even the stockroom to feel homey." He looked around. "Something they'd enjoy every time they came to work."

"I will." She smiled at him, making him squeeze the doorway. "I heard you're planning on opening more restaurants. How many?"

Sal hadn't really thought of an exact number. He just always thought more. "I dunno. Maybe four, five more?"

"Really? Why so many?" She didn't wait for him to respond; she was still taking in the old wooden canisters for the different spices. "Personally, I would want just one. I'd live to perfect it. It would be my baby." She turned to look at him. "But then there are three of you and you have a sister right?"

"Yeah, but she's a writer. She writes for a magazine and she's working on a novel. She' s content with just coming in and working a few days out of the week. She's not looking to run her own restaurant."

Grace tilted her head. "So then three restaurants for three brothers would seem like the perfect number to me." She shrugged. "But that's me. I don't usually think on such a grand scale like a lot of people do. My desires out of life are far more simple than most."

Sal thought about explaining that it wasn't just about the number of restaurants. It was his way of paying homage to his parents and grandfather. He wanted the Moreno name to be respected and honored for the hard work his father had put in for so many years — pay him back and show him that his extended education had been worth it. But he didn't think it was a good idea to get into all of that now.

"Is that what your plans are? To open your own restaurant?"

Her face tinged slightly with color and she nodded. "Someday. It doesn't have to be all this. I just want my own little restaurant where I can do what I love best — cook like my grandmother taught me."

Grace's dream was to have her own restaurant. She said she'd live to perfect it. The very thing he'd been trying to do with his family's business for years and now he'd be dedicating his life to this. A smile almost escaped him, thinking about the hours he could spend talking to her about just this. But he sensed a change in her mood and thought better of asking any more.

After a full tour of the stock room, he took her upstairs to show her the banquet rooms. Only one was in use today so they skipped it. Her eyes didn't disappoint when he opened the door to the remaining part of the huge room.

"It's one big room with dividers," he said, pointing at the ceiling. "We can break them up into smaller rooms."

Adding to her expressive eyes, her lips parted slightly, distracting Sal for a moment.

"Has anyone ever had an event that would use the

whole place?"

Sal chuckled. "My brother Angel's wedding."

She stopped looking around and turned to Sal. "It was this big?"

"Yep, a little over a year ago and let me tell you, this place was packed."

"You're kidding. You guys know that many people?"

Sal shrugged. "The majority of it were friends and business acquaintances of my parents they've met over the years through the restaurant. We also had a lot of family come over from Mexico."

"All the weddings I've ever been to, have either been in someone's backyard or didn't even have a reception." Sal stood at the door as she walked across the room to admire the mural on the wall. "Who did these paintings? They're beautiful."

"A friend of the family's. He did the ones downstairs too."

She turned to him, something changed in her eyes. "The one of the old lady?"

"Yeah, all of them."

She seemed to stare out into space for a moment then looked back at the mural. "He's very talented."

Again, there was a shift in her disposition. The excitement she'd exuded throughout the tour of the restaurant was gone. She walked back toward him. "Thanks for the tour. I should get back to work now."

"Something wrong?"

Her eyes met his for just a moment. "No, not at all. You have a beautiful restaurant. I just hope I get the opportunity to show you what I can do in the kitchen soon." She walked past him and out the door.

Once back in the office Sal tried to concentrate on

the inventory but his thoughts kept going back to Grace. Then he overheard her laughing with Melanie and damn it if it wasn't the cutest laugh he'd ever heard.

When he was finally done, he went out into the dining room. Brunch was still in full swing. Alex was talking to a couple of women in a booth and he flagged him over. Both women turned to see who Alex had flagged down and smiled when they saw Sal.

"Sal, you remember Tracy from high school don't you?"

Sal hadn't the faintest. Before he could say anything Tracy stood up and threw her arms around his neck. "Oh my god! You guys haven't changed at all. You're just like I remember." She pulled back and smiled. He still didn't have a clue who she was but she was attractive that was for sure. She'd slipped her hand in his after the hug and she didn't let go. "This is my cousin, Suzie."

Suzie held out her hand and smiled. Sal shook it wondering if he could bluff his way out of this. "Yeah, it's been a while." He glanced at Alex who smiled like he knew Sal didn't have a clue. He probably didn't either, the ass.

"I'm only in town for a few days. I don't live out here anymore." Tracy turned to Alex. "I know you're married now." Then turned back to Sal. "Maybe you and I can get together and hang out."

Those last two words coupled with the twinkle in her eyes had a certain connotation he'd heard all too many times. Alex excused himself when he got a call. The idea wasn't a bad one, but he doubted he could bluff the entire night. Not that he thought admitting the truth now would revoke the invitation.

He pretended to consider it and continued to make

small talk when he got the distinct feeling he was being watched. He remembered Melissa would be stopping by and he wondered if she was already there somewhere. Casually, he scanned the restaurant when he noticed Grace staring in his direction from behind the bar. She specifically stared at Tracy who was still holding his hand. The moment her eyes met his, she averted her stare and walked away from where she'd been standing.

*

"Good job today, Gracie," Alex smiled, putting his hand over the receiver on his phone.

"Thank you." She smiled back.

She'd walked in the back office at the end of her shift to get her things, and overheard him talking to his wife. He was so sweet and forever worrying about her well-being, Grace couldn't stand it. Why couldn't she ever meet a guy like that?

He winked at her and continued with his conversation. "I know, baby, but the doctor says you have to…"

Grace sighed. She was so glad he'd been there the day she showed up to actually talk to Sal. Knowing what she knew now, she'd still be out of a job if Alex hadn't been there. She thought Sal had finally started warming up to her Friday night, when he apologized for his behavior, but today he was back and forth from sweet to his ornery self. Even when he showed her around she couldn't shake that feeling that he just wasn't comfortable with her. He obviously still had his reservations about her.

She walked out to the parking lot where Joey said he'd be waiting. She felt bad that Joey was chauffeuring her around, but he insisted it wasn't out of his way. The gym where he'd started working out wasn't too far from the restaurant. Plus, he said there was no way he nor Taylor would let her take the bus home in the evening. She smiled, thinking about it. She *did* have guys who worried about her. Now if only she could find one who wasn't gay!

As she turned the corner to the parking lot, she saw Sal engaged in what appeared to be another amorous conversation with a different girl. Grace focused on Joey who sat in his car waiting for her. No way was she getting caught staring at Sal and his girl again like she had earlier. She felt so stupid. She'd just been curious. Not only was Sal completely out of her league, older, wealthy, beautiful and from what Melanie had told her, he'd just earned his master's in business—he also didn't like her. Grace had wanted to see what it took to impress a man like Sal. He seemed smitten at the time, but obviously not enough because here he was already, with another lovely candidate vying for his attention.

Grace opened the door and got in Joey's car.

"I can't believe you get to look at that *papacito* all day long. You lucky girl you."

Grace shrugged. "What good is looking?"

"Hmm, do I detect something in that tone?"

"No you don't." She put her seatbelt on as they drove by Sal and his girl. Sal's eyes were on Joey then he glanced her way. She waved and he waved back. "He's my boss, Joey. And remember I told you I don't think he likes me."

"Still?"

"Yes, still. I've only worked with him two days. He wasn't here yesterday."

The disappointment she'd felt when she realized he

wouldn't be there at all yesterday, had come as a surprise. While she felt so much more at ease, knowing she wouldn't have his scrutinizing eyes there, his apology Friday night had left her hopeful that she'd be a little closer to showing him what she was made of in the kitchen. Unfortunately, the vibe she'd picked up several times from him today was still a negative one.

"He'll come around, sweetie. You'll see. There is no way anybody can be around you for too long without falling in love."

Grace didn't know about all that. But she knew better than to argue with Joey.

"So you have to come over tonight, Grace. George is coming over with some old-ass movie he says we *have* to watch. I'm gonna be dying."

George was Taylor's much older ex-boyfriend. Grace had only met him once but Joey had told her all about him. She still didn't get how Joey could be okay with his boyfriend's ex hanging around. But according to Joey he was fine with it. George was thirty-five and into men his own age now. Taylor and George had been friends before they got together and vowed to stay friends even though their relationship hadn't worked out.

"What movie is it?"

"Jacob's Ladder." Joey made a face. "He said he's seen it many times and still doesn't get it. We made fun of him so now he's challenging us to watch and see if we get it. From what he described, it sounds pretty freaky."

That sounded interesting to Grace. "Can we pick up Rosie? I'm not sure if my mom is home and I'd hate for her to be alone with that pig."

"Of course."

Grace texted Rose to be ready and they picked her up. After watching the movie, which Grace thought she got, until the very end, they ate some of Joey's carrot bread. It was one of his specialties and absolutely delicious. He and Taylor planned on opening up a bakery when he was done with school. He'd made her the most fabulous cake for her twenty-first birthday. As far as Grace was concerned, baking and creating masterpieces was Joey's calling.

They all stood around in the tiny kitchen oohing and aahing over the delicious cake. "Oh my God, Taylor. You have to check out Grace's boss. He's a walking wet dream."

Taylor shot Joey a look. "Is he gay?"

Grace laughed. "Not even close."

"I was gonna say." Taylor licked his finger. "Your ass better not be checking out her gay boss."

Joey nudged him as he walked by toward the fridge. Joey and Taylor couldn't look more different. Joey was taller. His hair was black and he wore it very clean cut. He was the pretty boy of the two. Always perfectly ironed and matching.

Taylor had long dark blonde dreadlocks, usually pulled back in a ponytail like he had it now. Most of the time he went barefoot and he had a permanent five o'clock shadow. While Joey's eyes were as dark as coal, Taylor had the most amazing green eyes.

One thing that Grace finally got used to, was the way Taylor would flirt with her outrageously, even in front of Joey. Obviously, he was gay. But he had these bedroom eyes that could just melt you, male or female and he knew it too. He loved talking to her in this sensual way, always saying things with double meaning and watching her squirm.

"I've been to Moreno's. Good food and yes I've seen the eye candy that runs the place but what's it like working for them?" George asked, taking a seat at the small kitchen table. "The arrogance must be endless."

Clean cut pretty boys were hands down Taylor's type. George had clean cut and pretty boy written all over him. Taylor did his internship at a radio station where George was an executive. That's how they met.

"Actually no. Alex, not the one Joey saw, couldn't be sweeter and he spends most of his time checking up on his pregnant wife," she smiled. "He's like a big muscular teddy bear. He was a little smug the day I met him, but I wouldn't call him arrogant." She shrugged. "But then he's the one that took a chance on me while Sal... didn't even give me the time of day, so maybe I'm a little biased."

"Oh, he must be the one I saw when I was there. The guy was huge," George said.

"Yeah that's Alex. I haven't met their youngest brother, he runs the Moreno's on the Marina with his wife, but I've seen pictures in the back room. He's just as good looking as these two. He's also happily married but holding off on the baby making because they just opened the new restaurant last year. At least that's what the girls at work say."

She turned to George. "Sal on the other hand, the only one still single, is as expected — a chick magnet. Just today, he had two all over him. From what the girls tell me they've seen him with plenty of girls — none he ever sticks with for long. But I haven't really picked up on any arrogance."

George chuckled. "Smart guy. If it were me, I'd be working my way down the line, too."

Grace smiled though she wasn't feeling it.

"Oh, but you have to see him, Taylor," Joey gushed. "You'll just die."

Taylor rolled his eyes. "I'll have to check this guy out now."

They talked a while longer about the Morenos then thankfully, they moved on to another subject, deciphering the movie's ending. After a while of that, no one agreed. Finally, they called it a night and Joey drove Grace and Rose home.

"They're always so much fun," Rose said as Grace climbed in bed next to her. "Taylor is so hot, I can hardly stand it!"

Grace smiled and even as she lay there thinking about her evening with Taylor and Joey, thoughts of work came back to her, most notably, Sal. She didn't care if he didn't like her so much as she disliked the tension she felt when he was around. Alex had asked if it was okay if he scheduled her a full forty hours this week. She could definitely use the money but it would be cutting into her schoolwork time. Still, she agreed. There was no way she was passing up the extra cash. Her plans hadn't changed. Save up and move in with Joey and Taylor as soon as possible.

*

Sunday evening Sal had stopped by his parents' on his way home. He hadn't had a chance to tell his dad about the meeting until then. As expected, he wasn't happy about it. "I don't want them changing shit."

Sal assured him he wouldn't sign or even think about signing anything with anyone without checking with him and his mom first. His mother hadn't been in the best of moods either. Her plans to throw Alex and

Valerie a huge baby shower were spoiled with the news that Valerie would be confined to her bed from now until the babies came. She was carrying the babies too low now and at this point, the doctors didn't think it was wise that she be walking around if she expected to carry to term. Alex had his hands full, trying to keep his energetic wife following doctor's orders.

Sal's younger and only sister, Sofia, walked in from the back door. She was in her running gear and pulled her earphones out when she saw Sal.

"Hey, big brother." She smiled, hugging him at arm's length. "I'm all sweaty."

Sal leaned over and kissed her on the forehead anyway. "How's it been over there?"

Sofia had been helping out at Angel's restaurant for the past week. They'd been short-staffed but she'd be back at Alex's this week. Not a moment too soon either, since Sal could tell already, Alex's days were numbered. It would only be so long before Alex couldn't stand not being home with Valerie to monitor her every move. As it was, he was on the phone with her every ten minutes.

"Busy," she said, grabbing a water out of the fridge. "They're gonna have to hire more help. I heard we got a new bartender. Is he any good?"

Sal almost frowned. He'd managed to squash any thoughts of Grace at least for a few hours. "He's a she," he said. "And yeah, she's good—fast."

After draining nearly half the bottle of water, Sofia wiped her mouth with the back of her hand. "Really? Good, that's what we needed."

He was at his parents' house until well after nine. So many things crowded his mind. Another meeting with the investors was on the agenda this week. Sal had to decide if he was going to go forward with this or go a different route. In Valerie's delicate state, he wouldn't be able to count on Alex for much, soon. He was looking at taking the restaurant on full time at least until Valerie had the babies. There was no way he could commit to anything that would take him away from the restaurant until after the babies were born. Even then, he couldn't imagine Alex wanting to leave Valerie and his babies too soon.

Then there was the matter of getting more qualified help as soon as possible. He'd want to be there if Angel was going to do any hiring. That guy was worse than Alex when it came to being soft. It amazed Sal how two hard asses like his brothers could be so soft when it came to their families and employees.

Most annoyingly on his mind? Grace. He still didn't get it. He was a grown ass man with too many plans to be thinking about this. How was it that this little twenty-one year old culinary student trying to prove herself to him was beginning to get under his skin?

CHAPTER 6

Every day Grace went into the restaurant, she prepared herself for the unease she felt being around Sal. She wondered how long it would be, before she was comfortable around him. She'd been off Monday and Tuesday. Wednesday had been fairly painless. Sal had spent a lot of time out of the restaurant. He'd had a meeting and Thursday he spent at Angel's restaurant on the Marina interviewing potential hires.

Friday she came in and again, was overcome with the same disappointment of not seeing him. Something she refused to admit to anyone, not her sister, not even Joey or Taylor. She felt like a silly schoolgirl waiting for the cute guy to show up to class. This was her boss for heaven's sake. A boss that hadn't even wanted to hire her. A man she'd labeled a jerk.

They'd since hired another bartender and a new cook. She watched the cook, who was not yet head chef, as he prepared his dishes. He didn't seem very confident, at times it even seemed that his nerves got the best of him and he'd begin to panic. Really? She'd been passed up for this?

Grace was busy making three margaritas when she glanced up and nearly spilled what she was pouring. Sal walked in wearing a black on black business suit—everything black including his tie. He looked amazing—more than amazing. Jesus, she felt like those shallow girls in her pastry class. She didn't even realize she was gawking until Melanie nudged her. "Take a number," she giggled, handing her a towel to clean what she'd splattered.

Feeling her face flush she took the towel and tried sounding genuinely confused. "What do you mean?"

"Are you kidding me? Sal gets that same reaction from all women. Isn't he mesmerizing though? If I wasn't already engaged, I swear I'd be all over that."

Grace chewed on the inside of her cheek. Something about that second statement made her feel so ridiculously insignificant. She didn't want to get lumped in as one his groupies. So he was good looking. Big deal. She'd been around plenty of good looking guys. This was the man she worked for. It was completely inappropriate to be gaping at him that way, not to mention embarrassing as hell.

Trying not to show her agitation about having been so obvious, she wiped her hands on a wet towel. "I don't look at him like that."

"Oh really? Could've fooled me."

Grace felt her face flush again but refused to concede. "He just looks different today. That's all."

"He must have a date or something."

A sudden heat now accompanied Grace's flushed face. She placed the margaritas on the tray Julie had left on the counter. "Damn," Julie said, as she walked up to take the tray. She was staring in Sal's direction. Grace busied herself with the next order of drinks. "I wonder who the lucky girl is tonight." Julie stood there for a moment blatantly staring his way. "Oh, here he comes. Back to work."

She grabbed the tray and walked away. Melanie had walked over to the other side of the bar to take someone's order, leaving Grace alone. The discomfort she normally felt around Sal had spiked to a new height.

He was still a few feet away and she could already smell him. He wore the most alluring cologne she'd ever smelled and she closed her eyes for a second, taking it in.

"Hey, Grace. Has it been busy?"

Unwilling to take him in, in this close proximity, she pretended to be engrossed in the drink she was preparing, even bent over to grab something out of the refrigerator just to avoid looking at him. "Off and on." She indulged herself with a quick glance, regretting it almost instantly. As good looking as he'd been even on her first day when he arrived suited up from his meeting, today just wasn't fair. Something about the all black suit brought out his amazing eyes out and those heavy lashes taunted her. "You know," she cleared her throat annoyed that her stupid voice that nearly gave out on her, "...how it is. They come in herds."

"Let me go tell Alex I'm here so he can take off. I'll be back, I have something for you."

He finally had her full attention. Not that he hadn't from the moment he walked in but she allowed herself now to really look at him. He smiled that beautiful smile of his and began to walk away. "I'll be back."

Panicked and not having a clue what he might have for her, she rushed over to the bowl with the peppermint candies. She stuck one in her mouth then glanced at herself in the mirror behind the bar. Of course, she had one strand of hair sticking straight up like a cockatoo. *Damn it.* Why hadn't anybody told her?

Grace was still fixing her hair when she heard Alex's voice coming from the hallway to the back. Sal was with him when they turned the corner and walked toward her. She grabbed a towel and began cleaning off the bar area diligently. "I'm outta here, Gracie. I'll see you tomorrow."

Alex waved at Melanie and said his goodbyes to a few of the other servers before walking out. Sal walked over to her, holding a baseball cap. He handed it to her as soon as he was close enough. "This is yours."

She took it, examining it. It had the restaurant's logo embroidered on it and the phrase, *Slam-dunking for over 30 years*, around the back. She glanced up at him confused.

"March Madness is going on right now. We get a lot of people in here, watching the games. So on game days all the bartenders wear these. I'm ordering jerseys with the logos as well." He flashed that killer smile. "Team Moreno's."

Something about being part of a team, *his* team, even if it was just metaphorically, excited her and she smiled — probably a little too much.

"This is just a temp," he added. "I'm having your name embroidered on one. Is Gracie okay?"

As silly and as trite as that was, that excited her e-ven further. "Yeah, Gracie is fine." She turned to the mirror and tried it on, pulling her ponytail out of the back opening. She turned back to Sal with a giddy smile. "How's that?"

He stared at her for a moment before saying, "L-ooks good."

Just like that, the moment they were having was lost. She'd finally felt at ease with him, even if it was on for a instant over a silly cap, when that hardened look she was so familiar with now washed over him.

He glanced over her shoulder. "Melanie, you still have your cap from last year?"

"I think so. It's somewhere at home."

"Let me know if I have to order you another one."

Sal's eyes met hers one last time as she removed the cap before he excused himself saying he had to make some calls. Grace sighed. She'd never figure him out.

She slipped the cap under the bar, but after spilling something that almost dripped down there, she decided to take it back and put it in her cabinet. She slowed as she reached the open office door. Sal was on the phone.

"Melissa, you have a way of always turning my words around."

Grace held her breath, glancing around to see if anyone was watching her. No one was.

"Sweetheart, I think I'd remember if I said that."

Someone walked out of the kitchen forcing Grace to keep walking.

"No, I'm not calling you a liar I'm just saying —" he stopped talking when Grace walked in.

Grace motioned that she was just putting the cap away.

He nodded and continued. "I'm just saying you obviously misinterpreted what I said."

She could not get out of there fast enough. Sal laughed as she walked back to the bar, rolling her eyes. *Chick magnet.* The man had them coming at him from every angle.

*

Melissa's phone calls were starting up again. Sal knew he should have never agreed to see her again. After a hair-splitting phone call with her, where she conveniently mistook him saying *I'll see you around,* to mean *I want to see you again,* he finally got her off the phone without having to promise to get together with her.

He checked his e-mail to see if the investors he'd met with today had sent him the proposal they promised to have for him by the end of the day. It was still a little early, but he was anxious. This was the first time since he started looking into teaming up with others to expand the restaurants, that they were more interested in being silent partners than having a hand in everything. But they did say they had a few stipulations of their own. Stipulations that would be outlined in the proposal.

Sal almost went home first to change, but he'd hardly been in the restaurant this week. He was anxious to get there already. He told himself it was because Alex was waiting for him so he could go home to Valerie, but there was more to his anxiety about getting to the restaurant. Something he wasn't even ready to admit to himself yet. He pushed it to the back of his head until he saw Grace when he walked in. Even then, he reasoned the thrill that he felt was nothing more than the comfort of being back in a familiar place with familiar faces. But after a few doses of her wide-eyed excitement, topped with how sweet she looked in the ball cap on he had to get it together—had to snap out of it.

One look at his inundated email inbox and Sal's head nearly hit his keyboard. He kept saying he would go through it soon. Now was as good a time as any. He spent about an hour clearing it out and still, no proposal.

With his head swimming from all the emails he had to go through, he left the office to grab something to drink. He ran into Grace who hurried into the back.

"Sorry," she said, smiling, her hand on his chest.

Her touch sent a bolt through him as if it were the first time he felt a woman's touch. "Where's the fire?" He managed to keep his voice steady.

"I'm off now and my ride is here." She looked up at him.

This was the closest he'd been to her and Sal had to fight the incredible urge to get even closer. He moved out of the way, letting her by and walked into the dining room. It was still a few hours before closing time. Grace usually worked the closing shift but she must've come in earlier today.

Julie was manning the hostess desk at the front of the restaurant. He walked over to check if they had any late reservations or if tonight would be all walk-ins. There was a scruffy guy at the door in dreadlocks, as Sal walked up to the hostess desk. Sal didn't miss the way the guy checked him out thoroughly. So much so, he made it a point to address him. "Have you been helped?"

The guy's smirk was a bit too smug. "No, I'm good."

What the hell did that mean? Sal looked him over for a second, before deciding he was probably meeting someone and turned to Julie.

He glanced at the night's reservation list when he heard the guy purr, "Hey beautiful." Sal looked up just in time to catch the guy wrap his arm around Grace's neck and kiss her temple.

She turned to Sal and Julie and waved as she walked out with the grunge freak. Sal stood there stunned — or something. He wasn't sure what it was feeling, but somehow the scene had left him rattled. *Another boyfriend?*

Forgetting about the reservation list, he stalked

back toward the office. He didn't even realize he was pissed until he slammed the door shut. He sat back in his chair, breathing hard and stared at the ceiling. What the hell was wrong with him?

*

"All right, I'll give Joey this one. Your boss *is* smokin' hot."

Grace was getting tired of hearing this now. First from the girls in class, then Joey, then the girls at work, and now Taylor. It wasn't like she needed to be reminded of the obvious. She only wished it didn't bother her. Why should it? She nodded but said nothing to further that topic.

Taylor pulled up to the front of her apartment building where there were two homeless men arguing outside. "You want me to walk you in?"

"No, I'm okay. Those two are always going at it." She smiled as she watched Randy and The Snake shake their fists at each other. "They're harmless."

Taylor stared at them, taken aback. "Are you sure?"

"Absolutely."

She turned back, leaning in to give him a kiss on the cheek. He turned his head and she stopped just before their lips met. She frowned — same old trick — Taylor smiled. "One of these days you'll fall for it."

Grace nudged him before opening the door. "I'll make sure it happens when Joey's around. You'll be walking crooked for a week."

Taylor squeezed his legs together and winced. "Why do you always have to go there?"

Gracie laughed then thanked him for the ride. Taylor always did things like that. Even in front of Joey.

Joey played the part of being jealous, but if anyone was the jealous one, it was Taylor. She'd seen it once and it hadn't been pretty.

Yet, for as much as Taylor flirted, she'd never seen so much as a spark of real jealousy from Joey. He knew Taylor would never actually do anything.

As was the norm at her place, Ruben lay sprawled out on the sofa—beer cans and a bag of chips on the floor. Her mom peeked in from the hallway. "Pssst!"

Grace lifted her hand in the air and mouthed, "What?"

Her mom motioned for her to come over and put her finger over her lips.

Grace closed the door as quietly as possible. Ruben continued to snore like a bear. She held her keys tight in her hands so they wouldn't jingle. They made it to her room and her mom closed the door behind her. "Frank wants to see you again."

"What?" Grace felt sick to her stomach.

Rose was on her bed with the laptop on her legs. She glanced at Grace giving her that 'I feel for you' look.

"He called earlier today and said he really enjoyed the time he spent with you and he'd like to do it again. I was just thinking—"

"No!" Grace was done doing these things for her mom.

"If Ruben gets the job he'll be gone most of the week."

Grace and Rose's eyes locked. One of the things that gnawed at her most of the day was wondering how much time Rose had to spend locked in her room for fear of walking out into the kitchen or living room and being harassed by Ruben.

"What does me seeing Frank again have to do with Ruben getting the job?"

Her mother frowned. "It's not a done deal yet. Spending another evening with him just might seal the deal." A calculating smile spread across her face and she turned to Rose. "Won't it be nice when Ruben starts working and he's only home late in the evening and gone before we're all up?"

Another glance at her sister and she knew what Rose was thinking. If guilt was a facial expression, Rose wore it on her lips like a tight rope wire. As much as she hated it the idea of going on a fixed date with this man, it was totally worth it, if it meant getting Ruben out of the house. She turned back to her mother who didn't even try to hide her anticipation and sighed. "When?"

Her mother nearly jumped. "Sometime next week."

"Remember I have work and school."

"Yes, yes." Her mom reached out and held her by the shoulders. "We'll work something out." She crushed Grace into a hug. "*Ay, mija,* thank you so much. You won't regret this!"

Grace closed her eyes, taking a deep breath. She already did.

CHAPTER 7

Saturday morning Sal went through the online applications for employment at Angel's restaurant. Angel had given him the go-ahead to take over the hiring. Like Alex, he didn't care much for scheduling or conducting interviews. Sal called back the few he'd consider. To his surprise they were all available for an interview that very afternoon. He scheduled the interviews at Angel's location and was out before Grace's shift started.

The menu at Angel's restaurant was almost identical to Alex's but the one difference was that they were on the marina competing with a bunch of seafood restaurants. Therefore they boasted a lot more seafood specials. And no restaurant on the marina was complete without the lobster-filled aquarium at the entrance.

Sal stopped as he walked in to assess the lobsters in the aquarium.

"Hey, Sal." Sarah, his sister-in-law walked over and hugged him. "You look all spiffy." She tugged his tie, smiling.

Sal kissed her forehead. "Interviewing today—how's everything here? Where's Angel?"

Sarah gave him a look. "You didn't see him out there?"

"No." Sal turned back to the door.

"Some of the other restaurants are offering dinner cruises. There are a lot of sight-seeing and touring reps that have been coming around leaving their brochures.

But it sounds complicated to me. Angel thinks it's a good idea for the summer."

Sal thought about it. In theory, it was a good idea, but getting one of those boats to meet code regulations with the health department would be a bitch. "Maybe appetizers and drinks. I don't know about a full blown dinner."

"The Surf Club is already doing it. Angel went over to talk to them about it the other day, but he said they didn't offer too much information."

Sal walked toward their back office with Sarah. This was where he spent most of his time, when he was here. "Yeah, they're not going to. Angel's better off asking the cruise services."

"Well, that's where he is now. It makes me nervous. Anything goes wrong, and we'll be responsible."

Sarah was right. Maybe he could get Carlos, his godfather and the family's longtime attorney, to look into the details. "I'll look into it."

"Good," Sarah smiled. "So how many people are you interviewing today?"

"Three, a cook, a waiter, and a bartender." He took the seat at the desk.

"I heard about your new bartender. Oscar was over here yesterday. He said she's really good," Sarah smiled. "The way he went on and on about her, I think he may have crush."

Sal pretended to be into what was on the computer screen, but he had to ease up on the mouse in his hand when he heard a cracking noise.

"Hey, dude." Angel walked in. He kissed Sarah as she walked out.

Sal glanced at him in time to see Angel pat her behind.

"I hope you're not gonna do what you've been doing at Alex's place."

Sal turned to him with a frown. "What's that?"

"Be all picky and shit, about the hiring. I just need help. We keep getting swamped, especially on Sundays."

"You have to be picky, Angel. You can't just hire anyone."

"Yeah, but," Angel said, taking the seat next to the desk. "you don't understand, Sal. People start getting pissed when the service is so damn slow and we're moving as fast as we can. The last thing I need is for the word to get out that the service sucks."

Sal stared at him and scratched his forehead. "That bad, huh?"

"Yeah, I had a few people walk out last week."

"Shit. Why didn't you tell me?"

"I'm telling you now!"

Sal turned back to the computer and clicked on a different screen. "I'll see if I can get a few more people in today to interview. I didn't realize how bad it was."

Angel sat back, pulling the pencil out from behind his ear. He tossed it in the air in front of him. "Oscar told me about the new bartender over there," he grinned. "Said she's *real* good — in more ways than one."

"How the fuck would he know?"

Angel stopped tossing the pencil. "Easy!"

Sal gulped hard but refused to look at Angel.

"He said she knows what she's doing and she's fast. He didn't say anything *bad*." He tossed the pencil up again. "But he did say her cute accent goes with her personality."

What did that even mean? Sal wouldn't ask. He clenched his teeth and continued scanning through some of the other applications he'd dismissed that morning. "What's more crucial right now? Waiters or cooks?"

"Both," Angel said. "But I'm short on waiters. I have one on maternity leave and Sofie's going back to Alex's today."

"I can have her stay and help if you need her."

"Nah, we should be okay today. I have one back from vacation and Debbie who was out sick most of the week came back yesterday. I just need some new hires now, so they'll be good and trained for the summer when things really start kicking up."

"I'm on it."

"Did Sarah tell you about the dinner cruises?"

"Yeah, I'll have Carlos look into it first. I'm sure there's a lot of red tape involved."

Angel stood up and put the pencil behind his ear. "Some of the restaurants are thinking maybe booze cruises, just on the weekends."

Sal laughed. "I'll tell you right now. You're probably looking at a small fortune on the insurance alone for something like that."

"Well, ask Carlos anyway."

"I will."

Sal spent the rest of the day interviewing. In light of what Angel had told him about customers walking out, he found himself lowering his standards a bit. At least when it came to the amount of experience he normally was comfortable with. If he had to be there to train the less experienced himself, he would.

In spite of staying busy most of the day, his mind kept wandering back to Grace and her two boyfriends. What the hell was that about? He reminded himself, that her personal life was none of his business yet the annoying thoughts continued to plague him through out the day.

*

Another day of showing up to work and finding out Sal wouldn't be there. Nearly colliding with him last night, being that close—touching him, had Grace feeling things she knew she shouldn't. She'd nearly forgotten all about it when she got home and her mother dropped the news about Frank on her. But as soon as her head hit her pillow those thoughts were in high gear again. So much, she actually dreamed of him—talking to him and staring in his eyes, like she was never quite able to do in real life, without looking away.

As disappointing as it was that he wasn't there, it was better that way. This infatuation, if that's what she was going to call it, was beginning to get out of hand. The man didn't even care for her, much less see her in that way. Even if by some miracle he ever would, Melanie had told her about his love-em and leave-em tendencies. He seemed perfectly content with his bachelor status. In the short time she'd worked there, she'd witnessed his *action* with the ladies first hand. She knew better than to get caught up in that web.

Grace had just finished putting on her apron when a girl she'd never met walked in the back room.

"Hey." She smiled big.

Grace knew Sal was still working on hiring more people. This girl had long, thick, beautiful hair and was drop dead gorgeous. *Great.*

"Hey," Grace smiled but not nearly as big as the girl had. "You new?"

"No, actually I've been helping out at the other restaurant for the past week. They had a few people call in sick. But I'm back now." She pulled an apron out of one of the drawers in the cabinet. "I'm Sofia." The big perfect smile was still draped across her face. She tied the apron behind her. "You must be the new bartender I heard about."

Grace waited a second before responding. "I'm not the only bartender they hired recently."

"No, it's you. Sal spoke of a girl. I know he hired another guy but he didn't mention much about him."

And he had mentioned *her*? Trying not to sound too interested, Grace turned away from Sofia and placed her purse in the cabinet. "Really? What did he say?"

"That you're good. And he said you're fast. Which, let me tell you — we need fast, especially on the week-end." Sofia pulled her ball cap on. "Sweet Sixteen starts this weekend. You'll see what I'm talking about."

"Sweet sixteen?"

"March Madness." Sofia looked at her like she was from another planet. "The last sixteen college teams standing, they start battling it out this weekend. It's gonna get busy in here."

Grace was still thinking about Sal talking about her. Sofia said he'd hardly mentioned the other bartender. She shook it off, grabbing her cap out of the cabinet and began putting it on. "So uh, is Alex closing today?" That was one way of finding out if Sal would be there later or not. It was only either him or Alex who ever closed.

"No, he'll be in for a few hours, but I'm closing."

"You?"

"Yeah," Sofia smiled at her. She leaned over the desk and typed something into the keyboard of the computer. "Ugh, Sal has to be so damn anal about everything. Does he really think anyone has time to take their lunch and breaks when he schedules them?" She turned to Grace. "Seriously he does all this." She motioned to the screen. "And no one even bothers to look at it."

Alex walked in. "Hey, Gracie. Sof, you're back."

He leaned in and kissed the side of her head as Sofia continued to type something then laughed. "Don't tell Sal I did this."

Alex peered at the screen and smiled. "He's gonna know it was you."

"Doesn't he get it? After all these years?" She turned to Grace. "He still prints out recipes for the cooks that have been cooking here for years. I can just imagine the stuff he laid on the new cook."

Alex laughed. "Oh yeah, poor sap has his homework cut out for him."

"Homework?" Grace finally spoke up.

Alex sat down. "Just wait, Gracie. You'll see when you get in the kitchen. Sal's too much. I'm surprised he hasn't been riding you about the Moreno way of making drinks."

Sofia turned to Grace. "He hasn't given you the whole speech yet, about the way things work around here?"

Grace shook her head. "No, the most he did was give me a tour of the restaurant."

Alex and Sofia exchanged glances. "Maybe it was the way things went down with Grace. I hired her, not Sal," Alex chuckled. "He wasn't too happy about it either."

Grace tried not to frown at that.

"Why?" Sofia turned back to Alex. "He even said she was good."

"Ah." Alex winked at Grace. "Minor details on her résumé. You know Sal. But it's all good now. Gracie's in, and we got ourselves a hell of a bartender."

Sofia rolled her eyes then smiled at Grace. "Once you get used to Sal's meticulous ways, he's not so bad."

It wasn't until a few hours later that Grace got a revelation making her feel like an idiot. The whole time since Sofia had arrived, the way she spoke of Sal and how at home she made herself at the restaurant, Grace had begun to wonder about her relationship with Sal.

Then Sofia's fiancé dropped by and asked her something about her brothers. When Sofia told him only Alex was there, Grace nearly slapped herself on the forehead. Of course. She'd been so preoccupied with how pretty Sofia was and how Sal, who obviously did most of the hiring, and was so *meticulous*, had not only hired her, but given someone so young the responsibility of closing the restaurant by herself, Grace missed the resemblance entirely. She didn't even put it together when she saw the dimples Sofia flashed. Now it all made sense, even the way Alex had greeted her with a kiss.

What bothered Grace now was how relieved she'd been. What business was it of hers to care about who Sal hired and what inspired him to, anyway? She was forgetting her whole purpose for being here—time in the kitchen. That's what she should be focusing on. From that moment on, she vowed to stop with what was beginning to smother her every thought. But as much as she tried to stay busy and focus on doing her job, she couldn't help looking up and hoping it was Sal every time someone walked in. Even after they were closed, she looked up, hopeful it was him who knocked on the locked door. She smiled when she saw Joey, but couldn't help feeling let down.

Sofia unlocked the door and smiled at Joey as Grace walked out. "You working tomorrow, Grace?"

"Yeah, I close."

"Alex said maybe we can get you in the kitchen this week. I think tomorrow would be good. Most of the day it's a brunch but we do get some people ordering off the menu instead. Might be a good time to get you in there since menu orders are at their slowest on Sundays."

Grace glanced at Joey, he was already smiling. Grace nodded, feeling the sudden excitement. "Yeah, for sure."

"So come in early. We got enough people to cover the closing shift."

"Okay."

"Great, see you in the morning." Sofia closed the door.

Grace didn't even wait for her to finish locking the door. She turned to Joey who looked ready to burst and jumped in his arms. He picked her up and spun her around. Grace saw Sofia laugh.

"I told you, Gracie! This is it. There's no way they won't be impressed with your cooking."

Suddenly, everything she'd been obsessing about all day took a back seat. She was going to be cooking in Moreno's kitchen tomorrow. This was a dream come true. She leaned her forehead against Joey's. "Oh. My. God. How am I gonna get any sleep tonight?"

Joey laughed and she pulled away. They started walking to his car hand in hand. "You need to bring your A game tomorrow, so you *better* get some sleep. Don't blow this Grace." He squeezed her hand. "Oh, what am I talking about? You got this."

The whole drive home she talked Joey's ear off about the way she'd seen them prepare certain dishes and how Alex and Sofia had both said Sal was so anal about everything. She had her own way of cooking and she didn't do recipes. What if Sal insisted she did? She almost wished he wouldn't be there tomorrow, but at the same time she wanted him to taste her cooking.

By the time they got to her house, she was all talked out.

"Relax. You're gonna do great." Joey squeezed her hand then kissed it. "I'm so excited for you. Call me as soon as you get their first reaction. I'm sure they're gonna be floored."

That night Grace lay in bed, trying not to toss and turn too much. Her sister was sleeping soundly as u-sual. She'd told Rose about getting her chance in the kitchen tomorrow and she'd been just as excited about it as Joey had been.

As exciting as finally getting her opportunity to prove herself was, and as much as she tried to focus on that and that alone, her thoughts kept swaying in one direction. It wasn't about would *they* be impressed? All she could think of was, would *Sal* be impressed? She reasoned that it was because he was the one who ini-tially dismissed her as inexperienced but in her heart she knew there was more to it. For some reason the thought of impressing Sal Moreno in *any* way had sud-denly become a priority.

*

Sunday morning Sal rushed in early to get the week's inventory done as quickly as possible. He wanted to be out of there before the closing shift came in. He'd already called Jason. Sal was meeting him for a round of golf then he was stopping by Alex's. His mother was preparing a Sunday dinner over at Alex's house since Valerie couldn't get out of bed and she wanted everyone to drop by.

Staying busy was good. It helped keep his mind off of *other* things. He'd finally admitted to himself that maybe he *was* a little attracted to Grace, but after seeing her with boyfriend number two, it squashed any possibilities. Besides, it was out of the question. She was too young for him *and* she was an employee, it would never work. He was stupid to have even considered the thought.

He sat back staring straight ahead at the cabinets against the wall. It was just a physical thing. Even though at first he hadn't been very impressed by Grace, after being around her he noticed a few things about her that could be construed as attractive. Her big innocent eyes, the curves he hadn't been privy to on their first meeting because of the unflattering dress. The way there was no hiding her excitement even over the smallest things — a ball cap. And that laugh… there was no way he could hear it and not smile.

Alex walked into the back room. "What's with the cheesy smile?"

Sal straightened out. "I was just thinking about something." He spun his chair around to face the computer. "Are Angel and Sarah gonna be there tonight?"

Sofia walked in. "I heard dad on the phone last night so they better be." She giggled. "Is Grace here yet?"

Sal turned around. "No, she's closing."

"Well, she was," Sofia said, grabbing an apron out

of the drawer. "I told her to come in early. We're gonna give her a shot in the kitchen. I figured Sunday is a good day for her since—"

"Wait," Sal said, feeling uneasy. "Who okayed this?"

Alex laughed. "What do you mean? We said we were gonna give her shot so we're giving her a shot."

Sal couldn't care less about her in the kitchen at this point. He'd figured this attraction thing would go away with a few days of not seeing her. He'd planned it, damn it. Easy peasy. Monday and Tuesday were her days off. If he scheduled a few more interviews Wednesday and Thursday at Angel's, it would be almost a week before he'd have to be around her again. He would've been home free by then. Now they'd thrown a wrench in his plans.

"Yeah, and you should've seen how excited she was last night when I told her." Sofia added. "Even her boyfriend was excited. He picked her up and spun her around. He's a cutie!"

Sal squeezed the armrest of his chair. "Which one?"

"What do you mean?" Sofia stopped tying her apron.

Before he could gather his thoughts to respond, Alex's words made him hold his breath. "Speak of the devil."

In walked Grace. It had only been one full day since he last saw her and it felt like forever. Her hair was down. All this time he'd been witness to her hair in a bun or in a ponytail. Now it was down and hung loosely around her face, adding yet another thing he hadn't noticed about her before. How damn sexy she was. *Of course.*

CHAPTER 8

They'd been talking about her. Grace felt her heart speed up at Alex's words, but seeing Sal when she walked in the back room pushed her nerves into overdrive. "Morning," she said, to no one in particular.

"Good morning, Grace." Sofia was the first to respond.

"Ready to show us your stuff?" Alex asked, with a smile. He turned back to Sal, "I'm curious about this. If she's even half as good at cooking as she is at putting drinks together, I think we got ourselves a cook."

"Good morning, Grace," Sal said.

His stoic expression said it all. He didn't share the same enthusiasm as his siblings about testing her cooking skills. He looked at Alex. "You'll have to tell me about it. I'll be leaving in a little while."

"What? You're not gonna stick around and see what she can do?"

Sal's eyes met hers for a lingering moment. Then he added to her disappointment, "Nah, I'm meeting someone in a couple hours. I'll get a chance to another time."

With that, he turned around to face the computer.

"You'll have to put your hair up though, Grace," Sofia said, as she pulled her own hair up.

"Oh, I was going to. I just wore it down so it could dry on my way here." Grace started digging in her bag for the band she used to pull her hair up in a ponytail. She gulped trying not to think about Sal's aloof demeanor.

Her throat actually constricted, making her swallow hard. How could a few cold words from him actually make her feel like choking up? It was *so* stupid. *She* was so stupid. All night and all morning, it's all she had thought about — what *he* would think of her cooking.

She'd been a ball of nerves the whole bus ride there. Then hearing Alex's words stirred things up in her stomach even more but seeing Sal had done it. All day yesterday, she'd longed to see him, even if it was for just a moment. Now here he was and as usual, his indifference for her was palpable. Even as anal as they'd made him sound about the cooks, he wasn't the least bit interested in seeing how she fared in his precious kitchen.

Of course not, why would he? God, she felt ridiculous. This restaurant, as important as it was to him, wasn't his life. He had a life outside of this place and apparently, whoever he was meeting today took precedence.

Alex stepped out of the office to take a call from his wife. Sofia finished with her hair and apron before Grace. "I'll go check what orders, if any, are in the kitchen. But it's rare that anyone orders off the menu during brunch, especially because all the breakfast stuff is already out there."

Grace nodded, hurrying to get her hair done. She didn't want to be left alone too long with Sal. As soon as Sofia walked out the door, Sal turned to Grace almost as if he'd been waiting for Sofia to leave the room. "So which one is your boyfriend? Or are they both?"

His question came out of nowhere. She stopped what she was doing. "What?"

"The guys that pick you up after work." He stared

at her, the apathy now replaced with significant interest. He shrugged. "Just curious. Sofie mentioned your boyfriend seemed real excited last night when he picked you up. Does he know about the other guy?"

His tone was anything but *just curious*. It was almost accusatory. Wow, he wasn't kidding when he'd said first impressions went a long way. He still had her pegged as a liar. "They're both just friends of mine. Neither is a boyfriend."

She saw the insolence in his smile. "So do your *friends* know about each other?"

Was he for real? Alex walked in just in time to hear her response. "As a matter of fact they do. We hang out together all the time." She wasn't about to get into Joey and Taylor's relationship with him. It was none of his business. How dare he pass judgment on her with all the women he had hanging all over him?

She finished with her hair and reached for her apron.

"Sounds interesting." He turned around to face the computer again. "You'll need a jacket if you're going to be in the kitchen."

He almost sounded mad. Having his reservations about her as an employee because of the lie on her résumé was one thing. She'd give him that, even if she'd already apologized for it. But getting haughty over something he found questionable about her personal life was crossing the line. He had no right, no matter how anal he was about his employees' integrity.

She took a deep breath, glancing at Alex and held in what she really wanted to say. "Where do I get a jacket?"

"In the stock room. Sofia can show you."

She finished with her apron and shoved her bag in

the cabinet.

"Showtime," Alex said.

As excited as she'd been when she got there, she couldn't even muster a smile before walking past Alex out the door. If Sal had made up his mind about her already, then there was no need to even try to impress him. Apparently, the jerk had her all figured out.

*

Wait for it...Wait for it...

"What the hell was that about, Sal?"

And there it was. "What do you mean?"

Alex closed the door. "You know what I'm talking about. You pissed her off. What did you say to her?"

Sal turned around. Just a few weeks into it and Alex was already turning into the protective big brother. This was so like him. Sal shrugged. "Two different guys picked her up last week. I just asked her about them. She didn't seem mad to me."

"Are you kidding me? She looked ready to spit nails. What did you ask her?" Alex crossed his arms and stared at him.

Sal couldn't help frowning. Truth was she *had* been a little too defensive. "All I asked, is if they knew about each other."

"What?" Alex looked even more disgusted. "Since when do you get all involved?"

"I don't. I was just curious."

"Bullshit, that's straight out nosey. No wonder she was so pissed."

"So I'll apologize." It wouldn't be the first time. "I didn't think she'd be so bothered by it."

"What's going on Sal? What is it with you and this

girl? You still ticked off that I hired her even after you said she'd *struck out?*"

Sal stood up. He was done having this conversation. "Nope, I just asked her something that apparently rubbed her the wrong way. I'll go apologize, then I'm out of here."

He walked to the door aware that Alex was still staring at him. He opened the door and glanced back at him. Alex continued to stare at him but the scowl softened. Then suddenly he smirked. "You're into her."

"What?" Sal did his best to appear incredulous.

"You're into Grace."

Sal shoved the door closed. "No, I'm not."

"Yeah, you are." Alex laughed. "Why else would you ask her about the guys picking her up? You jealous, Sal?"

"I'm not *you*, you idiot."

Alex laughed even more now. "Oh this is great. Sal's got the hots for the new hire."

"Will you shut up?" Sal peeked through the door to make sure no one was within hearing range. "She's attractive. I'll give her that. But you know I can't get involved with anyone that works here."

"Why not? Sarah worked here before she and Angel got married."

"That's different." He couldn't believe he was even discussing this. "They were already involved when she came to work here."

"Man, you must really be into her to ask her something so ballsy. So what did she say? Is she really seeing two guys?"

"No!" Sal was letting Alex get the best for him. He needed to regain his composure here. "She said they're just friends."

Alex laughed again. "I see. So that's when you asked her if they knew about each other. Good one. I would've asked the same thing."

Sal wasn't sure if his brother and him sharing the same mentality when it came to reacting to women was a good thing. It was never in his nature to just react. That was Alex and Angel—not him. But the question had just slipped out before he even knew it. Just like his comment about Alex being married, her first day on the job. Now he was going to have to apologize *again*.

"I was out of line, Alex."

"Not really, Sofie said the guy picked her up and spun her around last night."

Sal worked his jaw. As much as that annoyed him, it still came down to one thing. "Friend or not, it's none of my business."

"Technically, I'm the boss here, Sal. I think she's pretty damn adorable. You wanna make it your business? Have at it. I don't have a problem with it."

Sal opened the door. That was impossible. There was no way it would work. Not only did she have guy *friends* who were a little too friendly for his liking, he'd managed to come across as a total asshole more than once now.

"Hey," Alex added.

Sal turned around.

"Just don't mess with her, man. *That* I'll have a problem with. I like her. She's a sweet girl and a damn good bartender. I don't want you giving her any reason to leave."

He almost walked out without responding then stopped and turned around. "Not a word about this to anyone, you hear me?"

Alex smirked.

"I'm serious, ass."

Alex nodded in agreement but not before getting in a few more laughs.

Grace was already busy in the kitchen when he got there, and she looked as comfortable as she did behind the bar. "You got breakfast orders?"

Grace shook her head without even looking up. Obviously, she was still mad. One of the other cooks addressed him. "She's helping out with the brunch, Chief."

Sal nodded, watching her for a moment. She *was* a natural. Julian, the other cook he'd hired, was still fumbling around after more than a week of being here. Grace had been in the kitchen less than a half hour and she seemed in complete control.

He walked toward her until he was just a few feet away. She still didn't look at him. "I wanna apologize," he said softly. "...again, I was out of line. What you do outside of the restaurant is your business. I have no place questioning you about it."

Finally, she looked at him. "Why *did* you?"

He was hoping she wouldn't ask that. "I dunno—curious, they both seemed a little too friendly to be just friends."

"They're gay."

His expression must've been as blank as it felt, because she laughed. "They're each other's boyfriend and my best friends."

"Oh." Was all he could think of to say, but he couldn't help smiling—this changed everything. "So you accept my apology?"

She smiled, nodding. "Yeah, I guess."

The whole time he'd been standing there she hadn't stopped what she was doing. She whisked eggs without even looking at them and the cheese filled green chilies she'd dipped in them was something she had put together effortlessly.

"That looks good."

"They are." She smiled, smug.

His phone buzzed and he pulled out and read a text from Jason.

On my way. See you there.

Damn. He didn't want to leave now.

"I gotta go. But maybe Wednesday, we can get you in here again and I can watch you work your magic."

He watched as her smile slowly evaporated and she glanced at his phone. "Sounds good. Have fun."

He hated to leave but he did. Now he was going to have to go almost three days before seeing her again. *Stupid plan.*

*

By the end of her shift, Gracie had impressed not only Alex and Sofia but some of the other cooks. She even made a dish that wasn't on the menu—one of her grandmother's specialties—a green chili chicken enchilada casserole. They had a whole list of enchiladas on the menu, all of which she could whip up with her eyes closed, but this was something her grandmother had come up with that could be made in huge quantities in half the time it took to roll up equal amounts of enchiladas. The casseroles were big sellers in her grandmother's restaurant. People bought them for parties back in Juarez.

Sofia walked into the kitchen as Grace finished clearing her area up. "You're a hit."

Grace smiled. Alex had already left, but he'd said

the same thing before he walked out. As good as it felt, she couldn't shake the disappointment of not having been able to show Sal what she could do.

"What's this?" Sofia pointed at the casserole on the counter.

"Enchilada casserole."

"It looks good. Who's it for?"

Grace lifted a shoulder. "Alex said he'd have a houseful tonight. My grandmother used to make these for parties. I thought maybe you'd want to take it with you."

Sofia's eyes widened. "Yeah, that'd be great. Sal will be there. He can get a sampling of your cooking."

Those were her thoughts exactly but now it made her nervous. Oscar was in the back room when she walked in to get her stuff. "You're off, too?"

"Yeah, they switched me last minute to open instead of close."

Grace didn't miss the way his eyes wandered. It wasn't the first time she'd seen him looking at her that way. It was so barefaced it was almost rude.

"Your ride here yet?"

She grabbed her bag out of the cabinet. "Nope, I'm taking the bus today."

"The bus? Where to?"

"Chula Vista."

Oscar's mouth fell open. "You take the bus all the way to Chula Vista?"

"Yep." She nodded as she walked past him.

Sofia walked in just as she got to the office door.

"I can give you a ride, Gracie."

Up until now, the only one she'd allowed to call her Gracie was Alex. There was something about him. It was sweet not predatory. With Oscar it felt weird. Still she didn't correct him.

"You don't have a ride Grace?" Sofia asked.

Grace stopped at the door. "Yeah, I do."

"The bus," Oscar said, as if it were illegal or something. "All the way to Chula Vista!"

"Oh no." Sofia shook her head. "If Oscar can do it, have him take you. I would, but I gotta close."

Grace took a deep breath, and agreed to have Oscar take her. Oscar was a talker. Good thing because she wasn't much in the mood for talking. He told her about the other car he was working on, some classic twelve-year-old car his uncle had bestowed on him. Grace was no expert but she was pretty sure it took longer than twelve years for a car to become a classic.

Then he told her about his daughter. "I like to be upfront you know, with any girl I meet about my d-aughter. She's not something I'm gonna hide, like some guys."

Girls he meets? Grace hoped he wasn't jumping to any conclusions. She knew she should've insisted on taking the bus. Oscar wasn't bad looking, but he was definitely not her type. She wasn't sure what her type was, she just knew it wasn't him. His blatant elevator eyes weren't reserved for just her either. She'd seen him do it many times with the other girls that worked there, not to mention some of the customers. The only one he wasn't so obvious with, but she'd still seen it, was Sofia. She was sure his refraining from ogling Sofia so openly had everything to do with her two *big* brothers around all the time.

Grace hardly got a word in the entire ride. It's not like she tried. Most of the way her mind wandered off to the usual. Only now, she had more to think about. Sal's questions about Joey and Taylor had come out of left field. Why would he act like such a jerk, then apologize and take it back? It made no sense. This was the second time he'd done that. Grace wondered if this was something she'd have to get used to. She hoped n-ot, because the longer she was around him, the more his surly behavior toward her was beginning to get to her.

"Are you?"

Grace came back to earth and realized they'd pass-ed her apartment building. "I'm sorry, Oscar. I live b-ack there. But you can stop here and I'll walk."

"No, that's okay I'll turn around." Once he'd made a U-turn he turned to her. "So are you purposely avoiding my question or did you not hear it when you were in la-la land?"

She turned to him, feeling terrible. She hadn't heard a thing he said for the past five minutes. "I didn't hear you."

"I asked if you're seeing anyone?"

"Uh, no. Not at the moment." She saw his lips curve into a smile. "But I am *talking* to someone. So you know... I'm just playing it by ear right now." She bob-bled her head, wondering if he'd bought it. She hated awkward situations like this. The last thing she needed was one more person at her job making her feel un-comfortable. "Here it is." She pointed at her apartment building.

She thanked him and got out before he could start talking again. Next time, she'd take the bus.

CHAPTER 9

Sal finished his round of golf with Jason. The entire time he'd thought of Grace. He kept thinking about the expression on her face when he'd asked her about the guys who picked her up. At first blank, then defensive, then downright heated.

He was one to talk about first impressions. He had to wonder what kind of impression he was making on her with his accusatory remarks and insinuations. If she thought he might be an asshole before, he'd just confirmed it this morning.

They reached the parking area. Jason turned to Sal before they went their separate ways. "Thanks for another good one. You sure everything is okay? You were real quiet today."

Sal nodded. "I'm good. I just got a lot going on at the restaurants."

"Anything I can help with?"

"Nah, nah, nothing bad. Just been real busy."

"All right, man." Jason tapped Sal's fist with his own. "I'll see you next time." Then he stopped. "Oh hey, almost forgot. I talked to Spence the other day. He's thinking Vegas for the bachelor party."

"Really Vegas? I thought you didn't want anything big."

"Eh, Spence can be persuasive. It won't be anything crazy, just a little gambling, drinking, and hanging out with the guys. You better be there."

"When is this?"

"In a few weeks. I'll let you know."

"I'll be there."

Sal hadn't taken but two steps when any thoughts of Jason were obliterated and Grace was on his mind again. It was almost annoying.

Alex's house was, as expected, loud and overflowing with food. Why his mom thought all this noise and company would make Valerie feel better was beyond him. But Valerie had managed to somehow get Alex to let her move from the bedroom to the front room where she lay in the oversized reclining chair.

Sal walked over to greet her as soon as he walked in. "Hey sweetheart, how we doing?" He rubbed her huge belly.

She gave him a half smile. "I just want all their little parts to finish growing already, so they can take these babies out."

Every time he saw her she was much bigger than the last, but he wouldn't tell her and make her feel worse. "Almost there, Val." He kissed her forehead. God, he felt sorry for her, she looked so damn uncomfortable.

Alex doted over her, bringing her another pillow and Sarah stood behind her, massaging her neck.

His mom had made too much food as usual. It was overkill. Sal leaned on the island in the kitchen, trying to decide what he'd try first. Sofia walked in with a tray and the first thing out of his dad's mouth was, "More food?"

"Yeah, our newest cook made it."

Just like that, she had Sal's undivided attention. Eric, her fiancé, walked in behind her and waved at everyone

"You got another cook?" Angel sounded almost

annoyed. "Didn't you just hire one last week?"

"Actually, this is the bartender Alex hired last week," Sofia said, setting the tray in front of Sal. "She's just as good in the kitchen."

Sal glanced at Alex who was smirking. "Try it, Sal. Alex and I had some of her cooking today. She's a keeper."

Alex finally moved away from Valerie and made his way to the kitchen, smiling. "Yeah, a keeper, Sal."

Real discreet. Sal didn't even look at him, he grabbed a fork and took the foil off the top of the tray. "What is it?"

"An enchilada casserole."

It looked good. Sal put a forkful in his mouth. It was good. *Really* good. He nodded, not wanting them to see just how excited he was about this. Of course, this was just one dish, but damn one thing was for sure — she could cook. "Pretty good."

He knew Alex wasn't buying his nonchalant act. Alex took the fork from him and dug in. After chewing for a second, he spoke with his mouth still partially full. "This is going on the menu." He turned to where Angel was sitting. "Angel, try this."

They were all standing around now, digging in and Alex took a plate over to Valerie, when there was a knock on the door. "Come in," Alex yelled.

Isabel, Valerie's best friend and roommate before she married Alex, walked in. "Oh, honey," she said, as soon as she saw Valerie and rushed over to her. She obviously hadn't seen her in a while.

Romero walked in behind her. "Damn, you're big!"

Alex shot him a look that shut him up before he could say anything else. Sal couldn't help laugh. Both Romero and Eric had grown up with Sal and his brothers. They lived right up the block from them. Since they were Angel's age they were closest to him, but they'd always been like extended family.

Romero and Isabel met at Angel and Sarah's wedding shower. It was almost funny how fast Isabel had brought womanizing Romero to his knees. They were married within months, something Sal hadn't been able to fathom but was now beginning to understand.

After eating, the girls all huddled around Valerie, chatting, including his mother who hadn't acted too impressed with Grace's cooking, but was on her second helping of the casserole.

The guys all stepped outside to the backyard minus his dad who nodded off on the sofa, after overeating, as usual.

They all stood under the patio. Alex had upgraded to a bigger house after he found out Valerie was pregnant with twins. This one was twice the size of his old one and had a pool and Jacuzzi. Since Valerie was an agent and managed her own real estate office, she'd gotten them a good deal.

"Say it, Sal," Alex said, after passing out beers. "I hit a home run hiring Grace."

The way he said it, Sal got the double meaning loud and clear.

"Who's Grace?" Romero asked.

"It's one dish," Sal said. "And Sundays are slow for specialty stuff off the menu. We still have to see what's she's like under pressure."

"Who's Grace?" Romero asked again.

"Dude, I saw her today. Things picked up after brunch and she handled it beautifully. That jerk-off you hired could barely keep up with her."

"Who the hell's Grace?"

"The new bartender at the restaurant." Eric answered Romero for them. "Sofia said she's real good. Not just at bartending but cooking, too."

Sal took a swig of his beer, ignoring Alex's smug grin. His brother was loving this.

"But that's a hell of a commute she's got," Eric added. "Sofia said all the way to Chula Vista, and on the bus?"

Sal stopped before taking another swig. "She gets picked up, though."

"No. Well, not today, Sof said she almost took the bus, until one of the guys offered her a ride."

Sal squeezed his bottle. "What guy?"

"I dunno, she just said one of the waiters."

There were only two male waiters on the payroll and Oscar was the only one scheduled today. Sal exchanged glances with Alex. The smug grin was gone. He was sure they were thinking the same thing. Oscar was a cool dude to hang out with—a guys' guy. He was funny as shit even, but he didn't know the first thing about treating women respectfully. He said they were only good for one thing. He openly joked about it. It was all in fun, so long as he didn't disrespect anyone at the restaurant. So far, he hadn't.

Sal took that swig of beer he'd held off on. The beer didn't go down as smooth as his first swig. He'd get things straight with Oscar first thing tomorrow.

*

This was the first time Grace had a job where she didn't look forward to her day off. To most people that would be a good thing. That meant they liked their job so much they loved being there, but Grace knew it was more than just the job.

She had to tell someone about this already. She needed someone else's perspective on it, someone who would tell her to snap out of it. The very notion that she could somehow interest Sal in *any* way, was ridiculous and someone needed to put her in her place. Two people who came from different worlds hitting it off was not unheard of. But when one of them was clearly uninterested and had much to keep him preoccupied in the way of feminine companionship, the other should accept it. It just wasn't happening. She needed to stop before she fell even deeper, especially since she was sure her experience with men in no way measured up to any of the women he was used to dating.

Still, Grace was falling fast. She could feel herself becoming delusional. The whole night before she thought of what Sal had said to her yesterday morning. At one point, she came to the conclusion that maybe Sal had asked about her personal life because he wanted to know what her status was. She nearly woke her sister up when the absurdity of it kicked in and she laughed.

After her first class, she met Joey at their usual Monday morning watering hole — the school's coffee shop. She'd already called him the night before, to tell him how it had gone with her time in the kitchen but she left out everything else that happened. They had exactly twenty minutes before their next class. Joey was so good at reading her, as soon as they sat down he said, "Okay, spill it."

"Really? It's that obvious?"

"Yes, tell me everything."

She ran her fingertips up and down the sides of her cup. She didn't even know where to begin. The stupid girls in her class, even Joey, Taylor and George had gone on and on about how good looking the Moreno brothers were. How could she let herself get sucked in? He wasn't even nice to her. She'd never been so shallow as to get taken in purely by a man's looks.

"Grace, I'm waiting."

"I feel so stupid." *Oh, no.* There it was. She was getting choked up again. She stared at her cup, willing the tears to go away.

Joey reached out and touched her hand. "Why, what's wrong?"

She gulped hard and for the moment, the tears seemed to subside. "I think I'm falling... " And there they were again. *Shit.* She looked up at Joey who was staring at her. "Promise me you won't laugh, Joey."

"Laugh? Honey, you're crying. Why would I laugh?"

"*Promise.*"

He squeezed her hand. "I promise."

She couldn't look at him when she said it, so she stared at her coffee cup again. "I think I'm falling for Sal. My freakin' boss."

"So why does that make you sad?"

She looked up at him and felt guilty now for making him promise not to laugh. His expression was nothing more than complete concern and compassion. "Because he doesn't even like me as a person, much less a ...love interest. Every time I see him, he does or says something that's even more telling of the kind of person he thinks I am."

"Like what?"

"Like yesterday." She told him about how he behaved when she arrived in the morning so excited to show off for him. When she finished telling him about

Sal's comments on him and Taylor, his reaction surprised her.

"I wish you hadn't told him we were gay."

"Why?"

"We could've had some fun with him."

Grace drank some of her coffee, feeling much more in control of her emotions now and so happy she'd told Joey. But she was confused. "How so?"

"For some reason it bothered him right? But it's none of his business. It might have been fun to lay it on extra thick every time one of us picked you up."

Grace rolled her eyes. "No, I wouldn't play those kinds of games. The point is he doesn't think very highly of me. *Obviously.* And here I am falling for him? How dumb am I?" She shook her head. "Tell me to get over it, Joey. Tell me what an idiot I am."

"No because you're not. Okay, lets think about this. What about him, besides his looks, has you *falling*?"

"Nothing! I'm telling you. He's been a total jerk to me, twice now. And the worst thing is while I'm sitting here on my day off talking about him and daydreaming about him every other moment of the day, he's out meeting girl after girl enjoying a life outside of the restaurant and all I can do is think about getting back there. It's pathetic."

"Then maybe that's it," Joey said, raising his eyebrows.

"What's it?"

"Maybe you like the cold, indifferent type."

Grace laughed. "Great, that seems like the best type of guy to get hung up on."

"I still think it's strange that it bothered him about me and Taylor. I mean, why would he care?"

Grace shrugged. "He's like that. Even Alex and his

sister said he's too much. Nitpicky almost to a fault. Maybe he found it offensive somehow?"

"Offensive to whom? Him?" Joey lifted his eyebrow even higher. "You know, that could only mean one thing."

Grace shook her head. "Oh, please let's not even go there. I already went over that possibility and it's too preposterous to even consider."

"Why?"

Joey couldn't be serious. "What possible interest can he have in me?" She saw that look on Joey's face, he was about to let her have it. Before he could, she continued. "He's twenty-five, Joey."

"And?"

"He's been around town and back. The man hasn't even lived at home for years. He's into women, not g-irls. Did you not see that woman he was talking to in the parking lot the other day?"

"The blonde in a foo-foo suit?"

"Exactly. That's what he's used to, and apparently into."

Joey shook his head. "You weren't there when he first stepped out to talk to her. If I had to make an observation, I'd say the ditz was getting on his nerves."

"Didn't look like it to me and neither did the one in the restaurant that same day. It was the same thing, she looked sophisticated and experienced in dealing with *men*."

"You have experience."

Grace gave him a look and sipped her coffee. Joey knew all about her experience or lack thereof. She just hadn't filled him in on all the detail of why but he knew she was still a prissy virgin.

"Okay, but what planet are you from that you think

a virgin wouldn't appeal to man?"

"I didn't say that. All I'm saying is he has all these beautiful, sophisticated women throwing themselves at him. Why on earth would he be interested in the little bus riding, wannabe cook from Chula Vista?"

Joey put his hand on his waist. Grace was in for it now. "Oh no you didn't. No you didn't just put yourself down, because of this guy." He shook his head. "Grace, I won't have this."

"But—"

"No! I won't let you turn into this little wimpy hoohaw, over some guy you just met. I've stood there all year and watched you cook the living shit out of every recipe those instructors have thrown at you. You've blown them all away time and time again. Are you actually gonna start questioning your talent, your *worth* because of some guy?" He pointed a finger at her. "You may be riding a bus now. But this." His finger went up and down in front of her. "This is where it all starts. You're gonna be great. More than great and why? Because you worked your ass off to get there, unlike Mr. Perfect over there. What did he do besides take over daddy's already successful restaurant? Wow, he should feel *real* proud of himself. What a man—"

"All right, all right." Grace was fine listening to Joey's little rant until he started putting Sal down. "I *am* aware that I can cook. I was just being melodramatic. And, for the record he went to school and got a master's in business management. He's incredibly smart and meticulously organized. It's amazing the way he's able to run not just one *very* busy restaurant but also help with the other one *and* be in charge of meeting with all these investors. Everybody at the restaurant seems to love him and although it's a lot of work to run the place and deal with the meetings he handles it all brilliantly. He's also planning on opening a lot more restaurants, so he didn't *just* take over his father's business."

Joey smirked. "But it's just his looks you're attracted to, uh?"

Grace picked up Joey's wrist, twisting it.

"Ow!"

She saw on his watch it was time to go and stood up. "We're gonna be late."

Joey shook his wrist making a face. "This—my l-ove—is not over. We'll have to get to the bottom of his odd behavior."

Grace was done trying to figure it out. There was only one thing short of quitting her job, which was out of the question, that she needed to do—get over it. She knew it was much easier said than done, but at this point, she had no other option.

*

Sal had a few stops he had to make before going into the restaurant Monday morning. He'd finally had a chance to go over the proposal in its entirety. For the most part everything seemed okay. Except for a few minor details like the possibility of television commercials, in which, neither Sal nor any of the Morenos would have a say.

Another detail was Sal's original vision was to keep all the restaurants relatively close by, preferably in San Diego county. The proposal stated they wanted to leave the possibility of branching out into other big cities, like Los Angeles, which wasn't too far, but there was even a mention of Vegas and New York. It was already a pain having to go back and forth from the two restaurants and they were only a half hour away from each other.

Granted it was all dependent on how well the local restaurants did first, but leaving it out there as a possibility was a bit nerve-racking. His brothers would all have to be in agreement before he signed anything. Just because the restaurants were out of town, or state even, didn't mean Sal would be okay with someone else making the decisions. As long as the Moreno name was on the line, he and his brothers would have final say on everything. That would mean a lot of traveling.

His mother had a huge breakfast waiting for him when he arrived at their house. "Ma, I told you, I was just gonna be in and out."

"Oh, you can eat just a little," she said, planting an overflowing plate of eggs, chilaquiles and the ever present beans and rice on the table. "Sit."

His dad was already eating. He also motioned for him to have a seat. Sal sat and started going over the proposal with his dad. All the while, his mother kept adding things to the table, tortillas, red salsa, green salsa, fresh Mexican cheese. Sal knew better than to argue. He'd just smile back at his mother, who seemed so happy to be serving him. In a way, he felt guilty for not letting her indulge him more often, lately. It's what the woman lived for.

Sal explained all the need-to-know stuff to his dad, about what the investors were asking. All his dad really cared about was the food and how things were run in general. Everything else wasn't worth trying to explain. His dad was anti-technology, so any explanation of the marketing and Internet use for the catering part of the business would be a waste of time. It amazed Sal he'd gone the years he did without any type of computers until he and his brothers were old enough to insist he get with the times, but he did mention New York and Vegas. "What? You plan on never having a family?"

Sal stopped mid chew, raising his eyebrow. "What do you mean?"

"Your mother and I are too old to be going back and forth to New York or even Vegas. This is gonna be all you and your brothers. You see how Alex is now about leaving Valerie and he's only fifteen minutes away." He shook a tortilla at him. "You don't think you're going to have a pregnant wife someday?"

Sal frowned and kept chewing. He'd managed to keep Grace out of his mind all morning and now his dad went and mentioned a pregnant wife. As ridiculous as the thought was, the first thing that popped in his head was Grace. "That's a big if, Pop."

"What? You don't want babies?" His mom stared at him horrified.

Sal turned to her. "No."

"Why not?" Her shrill voice went up a few notches.

"Mom, I do, I meant Vegas and New York are a big if."

"But you *do* want kids."

"Yes, mom, I want kids." Normally, Sal would've laughed at the turn the conversation had taken, but his parents had inadvertently shoved Grace back into the spotlight of his thoughts. Something he'd worked all morning to shut out.

After about another twenty minutes of going over things with his dad, and his mother casually slapping more food on his plate a few times, he finally got out of there. Between last night's dinner and today's breakfast

Sal was really going to need to get in the gym more often this week.

With his mind on his parents, the proposal and working out, he was finally clear of any thoughts of *her*. Then he got a text from Oscar.

Hey Chief not sure who's the boss today. Just letting you know I'll be a little late. I'll explain when I get there.

Even this brought on thoughts of Grace.

CHAPTER 10

Alex was already at the restaurant when he got there. Romero was there too, eating a burrito. He often stopped by to grab a bite before work or even during. Since he had his own security firm, he could come and go as he pleased. He hadn't been around in a while. Sal's phone buzzed just as he reached them at the bar. He frowned when he saw who the text was from, then raised his eyebrows when he read it.

"What's that look about?" Romero said, with a mouthful.

"San Diego State made it to the next round of the playoffs." Sal lifted his phone in the air. "Extra tickets for Saturday's game."

"You're shitting me?" Romero wiped his mouth. "Who has extra tickets?"

"Yeah, that's the catch. Some chick I'm having a hard enough time getting rid of. If I take her up on this, forget about it. She'll be dropping by here and calling not stop."

"You have any idea what those tickets go for, Sal?" Alex asked. "How many does she have? Maybe you can buy them off her."

"Dude, I don't even wanna ask. This is the one I told you about that got into my apartment in Los Angeles, remember?"

Alex laughed. "Oh, that chick?"

"Yeah, I rarely respond to her texts."

"Well, don't go with her. Take the tickets and we'll

go with you," Romero said.

Sal gave him a look. "You don't think she's gonna be there?"

His phone buzzed again and Sal read it. "Two tickets."

"Dibs!" Romero said.

"I can't go anyway." Alex frowned. "Valerie's ready to go any minute."

Sal started toward the back. "I'd rather not. It's not worth it."

"Ask her how much she wants for them." Romero followed him to the back. "I'll buy them. Those tickets are sold out for sure."

Sal stopped at the door. He knew Romero's persistent ass was not going to stop. He should've never said anything. He took a deep breath and texted Melissa back.

My friend is interested. How much do you want for them?

Her response was immediate.

Don't be silly. I'm offering them 2 you 4 free.=) But I was really hoping you'd go.

Sal glared at Romero. "She says they're free — if I go."

"So tell her you will. You don't have to."

"I can't do that."

"Then we'll go together. What's the big deal?

His phone buzzed again.

I'll drop them off this week. Gotta get back to my hearing. Ttyl!

"Great." Sal tossed his phone on the desk.

"What?"

"Now she has an excuse to drop by. She's bringing the tickets this week."

"Yes!" Romero did an inward fist pump. "So you going with me?"

"I guess," Sal said, taking a seat at the desk.

"'Cause if you don't want to I'll buy them off you and take Izzy."

"I wouldn't sell them to you, ass. But I gotta be there."

Romero drummed his hands against the doorway. "Then, let me know how we're gonna do this. I can drive if you want."

Sal nodded but didn't even bother to look back at him. Romero walked out and Sal could hear him boasting loudly. "Guess who's going too San Diego State's finals?"

Sal shook his head, annoyed. Over the years Romero had been the cause of many things gone wrong. It was only fitting that this too, was his fault.

*

Oscar walked in just after four in the afternoon. Sal eyed him as he strolled through the restaurant and into the back room. He finished the interview he was doing and hurried to the back. Alex was in there with him.

He turned to Sal when he saw him. "I was just telling Alex about my daughter. She was in the emergency room all morning because her fever was so high."

"What's wrong with her?" Sal asked.

"Ear infection. The doctors say if she keeps getting them they may have to insert tubes."

Alex winced. "Tubes?"

"Yeah, it's actually kind of common. When the ear doesn't drain, it gets infected so if they insert tubes it helps them drain."

"Doesn't that mess with her hearing?" Alex frowned, standing up.

"No, but the infections could, so it's better to get the tubes in, than to risk hearing loss from the constant infections. This is the third one she's had this year."

"Damn," Sal said. "Is she still in the hospital? You didn't have to come in, you know."

"Nah, she's home now. I'd rather be here anyway. I need the money."

Alex walked out, leaving Sal alone with Oscar. Oscar was busy pulling his stuff out of the cabinet. Sal wasted no time. "So I heard you took Grace home last night."

Oscar turned around. "Yeah, can you believe she takes the bus to Chula Vista? She acted like it's no big deal but shit, that's *far*."

Sal took a seat, and leaned back, giving Oscar all his attention. "Good looking out then. That *is* far."

Oscar grinned. "You know me," he winked. "I couldn't pass up the chance to be the charming gentleman."

Typically, this would be Sal's cue to wink back and grin with him, instead he ground his teeth, and began rocking back and forth in his chair. "I'm sure you couldn't."

"Actually, Grace is pretty hot in a reserved kind of way. They say those chicks are usually freaks in bed. They act all innocent and sweet, but get a finger or two in—"

"Whoa, what the fuck, Oscar?" Sal stopped rocking and sat up.

"What?"

"Can you have a little respect—she's a nice girl, and

an employee. I told you about this kind of shit already. You better not even think about messing with her like that."

Oscar lifted his hands in the air. "Dude, this is how I always talk. What's wrong with you?" He stopped and peered at Sal. "Wait. Are you who she's talking to?"

"What?" Sal was still trying to calm himself. He didn't mean to go off on Oscar, but hearing him say that stuff about Grace made him want to rip his head off.

"She mentioned she's talking to someone, and now here you're getting all crazy on me." Oscar grinned. "You son-of-a-bitch, you *are* talking to her. You sho-uld've told me." Alex leaned his head in the doorway. "You're still back here? C'mon, it's bad enough Sal's taking forever to hire people. The one useless waiter he did hire is back here chatting it up when we got a full house."

Oscar laughed and started out the door. He turned back to Sal who was now lost in thought. "Hey, man, peace." He held up two fingers. "I know now, so don't worry about it. Bros before hos."

Sal didn't even respond. He didn't care what Oscar thought, but he'd given him yet one more thing to ob-sess about when it came to Grace. Apparently, she was *talking* to someone. What the hell did that mean?

*

Monday and Tuesday completely dragged. It was now Wednesday morning and Grace was mad at herself. She was presenting her menu today for this week's fi-nal at school. A three-course meal that was to be prepared in under forty minutes. She remembered a time when this was exciting. Sitting in class now waiting for her turn to go up, all she could think about was the fact that she might be seeing Sal today. That is, if he showed up.

She went through the motions of her presentation perfunctorily. As expected, the instructor was thoroughly impressed, calling her menu a little ambitious, but that wasn't the first time she'd heard that.

The bus ride to work was torturous. Her insides were a hot mess. This was the first time neither Joey nor Taylor could pick her up and Joey had been beside himself, even offered to call George and see if he could pick her up. Grace assured him she'd get a ride from someone at work, though she had no intentions of asking anyone. She'd taken the bus before in the evening, it wasn't so bad. Everyone assumed taking the bus was the lowest form of transportation. She'd take the bus any day, over flirting for a ride like she'd seen so many girls at school do.

Initially, getting to work was a huge disappointment. Sal wasn't even there. Then she heard Alex say Sal was coming in to close so he could go home early because his wife might be having contractions. Though she felt for Alex, because he seemed so incredibly nervous, she couldn't help feeling excited. She had to remind herself she was supposed to be getting over this.

Seeing him when he walked in was more gut wrenching than expected. He wasn't in a suit like he had been so often lately, he wore jeans and a black polo. She tried playing the busy bartender when she saw him walk in, but it was impossible not to glance over at him. He seemed concerned when he spoke to Alex, but he still turned and smiled at her when he caught her looking.

Alex left and Sal came over to the bar where she and Melanie were talking in a rare moment of no orders. "I might be an uncle soon."

"We heard. Congrats," Melanie said. "Poor Alex, he was a wreck."

Sal laughed, those beautiful dimples melting Grace. "He'll be okay."

Oscar walked up to the bar and Melanie took the order he brought with him. Since Melanie started to make the drinks, Grace had no choice but to give Sal her attention. She smiled, trying to think of something to say but he beat her to the punch.

"How were your days off?"

"Okay," she said, trying not to read too much into the way he gazed at her. "School, homework."

He smiled. "I had some of your casserole."

"Oh?" Her insides were going wild. This was insane, he was just talking to her. How did those damn women do it and look so in control?

"It was delicious. Alex is putting it on the menu, so I hope you're prepared to share the recipe, and train all the cooks on how to make it."

"Really?" She smiled and for the first time since he got there, she felt excited and not completely lovestruck.

He smiled even bigger. "Yeah, really. Alex and Sofie were completely impressed by your cooking. You'll be spending a lot more time in the kitchen. I think I've been overruled."

"Why? You're still not impressed?"

Sal leaned over and spoke closer than he ever had. "Oh, I'm impressed, Grace." There was no denying the undertone of his words. She didn't know how to respond, especially since he held her gaze and his smiling expression faded into a smoldering stare. Something jolted him and he reached for his phone, pulling his phone from his holster and glanced at it. "It's Alex." He answered and walked away. "What's up?"

Grace let out a slow breath, her heart hammering away. If this is what it was going to be like from here on she didn't know how many up close conversations with Sal her heart could take.

For the following fifteen minutes, Grace did her best to stay busy and keep her mind off of Sal's last comment. It didn't mean anything. She had to stop reading into everything he said, but even if it *did* mean just what he said, and nothing else, that alone was enough to make her heart pound. Sal *had* been impressed. So what if it was just with her cooking? Her heart inflated anyway.

She saw him hang up and make another call and then walk back toward her with the smile that had begun to haunt her dreams. "He's meeting her and her dad at the hospital. Unless the doctors can stop the contractions Alex just may be a daddy tonight." Sal chuckled. "And he's nervous as shit."

Grace remembered the look on Alex's face just before he left. She thought he might be sick. "I can only imagine; he's been so nervous all these past weeks."

"It should be okay. I'll swing by the hospital tonight after we close up. See if I can't calm him down a little. My parents are already on their way."

Oscar approached the bar, wiping the smile right off of Sal's face. Before Oscar even said anything, someone from the kitchen called Sal. He excused himself and Grace started on the order Oscar rattled off. "So how come you didn't tell me?"

"Tell you what?"

"You know." He motioned toward the kitchen. "About who you're *talking* to?"

Grace glanced back at the kitchen then met Oscar's eyes again. "I don't know what you're talking about."

"Oh, I get it." He smiled, wickedly. "You two are keeping it on the down low." He picked up the tray with the drinks Grace just put on them. "Makes sense, him being the boss and all." He took the tray and walked away in a rush.

Grace froze, feeling the mortification sink in as Oscar walked away. Was she *that* obvious? She turned to see Sal walk out of the kitchen and into the office. What if it got back to him? What if Oscar mentioned it to Sal? Melanie *had* told her that Oscar and Sal went way back to Sal's early college days. She felt her face warm. This was a nightmare.

Oscar was on his way back to the bar and Grace made sure to get his attention. He walked over to her side of the bar. "What's up?"

"Where uh... " She wiped off the counter, avoiding eye contact and cleared her throat. "Where would you get the idea that me and Sal are...?"

Oscar laughed. "He told me." Grace stopped wiping and looked at him. "But don't sweat it. I won't say anything to anyone. I need a pitcher of Bud and two mugs."

"What do you mean he told you?" She took a step back to grab a pitcher out of the freezer but never once took her eyes off Oscar.

Oscar shrugged. "Look, I'm sorry. He didn't say it was a secret; maybe I wasn't supposed to tell you he said anything."

Grace began pouring the beer into the pitcher.

"What exactly did he say?"

"He just asked about me taking you home the other day." Oscar looked away from her, scratching his head. "He got a little pissy and just made it clear that you were off limits."

She finally had to take her eyes off him when she felt the cold beer on her hand from the overflowing pitcher. "Damn it."

"Here he comes. Don't tell him I told you."

Grace glanced back at Sal, her stomach completely in knots now. *Pissy?* She cleaned up the pitcher and put it on Oscar's tray along with two chilled mugs. She caught the exchanged glance between Oscar and Sal just as Sal reached the bar.

"Any word on them babies?" Oscar asked, picking up the tray.

"Looks like they'll be here tonight. The doctors can't seem to stop the contractions. The whole crew is down there except Angel who said he might close down early and head to the hospital. I might do the same, so you guys may get to leave early tonight."

"I'm off in ten minutes anyway," Oscar said.

Sal glanced at Grace. "You're closing right?"

"Yeah." Suddenly she couldn't look him in the eyes.

"I'll let you know." He glanced around the restaurant. "Looks like it's slowing down." He checked his watch. "Yeah, more than likely I will." He headed to the front and Oscar walked away, leaving Grace there to try to make sense of what Oscar had said. *Off limits?*

She hoped to catch Oscar before he left but she got caught up by a sudden rush and before she knew it, he was gone.

Sal began closing up as soon as the last of customers were out just after seven so she at least wouldn't have to stand at the bus stop after eight.

Melanie rushed out and Grace was pretty sure there was no one else left in the restaurant besides her and Sal. Oscar's words still rang in her ears as she pulled the apron off over her head. *He got a little pissy and just made it clear that you were off limits.*

"Your ride isn't here yet?" Grace nearly jumped, hearing Sal's voice as he walked into the back room.

She placed the apron in the cabinet and pulled out her purse. "No. They're not coming tonight."

Sal stopped what he was doing at the desk and turned to her. "So how you getting home?"

"The bus." She smiled but saw the look on his face. "I take it all the time."

He shook his head. "I'll take you home."

"No, really it's okay." Her heart sped up at the very thought of being alone with him in a car. "I don't know why everyone acts like it's such a terrible thing. You have to go be with Alex, remember? Poor guy's probably falling apart over there." She laughed nervously making her way to the door.

"Gracie." Unlike when Alex called her that, hearing it from Sal made her heart flutter. "I can take you. I insist."

"But what about Alex? What if you miss the babies being born?"

"It's not like I'm going to be in there when they're born anyway. I'll see them after."

"But—"

"I'm taking you, Grace." He grabbed the keys off the desk and turned off the monitor. "You ready?" The smile nearly did her in.

She nodded, smiling back. It was just a ride, damn it. So why did she feel ready to swoon?

CHAPTER 11

Most of the evening, hell most of the last few weeks, Sal had contemplated what, if anything he should do about his obvious growing attraction to Grace. Alex said he'd be okay with it but things would definitely be awkward for the other employees. Then there was the possibility of things not working out. What then? Would he be okay being around her once things were over between them?

He shook his head. The most glaring obstacle now was the fact that she was *talking* to someone. He'd been tempted more than once to ask Oscar exactly what she'd said and how the subject even came up. But it could only be one of two things. Either he asked her straight out, which he wouldn't put past Oscar, or she'd brought it up on her own. She'd revealed very little about herself except that her friends were gay, and that was something he sort of forced out of her with his completely out-of-whack accusations.

After setting the alarm, he finished locking up. Grace waited for him just outside. "Are you sure about this, Sal? It's completely out of the way."

"Not really. She's at St. Mary's." Sal clicked the car doors open with his keychain. "Don't worry about it." He opened the passenger side for her. "I'm taking you home so get in."

He saw her take a deep breath just before getting in the car. Sal had just turned the car on when he got a text from Sofia.

She just delivered the first one it's a girl! OMG Good luck! Alex will go gray before he's thirty! lol

Sal smiled, feeling a little choked up. "She had the first baby." He turned to Grace. "A girl."

The doctors had known for months the gender of both babies but Valerie insisted on it being a surprise so they had no idea. But the one thing they did know was the babies were identical. Which meant only one thing: Alex would be the father of two baby girls. Whoa.

Gracie smiled bigger than he'd ever seen her smile and she put her hand over her mouth. "Really? You're an uncle! How exciting. Congratulations!"

"Thanks. It feels weird." He texted Sofia back as it sunk in. A new addition to the Moreno clan and there would be another one any minute. "You wanna come with me to the hospital?"

Her smile disappeared and she blinked. "Oh, I wouldn't want to intrude. It's just family right?"

Sal backed the car up. "You're an employee which, if Alex has anything to say about it, means you *are* family now."

The apprehension in her face didn't disappear but Sal headed to the hospital anyway. The next text came about seven minutes later. When he got to a red light, he read it.

Second baby just born and they're all doing fine. I'm crying! Auntie is SO going to have to come to their rescue when they discover boys!

He laughed. "Second one was just born. Wow, two girls. Damn, my brother is going to have his hands full."

Grace smiled again, looking almost as excited as he felt. "Oh my Gosh. I had cousins in Mexico that were identical twins. They were boys and loved confusing people; only once they spoke you could tell the difference. One was so much shyer than the other, so no matter how much he tried to act like his brother, he never did quite pull it off."

"Yeah, well Alex has it coming. I can see it already. They're gonna drive him crazy." Sal shook his head. "You have any brothers or sisters?"

"Just one. A younger sister."

"Really how much younger?"

"She's fifteen."

Sal turned to her when he came to a stop again. "That's pretty big gap. Are you two close?"

"Very. Sometimes..." She looked out the window on her side. "Actually, many times it feels like it's just me and her against the world."

That piqued Sal's interest. It sounded a bit personal but he knew so little about her and she brought it up so he asked, "How so?"

"Ever since my dad died it's been just her, me and my mother." She continued to look out the window, a sign to Sal that the subject was not one she was comfortable with yet she continued. "Until my mom remarried that is. But even before then, my mom's always been... difficult. So we've always stuck close together. There's nothing we can't get each other through."

Sal knew it was a risk but again, she'd brought it up not him. "How long ago did your dad die?"

She finally turned away from the window and their eyes met for a moment before she stared straight ahead. "I was eleven. That's when we moved to the states. My mother didn't want to be in Mexico anymore. Since she was born in El Paso and was a U.S. citizen, she knew she had a better chance of getting a higher paying job this side of the border."

They pulled into the hospital parking lot. "You said your grandmother owned a restaurant in Juarez right? Does she still?"

He saw her eyebrows pinch and he knew he'd hit a nerve. Shit.

"She had to sell it when my mom said we were moving to El Paso. She was my dad's mom and aside from him, we were all she had, so she gave up the restaurant to follow us."

Sal parked the car and turned to her. "But Juarez is right over the border. Why didn't she just keep it and visit you guys?"

Grace shook her head and Sal saw that her eyes glistened. "She was getting older. My dad had pretty much been running the restaurant for years. She couldn't do it without him and my mom wanted nothing to do with the restaurant." Grace opened the door and got out.

When Sal got out and faced her over the hood of the car, he saw her wipe away a tear. "Hey, I'm sorry if I brought up a sore subject for you."

"No. I'm sorry. This is supposed to be a happy day. Let's just not talk about this anymore." Her forced smile was hardly convincing. "Let's go see those babies."

Damn it. He knew he should've stopped when his gut told him to. "Okay." He said, refraining from asking or saying anything more.

They walked into the hospital silently. When they reached the waiting room where everyone was, he saw they surrounded a very red-eyed Alex, still in scrubs.

Sofia turned when she saw Sal. Her eyes were all misty as well. The closer he got the more he noticed everyone was teared up. "Everything okay?"

"Yes perfect," Sofia said, hugging him. "Sienna and Savannah—those are the names of your two beautiful nieces."

Sal swallowed hard, feeling silly about the lump in his own throat. He walked over to Alex and hugged him hard. "How's it feel little brother?"

Alex nodded but was clearly still feeling emotional. "I gotta get back in there. They're gonna be in the NICU for the first forty-eight hours but the doctors said it's just precautionary. The girls are actually looking very good."

"How much did they weigh?"

"They were both just shy of five pounds. So as soon as they hit that five pound mark we're out of here."

Their mom hugged and kissed Alex. "You're going to be such a good father, *mijo*."

After letting them in on a few more of the details about the birth and how Valerie was doing, Alex went back in.

Sal's mother finally turned her attention to Grace then looked at Sal. "Mom this is Grace. She's the one that made the casserole."

"Oh," his mother reached out her hand. "You're the new cook. Your casserole was delicious."

"Thank you," Grace said, obviously a little self-conscious.

"She's a natural in the kitchen, mom," Sofia added.

"So you're the new cook we're gonna have to steal?" Angel said, wrapping his arms around Sarah from behind.

Alex saw Grace's face flush a little. She obviously wasn't used to being the center of attention.

"You'll have to go through Alex to steal her. He's

very proud of being the one who *discovered* her." Sofia smiled at Grace.

The only glimpse they got of the babies was through a window but it was hard to really see them since they were in an incubator. They stuck around and waited for a chance to see them up close but after Alex came out to let them know it wasn't happening tonight, everyone grudgingly started to make their exits. Sarah and Sal's mom still insisted on at least seeing Valerie.

Sal and Grace said goodnight to everyone and left. As they exited the hospital, they ran into Romero and his Izzy. Since Isabel and Valerie were so close, Sal actually been surprised that they hadn't been at the hospital when they got there. "Hey, you out already?"

"Yeah, we're not going to be able go in to see the babies tonight. We were already in there for a while." Isabel's expression fell. "But you can see them through the window and go in to see Valerie. My mom and Sarah are going to." Isabel smiled and glanced at Grace.

"This is Grace," Sal said, then added, "One of our newer employees at the restaurant."

Once everyone was introduced, Romero asked, "So did you get the tickets?"

"Oh my God. He hasn't stopped talking about those tickets," Isabel laughed.

"It's the Elite Eight!" Romero looked at her like *she* was the crazy one.

Sal started down the stairs of the front entrance, shaking his head. "Not yet but I'll get them this week." He turned to Grace who was a couple of steps behind him and felt the crazy urge to put his hand out for her to take but he didn't.

She crossed her arms in front of her when they

reached the bottom. "Alex looked so happy. Who would've thought such a big lug could get so emotional? But I guess seeing your baby for the first time will do that to you. And this was a double whammy for him."

"Oh yeah." Sal turned just as the wind blew a wisp of her hair across her face and she used her tongue to move it away from her lips. He nearly lost his train of thought. "That guy's always been a softie on the inside. As hard as nails as he is on the outside, when it comes to Valerie and his baby girls they're all gonna have him wrapped around their fingers."

"That's sweet." She smiled, making Sal glad she'd forgotten about the conversation when they arrived at the hospital. "As intimidating as he looked that first day I met him I could tell right away he was a sweetheart."

Sal pressed his lips together, remembering how he'd immediately noticed how comfortable she'd been around Alex that first day he hired her. Sal had always been far more guarded about showing his true feeling than either of his brothers. Those two wore their hearts on their sleeves whether they were bursting with happiness or enraged. Sal was always too worried about being professional even in his personal life.

They reached his car and he looked over the hood. "So were you surprised we were brothers?"

"No, you look so much alike."

"I mean because I know you weren't exactly thinking I was a sweetheart when we first met." She stared at him from across the car and he opened the door and got in.

"Actually," she said as she got in and put on her seatbelt. "I meant to apologize for that. I remember you saying something about first impressions and I know I made such a horrible one. I walked in there with this huge chip on my shoulder because I'd been shot down so many times already by other restaurants, you must've thought I was such a bitch. And then you find out I lied on my application. I don't blame you at all for not calling me back."

Sal drove out of the parking lot taking in what she just said. "I'm glad you came back." He turned to look at her. "Really glad. What do you say we start over? I've already forgotten about that day and I understand why you lied now. If you can forget what an ass I've been we can start fresh."

He was beginning to really love that sweet smile of hers. "Deal."

The rest of the way they talked about one of her favorite topics—cooking. She told him a little bit about her school but never once mentioned seeing anyone. He hoped for an appropriate moment where he might bring it up, but there never was one. By the time they reached her place, he knew all about how she'd met her best friends Joey and Taylor. He was especially glad that they were in a happy committed relationship because he'd heard of guys that swung both ways and the way she gushed about them he would've had his doubts, gay or not.

"Thank you so much for letting me tag along with you to the hospital. I can't wait until they're old enough so he can bring them into the restaurant and I can hold them." She tilted her head to the side. "And thank you for the ride. You really didn't have to."

"Get used to it. If you don't have a ride at night, I'll make sure someone gets you home. I don't care what you say. The buses are dangerous, Gracie, especially at night." He got away with calling her Gracie earlier and he liked it. She smiled again, not correcting him. He might never go back to Grace now.

"If I have to. I will." She opened the door and got out but leaned her head in the door. "You can't make it your job to *get* me home."

"You wanna bet?"

She shook her head but the smile escaped her. "Goodnight Sal. I'll see you tomorrow."

Sal sat in his car until he saw her walk all the way into the apartment building. He glanced around the area. A couple of bums were lying out front by the b-uilding next to hers and some drunk looking guys wal-ked down the sidewalk arguing. She was nuts if she thought he was going to let her take the bus home. Af-ter spending more time with her tonight, his attraction to her was irrepressible now.

*

The first thing Grace did when she got to work the next day was corner Oscar in the back room. After spending the evening with Sal, she was certain she felt some-thing from him but she was terrified of getting her hopes up. It didn't help that Melanie and Julie made him out to be the biggest ladies man they'd ever en-countered. "I promise this will be the last time I ask you."

Oscar turned to face her. She glanced out the door to make sure Sal wasn't there yet. "He really said I was off limits? Those exact words."

Oscar seemed a little uncomfortable. "I don't re-member the exact words but he warned me to not even think about trying to you know... get with you or anything. Said you were an employee, but I got what he meant loud and clear."

Grace took in the new information. That made more sense now. Though she didn't think he was so bad, Alex and Sofia said he was anal about everything. Maybe employee relationships were frowned upon. Sure, she'd begun to get a vibe from him but for some-one who hadn't made any kind of move, he sure would be taking an awful lot for granted to just blatantly tell another guy she was off limits for any other reason. But then why wouldn't he take it for granted? Look at him and look at her. She frowned.

She saw Oscar made a face. "Why? Does that make you mad?"

"No. I'm just surprised." She supposed if it were really what Oscar was thinking it *should* make her a lit-tle mad. Maybe if she wasn't busy trying to keep from reading too much into it, it would. "Thanks, Oscar. Please don't tell him I asked you."

Oscar laughed. "Don't worry. No way am I bring-ing that subject up again."

She still had a few minutes before her shift started. Grabbing her phone, she went outside. She needed to talk this out with someone. Joey was out of class now. Before she could even dial, her phone rang—her mom.

Irritated that she'd probably take up the few min-utes left before she started work she answered. "Hello?"

"Hi, *mija*."

Her mother only called her that when she wanted something. "Yes?"

"Frank is in town. He wants to get together tonight. Nothing fancy like last time. He said just a stroll on the pier and maybe a few drinks at Finny's."

"A romantic stroll on the pier? No way!"

"How romantic is it going to be, Graciela, with me and Ruben there?"

"Still, I don't want him getting the idea that I'm actually into this."

"It's only until Ruben gets the job." She heard her mom huff. "Fine, I'll think of somewhere else. But it'll be casual so don't worry about changing when you get home."

Great, she didn't have a ride again. Unless Sal insisted on taking her home she probably wouldn't even be there until almost ten. And she had that final tomorrow morning.

She stalked back into the restaurant already annoyed. Working fast to pull her apron on she rushed into the restaurant. She was shocked at what she felt when she saw Sal near the bar with that same girl he'd been talking to in the parking lot weeks ago. The girl was blonde and wore a pantsuit—the same kind she'd worn the last time only this one was black and hugged her body perfectly.

She was already tall and she wore ridiculously high heels. But most pointedly she was completely flirting with him and he seemed to be enjoying it. She kept touching his arm when she spoke. It killed Grace to admit it but they looked perfect together. She'd seen pictures of Valerie in the back room. She was blonde, too. Maybe Sal was partial to blondes also. God, what was she thinking? Of course, this would be his type— beautiful and sophisticated. She felt so stupid now. She gulped hard, trying to hold it together but the truth was she felt ready to fall apart.

He leaned against one of the bar stools and glanced at Grace as she approached. "I didn't know they were floor tickets—my friend is gonna go wild. He's already excited about just going."

"Oh, it's going to be awesome. Then after we're all headed to Brewster's in Oceanside to crack open some crab legs. Some of the players will be there as well. You have to go, Sal. The whole place is reserved just for our group. It'll be so much fun. Your friend is welcome to come, too."

"Players are going to be there? Shit, I know he's gonna wanna go."

"Good, then it's a date."

Grace turned her back to them, feeling her gut kicked in, then she heard Sal laugh. "I haven't agreed to anything yet, Melissa."

"Oh, but you will." Melissa's voice was so suggestive Grace wondered what else he'd be agreeing to on their date.

Feeling like a complete idiot for even allowing herself to consider the possibility of her and Sal, she rushed to the ladies' room before she lost it right there in front of them.

CHAPTER 12

Relieved that Grace had stepped away, Sal was still pissed at the fact that she overheard his conversation with Melissa. He wasn't sure what was going on with her and whoever she was talking to, but he didn't like the idea of her thinking *he* was off the market. He already felt her apprehension about opening up last night when she told him about her dad. The last thing he needed was to put up another wall. Melissa could be that very wall, especially if her crap started up again. Why the hell had he listened to Romero?

When Melissa finally left, he walked around casually, looking for Grace but she had completely disappeared. She was back at the bar when he emerged from the back room after an hour long conference call. Feeling like a giddy high school kid, he walked up to the bar. "So you have a ride tonight?"

She turned to him but went back to making the drinks she was working on. "I do."

Disappointed he glanced around the restaurant, trying not to show it. "Joey or Taylor?"

"Neither."

He turned back to her. "Who's picking you up?"

She continued making the drinks without so much as looking up. "The RTD."

He smiled, feeling relief wash over him. "Nah, I'll take you home."

"Sal—"

"Don't argue, Gracie. You're not taking the bus. I'm

taking you home." He walked away before she could protest.

He had to make a move soon. He could hardly look at her anymore without staring at her lips and thinking about how much he wanted to kiss them... taste her.

Julie informed him they were solidly booked for the night with reservations. He really needed to step up the hiring. He thought he'd gotten better at not being such a hard ass, as Alex put it.

He walked back to the bar. They were fully covered but the kitchen was lacking. He watched Grace as she so effortlessly made her drinks. "How do you feel about working the kitchen tonight?"

She looked up at him her eyes suddenly huge. "Really?"

Jesus, what her bright eyes did to him. "Yeah, really. C'mon." He motioned with his head.

She followed him to the back room. "Just put on a coat. We're getting busy and I need someone that knows what they're doing back there."

She put the coat on and walked right up to him. "Thank you. I won't disappoint you. I promise."

Sal had to refrain from saying what he really wanted to—that at this point, there probably wasn't a thing she could do to disappoint him. "I know you won't. Your skill, but most importantly, your ease in the kitchen is truly impressive. Get in there and kill it."

He couldn't have paid enough for the smile she indulged him with. "That means so much to me. You have no idea."

She had no idea what she was doing to him. For the next hour she worked the kitchen as naturally as she had worked the bar all night. He watched feeling a little irritated at how much the other cooks seemed to embrace her so quickly. The rapport she built with them, especially speaking Spanish, was almost immediate.

A half-hour before closing they had no more customers. It was winding down and Sal was looking forward to his time alone with Gracie when he drove her home. He walked out into the main dining room and saw her on her phone. He went back to the kitchen to make sure it was ready for closing. The busboys had their music on and it was loud in there. "Almost done, Julio?"

"You bet, Chief!" Julio put his hand at his waist shaking his hips, as the song kicked it up a notch.

"Just finish," Sal said, laughing as he walked away.

He walked into the back room where Grace was taking off her apron. "I won't need that ride after all, but thanks."

Sal watched her as she took her purse out of the cabinet. "You got a ride?"

"Yeah," She nodded, but said nothing else.

He sat down at the desk, trying not to wonder about who was picking her up but he couldn't. "It's not the RTD right, Gracie?"

"No."

Since she was obviously not going to offer more information, he shut down the computer and headed out front to make sure everything was wrapped up. He walked to the front to lock the front door and saw a Cadillac parked right out front and a man leaning against it, holding a bouquet of roses.

Sal took a deep breath, feeling his heartbeat speed up. This couldn't be her ride. The guy was too old. Feeling a weird unease come over him, Sal looked around to see who else was still in the restaurant. He knew Melanie's fiancé and it wasn't this guy. Grace rushed to the door. "Is it locked?"

"No." He watched from the hostess stand.

"Goodnight then."

"Is that your ride?" These moments of complete inability to keep his thoughts to himself were happening a little too often now.

She nodded but didn't turn to face him and pushed the door open.

"Is he gay, too?"

She turned around and met his eyes. "No, he's not."

Unable to take his eyes off her, he watched as she walked right into the guy's arms, giving him a quick hug, then taking the roses with a smile. He gulped hard, trying to understand how someone he'd only begun to get to know could affect him so profoundly.

*

Mortification and anger were the two emotions Grace felt as she sat in the front seat of Frank's car. She was going to kill her mother. She'd told her over the phone they would all be stopping by to pick her up, not Frank by himself—with roses. And did he really have to be standing *right* in front of the restaurant?

This was the last thing she needed to deal with after the day she'd had. Seeing Sal with that girl and listening to their banter while the reality of her delusional mentality sunk in had been far more emotional than she would have ever imagined. The day she got choked up when she told Joey about the feelings she was developing for Sal had been surprise enough. But breaking down and crying in the restroom for as long as she did today, was utterly ridiculous. How was she going to continue working there? Inevitably, she was going to keep seeing him with women, probably hear about them, too. Was she going to turn into a blubbering mess every time?

Grace hardly heard anything of what Frank was saying as they drove back to her place to pick up her mom and Ruben. Something about his hotel and the restaurant coming along and how he was looking for more cooks. Grace did a lot of nodding. This was the *last* time she'd agree to going out with Ruben. The flowers obviously meant he thought more of these little get-togethers than she wanted him to.

She knew it was rude to text while he was talking to her but she didn't care.

FYI I'm not staying out late tonight. I have a test tomorrow morning and I'm already tired so I need to be home early.

She sent that one off to her mom then send another to Joey.

I really need to talk to you but I can't now. Will you be up a little later.

She glanced at Frank who was still talking about the restaurant and smiled.

"I was telling your mom, you guys should come out and visit soon—maybe this summer. It's not a big fancy hotel but it does have a nice size pool and I'm working on getting a lounge act on the weekends."

"Sounds nice."

No way in hell. But if he'd already told her mom she had a feeling her mom would be pitching the idea to her anyway. Grace was ending this tonight. She drew the line at Frank already acting like he was a suitor. She glanced down at Joey's response to her text.

Sure hon. Call me as late as you want. =)

They picked up her mom and step-dad and Grace went through the motions of the evening. After the walk on the pier that her mother did nothing to change like she'd said she would earlier, they had a few drinks and Grace made her move.

"I really have to get home now." She turned to her mom who was already getting ready to protest. "I have that test in the morning, mom. I *have* to be in bed early." She turned back to Frank. "And I'm very tired. I had a long day."

"Certainly," Frank said, finishing up his drink.

Grace didn't care. Her mom could glare at her all she wanted. When they got in the car she texted her mom from the front seat.

I'm not doing this again. EVER so don't set any of this stuff up again or Frank is getting stood up.

Her mom texted her right back.

We'll talk later. Stop texting while he talks it's rude.

As soon as they were home she said good night and went straight to her room. Her sister was already asleep, and that girl could sleep through a hurricane, so Grace didn't feel bad about talking on the phone. She sat on the floor and called Joey. She grabbed a box of tissues because she could already feel it coming.

He answered. "What happened?"

"I'm so stupid." The tears were immediate.

"Why? Are you crying? Oh sweetie, what's the matter?"

Somehow, through all the sniffing and whimpering she managed to tell him about what Oscar told her and the night before. She especially felt stupid about how she'd actually thought she felt a vibe from Sal. Then she told Joey about the Barbie doll that visited Sal today and how she'd spent nearly a half hour in the restroom crying like an idiot over this man who clearly is interested in bettering his restaurant; so of course he's going to be nice to her if he thinks she'll make a difference in the kitchen. "And then to top it all off, Frank, that man I told you my mom wants me to hang out with so that Ruben can get a job already, picks me up right at the door with roses."

"Did Sal see?"

"Yes! And he asked me if Frank was gay too. I was so embarrassed."

"You see? Why would he ask something like that if he *wasn't* interested in you?"

"I don't know, Joey. But based on the women I've seen him with I'm definitely not his type. He's going on a date with her this weekend. I can't get caught up on a guy like this, but I'm afraid I already am. How do I stop this?"

She heard Joey exhale. "You don't."

"I have to!"

There was a knock on the door then her mom peeked in. "What's wrong with you?"

Grace wiped her eyes. "Nothing, I just had a long day at work. Can you give me a minute? I'm on the phone."

Her mom smiled. "I just wanted to tell you. Ruben starts working next week."

Grace gave her a thumbs up but couldn't manage much of a smile. "Good, 'cause I'm done going out with him anymore."

"We'll talk later."

Her expression said it all. Grace might be done but her mother wasn't. She had more up her sleeve. Her mom closed the door and Grace apologized to Joey for the interruption.

"Okay let's think about this. You get one ride from a co-worker and that warrants a warning right off? He's already questioned who me and Taylor were. He took you to be a part of something so intimate with his family and now he's asking about the guy with the roses?"

Grace shook her head. "I can't Joey. I have to stop r-eading so much into nothing. I'm being delusional and look what it's doing to me. I'm a mess."

"Why don't you do this? Wait and see if he has any-thing more to say or ask about Frank tomorrow. Then casually ask him about the blonde bimbo and see if he gets the connection. If he's so smart he should pick up on it."

Grace threw the tissue in the small wastebasket by her bed. "The problem is he probably *will* ask about him but not for the reasons I'm thinking and I have to stop making more of it. It does me no good."

"Then maybe honest and straight forward is the best way to go—enough of the wondering. If he asks you ask him why he wants to know and while you're at it, ask him why he told your co-worker you're off limits."

Grace thought about it. Maybe Joey was right. What's the worst thing that could happen? "You don't think he'll think I'm full of myself or worse think it's laughable?"

"No and I'll tell you this. I'm going to be dying to know what his reasoning is for saying you're off limits. You're a sexy mama, and you don't give yourself enough credit, Grace. I wouldn't be surprised at all to hear he *is* interested in something more with you."

Grace blew her nose and wiped away the rest of her stupid tears. "Okay but if I do this and there are perfectly logical answers to my questions meaning he's *not* interested you have to stop saying stuff like that. Promise me, because it's already hard enough and I really, *really* have to get over this. I can't afford to quit but if I have to, I will. "

"You are *not* quitting, Grace. At least not until you have enough experience and you can get a job somewhere better."

Grace couldn't even imagine working somewhere better than where she got to see Sal everyday.

She took a deep breath and gathered her thoughts. She really needed to get it together. Because there were other bigger things she had to focus on. She couldn't—wouldn't—let her feelings for Sal get in the way of her dream. The dream she'd originally set her sights on when she applied at Moreno's in the first place.

*

Sal stopped at his parents' on his way home to talk to his dad about the conference call he'd had that day but mostly because he needed the distraction. He couldn't stop thinking about Grace and the date she was probably still on.

To his surprise, Alex was there. His mom had a whole dinner set up for him.

"Hey, how's the family?"

Alex nodded as he took a bite of a king size burrito. Once done chewing he responded, "They were all sound asleep when I left. I needed to get some sleep myself. I just woke up, but I'm going back as soon as I'm done eating. The docs say they should be ready to come home in a couple of days."

Sal had gone back the morning after they were born

and was able to go in and see them up close. His nieces were absolutely beautiful.

"Salvador, I'm making you a burrito."

"Mom, I'm good."

"You'll be better with a burrito."

Sal didn't even know why he tried arguing and turned back to Alex. His dad had joined them at the table.

"You've had enough." His mother scolded his dad.

"I didn't say anything!" His dad protested.

"But I know you. And then your heartburn will keep you up all night."

Sal told both his dad and Alex about the conference call.

"So what do *you* think?" Alex asked him.

Sal shrugged. "I dunno. I'm beginning to think maybe we should just move slower. Do one restaurant at a time." Thoughts of opening up another restaurant and taking Grace with him as the head cook had been on his mind all week. But he didn't dare tell Alex that.

"Up to you, man," Alex said. "But you know with school and the babies I'm gonna have my hands full for a while."

Sal bit into the giant burrito his mother made him and nodded. After swallowing he said, "I let Grace work the kitchen today."

"Yeah? How'd she do?"

"She took over. The girl's incredible."

Alex stared at him, the smile increasing as he chewed his own food.

"Stop." Sal knew exactly what he was thinking.

"What?" Alex chuckled.

Both his parents were staring at him. "Stop what?"

"Nothing, mom." Sal gave Alex a warning glare.

"What are you two talking about?" his father demanded.

"Nothing." Sal repeated.

"Just tell 'em. He's got a *thing* for Grace."

Sal let his head drop back. Damn Alex.

"The one you brought to the hospital?" His mother eyed him.

Sal stood up, wrapping his burrito in a napkin. "I gotta go."

"No. I asked you a question." His mother put her hand on her waist.

Alex laughed, sticking what was left of his burrito in his mouth also standing up. Sal pushed him. "Ass!"

Sal walked over to his mom and kissed her forehead. "Yes, mom, the one I brought to the hospital."

"You got a thing for her? What does that mean?"

Sal shook his head, glaring at Alex. "Means she's driving me crazy, but she's on a date right now so don't start planning any parties yet."

"She is?" Alex asked. "How do you know?"

Sal bitterly took a bite of his burrito and felt like flinging the rest in the trash but his mother would have a fit. After a hard swallow, he turned to Alex before heading out. "The guy picked her up at the restaurant. Roses and all." He turned back to his mom and hugged her. "I gotta go mom." Then walked over to his dad and clapped him on the shoulder. "I'll keep you updated about the investors. I still gotta meet with them a couple more times."

Just before he walked out Alex got his attention. "Hey, Sal."Sal turned back to a very serious looking Alex. "Remember what you told me when I thought it was too late for me and Valerie? Doesn't mean anything, bro." He shrugged. "Just 'cause she's on a date doesn't mean it's hopeless. But you gotta make a move, dude, before it is."

Sal nodded, knowing it was true. Making a move wouldn't be the hardest part. Her shooting him down or things not working out and having to be around her after would be the worst. So was it worth the risk? The answer to that screamed in his head... absolutely.

CHAPTER 13

For the first time since Grace had been attending school, she fumbled through her final, barely able to finish in time. The good thing was she still managed to get a decent meal out and now this class would be out of the way. Just a few more weeks and she'd be done with all her classes and have her degree.

Joey skipped his next class to drop her off at work. "You don't have to, Joey. I have plenty of time to take the bus."

He waved her off. "I wasn't going to my next class anyway. The professor is not even going to be there today. It'll be a waste of time."

They stopped to grab an iced coffee then headed to his car. "Taylor totally agrees with the straight up approach. People waste way too much time trying to figure out all the signs. Just go for it and ask him already."

Grace was so nervous about this, her stomach was in knots. "I'm gonna try but I'm not promising I won't chicken out."

Joey groaned. "You can't chicken out! It's a simple question. If he can ask you then you can ask him."

Grace asked to change the subject on the way to the restaurant. She was already one big ball of nerves. When they got there, she saw Barbie leaning against her Mercedes laughing it up with Sal. Sal was in a suit again and looked amazing. Unlike the first two times Barbie wasn't wearing a power suit. Instead, she wore a short frilly sundress with the highest, sexiest heels. Grace probably wouldn't be able to even stand in those shoes, let alone walk in them. Just like the last time, she kept touching him.

Grace instantly felt the lump in her throat. "Oh my God. What is the matter with me?" She turned to Joey. "I gotta get a grip."

"Grace, the guy is hotter than shit. You have to expect women to be falling all over him. The key is to find out if he is into the relationship thing, because obviously you won't be able to handle anything less. If he is, then these women will have to go. We'll make sure of it. But one step at a time, sweetie. Just 'cause this skank is all over him doesn't mean *he's* into *her*." Joey parked across from Barbie and Sal and eyed them. "Look at her body language. She is *so* obvious and look at his. I'm telling you, he's not into her, Grace. He looks bored."

Grace gulped not wanting to look in their direction but she would have to walk right past them if she got off where Joey parked. "Yeah, well bored or not they're going out this weekend. Can you pull around the back? I'd rather walk in that way."

Joey started up the car again, getting Sal's attention. He turned to look at them and Grace glanced in the opposite direction as they pulled around back.

She was surprised to see Alex in the back room when she got there. "Hey. What are you doing here?"

"I had a class today and I needed to get something I left here. How are you, Gracie?"

"Good. How are the babies and your wife?"

"They're all good." He smiled looking every bit the proud daddy. "Coming home in a few days, hopefully. Is Sal here yet?"

Grace turned around to face the cabinet. "He's outside with his girlfriend."

"Sal doesn't have a girlfriend."

Grace rolled her eyes, glad she wasn't facing him and tied the apron around her waist. "Well, girl *friend* then. Whatever she is, he's out there with her."

When he was quiet too long she turned to see if he was still there. He was grinning and staring at her. "What?"

"Does that bother you, Gracie?"

She felt her face warm and she turned back to the cabinet, taking extra long to adjust her things in there. "Does what bother me?"

"That he's out there with a girl."

"Of course not. Why would it?" God, she was so freaking obvious. If Alex noticed, it was only a matter of time before Sal did too.

"I dunno, sounded a little like it did. Kind of like when Sal told me about *your* date last night."

Grace spun around. "My date?"

"Yeah, the guy that picked you up with the flowers. Is that your boyfriend? Or just a boy *friend*?"

She ignored the last question but feeling a little thrilled, had to ask, "Why would it bother Sal?"

Before Alex could respond, Sal walked in the door. "Hey, I was wondering what your truck was doing out there."

"I'm just in and out. I had to grab something." Alex glanced back at Grace as she avoided looking at Sal at all costs. "Gracie thought maybe that was your girlfriend you were talking to outside."

Grace turned back to the cabinet, squeezing her eyes shut. Where were all the California earthquakes when you needed one?

Sal was quiet for a moment and she was sure Alex was grinning from ear to ear. "Nope. Not even close."

"You see? Told you, Gracie."

She didn't bother turning around. She couldn't. She knew her face was probably bright red so she simply nodded, hoping Alex would just drop it. No such luck.

"So I was asking her about the guy last night. Is *he* your boyfriend?"

Damn it. It was supposed to be Sal asking her not Alex. How was she supposed to turn this around now? "No he's not. Just a friend."

Sal took a seat at the desk. "Do *all* your friends bring you roses?" he asked.

Finally, Grace turned to face him then glanced at Alex, who was still smiling. "Do you two always ask your employees about their personal lives or am I just special?"

"No and yes," Sal responded.

Alex waved. "I'm out. I'll let you two work this out."

Gracie fidgeted with her apron, still trying to figure out what was going on. She watched as Sal stood up and closed the door. "I don't mean to pry, but I will since Alex brought it up. Who was that guy last night?"

This was it. Joey would kill her if she didn't do this. Sal was obviously calling her out. "He's a friend of my step-dad's." She cleared her throat. "Are you seeing that girl you were talking to outside?"

His eyebrow lifted and he smiled. "Melissa? No. She just got me tickets for the big game this weekend." He leaned back in his chair apparently enjoying the quid-pro-quo. "So why's your step-dad's friend bringing you roses?"

She shrugged. "I think my mom gave him the idea I

might be interested in him." She stared him straight in the eye, feeling her heartbeat thud against her chest and trying desperately not to read too much into what was happening here, but it was impossible. "I won't be seeing him again, but you're going out with Melissa right? After the game."

His expression went tense. "I'm not sure yet. I really don't want to. She's... well let's just say she's a long story." For the first time since she met him, he looked her up and down, unnerving her even further. "Where would your mom get the idea you were interested in that guy? He's a little old for you isn't he?"

Grace shifted her weight. "My mom gets a lot of crazy ideas. *She's* a long story, too." She bit her bottom lip debating on whether or not she should say what she wanted to and finally did, "Melissa sounded pretty convinced you'd be willing to go." She glanced at her feet then back at him. "It sounds like fun."

"Actually." He paused for a moment, staring at her. "I may not even go to the game."

Grace had to refrain from smiling. "But she got you tickets."

"I can give them both to Romero and he can take Isabel," he smiled. "What are *you* doing this weekend?"

She feigned a pout, feeling her heart speed up. "I work all weekend."

"After work?"

Grace struggled to remain poised. "Nothing."

"Maybe we can spend some time after work this weekend so we can share our long stories."

Grace wasn't sure she even wanted to hear about Melissa and she certainly didn't want to tell him about her mom, but spending time with Sal sounded like heaven. "Yeah, okay. That sounds good."

He smiled, flashing the dimples that were beginning to own her heart. "Then it's a date."

After agreeing and finally able to pull her eyes away from his, she was on her way out the door still unable to believe she had a *date* with Sal. As excited as she felt, she also could barely catch her breath. What if she was just *this* week's date for him? She'd already cried for this man and nothing had even happened between them. What was she going to do the next time she saw him with another girl?

"Gracie." She stopped and turned around to meet his eyes. "It's Friday so technically the weekend starts tonight."

Tonight? She planned on going over Joey and Taylor's tonight so they could help her mentally prepare. Now she was on her own. She gulped hard but nodded. "Okay. I didn't have a ride tonight anyway."

"Perfect."

Grace walked out into the restaurant's main dining room in a daze. Usually she left her phone in the back room but she brought it out with her in her pocket. She *had* to tell Joey but she didn't want anyone to hear so she texted him.

We're going on a date tonight!

She hadn't even put her phone back in her pocket when it buzzed.

Get out!

She started to respond but it buzzed again.

I knew it! Sexy Mama! I knew it!

This was making her more nervous. She didn't even know how to begin to be sexy. Taylor and Joey told her she didn't have to try, that's what made her even sexier. She always told them she didn't know what that meant. Joey said her accent had a lot to do with it. The accent she tried so hard to hide but apparently it was still present. She didn't know what was so sexy about it. She'd always thought people thought less of her because of it.

Gotta get to work but I'll call you tonight.

The day literally dragged, especially since Sal left to do some interviewing at Angel's restaurant. Sofia came in to cover for him while he was gone.

"Hey, you." Sofia walked up to the bar with a big smile. "I heard you handled the kitchen beautifully yesterday while we were busy."

"Yep. And it was actually Sal's idea."

"I know. He also said as soon as we get a couple more bartenders you'll be in the kitchen full time." Sofia held up her hand to high five Grace. "That's what you wanted right?"

Grace high fived her, letting the delight sink in. Everything was working out like she'd only dreamed, and spending time with Sal hadn't even been part of that dream until very recently. Icing on the cake if this didn't all blow up somehow. Things never seemed to work out for her like this.

"What are we high fiving about?" Melanie walked over and held her hand up for Grace.

Grace high fived her, laughing. "I'll be in the kitchen full time soon."

"What's cool is you're so young you'll add spice to the kitchen," Sofia said.

"But I'm old-school when it comes to cooking. I don't do recipes. I hope Sal realizes that."

Sofia laughed. "None of our vets do recipes either. Trust me. Just humor Sal if he ever wants you to. It's not like he'll have time to be policing you."

"Did he leave with that chick?" Melanie asked.

Grace bit her bottom lip, hoping she wasn't so damn obvious again about this subject.

"What chick?" Sofia asked.

"That one from the other day."

"Which one? Geez, my brother has a load of chicks."

Grace took advantage when she saw Julie walk up to the bar, by taking her order and she started putting the drinks together, trying not to think about what Sofia had just said. The bad feeling she had in her stomach about letting herself get caught up with Sal just got bigger.

"You know the blonde girl in the suits," Melanie said. "She's been here a couple of times. I wonder if he's actually getting serious with her."

"No way," Sofia said, as she walked away. "Sal doesn't do serious. She's probably just another one of his many. I don't think he left with anyone. He was on his way to Angel's." Sofia stopped and turned back to Melanie. "He's coming back. Why did you need something?"

"No," Melanie smiled. "Just being nosey."

Oscar walked up to the bar with another order for her, reminding her about what Sal had told him. Maybe she'd bring it up tonight. This time of day usually got busy and Grace welcomed the distraction—anything to get her mind off worrying.

By the time Sal returned, things were slowing down. She saw him stop and talk to Julie, giving her that smile she wished he could reserve for just her. Julie was the only other single girl around his age that worked at the restaurant and Grace could tell even on that very first day when she walked in for the interview that she enjoyed flirting with him. Her phone buzzed in her pocket snapping her out of her thoughts. It was a text from Joey.

I can hardly wait! You better not forget to call me tonight. No matter how late. =)

She frowned texting him back.

I won't cause I'm worried now.

She didn't bother putting the phone back in her pocket she knew he'd be texting right back. Her phone buzzed almost immediately.

What now woman?!

That made her laugh. Joey always said she was a worrywart. But she had very good reason to be this time. She'd never been this emotional about *any* guy much less one who she wasn't even in a relationship with. It scared her to death to think what it might do to her if something actually happened between them and like Sofia said—he didn't do serious. Joey had been right. She evidently wouldn't be able to handle anything less.

She texted back.

EVERYTHING! We'll talk tonight. =/

They'd gotten so busy and with Grace continuing to think about Sal she'd forgotten all about eating.

At the end of the night, everyone trickled out until it was just Sal and Grace. He walked up to the bar where she'd just finished cleaning everything. "So did you think about where you wanna go on our *date*?"

The smoldering stare was the same one that made her insides mush the first time he told her he'd been impressed by her cooking. There was an overload of mushing going on now. She cleared her throat. "I'm kind of hungry. I skipped my lunch."

His eyebrows pinched. "Why?"

"I dunno. We got busy and I just forgot."

"You can't be doing that, Gracie. I'm gonna have to write you up," He smiled and she had to take a deep breath. His smile this close was breathtaking. "So what do you feel like eating?"

Nothing sounded particularly appetizing, but then she had a thought. "I know. Why don't I make us something here? You can try out another one of my grandmother's recipes."

His brows shot up. "Sounds good to me. But it's still a date, Gracie. Just so you know."

"Got it." She started walking toward the kitchen; her insides were completely out of control now. He had to stop saying that. She was ready to swoon again. And as obvious as her emotions were to everyone else, he was bound to notice.

It took a few minutes to get everything she needed gathered over by the stove. She knew exactly what she would make for him.

"I'm gonna grab a beer. You want something?" he asked, walking out of the kitchen.

"I'll take a beer too."

A few minutes later Sal walked back into the kitchen, carrying a tin bucket of Coronas on ice and small bowl with sliced up lime wedges. "So what are you making?" He opened up a beer bottle then stuck a wedge of lime in it and handed it to Grace.

She took the beer. "It's a surprise." She squeezed the lime into the beer and pushed the wedge all the way in. It wasn't until she sprinkled the salt on the rim that she noticed he was staring at her. Her heart fluttered and she took a longer drink than she normally would, hoping it would take a little edge off her nerves. "This isn't on your menu either, but I think after you taste it you'll consider adding it."

Sal opened a beer for himself and leaned against the counter. "Consider? If it's anywhere near as good as your casserole I'll be demanding it is."

Grace regretted taking such a big drink of her beer because she needed to burp now. It wasn't happening in front of Sal. She turned her back on him and placed her hand on her mouth praying it wasn't loud. Thankfully, it wasn't and she turned around to face him again.

"You okay?"

She assured him she was and put the beer down to begin cooking.

"Oscar said you're seeing someone. Yet here you are on a date with me. So what gives?"

Grace looked up at him completely taken off guard by his question. She knew they'd be talking tonight but this was totally unexpected. Even when he mentioned this being a date several times, she didn't actually expect him to take it this seriously. His eyebrows went up and he didn't smile. Apparently, he was very serious.

CHAPTER 14

Grace's expression wasn't what he expected when he asked the question and Sal wasn't sure if that was a good or bad thing, so he waited while she picked up her beer and took another drink.

"You asked him if I was seeing someone?"

"No. He just mentioned it the day after he gave you a ride home—said you were *talking* to someone."

She put the beer down and began pouring rice into a saucepan. "Did you say something to him about staying away from me or me being off limits?"

Sal laughed. "He told you?"

She stopped what she was doing again and looked at him. "So you did?"

With a shrug he took another drink of his beer. "Something like that."

"Why?" She walked away to pour water into a cup.

Sal took advantage of the moment to size her up. The craziest thing was happening. The more he had her here to himself the more intense his need to know if she was free for him to make his move got. "Oscar's a good guy but he tends to look at women like objects. I just reminded him not to do that with you or any of the employees."

Grace glanced at him before pouring the water in the saucepan with the rice. She hadn't fried it before-hand and she added nothing else but a little salt. Steamed white rice was not something he'd ever considered putting on their Mexican menu.

"Oh. I think he took it differently," she said, looking up at him.

"I know he did, and I'm glad." Sal stared at her. "Means he'll definitely be staying away. But Gracie...you haven't answered the question."

"Can I ask you something first?"

Sal took a deep breath. He didn't care what it took he was getting an answer tonight. "Go ahead."

"Why does it matter?"

He squeezed the bottle of beer. "Why wouldn't it? We *are* on a date right? I'm not in the habit of dating girls who are seeing someone else. That's not my thing."

"What is your thing?" She took a pan down from where it hung and splashed a little cooking oil on it, setting it aside. "Because I hear serious relationships are not it."

Sal was usually very patient but for some reason this really irritated him. "Who said this? Oscar?"

"No, your sister did, actually." She began dicing peppers.

Sal noticed how at ease she seemed in spite of the nature of their conversation and his obvious growing impatience. She appeared a little nervous earlier but it was almost as if being in her element had calmed her. He wished he could say the same for himself. He'd grown more anxious by the minute.

She shrugged. "Just seems that if that's the case, dating someone who's not looking for anything serious because they're already seeing someone else would be ideal."

He clenched his jaw, surprised at how much that irritated him. "No. It wouldn't. And for the record, just because I've never had a serious relationship doesn't mean I don't do them."

She hadn't looked at him since she begun dicing but she stopped now and glanced at him. Then she took a drink of her beer, but still didn't answer his damn question.

"So is that a yes?"

She shook her head and he exhaled slowly. Now for his next question: something he'd thought about all night. "So whatcha do last night? With your dad's friend."

"Step-dad." That had a little bite to it and she began dicing a bit faster.

"Okay, step-dad's friend. Were you two on a date?"

"Sort of."

Sal clenched his jaw. Was she being vague on purpose? "What does that mean? Are you into this guy?" He was going to throw all the questions at her tonight. He had to know now.

"Just because I go out with someone doesn't mean I'm into them."

Ouch. "Is that right?"

"Yeah, my mom wanted to make sure my step-dad got a job with this guy so she asked me to entertain him a few times."

"What? Your mother asked you to? What kind of entertaining?"

Adding to the incredible annoyance he now felt, Grace laughed. "Nothing bad. Just go out and have dinner one time and last night we took a walk on the pier then had a drink. "

Even that pissed him off. What kind of mother asks her daughter to *entertain* a man to get her husband a job?

"So tell me about Melissa." She started frying chorizo in the pan.

At this point Sal had given up trying to figure out what she was making. He'd fill her in on Melissa, but he was getting back to her mom. She *did* say it was a long story and they had all night. At the time her mother hadn't interested him much but now she did. He knew where Grace came from, she couldn't have the best lifestyle but having a mom that pimped her out was a whole other ballgame. He wanted to know more.

He told her about how he met Melissa, not mentioning too much about Melissa being so clingy, but he did make it clear that he wasn't interested in her.

"So you were just using her for her basketball tickets?" She smirked, taking a break from her cooking and drinking the last of her beer.

Sal took the empty bottle then opened another one for her. "No. I wasn't even going to respond but I made the mistake of mentioning the tickets to Romero and he went all crazy, insisting I get them. Otherwise, trust me I wouldn't have."

Grace went back to cooking, taking the done rice away from the heat then sautéing the peppers, onion and chorizo with a generous amount of shrimp. "*She* seems very into *you*."

"She's persistent. I'll give her that." He was beginning to love watching her cook. He'd watched many cooks at work in his time but none were as graceful as she was. His mom was the only one that came close, but he'd never look at Grace like he did his mom, so there was no comparison. "You said your mom was a long story too. Tell me about her."

The smirk went flat as she cracked an egg off the side of the pan in which she was sautéing the vegetables and shrimp and began scrambling it. She took a deep breath. "My mom is actually my step-mom, but I've always called her mom because she's the only mother I've ever known."

Feeling an ache for her, he had to ask. "What happened to your real mom?"

She dumped the rice into the large frying pan in which she'd been sautéing and added more spices. "She died giving birth to me. In Mexico, it's not like the states. There is no insurance. My dad couldn't afford to take her to the hospital so a mid-wife was called in. There were complications and they rushed her over the border to a hospital in El Paso. They barely made it to the hospital in time to do an emergency C-section. I nearly died, too, from what my grandmother told me, but my mother didn't make it. My dad never really talked about it."

She paused to take another drink of her beer and Sal wondered if she was getting upset again like the night she told him about her dad. He was afraid to ruin the night so he wouldn't push for more unless she offered on her own. She did. "It was just me, my dad, and grandmother for years. Then when I was five, my dad started dating my step-mom and I begged him not to marry her. I didn't want anybody else in our family. He promised he wouldn't, then a few months later she was pregnant and he said he had to do the honorable thing. They were married and my grandmother assured me having a sibling would be a good thing." She finally smiled. "She was right about that. Rose was my little doll, then she became my little shadow. But my step-mom didn't seem to have the same adoration for her as the rest of us did. My grandmother told me when I got a little older that some women just weren't meant to be mothers and my step-mom was one of them."

When she paused for another drink, Sal decided to change the subject even if it was just for a moment. It was getting somewhat heavy and even though he now wanted to know everything about her, he didn't want her getting upset. He knew she was probably near the part about how she lost her dad and it made him nervous.

"That smells delicious, Gracie. Are you gonna tell me what it is now?" It really did smell great. The mixture of the spices with the chorizo and shrimp was heavenly.

She turned back to her creation and covered it, smiling. "There was only one Chinese restaurant near the area where my grandmother's restaurant was in Juarez. So it was pretty popular. One of their most popular dishes was their shrimp fried rice. My grandmother decided she could top it, adding a Mexican flair to it and put it on the menu. It was an instant hit. Even the owner of the Chinese restaurant came over one time to compliment her on it."

"Mexican shrimp fried rice?" Sal eyed her, then leaned over and lifted the lid to get another look. His arm brushed against her and just like the time she nearly collided with him, just being that close to her excited him. It was like nothing he'd ever experienced. Maybe it was that she was an employee and it felt a little wrong or maybe it was that he remembered her aversion to him in the very beginning and the thought of any chance with her seemed like an impossibility at the time. Whatever it was, the feeling got stronger with each moment he stood next to her.

Another look at her dish and he had to admit it looked as good as it smelled but he could hardly concentrate. Now all he could think of was touching Grace. "Is it ready?"

"Almost, it just has to sit for a little bit. You can make it with chicken or beef also but shrimp was always my favorite. This was also another one they used to order a lot for parties because it can easily be made in large quantities."

Sal turned to her. Standing this close he was tempted to lean in and kiss her but really had to be careful. Sure, she agreed they were on a date, but things would get incredibly awkward if he tried something she wasn't ready for and she rejected him, especially since they'd still have to see each other every day. She blinked her big almond shaped eyes. "It's actually really good served with Cadillac Margaritas."

"Well let's do this." Sal pointed towards the bar. "Who better to fix them than you? I want the whole experience here, Gracie."

She smiled and started toward the door. God what she did to him was insane. He walked behind her, wondering how long he could put off making a move. Even if it wasn't a physical one. Not much longer that was for sure. Getting her to agree to give him a chance would more than suffice for now.

Grace went to the bar. Sal grabbed a lighter from just under the counter and walked out to one of the booths in the corner to set it up.

"What are you doing?" she asked from behind the bar.

"I'm setting up the table. I told you already. Just because we're here doesn't mean it's not a real *date*." He lit the candle in the middle of the table, glad he managed to derail any more talk about her mom and dad. He wanted to know all about it — all about *her* — but the intense stuff could wait for another time. Tonight he had other subjects he wanted to touch on. Like what his chances with her were. She'd already mentioned dating someone didn't mean she was into them. He knew she'd been referring to her date last night but it could've been her subtle way of hinting he shouldn't be putting too much weight on tonight. He'd get it straight before the night was over. After grabbing a couple of the pre-wrapped silverware, kept under the hostess desk up front, he walked back to the booth. Grace had already poured the margaritas and walked them to their table. She placed them on the table then smiled at him. "I'll be back with the food."

No way could he stay away from her now. "I'll help you."

He followed her into the kitchen and watched as she pulled out two plates. Sal inhaled deeply. "God, it smells good."

"I haven't made it in a while, but I think I got everything it needed." She spooned some on both plates.

Sal inched his way closer to her, taking in the mixture of her warm skin and lotion maybe. He leaned in to help pick up one of the plates, when she turned her face their lips were just inches apart. "We could—" She stopped and stared at his lips then her eyes wandered up and met his. "I was gonna say we could also warm tortillas to go with this if you want." He saw her gulp but she didn't move away from him and he was sure she was feeling the same thing he was.

"Gracie." His voice was hoarse and a near whisper.

"What?" She searched his eyes. The ease that had kicked in while she was cooking was gone and he saw the nerves were back.

"I wanna kiss you so bad."

Her eyes moved down to his lips again. "You do?"

"Yes. But I don't want you to—"

"Do it then." She brought her hand up to his face and caressed it, making his legs nearly give out on him.

Putting the plate down, he leaned in and kissed her softly not wanting to come on too strong, but he did trace her lips with his tongue. The taste of her mouth was incredible, just like he'd imagined. Noticing her inexperience almost immediately only excited him more, but he forced himself to go slow and be gentle. It wasn't easy.

He continued gently, placing his hand behind her neck and she leaned back allowing him better access. Then she eased her mouth open, inviting his tongue in and he really had to restrain from devouring her mouth. She followed his lead as his tongue moved around hers and he moved in closer, feeling her breathing become slightly labored. He didn't want to stop but he had to before things got too heavy. He still had the rest of the night with her. Forcing himself to, but not before giving her a few more soft pecks, he pulled away and stared into her eyes. She licked her lips. "You don't want me to what?"

At first, he didn't know what she was talking about. The kiss had clouded everything out but then he remembered. "I don't want you to think I'm coming on too strong on our first date."

She glanced down pulling a strand of hair behind her ear. "So there's gonna be more?"

"Of course," he said, pulling the other strand behind her other ear. "That is, if you want there to be."

She nodded, smiling. "I do."

"But I meant what I said about not dating anyone that's already seeing someone else." He had to get this one straight. "You're really not then right?"

"No. I'm really not."

Sal peered at her. "So who were you talking about when you told Oscar you were?"

"I just said that so he wouldn't get any ideas about asking me out." She shrugged. "I didn't want to be mean, especially because I knew I'd have to work with him."

The relief felt too good. Sal didn't even try to hide his excitement. He cupped her face with both hands and he kissed her again. This time just a quick one. "But you'll be okay with *this*, right?"

She bit the corner of her lip and hesitated. "I'm not sure."

He pulled back to look at her better. "Why?"

"You've never been in a relationship. I have. I've never done the casual dating thing. I'm not sure if that's something I'd like or could handle. Your sister said—"

"Never mind what my sister said, Gracie. My family only knows what I want them to know. I was away at school for a long time. Believe it or not, I did have a relationship or two. Just nothing I would consider serious or very meaningful, so I never mentioned them to anyone." She stared at him and he knew what he'd say next was risky but she's the one that brought it up. "I wasn't going to say this tonight but I don't want you to take this casually. Not once have I ever considered dating someone that works for the restaurant. I never thought I would. Not until I realized I want more than just a date."

She blinked and looked away then turned back to him. Her eyes glistened. "I do, too," she whispered, her voice nearly breaking.

She was by far the most emotional girl he'd ever met. But he was glad she was emotional about this. It meant she really cared and it felt damn good.

This time he hugged her. Having her in his arms finally, felt better than what he'd expected. It felt perfect. Like that was exactly where she belonged. Keeping his hands off her while they worked was going to be a challenge. But a challenge he more than welcomed.

CHAPTER 15

Originally the booth set up had the place settings across from each other but after that kiss and their talk Sal said there was no way he wasn't sitting next to her. So they sat on the same side. He said he loved the Mexican fried rice and it would be a perfect addition not only to the menu but to the Sunday brunch. Grace still couldn't believe this was all happening to her. It felt too good to be true.

Not wanting to move into any subjects that were too nerve-wracking or that might have her in stupid tears again she asked about something safe. She really did want to know more about his plans on expanding the restaurants into a franchise. He told her more about it but said he was having second thoughts.

"Actually I thought about what you said the day I gave you the tour. It might be smarter to keep it on a smaller scale and work on perfecting the restaurants rather than expand into too many, because I know I wouldn't have the time to manage them all. If I don't have a close hand in it all it won't be the same."

She frowned. "You have to trust other people's judgments, too. You can't do it all."

"I can if I stick to fewer restaurants." He'd already helped himself to a second plateful of the rice and he was nearly done with it. That made her smile. "No one cares about this as much as we do. The family has their hands full even with the two restaurants we have now."

"Well maybe you should just do one at a time. Once you're managing all three smoothly, then you can try for another until you feel like you can't take any more on."

Sal smiled and kissed her. "That's exactly what I was thinking."

Grace stuck to safe subjects for the rest of the night. She was amazed that this whole restaurant business started with his dad in a catering taco truck. Sal was obviously very proud of how far his dad had come. It gave Grace hope that someday she'd be able to do the same.

By the end of the night, Grace felt almost drained from the amount of emotions that evening. She was so glad when he'd changed the subject from her mom and dad earlier. She'd been pretty close to getting emotional about that again and she would've hated for him to remember their first date that way.

When he dropped her off, he kissed her again the way he had in the restaurant. She didn't want it to end and it did go on much longer than their first kiss. He leaned his forehead against hers when it was finally over and gazed in her eyes. "You have no idea what you do to me." Then he smiled. "Hell, I don't even know how to explain it."

The way he looked at her at that moment made her wonder if he could actually be feeling what she was feeling. "I can't explain what I'm feeling either. All I know is... it scares me."

"Don't be. I'm not scared." He lifted his eyebrows. "Okay, maybe a little. But it's a good kind of scared, like I just boarded the ride of my life." He kissed her nose and whispered, "Hold on tight."

Even after talking to Joey for over an hour, going

over every detail of her date and him reassuring her this was not only a good thing it was great she still couldn't sleep. But it was like Sal said—a good thing. She was too excited.

Every time she closed her eyes she relived those incredible kisses.

*

Grace wasn't sure what to expect when she arrived at the restaurant the next day. Their eyes met as soon as she walked in and he greeted her with most breathtaking smile. Her insides had already been going wild even before she got there. As she put on her apron in the back he startled her coming up from behind. She nearly let out a yelp before laughing when she realized it was him and he planted a long smoldering one on her.

"Is the door locked?" Grace asked when she came up for air and she was able to gather her thoughts.

"I think."

"What do you mean you think? What if someone walks in?"

He shrugged going in for another one. "Sal, I don't want anyone to know."

He pulled back immediately with a glare. "What? Why?"

"Aren't you the one all about professionalism? Isn't it gonna be weird for everyone to know me and you are... a thing now?"

The glare softened into a smile. "I like that. Okay, I'll be discreet to an extent. But Gracie, if anyone gets wind of this or somehow finds out, I really don't give a shit. It's our business, not theirs. They'll just have to deal with it."

With that, he kissed her again and the ride began. Gracie decided not to fight it and just hold on tight.

*

That afternoon Sal got a text from Romero. He was at the game with Isabel.

That Melissa chick really pissed me off. Just an FYI you'll probably be hearing from her.

Sal frowned and texted back.

What happened?

He sat back in his chair and waited for a response. Grace walked into the back room and he threw the phone on his desk, standing up. That could wait, this couldn't. She smiled when he pushed the door closed and pulled her to him. "You on a break, or are you just here to see me?" He kissed her before she could answer and she giggled against his mouth.

The door handle jiggled and Grace pulled away. It irritated him that she cared so much about people finding out. Grace spun around and opened the cabinet when the door opened. Sofia walked in. "I thought you were interviewing today at Angel's."

"Nah, I moved those to Monday. I'm only gonna do them on Monday and Tuesday now."

Grace said hello to Sofia and walked out with her phone in her hand, in too much of a rush. Sofia looked at him funny, lifting an eyebrow. Sal sat back down at the desk not acknowledging her suspicion and grabbed his phone that had buzzed twice since he threw it down. He read the first text.

She got rude with Izzy when I told her she took your ticket and well you know me. I wasn't having it.

"Godamnit!"

"What?" Sofia asked as she put her apron on.

"Romero."

"Ah," Sofia laughed. "'Nuff said."

Sal read the next one.

I told her I'd pay for the damn tickets but she said you'd be paying her for this one way or "another." I told the bitch that's probably what she needs. Ha! She didn't think it was funny. >=)

Sal shook his head, exhaling loudly.

"What did he do?" Sofia asked.

"Just made another mess for me." He tossed the phone back on the desk and turned his chair around. "Grace has another great dish for us. Mexican shrimp fried rice."

"Ooh, sounds good."

"It is. I was hoping to get it in tomorrow's brunch 'cause she said it can easily be made in large quantities. I already told Alex and he said he'd come in just to try some, but I was hoping you can come in to help in the morning. I totally forgot I'm meeting my buddy in the morning for a few rounds of golf. I already told him we'd have to do it earlier than we planned so I can get here early and see how it goes."

He also wanted to spend as much time with Grace as he could before her two days off. He would've gladly just canceled the whole thing but Jason had beaten him to it, calling to tell him he was looking forward to it because he really needed to talk.

"Yeah, I can come in and open. As long as I can leave early. I have somewhere to be in the afternoon."

His phone rang and he picked it up to check the caller ID. Melissa. *Shit.* "You can leave as soon as I get here."

Sofia nodded and started out the door. "Can you close the door behind you?"

She did and he answered. "Hey, Melissa."

"I can't believe you gave that asshole those tickets." It was really noisy and Sal couldn't tell if she was yelling to be heard over the crowd or because she was that mad.

"I was supposed to go with him. But something came up last minute."

"And what about tonight? Will I see you there?"

He sat back. "No. Can't do it."

"What do you mean you can't?"

"I just can't. I'm sorry."

"What? I can barely hear you."

"I said, I just can't."

She was quiet and he wondered if she'd heard him. "You can't just brush me off like that. Do you know what I had to go through to get those tickets?"

"Sweetheart, I didn't ask you to, but I do appreciate it. I'm sorry it worked out this way but I won't be there tonight." He was trying to be as nice as he could. He knew what she was capable of.

There was a sudden roar in the background and she didn't speak until it died down a little. "I can't hear you. I'll call you later."

The line clicked and he threw the phone down again more frustrated than ever. He'd pay her for the fucking tickets if he had to, but he wasn't responding to her calls anymore. He shook his head. Never again.

*

The evening was spent pretty much the same as the one before only a little less formal and the food Grace prepared was a bit more simple—*tacos al pastor.* They ate them in the kitchen with beer. She sat on the counter.

Just like the night before while she cooked she felt completely under control. It was only when she'd sat on the counter and Sal walked up to her, pushing her legs apart to get closer to her that her heart began to hammer away. She thought of how experienced and put together Melissa seemed. She'd probably done things to him that Grace had only read about. How could she possibly live up to that? She still held her bottle of beer in her hand as she draped her arms around his neck keeping up with his deep kisses. He groaned and whispered against her lips. "You're getting so much better at this."

She pulled back a little. "Why? I wasn't good before?"

He let out a laugh. "Jesus, your lips have been perfect from the moment I first laid eyes on them and they taste even better, but you were a little tense in the beginning. I wasn't sure you were enjoying it as much as I was." He slid her closer to him and she felt his strong hard body against her, making her breathe a little harder.

"This is all a little new to me. But of course I'm enjoying it."

She saw the confusion in his eyes. "You said you'd been in a relationship. I was gonna ask but I'm not sure I wanna hear about it."

"I meant the only times I've ever been involved with someone it wasn't just dating. Both times it was understood we were in a relationship, but neither lasted very long and I've never..." She felt her face flush when his eyes widened. "I was real young, too. It was right before my grandmother passed."

Ah hell. She felt the lump in her throat forming. Not wanting to ruin the moment with her damn tears again, she kissed him, this time putting more into it than before. She put the bottle down and ran her fingers through his hair, kissing him frantically. The arousal she felt was electrifying. Any thoughts of crying vanished, instead all she could think of was the possibility that Sal would make love to her one day — maybe soon. She moaned in his mouth and he moaned in response. His hands caressed her back and she wished she had the nerve to tell him to do more. Even though his body was pressed against her and he kissed her just as madly as she kissed him, he was incredibly gentle in every other way.

Grace moved up even closer to him so her legs straddled him completely. Feeling brave, she wrapped them around him and felt just how aroused he truly was when he pushed up against her. He pulled away from her mouth and made his way down to her neck. Feeling his tongue as he kissed and sucked it made her squirm. She'd made out a few times but it'd never felt like this. "This is *crazy*," she said breathlessly.

He stopped and looked at her. "What is?"

She stared at him and infuriatingly she felt the lump in her throat again. "The way you make me feel." She hugged him burying her face in his neck. No one had ever made her feel this way. *Ever.* She didn't know what to make of it, but it was getting embarrassing.

His caressed her slower now and he kissed the side of her head. "Gracie, you have no idea how glad I am that you're feeling it, too."

She took a deep breath before she pulled away from him and looked in his eyes. "Really? What is it, because

I don't understand it. I've never felt anything like this."

"I'm not sure. But I'm older than you and like I said yesterday. I've never felt it either." He kissed her softly. "Just go with it, Gracie. Whatever it is, it feels damn good."

He tilted her chin up and gazed in her eyes for a moment before devouring her mouth again.

*

Sunday morning Sal ignored three calls from Melissa and didn't respond to any of her texts. He'd talk to Jason on the golf course about possibly getting Kat to talk to her about backing off. The last thing he needed was her causing any problems with him with Grace.

Since it was a last minute change in time, they weren't able to start as soon as they got there and he wouldn't be done as early as he hoped. Jason had walked off to get them both coffee and Sal read Melissa's latest text.

You know better than to ignore me. I'd say after what you did yesterday the least you could do is offer to make up for it.

He texted her back.

I'll pay you for the tickets.

He could kick himself for having listened to Romero. His phone buzzed again.

U know that's not what I mean. You owe me a night out, Salvador!

Exhaling, he knew what he had to do. He may as well get it over with.

Can't do it. I'm seeing someone now. Sorry.

Jason got back with the two coffees and Sal put his phone away. He could go back and forth with Melissa all day if he left it up to her.

"So the bachelor party is in two weeks. You're gonna be there right?"

Sal had forgotten about the damn party. Just being here right now when he could be back at the restaurant with Grace had him feeling antsy. He didn't even want to think about giving up a whole weekend with her just to go to some stupid bachelor party, but there was no way out of this one. He'd already agreed and Jason and him went too far back. Plus there was no way he was explaining that he didn't want to be away from a girl he'd only just started seeing. "Yeah, I'll be there."

"Good." Jason smiled, getting in the cart. "We're all flying out Friday and coming back Monday."

Hell no. Sal climbed in on the passenger side of the cart. "I can't do all that. But I'll meet you guys up there Saturday, then I gotta get back Sunday."

Jason's shook his head. "You work too much, man. You need a vacation."

"Partying all weekend is not my idea of a vacation. I'm only doing this because it's for you."

"Well you can't show up and be a dud either. This is Vegas we're talking about remember? What happens in Vegas, stays in Vegas."

Sal took a drink of his coffee and glared at Jason. "Dude, you're getting married."

"I'm not talking about me, I'm talking 'bout you."

"I'll have a few drinks with you. I'm not flying out there for nothing. But I'm not doing anything crazy either." He had Grace to think about now. Jason was lucky he was even going.

Turned out what Jason wanted to talk about was the cold feet he was beginning to feel. Sal did his best to assure him it was normal. The guy had been living with his girlfriend for years now. What difference would it make if he got married?

Talking about marriage inevitably made him think of Grace. Though in the last couple of days *everything* made him think of her. Even the phone that continued to buzz in his pocket made him think of her. He was really going to have to do something about Melissa before she did anything stupid.

CHAPTER 16

Grace tried not to let the disappointment of knowing Sal wouldn't be there all morning take from the excitement of adding her new dish to the Sunday brunch. She knew this was huge. There were many waiting to be seated already and her newest dish would be out there. Sofia had tried it and loved it. Alex was coming in *just* to try it. Her dream was slowly being realized.

She was showing the cooks the basics on how to make it just like her grandmother had always taught her. A quick but informal lesson, and they had it. Unlike Sal, she believed in their ability to make it work. The recipe wasn't that complicated and she hadn't even written it down.

Sofia walked into the kitchen after a couple of hours. "Grace. They're loving it. It can't be replaced fast enough. Mexican shrimp fried rice is the bomb! Angel is gonna be so pissed!" She laughed.

Grace didn't think her week could get any better. "Are they really?"

"Would I lie?" Sofia walked over and hugged her. "Sal is gonna flip!"

After Sofia walked out she was still walking on air then Alex walked in with a plate in his hands. "Are you shitting me with this?"

Sofia looked up from the stove she'd been cleaning off. "You don't like it?"

"Hell yeah, I like it! It's delicious!"

Just as she was allowing the awesomeness of this

day to sink in, there was a commotion out in the restaurant. Someone was complaining a little too loudly.
Alex turned around and put his plate down. "I'll be
back."

Grace walked slowly to the door and watched as
Alex charged out into the dining room.

"I need to see Sal." She heard a woman demand.

"He's not here," Alex said. "What can I do for
you?"

Grace reached the door in time to see it was Melissa
smirking at Alex. "Oh, you could do plenty I'm sure,
but I need Sal."

Alex glanced around the restaurant. "Like I said,
he's not here."

Melissa didn't look like her usual power chick self.
She wore denim shorts and a tank top. But her hair and
make up were still flawless.

"Your brother's blowing me off, Alex. I don't get
blown off. He tried throwing the 'I'm seeing someone
else now,' crap on me. I don't buy that."

Grace's days of going nose to nose with bullies
came back to her in a flash. She'd kicked some ass back
in her day. She had to. Being new to the states with an
accent had made the kids tease her endlessly. When the
words didn't come fast enough to defend herself, the
fists went flying.

If Sal actually did tell this bitch he was seeing
someone, then he *was* serious.

"I don't know anything about it, and he's not here,"
Alex insisted.

"When will he be? Because he if he thinks he can
just blow me off, he's sadly mistaken."

Before Alex could respond, Grace walked up from
behind him, pulling off her earrings off one by one. "H-

e's seeing me now. Do you have a problem with that?"

Melissa seemed stunned for a second then she smirked. "No way. I knew he probably did the *help* but to tell them he's seeing them?" She turned to Alex and scoffed. "That's just low."

Grace almost jumped at her but she felt Alex's hand around her waist and before she knew it, he was in front of her and spoke through his teeth. "Get the fuck out of here, Melissa."

"I'm not going anywhere until I talk to Sal."

Sofia got in front of Alex and he pulled her back too. "No, Sof." Melissa had the attention of everyone in the restaurant. Alex turned to Oscar, who stood by the bar. He still held both Grace and Sofia back. "Help me out here. Walk her out, man."

"Tell your brother he owes me." Melissa glared at Alex. Then she looked at Grace. "You're a joke. What on earth could your wetback ass have to offer Sal, besides an easy lay?"

Grace tried but there was no getting around Alex. Sofia almost did though. "Get her out!" she screamed, surprising Grace. "Before *I* throw her ass out!"

"Stop, Sof!" Alex obviously had a good hold on Sofia because she didn't budge from his side.

Oscar managed to walk Melissa out, but not before she made quite a scene, flinging her arms and shouting obscenities at his attempts to take her by the arm. Grace walked back into the kitchen still reeling from the sting of Melissa's words. Her entire life she'd been judged by her looks and accent. This was not the first time she'd been referred to as a wetback. Having it spat at her in front of Alex and Sofia and the rest of the staff was humiliating.

"You okay, sweetheart?" Alex hurried into the kitchen behind her.

She nodded unable to even look at him. One of the other kitchen helpers touched her arm. *"No te aguites por esa pendeja."*

Grace put her earrings back on but didn't respond. She was surprised she didn't feel the emotion that lately had overwhelmed her. Instead, she felt the same anger that had consumed her for so many years when she was younger. Anger of having been forced to come to a country where she always thought people like Melissa would never take her seriously. People who assumed an accent meant she was stupid or less then them somehow.

She watched as another tray of the Mexican shrimp fried rice was prepped to go out into the dining room.

"Grace, you can be sure I'm telling Sal I don't wanna see that bitch in here ever again," Sofia said, standing behind Alex.

Grace turned to both Alex and Sofia who were staring at her looking very concerned. She'd put it out there so they knew. Hell, anyone within hearing distance knew now and Sal said he didn't care if anyone found out. She didn't either. Joey would be proud. "I'll be sure to tell him, too."

*

Sal got the call just as he drove up to the restaurant. He had a few voicemails but hadn't bothered to listen to them, assuming they were from Melissa since he had so many missed calls from her number. "What?" He brought the car to a grinding stop.

"She made a fucking scene and she insulted Gracie." Alex was his usual furious self.

He felt his own rage begin to go off. "How's Grace? Is she still here?"

"Yeah, she's still here. She actually handled it pretty well. I had to hold her back though. Dude, I hope y-ou're done with that chick. If she ever comes back in here and Sofia is here it's gonna get ugly. She was re-ady to go at her today."

Alex filled him in on the rest of the morning as Sal sat in his car, resting his forehead against his hand. His other line had been beeping the whole time. As soon as he hung up with Alex he answered the other line.

"You can't be serious with that girl, Sal. Are you? What does she work for free or for food? I mean—"

"I'm gonna pay you for those fucking tickets and then you're going to disappear, you hear me? I'll give the money to Jason. I don't want you anywhere near the restaurant or my place."

She laughed. "I just wanted to talk to you. Her ghetto ass is the one that came at me. But what do you expect from someone who probably just came over the border. It's laughable. What can you possibly see—"

"She has the one thing you've never had, Melissa. My respect."

He hung up on her and got out of his car. Rushing into the restaurant, he scanned it, looking for Grace. He didn't care who knew now. All he wanted was to make sure she wasn't upset. He hurried into the kitchen, his heart fluttering when she came into view. She was smiling, talking to one of the other cooks. As much as it irritated to him to see how chummy the cooks had got-ten with her so quickly, he was glad she didn't look upset. He walked to her with only one thing in mind. She looked up when she heard one of the other cooks greet him.

"I'm so sorry about what happened," he said as soon as he reached her. Unable to hold back he pulled her to him.

Surprisingly she didn't protest. "It's not your fault." She caressed his face and smiled. "I'm fine."

"You sure?"

She nodded, smiling even bigger, making it impossible for him not to kiss her right there in front of everybody. Someone whistled while a few others sniggered and made jabs. He pulled his lips away from her, giving them all a warning look and they all pretended to go back to being engrossed in their work.

"The rice is a hit," she said.

"I heard. I knew it would be." He pulled her by the hand through the kitchen door and into the back room. Alex and Sofia were in there, looking at something on the computer. Alex turned when he heard them walk in and smiled when he saw Grace's hand firmly in Sal's. "I just finished the schedule for next week. You said you'll be at Angel's on Mondays and Tuesdays right?"

"Yeah. Most of the mornings anyway. Can you guys give us a minute?"

Both Alex and Sofia looked at him knowingly but made their way toward the door without saying a word.

"You okay, Grace?" Alex asked, as he walked by her.

"Never been better."

Sal squeezed her hand. He didn't even wait until they were completely out the door before sitting on the edge of the desk and pulling her to him. He spread his legs placing her in between them, cupping her face. "Listen to me. I promise you. That'll never happen again."

"You said you never had feelings for her right?"

"Never."

She leaned in and kissed him. "I was a little surprised when I heard her say you told her you were seeing someone, but I was happy to hear it."

"I told you. I don't give a shit who knows. In fact," he pulled her closer, "the babies are coming home this week. My mom's already planning that shower she never got to throw. The whole damn family and half of La Jolla will probably be there. I want you there. I'll make sure you get Saturday off. So you won't be off tomorrow. Is that all right? You can come with me tomorrow to Angel's restaurant and catch his cooks up on the new recipes. I'm sure he's gonna love the rice, especially since it's shrimp and seafood is their thing." The whole time she listened intently, her bright eyes getting wider with everything he said. "I wanna meet your family, too." That's when her eyes lost their excitement and he had to ask, "What?"

"I want you to meet them, too," she said. "It's just that... "

"Too soon?"

"No. It's not that... my step-dad isn't exactly the most dignified person out there and my mom... well. I told you she's not my real mom so we're real different."

"I don't care —"

"I mean *real* different, Sal. I wouldn't want you to get the idea that I think like them."

Sal laughed. "Sweetheart, my brothers are ticking time bombs. Not to mention my pistol-whip of a sister. Just because we're related doesn't mean their personalities reflect on me. I would never judge you by your

family. I'm not gonna judge you period. I already know enough to be convinced that I wanna be with you.
That's all that matters. Don't worry about anything
else."

"I'd love for you to meet Rose. I can bring her to the
shower if that's okay?"

"Absolutely. I can't wait to meet your little *shadow*."

That made her smile. "That reminds me. Since y-
ou're closing and I'm getting off early today, Taylor an-
d Joey are picking me up. We're taking Rose to the mall. She got invited to the prom so we're helping her pick
out a dress." She played with the buttons on the front
of his shirt. "I can introduce you to them today when
they pick me up. They're not family but they mean the
world to me."

Sal swallowed hard, knowing he shouldn't have an
issue with these two guys meaning the world to her.
Now that he knew the truth, he saw it in Joey who was
a little more obvious. But Taylor had really struck a
nerve, especially the way he called Grace beautiful.
Still, he took a deep breath and forced a smile. "Sure.
I'd love to meet them."

After their talk and a few more lustful kisses Sal finally had to let Grace go back to work. Sofia left and
Alex came in the back to have a word with him. "So I
see you made a move?"

Sal nodded still facing the computer, he was switch-
ing Grace's days off. "Not just a move. I'm having her
come to the shower this weekend. I want everyone to
meet her."

"Wow. You don't waste time do you? That's cool
though. Gracie's pretty awesome. Just one thing." Sal
turned to look at him. "You better let all your little girlfriends know you're off the market now, because you

are, right?"

Sal frowned. "I don't have girlfriends."

"Well anyone else that might get any ideas about coming in here to face off with Grace. That wasn't cool. She played it off, but I won't have her being mistreated like that. She doesn't deserve it."

"You really think I'm gonna let that happen again? Melissa's the only one that would do something like that and I already talked to her. She won't be coming around here again."

Alex didn't seem convinced. "I really hope everything works out, Sal. Sofie was a little worried too when she realized what's going on. I don't think Grace will stick around if it doesn't."

Sal had every intention of making things work with Grace. It had to. "Trust me. I'm not taking this thing lightly, if that's what you're worried about."

They talked a little longer. Alex was clearly concerned not so much about Grace leaving but about her feelings being hurt. He said he hadn't even thought about how she'd handle all the women in Sal's life.

It annoyed Sal that Alex and Sofia made him out to be such a player. Just because he'd never brought anyone home to meet the family didn't mean all that. He just hadn't found anyone he felt he wanted to and now that he had he was wasting no time. In that sense, he had to admit he was like his brothers. They both knew when they met the one that she was it. Even though it took his knucklehead brother Alex years to figure it out he'd been stuck on Valerie from the moment he met her.

The day went by too quickly. Before he knew it, Grace was in the back getting ready to leave. He walked in as she pulled her things out of the cabinet. He hated that he wouldn't be spending time with her tonight like he had the last two nights.

"Joey couldn't make it after all," Grace said, looking up from her purse. "His mom showed up last minute from out of town so he's spending the day with her. But Taylor is still picking me up."

"You guys still going to the mall?" He asked, hopeful that it'd been cancelled and he could pick her up once he closed the restaurant up.

"Oh, yeah. My sister is dying to go and even though Taylor's not the shopper of the two, he said he didn't mind. We'll probably catch a movie after."

Sal let that simmer, reminding himself Taylor was gay and in a happy relationship. She turned back to the cabinet and Sal walked up behind her, kissing her neck. "So I'll pick you up tomorrow and you can come with me to Angel's?"

"What time? I have class in the morning."

He sucked her neck now, feeling the tightening of his pants, but he couldn't stop. Julie walked in the room and Grace pulled away, annoying the hell out of him.

"Uh... your ride is here, Grace."

Grace was visibly embarrassed; her face even flushed a little. "Thanks. Can you let him know I'll be out in a minute please?" Julie walked out and Grace turned to Sal, who reached for her hand. "I get off at noon. I can meet you there. I'll just have to figure out the bus route."

Sal hated thinking about her on the bus. No matter what she said, it was dangerous. He'd have to come up with a way to get her off it. As much as he wanted to he knew he wouldn't always be able to pick her up and drop her off. He didn't like her relying on anyone else either. "No, I'll pick you up at school."

"You sure?"

"Of course, I'm sure."

She smiled. "Okay. C'mon. Let's go introduce you to Taylor."

"Oh yeah, *that*."

She looked at him weird. "What does that mean?"

"Nothing I just forgot about it."

They walked out of the office and took the dreaded walk to the front where Taylor stood near the front door. Sal hadn't noticed the green eyes that first day he picked her up but now he noticed every detail, including the smoldering way he looked at Grace as they approached him. "You ready, beautiful?"

Sal didn't want to hate this guy but he was really starting to. Hell, he hated him the first time he saw him leave with Grace. "Yeah, I'm ready, but I wanted you to meet Sal." She turned to Sal, letting go of his hand to stand by Taylor. "Sal this is one half of my two best friends, Taylor."

Taylor reached his hand out to shake Sal's. "Nice to meet you. The other half is with his *mommy*." Taylor sounded annoyed and that made Sal feel a little better. The guy was mad that his boyfriend flaked on their shopping date. Although, it didn't help that his arm was now draped over Grace's shoulder.

"Good to meet you, too. I've heard a lot about you and Joey."

"Likewise," Taylor smiled. "She's talked our ear off about you as well."

Grace seemed embarrassed by that. Sal took a step forward, reaching out for her hand. "Well, hopefully you'll be hearing a lot more."

"I'm sure we will." Taylor turned to Grace. "Your

sister's waiting. Are we out?"

Grace laughed. "Yes! She's already texted me twice." She started to take her hand out of Sal's. "I'll see you tomorrow then."

Taylor took his arm off her and pushed the door open. She turned to walk out.

Hell no. Sal pulled her back toward him before she could take a step. "Aren't you gonna say goodbye?"

Her eyes went wide. Yes, he knew they were in the restaurant and everyone was around but after what happened today, he felt compelled to make a statement. So he brought his hand behind her neck and kissed her softly. Not too long but long enough. He would've kissed her even longer if he didn't think it would make her completely uncomfortable. Everyone would know now and that's exactly how he wanted it.

CHAPTER 17

To say Taylor was livid when Grace told him about the Melissa incident was putting it lightly. He did, however, *love* that both Alex and Sofia had backed her up the way they did. And he was more than ecstatic about the way things were turning out with her and Sal. "My God, Grace. I don't know how you ever had a doubt this guy was hot for you."

"Well, I'm not a mind reader," she said, texting her sister that they were outside waiting for her.

"You don't have to be with this guy. He *does* realize I'm gay right?"

Grace looked at him. "Yeah, he knows all about you and Joey."

"Did you not see the way his eyes nearly flamed up when I put my arm around you?"

"They did *not.*"

Taylor opened his mouth wide in amazement. "Grace, I almost jerked my arm back, afraid he was gonna kick my ass. I can't believe you didn't notice."

Grace laughed. "You're such a liar."

"Ah, shit. This guy has probably been hot for you since day one and you didn't even notice."

Grace thought about Sal's comment, *Oh that,* when she reminded him she wanted him to meet Taylor. But it was total nonsense, he knew Taylor was harmless.

"I know now. That's all that matters." She smiled, feeling giddy. "He wants me to meet his entire family."

"Wow. But I'm not surprised. I'm telling you, Grace. This guy's body language is so obvious it's ridiculous. You gotta be blind if you don't see it. Just wait 'til Joey sees him around you. I'm surprised he hasn't said he loves you yet."

That made Grace's heart pound. "No way. We haven't known each other long enough." But she *had* cried for him already — several times.

"You don't need to know much more than how he makes you feel." He reached out and cupped her chin with his thumb and finger. "Brace yourself, Gracie. I saw the way you looked at him when he kissed you. If I hadn't seen the way he looked at you, I'd be worried."

Rose got in the back seat.

"Hey, Rosie." Taylor reached in the back and squeezed her knee. "Ready to shop 'til you drop?"

"Yes!"

Grace's heart was still pounding and Taylor patted her knee. "Relax." He smiled. "It's a good thing."

They started toward the mall with Rose talking the whole way about the prom. It calmed Grace a little to take her mind off Sal and the enormity of what she'd been thinking all this time but Taylor forced her to confront. She was falling and she was falling *hard*.

Grace smiled, trying to push aside the memories of her own bittersweet prom night. For the first time, something had actually gone perfectly for her. Her date was wonderful, her dress — spectacular. It was everything a girl that age could dream of, and then just as they were on their way to the after party, she got the devastating call that her grandmother had suffered a heart attack. She swallowed back the lump that had begun to grow in her throat. She wouldn't ruin this for Rose.

After several hours of shopping, they stood in line to buy tickets to the show. Her phone buzzed and she checked the text, feeling that familiar sputter of her heart that was happening all too often these days.

I miss you.

She smiled allowing herself to feel what she'd been so afraid to until now. Now that she knew Sal was genuinely interested in a relationship with her, she was happier than she could ever remember being. She texted back.

I miss you too. Can hardly wait to see you tomorrow.

After sending it, she glanced up. Both Rose and Taylor were staring at her, smiling. "What?" She felt her face warm.

"Wow," Taylor said. "Look at you."

Grace rolled her eyes but knew exactly what he meant. Excited didn't even begin to explain how she felt about the whole situation with Sal.

"Grace, you're glowing," Rose said.

"I *am* not!" But she felt it.

It finally hit her. She and Sal were an actual couple now, and Sal wanted everyone to know it. As if her heart weren't already racing her phone buzzed again.

Tomorrow? =(I don't think I can wait until then. What have you done to me Gracie?

She brought her hands to her mouth, smiling, and took a deep breath. She didn't care that Taylor and Rose were still staring at her. The movie would be over a little after seven. She just might be able to work something out.

*

This was crazy. He'd just seen her a few hours ago. He spent the whole day with her and here he was waiting impatiently outside the movie theatre. When Grace mentioned that the movie was ending early, Sal jumped on it, asking if he could meet her after somewhere. She agreed to have him pick her up. Taylor would take her sister home and she and Sal could go out to dinner.

He saw them come around the corner and immediately he smiled. Her sister was a younger version of Grace, just as pretty.

Grace smiled when their eyes met. The second she was close enough, Sal reached for her hand. "Sal, this is my sister, Rose."

"Hi, Rose. It's very nice to finally meet you."

Rose smiled, a bit timid, but gave him a little wave. "Hi."

"So how was the movie?" Sal asked them all.

"It was okay," Grace shrugged. "Kind of cheesy."

"Aren't all chick flicks cheesy though?" Taylor asked.

"I liked it," Rose announced. "I bet you Joey would've liked it too."

"Oh God," Taylor laughed. "He *so* would've, and he probably would've been the loudest one laughing. *And* crying."

Both Grace and Rose laughed. "You know he's gonna be mad we saw it without him," Grace added.

"I'll come watch it with him again," Rose said with a smile.

After explaining to Rose what to tell their mom when she got home, Grace and Sal said goodbye to Rose and Taylor and started toward Sal's car. The second they reached it, Sal had to stop and kiss her. It was a bit alarming how much he felt for her so fast, but he didn't care if she noticed.

She smiled when he finally pulled away. "Your sister seems sweet, and she's almost as beautiful as you are."

"I'll tell her you said that. But I'll leave out the almost."

"Yeah, don't tell her that part."

They got in his car and he started it up, turning to her. "What do you feel like eating?"

Grace gave him a wicked smile. "Pastrami?"

"That sounds good. I know just the place, too."

"You think maybe we can go through a drive-thru and go some place where we can be alone?" Grace squeezed his hand with a hopeful expression. "I've had enough crowds for the day."

She'd read his mind. He wanted nothing more than to be alone with her. "We could take the food back to my place if you'd like. Unless you'd rather not."

"No. I'd love to check your place out," She grinned. "I'm nosey like that."

"All right then, my place it is."

They picked up the pastramis and headed to his house and Grace told him about everything they bought for her sister, mentioning how she'd have to pay Taylor back since he offered to pay for the dress that just wasn't in Grace's budget. "Your mom didn't pay for any of it?"

Grace rolled her eyes. "My mom hasn't paid for anything extra for me and Rose in years. The only thing she paid for since I got my first job, was the tuition for me to get my bartending license. And even that wasn't a selfless act. She did it so that I could get a better paying job to help her pay the bills."

Sal tried not to frown. He didn't want her to know

that the more he heard about her mother the less he liked the woman. The thought of her asking Grace to go out with men for her own selfish reasons almost made him hate her. But he wouldn't. She was the only mother Grace had. Grace was already leery, thinking he would judge her. He didn't want her getting the wrong idea if he expressed himself negatively about her mother.

They got to his place and Sal watched as Grace's eyes widened with every room they walked through. He hadn't originally planned on purchasing such a large home, but Valerie talked him into it. She said it was a good investment and she'd worked her magic to get him the best deal possible. He couldn't pass it up. He only hoped it didn't intimidate Grace. His neighborhood was a far cry from the area she lived in.

Her conversation had begun to wither as they drove through the winding streets up to his house and she stared at all the homes. The one thing he loved the most about his house was the backyard view. Situated up in the hills of La Jolla, the view was spectacular. "We can eat out back. It's nice out tonight."

Grace followed him out the sliding patio door, and he set the food down on a glass patio table which sat twelve. His mother had helped pick it out, making sure there was enough room for everyone, because it was rare for just one of his family members to show up without all the others showing up, too, and that included Romero and Isabel.

He turned to Grace, who had stopped at the door, taking in the view. The ocean was visible off to one side while the cityscape of downtown La Jolla was visible at the other end. Then her eyes went to the outdoor kitchen. The only time he'd ever used it was when his family had come over and his mother and Sofia had made him a birthday dinner. That was the end of last summer, when he'd first bought the place. Even then, he hardly touched it except to figure out how to get it going then his mom took over. Sal had been home less and less since then, especially now that he was helping Alex out with running the restaurant.

"It's beautiful." She turned to Sal. "And you get to see this everyday?"

He smiled holding out his hand for her. "You could, too, you know, if you come over every day."

She took his hand and came over to sit next to him at the table. He wouldn't tell her just yet, but the thought of having her around all the time was definitely something he'd be suggesting and a lot sooner than he would've ever imagined. He was certain what he was feeling, like today when he closed up and could think of nothing else but wanting to be with her was not going away any time soon. In fact, he anticipated the need to be around her only getting worse.

Other than her eyes widening, she didn't appear to be put off by the suggestion. "I should've known your house would be amazing, but I just didn't expect all this."

Sal shrugged. "My sister-in-law knows her real estate. She did a good job helping me find this gem."

"I'm sure you had plenty to say about the details." She grinned.

He leaned over and kissed her. "You don't know that."

They ate quietly at first. She must've been as hungry as he was because she dug right in. After a few bites, she wiped her mouth, staring out into the view again. "Before we moved out here, I'd never even seen the beach." She turned to him with the napkin still over her mouth. "I didn't even know how to swim."

"Did you ever learn?"

She held her hand out opened and moved it side to side. "More or less. I still get nervous, though."

Sal motioned to his pool. "You can come over and practice any time you want. Bring Rose, too."

He loved seeing her excited smile. It reminded him of how young she was even though she was mature beyond her years. Obviously everything she'd been through had forced her to grow up far before her time. "When I was a little girl we used to go camping every year to a place called Elephant Butte in New Mexico. It was our summer trip. They actually closed down my grandmother's restaurant for a week so we could go on vacation. It's the only time I ever got to swim, but I loved it. I just never got very good at it." She gazed out into the his backyard view again. "I loved camping — those are some of the best childhood memories I have. Swimming all day, then fishing. Dad and I caught a real big one, one time. My grandma gutted and cleaned it and we had it for dinner. And there was nothing like sleeping in a tent, roasting marshmallows... for some reason a simple sandwich or in our case a cold *torta* tasted so much better when we were camping." For once, she looked so at peace and actually smiled when speaking of her past.

"Elephant Butte, uh? I heard of it somewhere. What's up with that name?"

"It's named after some island in the lake that supposedly looked like an elephant butt, but I didn't think it did." She took another bite of her sandwich and stared out into the view again for a moment before turning back to him. "My dad always said he'd take me to the beach someday but..." She took a deep breath. "Rose only got to go camping with us a few times. She probably doesn't even remember. My mom didn't like camping so she wouldn't come on the trips. After a few years she made my dad feel so guilty about leaving her behind, we stopped going." She stared at her fries, lost in thought.

Sal squeezed her hand. "So how'd your dad die?" Uncomfortable or not, this was obviously a significant aspect of her life. Sal wanted to know everything. What made her smile, what made her laugh, even what made her cry.

She looked up from her food and met his eyes, but she didn't cry. "He was murdered."

Sal tried not to react, in hopes she could get through the story without crying but he was *not* expecting that at all.

She continued, dry-eyed. "It was no secret that my grandmother's restaurant was doing well and Saturdays were especially busy. It was getting so busy that like you, he'd begun to talk about expanding when I was old enough to run a restaurant on my own. It would be on a smaller scale but it would be all mine." Her eyes were excited for the moment. "One Saturday night just as he closed up, three men walked in and robbed him at gunpoint." Sal squeezed her hand again when he saw the grimace and the tears begin. He was surprised she'd gone this far without crying. But she took a deep breath and continued. "He gave them all the money he had, did everything they asked and they still shot him. My sister and I were already home with my grandmother. My mom is the one that found him. She'd gone out to move the car around front, while he closed everything up. It was the reason why the back door wasn't locked. Since he was shot at such a close range he was gone before the medics ever arrived." She wiped a single tear that escaped from the corner of her eye, took a deep breath and went on. "It was all over the local papers for weeks, that's how I found out we were selling the restaurant. They hadn't told me yet but my mom had mentioned in an interview that the restaurant would be up for sale and we were going to be moving. It happened during the summer. By Christmas we were living in El Paso."

Sal leaned over and kissed a tear away that trailed down her cheek. His heart ached for her. "Did they ever catch the guys that shot him?"

She let out a sarcastic laugh. "I doubt they ever even tried."

Sal pulled her chair to him, suddenly needing her closer, and caressed a few strands of hair away from her forehead. "I'm sorry that happened. I can see it's something that still hurts a lot."

Grace tilted her head and her eyebrows furrowed as she cleared her throat. "The funny thing is I only cried when I first got the news. I was in complete shock and denial. I didn't want to believe it. But after that I refused to cry because I didn't want Rose to see me cry. She was only five and though she was sad she didn't quite understand the enormity of it. She didn't really get that he was *never* coming back, so it wasn't as devastating for her as it was for me, and I didn't want it to be. She caught me crying one time when I thought she wasn't home and it really scared her. So I vowed it would never happen again. Though sometimes I did where I knew she couldn't catch me, like in the shower or at night when she was asleep and she's always been such a sound sleeper I didn't worry about her waking.

But I put up a front for so many years. Then when my grandmother died something changed." Sal played with her hand and she glanced down at it. "Even though I tried, like with my dad, to hold it in for my sister's sake. As the years passed, I've gotten so much more emotional about it all now and I don't understand why."

Sal kissed her hand, wanting more than anything to take her pain away or at the very least lessen it. "Grief is a process, sweetheart. Even though you thought you understood it at the time, you really didn't." He was glad now for choosing to take that extra semester of Psychology. "You can't heal if you don't allow yourself to grieve and it sounds like you never did. But it's inevitable and it *will* happen. I think it's what's happening now. You're finally letting the emotions manifest." He kissed her forehead. "It's a good thing."

One side of her mouth went up slightly but it was hardly a smile. "I'm such a downer." She sniffed.

"No. I *wanted* to know. You really think I thought you wouldn't cry? It's natural, Gracie. I'm gonna ask you something else and I don't want you to hold anything back either." Her eyebrows shot up. "How'd your grandmother die?"

She didn't give it much thought before answering. "Heart attack."

Sal cringed. It couldn't have been anything less sudden? But Grace didn't cry. Instead she reached for her purse on the other seat and fished out her wallet, then pulled a picture out and handed it to Sal. It was a snapshot of herself in a formal gown with her hair up. She was younger and looked stunning. His jaw involuntarily clenched at the sight of the guy holding her hand in the picture but he pushed the unreasonable jealousy away. He knew this had nothing to do with him. A short older woman with a white braid and a big smile held her other hand.

"This was the last picture I took with her. It was hours before she had the attack. I was actually on my way—" She stopped when her voice betrayed her and she brought her hands to her face.

Sal wrapped his arms around her, feeling a deep ache inside for her. This happened on her prom night? "It's okay, baby. Let it out. You'll feel better."

She didn't cry long enough, pulling away after only a few moments. Sal frowned, handing her a napkin. She wiped her face and went on with her story, clearing her throat. "We were on our way to an after party when I got the call." She took a deep breath but no longer cried. "By the time we arrived she was gone." She gave him a crooked smile as he handed her the picture back and she tapped her finger over the guy in it. "To top it off, we broke up that night."

"He broke up with you that night?" That pissed him off. How could the idiot do that to her *that* night?

"No. I broke up with him. We had talked about that night being our… first time." She glanced away from him and he took a very deep breath. The conversation had taken an unexpected turn but he wanted to continue to be supportive, so he worked on keeping his expression the same. "I never quite agreed to it, because I wasn't completely sure I was ready. Then after everything that happened with my grandma, of course it wasn't happening. I guess because when I saw my sister at the hospital so broken up, I tried my hardest to be strong. I cried, but not as much as I wanted to. I put up a front again. I needed to be strong for her. Well, my *boyfriend* who wasn't close to any of his grandparents took it as a sign that it wasn't that big a deal and when we got back to his car he told me about the room he'd already paid for and was planning on surprising me with. He actually suggested we still go there."

Wow, and here Sal thought the guy was an idiot *before* she explained it.

"I was so unbelievably disgusted there was no way I could continue a relationship with him." She pulled away from Sal's embrace and sat up straight. "Anyway, I'm glad you asked. Those two instances in my life are probably the most painful of all, but there have been a lot of good times, too."

Grace insisted on hearing more about *his* family. Sal told her more about how close they'd always been and she laughed when he told her about how poor Sofia had to deal with all of them including Eric and Romero watching over her so closely when they were all growing up. "We were all bad, but Alex has always been the worst. You'll probably notice he'll get that way with you eventually. He's very protective over his family and friends."

She smiled. "I think I already did a little bit. If Melissa wasn't female I have a feeling he would've hurt her today."

Sal winced. "I'm sure he would've. Damn. I'm sorry about that, Gracie."

"Stop. I won't allow you to apologize for her. It wasn't your fault. Maybe I shouldn't have confronted her the way I did."

Sal laughed.

"What?" She stared at him in that cute confused way, she did so often.

"Alex told me what you said and about you pulling off your earrings." Grace's face flushed. "Don't be embarrassed." He hugged her again, chuckling. "You're gonna fit right in with the rest of my family and friends. Don't even get me started on Romero."

They moved to the lounging sofa with the overstuffed pillows that faced the pool. Sal sat back, pulling her to him and she leaned against him. "It's so beautiful out here. If I lived here... " She stopped.

"If you lived here what?" Sal liked where this was going.

She turned to face him. "I'm just saying *hypothetically.* I don't want you to think that—"

"Oh, I'm thinking it, Grace. If I have it my way, you will." He kissed her. "So go on."

Her eyes were glued to his for a moment, taking in what he just said. "All I meant was if I lived some place like this, I'd be out here *every* night. I'd probably never cook inside. Except maybe when it was too cold." He saw her glance at the outdoor fireplace. "Even then I'm sure I'd figure out how to stay warm."

"I'll tell you what," Sal said, leaning further back, bringing her with him so they were practically lying down. "I'd like nothing more than to have you here every night, so if you're game we can come back here every night and hang out from now on."

Her eyes brightened and it drove him crazy. Unable to hold back any longer he kissed her long and deep. They made out for the longest time since he'd first kissed her and though there were moments he thought of trying for more than just kissing and enjoying her soft delicious neck, he didn't. He remembered her mentioning she'd *never.* If that meant what he thought it meant, as torturous as it was to hold back, he had to take things real slow. She was absolutely worth waiting for.

CHAPTER 18

Sal picked Grace up after class the next day. Even as they drove to Moreno's on the Marina, everything still felt so surreal. She'd hardly been able to concentrate in class, daydreaming instead about the past several evenings with him.

So far, Rose had been the only one who'd met Sal and hadn't gushed about his looks. While she said he was good looking, she didn't like that he seemed too serious, reminding Grace of her first impression of him that now felt like a lifetime ago. Never would she have imagined the day he interviewed her that things would turn into this.

It didn't take very long for her to teach the two cooks that were there at the time how to make the new dishes. As Sal had anticipated, Angel was especially excited about the shrimp dish. That afternoon when Sal was done with all the interviews, they took a walk on the pier of the Marina. It reminded her of the awkward night she'd spent walking the pier with Frank. It amazed her, how different it felt with Sal now and how at ease she was with him. She leaned into him, taking a deep breath, glad that she was almost done with school so she didn't have to rush home to do homework.

They walked up to the rail and looked over into the water. Sal stood behind her and kissed her temple.

"Only two more weeks," she said.

"For what?"

"And I get my culinary degree."

"Perfect timing. Although," he chuckled, "you don't even need it now."

She turned to look at him. "Of course I do. You never know what the future holds. I know better than anyone that things can change in a blink of an eye. I'm always prepared for the worst, so if it happens, I'm ready. "

His expression went hard. "You mean with your job or with us?"

"Both."

"That's a little pessimistic isn't it? I have faith that both will work out."

She shrugged, turning all the way around to face him. She wished she could be more optimistic, but it was hard. "They do go hand in hand. I just wanna be prepared."

He leaned in, his hard body pressing against hers making her heart speed up. "I'll tell you right now. Unless something unthinkable happens, my feelings for you are already so concrete, I don't see how things *couldn't* work out."

Her heart swelled, but she had a hard time concentrating with his body pressed against hers. The night before things had gotten pretty heated, but as usual, he didn't push. She wondered how many more nights they could spend on that sofa in such a romantic setting before things moved forward. Just the way he looked at her even now warmed her insides. Before she could respond, he kissed her so passionately, she held on tight feeling her legs go completely weak.

*

As promised, the rest of the week they went back to his place every night, including her day off Tuesday. Every night, they spent hours talking, then getting very cozy on the lounge chair that was now Grace's favorite place to be — under the stars, with an amazing view — in Sal's arms.

Her mother hadn't asked her much until Friday night when she'd texted her at work to tell her Frank was in town and wanted to see her.

She tapped out an answer, furious. *Absolutely not!*

It was closing time and they'd be headed to Sal's place again, just like they had all week. The text had been sent an hour earlier, and she'd just noticed it. She dropped the phone in her pocket, knowing her mom would be texting her again.

Sure enough just as she walked back toward the kitchen where she'd worked all day it buzzed in her pocket.

Graciela be reasonable the man is Ruben's boss. All he wants is a few hours then he's gone again possibly for weeks.

Her mother was outrageous. Did she really expect Grace to continue this charade for good? All week she'd gotten home so late her mother had been asleep. She knew she was out with someone but Grace hadn't had a chance to tell her about Sal. Before she could text back her phone buzzed again.

He's picking you up at work. When you didn't respond to my last text I assumed you were okay with it so I told him to go ahead. He's on his way there now. Just be nice one last time. Ok mija?

"Something wrong?"

Grace almost jumped. Her face must've been as white as it felt because Sal stared at her, concerned. "Uh… no, it's just my mom."

"She okay?"

"Oh yeah, she's fine." As inconspicuously as she could, she glanced past his shoulder to the front door and her heart sunk. Frank stood out there, leaning against his car, just like the last time, holding a bouquet of roses. Her eyes were immediately on Sal again. There was no other way out of this but to just tell him. "She set up another date with me and my step-dad's boss."

Taylor had hit it on the nose about Sal's flaming eyes, because she saw them flare now. She reached for his arm. "It's not like I'm even remotely interested in him."

His eyes opened wide. "So you're going?"

She turned towards the front door, feeling defeated. "What am I supposed to do? He's already here."

Sal's head jerked toward the front of the restaurant as soon as she said that. "You tell him you don't want to go. That's what." He started walking. "I'll fucking tell him."

Grace squeezed his arm. "No, Sal. Please."

Sal glared at her. "Do you want to go with this guy, Grace?" His loud words turned the heads of the few employees that were still there cleaning up and they glanced out the front to see who Sal was talking about.

"No. Of course not."

"Then don't go."

"I won't." Her heart was going a mile a minute now. She never expected his reaction to be so explosive. "But let *me* tell him."

Sal pulled the keys out of his pocket. "Lets go."

He held her hand firmly all the way to the door then unlocked it for her. He started to walk out with her but she pulled her hand out of his. "Wait here, please."

He stopped, but obviously had no intentions of going back in without her. She tried to give him a reassuring look but he was busy staring Frank down.

Frank smiled as she approached him. "Hello, Grace. You look very nice tonight."

"Thank you. Listen Frank I'm really sorry but I can't go with you tonight. I already had other plans my mom didn't know about. I didn't get her text until just now."

There was no hiding his disappointment. "That's too bad... and there's no way you can change them?"

"No, she can't." Sal slipped his hand in hers. Grace wanted the earth to split open and suck her in. This was the most awkward situation she'd even been in and it was all her mother's fault. "Not tonight or any other night. Got it?" Sal pointed at the roses. "And you can keep those. Take them to her mother. She'd probably like them."

Frank looked flabbergasted. He cleared his throat. "I see." He nodded at Grace. "I'll give your mom a call." He didn't even glance at Sal, before spinning around and walking to the driver's side of the car.

Sal didn't wait for him to leave before heading back inside, holding Grace's hand in his. Some of the busboys stood just inside the door. "It's cool guys, get back to work." They all walked back toward the kitchen. As soon as he locked the door, he turned to her, his eyes still on fire. "Why didn't you just tell him the truth?"

Grace gulped. The intensity practically radiated off him and though it unnerved her, she stood her ground. "I just wanted to get rid of him as fast as I could, and let my mom do the rest. It's her fault—let her deal with it." Remembering how she felt when Melissa showed up wanting to see Sal, and how Sal had told her al-

ready that he was seeing someone, softened her. He h-
ad every right to be angry that she'd even consider going out with Frank, even one last time. She brought her
hand to his face, caressing his cheek, and he leaned into
it. "Don't be mad. Please? I promise to set my mom
straight as soon as I get a chance to talk to her."

He pulled her too his chest, hugging her tight, and
she felt how hard his heart pounded. "Well, I set *him*
straight already so if his ass ever shows up here again,
he'll be answering to me. I thought you said your step-
dad got the job already. Why is your mom still asking
you to *entertain* this guy?"

"I don't know. He owns a hotel casino in Laughlin,
and I guess she wants to stay in his good graces. Guess
she thinks he might come in handy someday."

Grace was so furious with her mom, especially because she knew her mom didn't give up that easily.
She'd seen Sal's attempts to hide his contempt for her
mother whenever Grace spoke of her. He didn't even
try hiding the disgust now. She could only hope Frank
had enough sense to listen to Sal and not her mother.

*

That night, after spending another incredible evening
with Sal in his backyard, he dropped her off late again.
Only this time, her mom was waiting up. She'd texted
Grace earlier, but after Sal had calmed down about
Frank. She dared not even read another one of her
mother's texts for fear that he might ask her about it.
She could only imagine what her mother would be tex-
ting her after talking with Frank.

Her mother sat slumped at the table in what was
beginning to feel like an increasingly small kitchen. Sp-

ending so much time in Sal's huge house made her realize how small this place really was.

"Who did you get to scare Frank off?"

"My boyfriend." It felt so odd saying it out loud.

"Your boyfriend?" Her mother sat up straight.
"Since when do you have a boyfriend?"

"Since last week. I hadn't had a chance to talk to y-
ou all week."

"Who is he?"

"His name is Sal Moreno."

She literally saw the cha-ching go off in her mother's brightened eyes. "Is he the owner of Moreno's?"

"One of them. His family owns it. His parents are
retired and he and his brothers have taken over."

"I've heard a lot about Moreno's. My girlfriends go
there often for Sunday brunch. I didn't realize you were involved with one of the brothers. I heard they're all
very good looking. How many are there?" It seemed
her mother had suddenly forgotten all about Frank.

"Three. He wasn't happy about Frank showing up
there, mom. You can't do that anymore."

Her mother frowned. "I know. He told me. I didn't
know what to say. I thought maybe you just put up one
of your co-workers to make him go away because you
were being stubborn. I felt so bad that I invited him
over tomorrow for lunch."

Grace let out an exasperated sigh, then remembered
and smiled. "I won't be here." She started to her room
done talking to her mom.

"I thought you said Saturday was your day off this
week?"

"It is. But I have a baby shower to go to. I'll be gone
all day." She needed to get to bed. She was looking at a
long day tomorrow. She'd made plans to have break-

fast with Taylor and Joey, since they were both whining about being abandoned ever since she started seeing Sal. She'd kill two birds with one stone because while they were out she could pick up a gift for the shower.

*

Since Alex refused to take the babies out yet, even though they'd been cleared by the doctors to leave the hospital and were home now, the shower was being held at Alex's home. As usual, his parents had gone overboard. When it came to throwing parties, their mother was insatiable. Nothing was ever too much.

Sal spent the entire morning helping get things together. He felt bad that they'd all gone over to help start setting things up last night and he'd chosen to spend another evening alone with Grace instead, so he'd headed to Alex's early that morning.

The place was a madhouse already, as was usually the case the morning of any Moreno family party. Alex's covered deck was big enough, but his mom still insisted on adding a huge canopy over the pool area to allow for extra tables and chairs around it, which only meant one thing—she'd invited *everyone*. He was surprised only a handful of family members from Mexico were there, but the day was still young.

He walked over to where Alex was setting up a popcorn machine. Next to it was a cotton candy machine. Alex frowned when he saw him. "Can you believe this shit?"

Sal laughed. "I can't believe you're surprised."

"I told her I don't want all these people around my girls. Do you have any idea how many germs are going to be floating around here today? She's nuts if she thinks she's going to pass the babies around for everyone to hold." Alex slammed the back of the popcorn machine closed and moved on to the cotton candy machine. "You better talk to her. Because you know me, I'd never say anything to hurt mom's feelings, but when it comes to my girls, I'm putting my foot down."

"Easy." Sal clapped Alex on the back. He expected nothing less than a lion's roar when it came to Alex and all three of his girls. "I'll talk to her. Don't worry."

He walked back toward the house. Great. He was bringing Grace around for her first formal meeting with the family and already there was the possibility of a family meltdown.

His mom assured him no one would be passing the babies around. She had plenty of pictures of them to pass around instead. She'd also set up a screen outside that would play the babies' homecoming video—two hours of goo-gooing and gah-gahing and two beautiful baby girls who slept through the whole thing.

After helping for a few hours, he went back to the restaurant to check on the food that would be delivered to Alex's house a little later. Alex requested Gracie's casserole and she'd been incredibly flattered. The huge trays looked as good as the ones Grace had made.

He went home to shower and change then headed to pick up Grace. He worked his jaw when he remembered the man Grace's mom sent to pick her up last night. The guy was at least ten years older than Grace. But that wasn't even the issue. At this point, he wasn't sure he wanted to meet her mom at all. Just the notion that she'd use her own daughter like that infuriated him. Now that Grace was with him, there was no way he would put up with that kind of shit.

As he drove up her street, he pulled his phone out to text her that he was there. He noticed from the very first time he picked her up that she hadn't wanted him to come up to her apartment. He knew she had it hard. He wouldn't push anything that would make her uncomfortable.

Pulling up slowly next to a Cadillac that looked just like the guy's Cadillac from last night, he parked right out front of her apartment building. He couldn't be certain, but it was the same make and color and looked completely out of place in this neighborhood. He parked behind it and called Grace instead of texting her, taking in the Nevada plates as her phone rang.

As soon as she answered he asked, "Is that guy from last night here?"

"Yes."

Sal pulled the keys out of the ignition and bolted out of the car. "Why?"

"We're on our way down. I'll explain when I get out there. Just give me a second please." She hung up before he could ask anything else. He wasn't sure who he was more enraged with, her mom or the fucker for having the nerve to show up after he'd made it clear Grace was with him now. He certainly wasn't mad at Grace. He slammed the door to his own car and stalked toward her building. Maybe he hadn't been clear enough.

CHAPTER 19

Grace and Rose rushed down the stairs each holding a gift bag. "Just follow my lead, Rosie. I was hoping Frank wouldn't get here until after I'd left. Sal's not gonna be happy." Her only hope was that when Sal saw Rose he'd calm down a little. Although his intensity had almost excited her last night, she didn't like upsetting him. She heard it in his voice just now. He was *already* upset.

Sal stood at the bottom of the stairs looking up as if trying to figure out which of the endless identical doors was the one to her apartment. His hardened expression softened a bit when he saw them. She smiled big, hoping he would too, but his expression was hardly forbearing.

He nodded at Rosie then turned to Grace. "Why is he here?"

"My mother invited him over for lunch. I didn't know anything about it until last night." She slipped in her hand in his. Even though she felt a little weird about doing it in front of Rose, she leaned in and kissed his tense lips. "I talked to her last night. This whole thing with me entertaining Frank is over. She knows now. She and my step-dad can entertain him all they want. I'm out."

He still didn't smile, but he turned to Rose. "I'm sorry Rose, I didn't say hi." Then he glanced at the bags they carried and his expression hardened again. "Grace, you didn't have to get anything. That's not why I invited you today."

"Nonsense, I was going to anyway. It's nothing extravagant. But I thought they were adorable. You'll s-ee."

He frowned, glancing up at the building before turning around and they walked back to his car, her hand in his the whole way.

By the time they reached Alex's house, he was in a much better mood. He'd quizzed Rosie about soccer. Grace had told him about Rosie playing soccer since she was a little girl and how she was on her high school team now. She'd stopped playing on her club team a few years ago when her mother announced it just wasn't something she could afford anymore—as though she was bringing in the money that paid for it. Luckily, it didn't cost anything to be on her school team, so though she didn't get to play all year round like she did in club she at least got to play during soccer season at school. She was also on the volleyball team but soccer was her first love.

Grace, Joey and Taylor were regulars at her games, while her mother was a regular no-show. Rose didn't ask her anymore why she didn't show up. Half the time Rose didn't even tell her mom she had a game. She told Grace not to either, that it didn't matter. But Grace got the distinct feeling she did it so there would be a less painful reason why her mother hadn't shown up—the fact that she didn't know about it.

Sal had warned Grace about his family's over-the-top parties. He hadn't exaggerated. The only thing missing was a petting zoo and the clowns. Rosie's eyes were as wide as hers felt when they walked into the back and there were as many people there as when they were fully loaded at the restaurant. "Wow," she said, as they walked through the crowd, holding Sal's hand. "You weren't kidding."

After stopping at about half a dozen different tables full of family members as Sal introduced her and Rosie to them as his girlfriend and her *baby* sister, Grace's head spun. There was no way she'd remember all their names.

She saw the resemblance in many of them. The Moreno genes were strong throughout his family. The big smiles from some of the elders, were telling of the points she earned when she spoke to them in her perfect Spanish.

Most seemed surprised when they heard the word girlfriend. Some were outright blunt about it. "*No lo puedo creer!*" one of his aunt's exclaimed, making Grace cringe. Even his aunt couldn't believe Sal was capable of committing.

They finally settled at their own table. No sooner had they sat than more family members arrived and sat at the same table with them. Sal introduced them as his aunt and uncle and their sixteen-year-old son Vincent, whom he referred to as Vinnie, from La Puente. They'd driven more than two hours to make the shower.

Sal walked away to fetch them all drinks. Rose leaned into her. "They hired waiters for a baby shower?"

"They hire waiters for everything," Vincent said, with a smirk. "My aunt's known for outdoing everyone in the family with her parties."

His mom gave him a look and he rolled his eyes.

He had both Grace and Rose's attention. He resembled Sal and his brothers in many ways, except there was an edge about him. Grace noticed the tattoo of a skull and bones and words she couldn't quite make out, on his forearm and this boy was only sixteen?

"We've never attended any of the Moreno's parties."

He chuckled. "Well, if you're with Sal now, get used to it. It's like this *every* time."

"Where is La Puente?" Rose asked.

"About a half hour before Los Angeles. Ever been to the L.A county fair?"

Rose shook her head.

"Oh, well it's near there."

Sal arrived with a tray of lemonades for Grace, Rose and his aunt, then handed a beer to his uncle and a soda to Vincent. "Where's *my* beer?"

"You're funny Vin," Sal said, sitting down next to Grace.

Vincent continued talking to Rose while Sal pointed out more of his family to Grace, laughing at some of the anecdotes he told her about each one. "We'll go in and see the babies in a little. Valerie and Sofie were changing them just now."

"I can hardly wait." Grace squeezed his hand.

Both Sal and Grace turned when she noticed Rose and Vincent stand up. "Vincent is gonna show me the koi pond on the other side of the house."

Sal eyed his cousin. "Best behavior Vin. I mean it."

"You know me."

"Yeah, that's why I'm worried." Sal frowned as they walked away. He turned to his aunt and uncle who were engaged in conversation with the people in the next table and spoke softly. "Every family has a bad seed. He's ours. That boy's nothing but trouble. Always has been. Keep an eye on your sister."

Grace watched as Vincent and Rose walked away, talking. Unlike Grace, Rose had always made friends easily. It didn't surprise her that she'd already made a friend here. She turned in their direction again. "He's not *that* bad is he?"

"I wouldn't have let them walk away if I thought he'd be stupid enough to do anything wrong here. No need to worry." He leaned and kissed her. "She'll be fine here. It's just that I hate to say it because he's family, but he's definitely not someone you want your sister associating with too much."

Feeling a little relieved that her sister wasn't in any immediate danger she smiled. "I'm glad he'll keep her busy at least for a little bit. I was afraid she might get bored."

Sal stood up. "Just keep your eye out. C'mon let's go see my nieces." He looked her over as they walked toward the house. "By the way, you look beautiful."

Grace chewed her lip. "Thank you." She wondered how long it would be before she stopped getting that tingly feeling around him.

Alex's house was just as big as Sal's, only not quite as perfectly kept. But she figured having two newborns in the house must make it hard to keep up with everything else. Alex walked out of one of the hallways and smiled when he saw Grace. "Hey, Grace. You look nice."

Grace felt her face warm. She'd obsessed about what to wear all morning. Since she and Rose wore roughly the same size, she borrowed one of Rose's pale pink baby doll tanks and a white denim skirt. The skirt was also Rose's and a bit shorter than what she normally liked but Rose assured her she looked fine. She also straightened her hair. Since it's so damn thick it usually took her forever but Rose helped her with it this morning and they got through it in half the time. "Thank you. I can't wait to see your babies."

"Come on. Not too many people are going to get

past this hallway today but you're one of the few I'll make an exception for."

As they walked through the hallway, Grace took in some of the pictures on the wall. Alex must've met his wife way back in high school because there were a few of them together where they looked so young. Even back then, he was huge.

She and Sal followed him into the last room at the end of the hall with the double door entryway. His wife Valerie, a very attractive petite blonde woman with big brown eyes, smiled as she looked up. She sat on the huge bed, holding one of the babies while Sofia sat across from her on a rocking chair, holding the other one.

Grace brought her hand to her mouth as she approached. "Valerie this is my star employee, Grace. Grace this is my wife, Valerie."

Valerie smiled. "Finally I get to meet what all the fuss is about. Alex has been going on and on about you ever since he hired you. I was beginning to get a little jealous." She glanced down at the hand that Sal held firmly in his and smiled. "I guess I don't have anything to worry about."

"No, you don't," Sal said before Grace could answer.

Alex took the baby Sofia held. "Like any of my girls have anything to worry about. *Ever.*" He leaned in and kissed the baby on the nose. Then walked over to Grace with her. "This is my beautiful Sienna."

Grace put out her hands, feeling a little nervous about holding something so fragile. "Oh my God, Alex. She *is* beautiful." She had all of Alex's features, from the dark hair to the fair skin. Her eyes were closed so she couldn't see the color but she had the trademark full Moreno lashes.

Alex beamed. "And that other beautiful little thing over there." He gestured toward Valerie. "Is Savannah."

Sal walked over and took Savannah from Valerie's arms. "Hey, baby girl. She's awake." Sal smiled, walking back to Grace.

"Yeah, she stays up a little longer than this sleepy head," Alex said as Sal approached Grace so she could see her.

"Her eyes are huge!" Grace said, amazed at the sight.

They were in there for a while completely in awe of the two beautiful little creatures. Alex doted over them, until their mother walked in to ask Alex and Sal if they could come out and help bring in the food that had just arrived. Sal handed the baby back to Valerie and Valerie asked Grace to take a seat on the bed.

The baby felt so tiny in her arms. She had that wonderful baby scent. "I see Sal's staked his claim," Valerie said, smiling. "Alex wasn't surprised. He said he noticed something when Sal first told him about the interview he had with you. It's normal for Sal to over think things but Alex said this interview really struck a nerve with Sal and he'd gone on and on about it."

Sofia laughed. "I didn't notice until the day she walked in with her hair down. You should've seen the look on his face. It was classic and he tried so hard to play it off."

Though their comments made her feel good they also made her feel a little dumb. She hadn't noticed a thing until his, "Oh, I'm impressed." comment and even then she hadn't been totally sure. Taylor was right again, damn it. But she supposed it was easy to be blind to these kinds of things, especially when it seems just too good to be true.

"You're the first girl he brought home to the family, you know? Everyone is a little surprised, including my parents."

Grace had to ask. "Why is it so hard to believe?"

Valerie and Sofia exchanged a glance that made Grace nervous. "Honestly, I was beginning to think he'd never find a girl that he thought good enough," Sofia said, then added quickly, "Not that he thinks he's all that. But my God, that guy is so picky about *everything*."

"Tell me about it," Valerie said. "I nearly gave up looking for a house for him. He drove me *nuts*. Alex had even told me at one point to just forget about it and let him find another agent because there was always something that wasn't exactly perfect about *every* house I showed him. It took over a year." She leaned over to make sure no one was coming down the hallway. "I was so sick of him." Then she giggled. "Even after he finally settled on the house he bought, it was months before he remodeled and changed things to his liking."

"Yeah," Sofia said. "Don't let him do that to you."

"Do what?"

"Try to change you to his liking."

So far, Sal hadn't suggested changing anything about her. The closest thing was when he asked her why she tried to conceal her accent. *I love it. You wouldn't be Grace without it* were his exact words.

"I don't think he would," Grace said, cooing, at the baby who finally opened a huge pair of eyes and yawned.

"No." Valerie agreed. "I think Sal finally found someone who's completely intrigued him. Alex had talked about the way Sal is around you and I saw the way he looks at you. Grace, I think he finally found a keeper — that is — if you'll keep him."

Both Valerie and Sofia laughed. Grace's insides went wild. But she didn't want them to know just how much that excited her. "I'm pretty intrigued too." Was she *ever*.

Sofia sat the edge of her seat. "Growing up, I used to think I'd be the way my brothers were with me, when it came to their girlfriends. No one was good enough for their little sister. But so far I've been blessed with two wonderful sister-in-laws. I couldn't be happier that you and Sal have hooked up. I think you're perfect for him." Her eyes opened in excitement. "So since you're here today it must be getting serious, huh?"

Sister-in-law? Grace gulped. "I don't know. It's only been a week."

Sal walked in followed by Alex, Romero and Isabel.

"Isabel," Alex said. "You can hold my babies but I don't know about Romero."

"I'm not sure I want to," Romero said. Alex gave him a look. "I'm scared!"

"Of what?" Isabel asked. "Don't be ridiculous. You're going to hold them."

Romero raised his eyebrows at Grace to acknowledge her but looked genuinely nervous. "All right but only if I'm sitting."

Isabel smiled at Grace. "Hi again." She leaned over, looking as mesmerized as everyone was with the baby. "Oh my gosh. Look at those eyes!"

Grace lifted the baby, offering her to Isabel. Isabel took her, gushing. Romero sat on the bed. Grace giggled at the way he prepared himself backing far up so he was further away from the edge. He cradled his empty arms a couple of times.

Alex's brows pinched. "What are you doing?"

"I'm practicing!"

Valerie laughed, standing to hand him the baby. She placed it gently in his arms and Romero's eyes widened as she began to pull her own arms away. "Hold on. Hold on!"

"You got it," she laughed.

Grace had never seen anyone hold a baby so awkwardly and everyone laughed at how stiffly he sat. "Relax, dude," Sal said.

Isabel sat down next to him and he looked absolutely panicked. "Don't move me!"

"You've never held a baby before?" Isabel asked.

"How can you tell?" He inched a little further back into the bed.

"You better not drop her," Alex teased.

Romero's eyes opened even wider at the comment then looked back down at the baby. "She's beautiful, man."

Sal leaned over to Grace. "You wanna go check on your sister?"

Grace stood up. "Oh yeah, she's probably looking for me."

They excused themselves and walked out. She walked in front of Sal through the hallway and felt him lean into her ear. "Just so you know. I'm *very* serious about us. I hope you are, too."

Grace didn't think she could get more excited than what Sofia and Valerie had said made her. She turned to him just as they walked out of the hallway together. She'd wondered when he walked in, if he'd heard

Sofia's question. "I am. She just caught me off guard I wasn't sure what —"

He kissed her softly, before she could finish. "All I needed to hear were those first two words. Don't worry about anything else."

She felt her heart inflating a million times over as he stared in her eyes. What she felt for him this soon, was utterly illogical. She hadn't been scared before but now she was. *Completely*. She wasn't just falling in love with just him, she was falling in love with his entire family.

CHAPTER 20

They walked out into the backyard and Sal felt a little alarmed when he didn't see her sister and Vincent anywhere. Vincent had been one headache after another for years. The problem was his dad's younger brother hadn't been around much in the beginning of Vincent's life. When he finally was, Vincent was a preteen and already out of control.

His mother lived too far for Sal's dad to be too much help. The last he heard was that his dad was having to pay fines because the ass got caught tagging up the school walls after hours with his low life friends.

Grace glanced around. "You think they're still over by the koi pond?"

"Let's go see." He took her through the front instead of walking through the crowded backyard. They didn't have to walk very far. Vincent and Rose were sitting on the porch swing, talking. Rose was a very pretty girl and looked a little older than her fifteen years. Sal thought Vincent looked a bit too comfortable and the swing was big enough he didn't need to be sitting so close. Vincent smiled when he saw them. "Checking up on me already? I told you I'd be cool."

"The food's here. Why don't you guys come get something to eat?"

Vincent asked Rose something Sal couldn't hear and turned back to Sal. "Neither of us is hungry yet. We'll get some later."

Sal frowned, lifting his hands with Grace's hand

still in one of them and parted them. "Can you get a little space in between you two? Come on, Vin. There's enough room on that swing."

Vincent laughed. "You're kidding me, right?" But he complied and scooted over a little.

Grace squeezed his hand. "Sal!"

They turned back to the backyard. "I'm telling you," he said in a lowered voice. "That kid can't be trusted." He turned back to Vincent. "Don't go disappearing anywhere, Vin."

"We'll be *right* here." The wicked grin only spiked Sal's nerves.

They ate an excellently executed version of Grace's casserole and after the cake was served, Valerie began working her way through the enormous pile of gifts. Those babies were set with every baby gadget and product out there. Even Sal hadn't been able to help himself and bought the deluxe twin stroller that doubled as car seats.

Then came the clothes. Valerie made a comment pouting that she'd have no excuse to shop for them for at least a year. She wasn't kidding. She got to Grace's bags and Sal abstained from frowning, especially since Grace grinned silly when she saw Valerie pick up her gift bags. Sal knew Grace was on a tight budget. She'd even told him how she paid for a good portion of the household bills.

Valerie pulled out a pair of tiny San Diego Charger cheerleading outfits. Complete with pom-poms and matching booties. There were a lot of and awes and some clapping. "Yes!" Alex fist pumped. "But they're a little short."

Valerie rolled her eyes while others laughed.

After the shower, they drove Rose home, but not

before a disturbingly long goodbye to Vincent. Much to Sal's discontent, he'd watched as they exchanged phone numbers by calling each other on their cells.

"I can't stress enough, Gracie," he said to her as soon as Rose was out of the car and out of earshot. "The boy is bad news. I hope you warn her."

"He's so young and he has a tattoo."

"Yeah, that's how stupid he is." Sal shook his head.

They drove back to his place and sat in the back again. Sal was beginning to hate taking her home each night. He knew it'd only been a week since they'd gotten together but what he'd been feeling for her had grown over a longer period of time and he couldn't get enough of her now. Hearing her say she was serious too had made his day.

He also remembered her mention that she'd *never.* If that meant what he was sure it did, asking her to spend the night was out of the question. He'd have to be very patient. This wouldn't be his first time with a virgin but definitely the first time he'd ever been with *anyone* he had these kinds of feelings for, so in a way this was a first for him as well. This was huge. Taking his time around someone that drove him this insane wouldn't be easy. But he had no intention of doing anything that might make her uncomfortable.

*

Jason called on Tuesday to remind him of the bachelor party that weekend. "You got your flight booked?"

Now, more than ever, Sal couldn't imagine leaving for two days but he knew there was no way out of this. "Yeah, I'll fly out at five and be there by six on Saturday."

"In the morning, right?"

"Nah, man I couldn't get anything earlier." That was one fat lie if he ever told one. He only hoped Jason wouldn't check. There was a flight available as early as nine in the morning. But it was bad enough that he'd be missing his evening with Grace that night, he wasn't going to miss the whole day too.

"Are you kidding me? We'll probably all be bombed by then."

"At six? You're crazy. That's still early. Everything's just getting started around that time."

"Not in Vegas, baby."

Sal laughed. "I'll catch up when I get there. I promise."

He hung up before Jason got a chance to ask him what time his flight was the next morning. Curiously, there were plenty of early flights home Sunday. Knowing he'd probably be up late Saturday night, he made sure he didn't book one too early, but he knew even his eleven a.m flight would be too early for Jason.

Grace was off, but he'd be picking her up later that evening. He actually could pick her up earlier and he really wanted to. Sofia had come in and said she could close if he wanted her to, but Grace was spending the afternoon with Joey and Taylor. Even though they were gay, it still annoyed him that they were taking time that he could be spending with her.

Sal hadn't told her yet about the bachelor party. He was telling her tonight and he wasn't looking forward to it. The things Grace did with her friends when he wasn't around were things he didn't have to worry about. Like today they'd all gone to a farmers' market where some of their school friends were participating in a chili cook-off and then they were having an early dinner. He wasn't sure how he'd feel about her going out to a club without him. Or even to have a few drinks on a Saturday night at places where it was known people went to hook up. So he didn't want her to get the idea he was okay with even these kinds of things. He'd certainly have a problem with her taking off for the weekend, especially if she and her friends were planning ahead of time on getting *bombed*. After this damn weekend, she'd have a free pass.

The only hope he had of getting out of going this weekend would be if Grace told him she wasn't comfortable with it. He'd cancel his flight in a heartbeat. Jason would just have to understand and if that were the case, he wouldn't feel the least bit guilty. Grace's feelings were more important now. Unfortunately, since Grace hadn't shown any insecurity with Melissa, he highly doubted she'd be concerned about this.

She said she'd be ready by seven. Sal had driven around her block since he'd been there a little too early to text her. By the time she got in the car, he was so damn anxious to see her, their first kiss was ravenous. She licked her lips when he was done and she laughed. "I missed you, too."

Thank God for Sofia. He might've closed early, if she hadn't showed up. He was going to have to control himself. It was getting harder and harder to not push things further physically but she still hadn't shown any signs that she was ready to move forward and he refused to push her — refused to even mention it — not until she did first.

They got back to his place and Sal felt like a teenage boy barely able to keep his hands and lips to himself. Fortunately, Grace didn't seem to mind. Once back at their place, the oversized patio sofa Grace liked so much, he found a moment to bring up that weekend.

"My friend is getting married in a few weeks and he's having a bachelor party this weekend." He tried to read her expression but it was vacant. She didn't appear mad, but she certainly wasn't smiling.

"I might go to one someday when Joey and Taylor get married." Even as she said that she still didn't smile. "Will there be strippers?"

"No, we're just all going to Vegas for the weekend. I'm only going to be there overnight on Saturday."

Now she laughed. "No strippers in Vegas, uh?" She sat up a bit but Sal held her to him.

"It's supposed to be just a bunch of guys drinking and gambling. No one's mentioned strip clubs, but if it comes up I'll duck out."

"When will you be back?"

"Sunday morning. I'm not even leaving 'til late Saturday. You won't even notice I'm gone. I'll make sure you have a ride. Sofia's closing that night so she can drive you."

Finally, she smiled. "Oh, I'll notice you're gone. Trust me." She leaned in and kissed him so long and deep, he could hardly stand it. "You'll just have to make it up to me Sunday night."

He stared in her eyes, getting that same feeling he'd had when he looked up and saw her walking down the stairs of her apartment building the day of the shower, looking so incredibly beautiful she took his breath away. For an instant, he'd forgotten all about the idiot her mother had set her up with. He'd had that same feeling over and over ever since and he was sure of one thing now. "I love you, Gracie."

Her eyes opened wide and she pulled away from him. Not the reaction he was hoping for. Then her hand went to her mouth and she grimaced, her eyes filling with tears. "Don't say that," she whispered.

He sat up, straightening them both up. "Why?"

"Because I might believe you."

He kissed her hand with a chuckle. "I want you to. I wouldn't be saying it, if it weren't true." He cupped her face in his hands. "There is no doubt in my mind — none whatsoever. I'm *crazy* in love with you." He wiped the tear that slid down her cheek.

She leaned her head against his hand that caressed her cheek now and closed her eyes. "I'm afraid to love you, Sal, but I do. *So* much."

He swallowed hard, clearing away the knot in his throat that her words produced instantly. "Don't be afraid, Gracie. I'm not." He lay back down, bringing her with him, feeling how her heart beat almost as loudly as his did. They kissed, but not in the frantic way they'd been kissing lately. This had nothing to do with the physical desires that had been building between them. Kissing her suddenly felt different. Now that he knew she loved him too, he wanted to feel just how much she loved him in every stroke of her tongue — every beat of her heart. These were, by far the best kisses he'd *ever* experienced.

*

Friday night, Sal opened up a bottle of wine and they got in the Jacuzzi. Grace had been nervous about him seeing her in a bikini, but the look on his face when she walked out of the house wearing it, didn't disappoint.

Everything felt different now. Ever since Sal had told Grace that he was in love with her even water tasted better. He hadn't stopped telling her since and she'd never get tired of hearing it. Of course, she cried when she told Joey and Taylor. Joey cried with her and Taylor laughed at them calling them hopeless romantics.

She wasn't even worried about Vegas anymore. Admittedly, she had been when he first told her. The thought of him in Vegas, drinking with a bunch of strippers that would probably be willing to strip for him free, scared the hell out of her. Who knew what else they'd be willing to do? But after his heartfelt admission the only thing she was worried about, was how much she was going to miss him that night.

They sat in the hot Jacuzzi, sipping wine as music played softly from the speakers that looked like rocks in the landscape. She'd had a few glasses now and was really feeling relaxed. Sal pulled her closer to him and they began kissing softly. Having her near-naked body next to his hard bare chest did something to her insides. The wine made Grace feel a little less inhibited and she kissed him with more hunger than usual. She put her glass down and moved her body over his, straddling him.

He moaned when she pressed herself against him and her heart rate spiked when she felt just how aroused he really was. She pressed against him, making him moan even more.

Sal pulled his mouth away, breathlessly. "Gracie, maybe we shouldn't have any more wine."

She breathed heavily, staring at his lips. Finally, she understood why she'd avoided being intimate or even coming close to it with anyone. For the longest time she'd associated her first time with the death of her grandmother. She didn't think she could ever get past the disgust she'd felt that night when her boyfriend had suggested they still go back to the room, especially because anytime anyone asked why they'd broken up the thoughts inundated her.

Now all she could think of, sitting here straddling Sal, was how much she would love for him to be the one. She always said she'd wait for the perfect guy, knowing full well that no such guy existed. But here he was, staring at her and he was definitely far more experienced than any of the boys she'd ever gone out with. "Make love to me."

His eyes opened wide. "Grace have you ever—"

"Never." She leaned in, kissing him, wanting him to feel just how badly she wanted him.

When she finally stopped, Sal caressed her face. "I'd love nothing more, Gracie, but you've been drinking."

"So?"

"This whole week you were sober and you never felt ready to go there, but now you've had some wine and you are?" He traced her lips with his finger. "I want you…no I *need* you to be absolutely sure."

"No one's ever made me feel like you do, Sal. Not even close. I *know* you're the one. I love you."

"Baby, you have no idea how bad I want to, but it just wouldn't feel right tonight."

She glanced away not wanting him to see the disappointment she felt.

"Can I ask you something?"

Her eyes met his again. "Yes." She'd answered the hardest question she could think of already and now he knew without a doubt she was a virgin—a virgin who was offering herself to him. He could ask her whatever he wanted.

"How far *have* you ever gone?" He brought her hand to his chest and she felt his heart pound. "I won't lie. I'm feeling a little pressure, not to mention the incredible honor of being your first. When the time comes I just wanna know exactly how gentle I need to be."

Okay, so maybe there were still a few tough questions left. "Not far. I hadn't even kissed anyone in almost year. And before that I had a couple relationships in high school. But I was always too scared to do much."

She felt his hand slide up in between her legs and her breath caught but she didn't want him to think she was scared, even though her heart jumped to her throat. His fingers caressed her as he stared deep in her eyes. "Anyone ever done this to you?"

Feeling the sudden arousal of his touch, she took a deep breath and closed her eyes, shaking her head.

"Really? No one has ever touched you there?" His fingers continued to move in small circles and she felt tingly from the pit of her stomach all the way down to her toes. She couldn't even answer him. She shook her head again, breathing harder with every one of his slow strokes.

He kissed her neck then began to suck softly. A moan escaped her when she felt his fingers move the strip of her bikini bottom aside. Now there was nothing in between his fingers and her burning flesh. He continued to massage finding the spot that made her shudder. "Relax," he whispered against her ear. "You're gonna like this." Then he kissed her cheek softly.

She wrapped her arms around his neck, spreading her legs a little wider for him and felt his hard erection against her pelvis. "I already do," she whispered in his ear.

His fingers spread her and teased her, making her

heart pound even harder. Would he go there? Then they suddenly stopped. He pulled his face back so that their eyes could meet and he smiled. "I'm saving that for me." She felt his fingers move back higher to the place that had made her spasm moments ago and she buried her face in his neck, squirming as the sensation began to build. His fingers moved rhythmically but gently. He'd speed up then slow down, driving her crazy. She pulled her face away from his neck and kissed him.

As her tongue sped up so did his fingers. Until she had to pull away from his mouth to pant, her entire body trembling. "That's it, Gracie. Enjoy it."

It felt so incredible she cried out and squeezed her eyes shut, pulling herself away from him because she couldn't take his fingers anymore. He pulled his hand away but brought her back to him, hugging her tightly. "Goddamn, Grace. You drive me crazy."

She wrapped her arms around his neck breathing hard. She kissed his temple still enjoying the waves of pleasure that rolled through her entire body.

"Did you like that, Gracie?"

Still unable to speak she nodded.

"Good," he whispered. "I love you, baby."

Even though she'd heard him say it all week it still felt too good to be true. She still couldn't wrap her mind around the idea that Sal Moreno loved her. She wasn't sure if she'd ever fully believe it. "I love you too, Sal, with all my heart." *That* she was absolutely sure of.

CHAPTER 21

Knowing he'd be gone that evening, Sal made sure to schedule Grace for the opening shift Saturday. He picked her up and together they opened the restaurant. In the little time Grace had worked there she'd caught on to everything quickly. She walked in with him and helped him set everything up, get the registers counted and going, start the ovens, set up the kitchen and get everything else for the day—she was incredible. Only he and his siblings did as much with so much care. To all the other employees it was just a job, but Grace really cared, he saw it in her face. She wanted things done right, just as much as he did.

He walked up behind her as she worked in the kitchen, and wrapped his arms around her waist. "God, I'm gonna miss you tonight." He kissed her just above the ear.

"Just hurry home tomorrow." She spun around, wrapping her arms around his neck. He took her mouth in his, thinking about the things he'd do to her when he got back. Unable to hold back he kissed her even deeper. Hearing a small moan escape her drove him crazy. The kiss became even more frenzied now as he imagined doing things to her right here in this kitchen.

Someone cleared their throat loudly and Grace pulled away. Alex chuckled as he walked away from the kitchen door and into the office. Sal gulped trying to catch his breath as he glared a his brother's grinning face. *What an ass.* In Sal's hurry to pick up Grace, he'd forgotten Alex said he'd be in early to do the payroll.

"How embarrassing," Grace whispered, pulling even further away from Sal.

He pulled her back to him. "Don't be embarrassed. That guy has no qualms about attacking his wife in front of anyone. He's worse than Angel."

"Still," she said her face a bit flushed.

"No still." He kissed her, then hugged her tight, running his arms all over her back. "Damn, I can't wait to make love to you." He was already rock hard.

"I can't either."

Several times throughout the day he debated about just canceling his trip to Vegas and staying home to be with Grace. He could do to her tonight what he'd now have to put off for another time. But he didn't.

Romero showed up as expected to drive him to the airport that afternoon. They dropped off Grace at her apartment and after a very long goodbye, he finally got back in the car with Romero. "Next time get a room and I can come back to pick you up."

Sal smirked. "I can't believe your wuss ass can't come with me to Vegas. It's one night!"

Romero shook his head, pulling a fast U-turn. "Nope. Are you kidding me? And risk Izzy turning this on me and taking off sometime on her own? *Hell* no."

Sal stared out the window, hoping Grace would never think that way and make him have to worry about her taking off for the weekend to party with her friends. So far, she'd said nothing of the sort, but if she ever did, he'd just have to suck it up. One thing was for sure. This was the last time he ever left without her.

*

It didn't take long to find the guys at the bar in Vegas. Sal had checked in, gone to his room and settled in before going back downstairs. He'd texted Jason and knew which bar to head to. Most of the guys were already getting loud. He knew a few from school but there were others he'd never met before. Jason walked up to him with a shot as soon as he saw him. "You need to catch up." He handed Sal the shot, slinging his arm over his shoulders. "Everybody say hi to Sal, my college roommate."

Sal got a loud greeting from all the drunken idiots and he lifted his shot in the air before downing it. At first, Jason was on him, handing him one shot after another. Sal was glad he'd eaten before leaving the restaurant that afternoon. Grace had made him something special and they sat in a back booth eating together. But after several shots he began to feel the slow buzz. He figured he was in Vegas for that reason and he wasn't driving anywhere so he went with the flow, but he hated hangovers. He'd only had a few in his life and they weren't fun. Talk about wasting an entire day. So he had a plan. He knew lushes hated partying alone, but he also knew once drunk enough they were easily fooled into thinking he was drinking just as much. Since Jason already had a head start this should be easy.

Sal texted Grace a few times to tell her how much he missed her. Even with all the noise and everything going on around him, she was all he could think of.

A few hours later, Sal knew Jason was cooked. Jason hung on him, talking and Sal could barely make out what he was saying. Sal had had enough shots to be feeling a comfortable buzz but he was no where near the state Jason was." Maybe we should call it a night."

"No, man." Jason pointed a finger at him, smiling. "The girls are coming."

"What girls?"

"Kitty…" Jason laughed. "My kitty Kat and her bridesmaids are out here, too."

The waitress came to their table with a tray full of what looked like more shots. "These are compliments of some of your admirers, gentlemen."

All the guys spoke at once, cheering and asking her who sent the drinks and what they were. The waitress simply pointed at a group of women on the other side of the bar and said, "Tequila. Casadores." She turned to Sal with that unmistakable gleam he was so used to getting from women. "This one's for you."

Sal smiled taking it from her. Jason already held his and lifted it toward the group of women. "There's my kitty Kat."

Sal squinted barely able to make out the girls in the smoky crowded room. Jason handed him the drink and held his up for a toast. "You sure you wanna drink another one?" Sal asked.

"This is my bachelor party, man!" Jason slurred, hanging on to Sal's arm for support. "Don't get all Mother Teresa on me!"

Sal clinked Jason's glass with his then took a sip of the drink. Casadores tequila wasn't the smoothest tequila out there but he didn't remember it being this rough. Maybe it was because the Third Generation tequila they'd been drinking earlier was one of the smoothest out there.

Jason downed his. "Whoa!" He lifted his empty glass in the air then frowned at Sal's still almost-full glass. "C'mon! Don't be a pussy!"

There was no arguing with a drunk so Sal drank the rest instantly feeling his entire body warm. Jason smiled big. Another waitress walked up to them with a tray of drinks. Not shots this time but Sal didn't recognize the drink. "The ladies are intent on getting you guys loaded," she said passing out the drinks.

Sal rolled his eyes. As if Jason needed even one more shot. He took the drink the waitress handed him and smelled it. Whatever it was it was potent.

"What is this?" he asked with a frown.

She smiled. "Liquid Cocaine. It tastes better than it smells, trust me. Your ladies know their drinks."

Sal turned to the corner where the *ladies* were feeling a lot more buzzed than he had just earlier. It wasn't until those ladies looked like nothing more than a bunch of fuzzy bodies in motion that he realized just how buzzed he was.

He took the drink and held it up in the direction of the fuzzy bodies, losing his footing for a moment. Half the drink spilled onto his wrist and he licked it, holding on to a barstool for support. He'd never even heard of Liquid Cocaine but if he had to guess it was straight gasoline laced with acid.

There was a commotion by the bar with the guys and Sal looked over to see Jason on the floor between the barstools, laughing and telling everyone he was okay. Some of the fuzzies rushed over and one of them bent down to help the other guys get Jason up. Sal couldn't make out what the fuzzy said. She sounded like the adults in the Charlie Brown cartoons. After that so did everyone else. Someone else handed him another Liquid Cocaine. He wasn't even aware that he'd drunk the first one.

It got harder and harder to open his eyes after every

blink but he was sure no one noticed as he stood there, holding on for dear life to the bar stool next to him. Jason said something to him he didn't understand and he felt an arm link onto his. Stupidly, he let go of the barstool, apparently the only thing that was keeping him up. If whoever held his arm hadn't been there he would've gone down for sure.

It got real loud all of a sudden and there was a scuffle. Sal couldn't even make out who was shoving who but he heard glass break. Someone pulled him away from the shoving crowd and he struggled to stay upright. He blinked, the whole room blurring in and out as they stumbled toward the exit. He noticed people looking at him as he walked through the casino, but he could barely focus his eyes. Each time he blinked, it got darker until everything finally went black.

*

Rose's face lit up when she read her text and Grace frowned. Lately that had been happening a lot. Rose had never smiled so much from reading her texts. She knew exactly who the text was from. "Rose, I hope you're not getting too friendly with Vincent. Sal was adamant that he's bad news."

"How friendly can we get? He lives so far."

"He'll probably be driving soon."

Rose finally looked up from her phone. "Oh yes, he's gonna wanna drive all the way to Chula Vista from La Puente, just to see me. That's over two hours."

Grace slipped on the shorts to her pajama bottoms. "You'd be surprised what a man would do when he's really interested in a girl."

Rose laughed. "A man? He's sixteen. He can't even

afford to call me because we're on different carriers and he's not allowed to use up his mom's minutes or they'll take his phone away. Besides who said anything about him being *interested*?"

Grace gave her a look. Rose was showing her innocence, but ignored her question, not wanting to push that topic further. "Aren't weekends unlimited?

"Not his. His mom got the cheap package so even on the weekends they only have so many minutes."

Grace shook her head. She'd mentioned to Sal how Rose and Vincent had been texting. He wasn't happy about it at all. But Rose was right. Grace didn't see the harm in them texting, as long as nothing more became of it.

"He *is* going to Rosarito in a few weeks with his family and he asked if maybe he could meet me somewhere as he passed through here." Rose's eyebrows went up and she gave Grace an imploring look. "We're just friends."

"Nope, not happening."

"Why not? He just meant like grab a hamburger or something. His whole family is going to be with him. It's not like we're gonna be alone."

Grace plopped down on the bed. "Because Sal wouldn't be so dead against it if he didn't think it was dangerous."

"Did he tell you what he did that's so bad?"

"Tagging for starters." Grace lay back, resting her head on the pillow. "And what sixteen-year-old gets a tattoo?"

"Oh my God! Lots of them. A whole bunch of kids from school have them."

Putting her hand behind her head, Grace frowned at Rose who was looking at her incredulous. "Aren't you supposed to be eighteen or something?"

Rose laughed, lying down next to Grace. "No one checks your I.D. You just tell them you're eighteen and that's good enough for them."

"How do you know?"

"Because I know people that have gotten them." Rose lifted herself onto her elbow and faced Grace. "He's just misunderstood, Grace. That whole tagging thing wasn't even his fault, he was with the guys that were doing the tagging and they all got hauled in together. Even the tattoo he says he regrets. He and a few of his friends did it on a whim. He calls it his incredibly stupid, temporary insanity moment and he says he hopes that's as stupid as he ever gets. He's actually really smart."

Grace didn't like how empathetically Rose spoke of him. The few times Rose had spoke of any of her guy friends, she had very little to say. Maybe it was because this one happened to be her boyfriend's cousin, but Grace could totally relate to the excitement she saw in Rose's eyes when she looked down at her phone and realized the text was from Vincent. It was the same way she felt when she got a text from Sal. This was disquieting to say the very least. Her sister was only fifteen after all. Rose glanced down at her phone and her face lit up.

"What is he saying that has you smiling so big?"

She saw Rose try to wipe the smile but it was a fruitless effort. She did for a second, then shrugged and laughed. "He's just so funny. The way he speaks and texts is hilarious. Most people shorten words in texts like OMG and JK; he writes it all out. And you saw how he looks like this hard ass bad-boy with a tattoo and all, but the way he speaks is *so* not like that. I noticed it right away when he schooled me on the differences between koi and regular fish. Then just now I told him I was in my room talking to my sister and l-ook what he responds." She showed Grace the text and Grace read it out loud.

"I've heard the relationship between two sisters is far more profound than any relationship they'll ever encounter with anyone else. Would you agree?"

Rose laughed. "I mean who talks like that?"

"Does he actually *talk* that way or does he just text like that?"

"No, just like with his text, not everything he says is heavily worded but yeah, he threw in a few like that when we were talking at the shower. He used the word *consequently* when the subject of getting a job came up. He said 'Consequently my dad will be speaking to my uncle today about possibly hiring me for the summer at one of the restaurants.' He might come out and stay with your *in-laws* for the summer."

Rose's reference to her in-laws threw Grace. She was already beginning to panic about the idea of Vince being so close to Rose all summer, then Rose used the term and her mind went elsewhere. Ever since she h-eard Sofia mention her sister-in-laws at the shower with the implication that she might possibly be next, she'd been trying not to put too much weight on the thought. But now that Sal had told her he was in love with her and she'd begun to allow herself to accept it as the truth, the likelihood that she might actually be his wife someday was beginning to feel more and more plausible.

"Earth to Grace." Rose waved her hand in front of Grace's face.

Grace shook he head and remembered Vincent. "I

hope you don't plan on spending any time with Vince this summer. Sal hasn't mentioned him coming out for the summer and honestly the way he speaks of him, I highly doubt he'd be willing to have him work at the restaurant."

"But Sal only knows what he's heard through the grapevine. Vinnie said he's never been close to any of his cousins out here in La Jolla. I'm sure if Sal gives him a chance he'll see he's not so bad."

Grace rolled her eyes. "You've known him a whole week and already you know so much about him?"

Rose smiled sheepishly. "We text 24/7."

Grace's jaw dropped. "But you said you're just friends."

"Well yeah, what else can we be? We live so far from one another."

"That's what worries me. If he's in La Jolla, that just might change." Grace could totally see why Rose would be attracted to Vincent. He was a Moreno after all. The amazing-good-looks fairy had been more than generous when passing them out to that family.

Rose glanced back down at her phone and smiled brightly again.

Nothing good could come of this. She'd get to the bottom of Vincent coming down for the summer as soon as Sal got back from Vegas. She lay there, knowing it would be hours before she would actually get any sleep. So many thoughts swam in her head it was impossible to settle her mind down enough to fall asleep.

CHAPTER 22
The Hangover

Waking up to the worst hangover of his life and realizing he'd brought a woman back to his room was bad enough, but seeing who that woman was, nearly sucked the life out of him.

Sal stared at Melissa horrified. She stood at the door of the bathroom, holding two coffee cups, wearing a sundress, her hair and makeup perfect as ever. Did he really sleep through her getting ready that morning? "Why are you here?"

Her eyes widened and she looked him up and down with a smirk. "You don't remember?"

It dawned on him just then that he was still naked. He walked past her in a hurry, grabbing his boxers off the floor and slipping them on. His head throbbed. "Remember what, Melissa?" He held out hope, based on the fact that she was fully dressed that what had happened wasn't what he was thinking.

But she put one of the cups down on the nightstand and bent over to pick up the panties on the floor. "There they are. I couldn't find these this morning." She smiled wickedly and pushed them into her purse.

His patience gave way. "I asked you a question. Why are you in my room?"

"You brought me here last night."

"I brought you?" He didn't buy that for a second. Even in a drunk state, he would never do that to Gracie — not with any girl — but especially not Melissa.

"Yes." She smiled, taking a few steps toward him. "We were pretty drunk but not too drunk to..." She glanced at the bed. "You were amazing."

Sal put his hand up—a warning for her to not take another step. "Whatever happened was a mistake. I don't remember any of it."

"But last night you said—"

"I said I don't remember!" He raised his voice with every word, feeling the enormous dread sink in and the pounding in his head double. "How the hell are you gonna hold me to something I said when I don't even remember any of it?"

Her wounded expression did nothing to make him sympathize with her. They might've been drunk and he'd man up to whatever he'd done, but he knew somehow she manipulated this outcome. There was no way he'd allow her to even think she could make more of this than what it was—a horrible mistake.

"I don't understand why you're angry. We had a good time."

"Because this should've never happened." He wanted to punch a hole through the wall. Why the hell had he drank so much?

His phone rang somewhere near the bed and he glanced around then picked up his pants from the floor. He pulled the phone from the pocket and he saw it was Grace. No way would he take the chance of answering and having Melissa say something to make her presence known. "You need to leave."

"But I thought we were going to—"

"Melissa," he said through his teeth. "Whatever we did last night and whatever was said is a scratch. It's like it never happened. Do you understand?" It sure as hell felt like it never happened. If only he could take the entire night back.

He saw the tears in her eyes and he knew he should try to sound a little more sensitive but this was a disaster. All he could think of now was how he was going to fix this — was this even fixable?

"You can deny it all you want, Salvador. But it *did* happen, more than once and you loved it." She took a step forward, her tears — probably fake — gone now. "And don't say you forgot you had a little girlfriend because you texted her just before you fucked me."

His stomach nearly gave out and he glanced down at his phone, scrolling quickly to his texts. He found the thread between him and Grace and nearly choked at what he read. The first one he sent was just after two in the morning.

Having so much fun I may never come home.

She didn't respond until fifteen minutes later.

Then don't.

To his horror, his next text was even worse.

I'm really busy right now...if you know what I mean. ;) Can't text anymore.

She didn't respond after that, but he had missed calls from both her and Alex. More than one from her which meant this last call that he'd let go to voicemail wasn't her first that morning. "You need to go." He hurried to the door. "I really hope you keep this between the two of us. Nobody needs to know, Melissa."

She smiled as she reached the door he held open for her. "Don't worry I won't be telling your little girlfriend. By the look on your face when you read your texts, something tells me you already did."

"Nope. And I appreciate you keeping this between just us. I don't even want Jason to know."

She walked out and turned around to face him. Sal

fought the urge to slam the door in her face. "He probably already knows. He was pretty out of it himself, but he saw us together."

Fuck. Who else had seen? "I'll take care of him. Just don't tell anyone else... *please.*"

She turned around and stalked away without saying a word. Sal closed the door and began the damage control as soon as possible. He called Alex first.

Alex sounded anxious. "Hey. You okay?"

"Yeah, why?"

"I've been trying to get a hold of you. Grace is worried. She said she got a couple of drunken texts from your ass, then hadn't heard from you since. She's been calling you, too."

Sal put his hand on his forehead and paced. The continued throbbing of his temples didn't help the thinking process. He desperately needed to figure out how to deal with this mess. "Is she mad?"

"No. Why? What the hell did you text her?"

"Nothing. Just drunken gibberish. Did she say anything else?"

"That's it. Just said she was worried and asked if I'd heard from you."

"All right. I'll call her."

He called Jason next. No answer, so he called the phone in his room instead. A very groggy sounding Kat answered. "Hey, Kat this is Sal. Sorry to wake you, but I need to talk to Jason."

"Hmm hold on." He could hear her trying to wake him and then Jason moan. This was no good. He probably had no clue either about last night's events.

Finally he was on the phone. "Sal?"

"Yeah, dude. Hey, what happened last night."

"We drank too much and..." Jason paused. "Aw,

fuck my head is pounding."

"How'd I get back to my room?"

"The girls, I guess. All I remember was falling then being dragged back to the room by Kat and one of her other friends. Not sure how you got back, man. I was out of it."

Sal heard Kat say something about Melissa. "What was that?"

Jason chuckled then moaned. "I guess Melissa got you back to your room."

Sal held his hand to his forehead. "Did anything else happen last night that I should know about?" Mostly Sal was digging for anything anyone else might have seen, like him and Melissa making out or something in public.

"Nah, that's it. After that it was lights out."

With no more helpful information and Jason saying he was going to be sick, Sal hung up, his stomach in knots, wondering what was the best way to go about this. He hated to lie but there was no way he would tell her the truth. The truth *was* he was drunk and didn't remember sending the texts. He'd start with that.

Hitting speed dial to call Grace, he took a deep breath. The pounding of his heart was now drowning out the pounding in his head.

"Hello?" Hearing her voice made him feel even guiltier.

Maybe he should've done the cowardly thing and texted her instead. "Gracie, baby. I'm so sorry about those texts last night. I had way too much to drink and I don't even remember sending them."

She was quiet then asked, "Who were you so busy with?"

"No one." He squeezed his eyes shut. "It was all

guys. Bunch of stupid, drunk ass guys."

She was quiet again, intensifying the angst he felt, then finally spoke again. "Even if you were drunk, why would you text that to me?"

That's what he didn't get either. The thought that maybe Melissa had sent them crossed his mind but he couldn't know for sure. All that mattered now is that the texts had been sent and the damage was done. What he needed to work on now, was making sure Grace forgave him. "I don't know. I'm an idiot. Honest to God, I don't remember much about last night at all."

"So does that mean you *are* coming home?"

He felt a little relief. If she wanted him home then she didn't hate his stupid ass. "Yes. I'll be there in a couple of hours. You forgive me?"

She didn't respond for what felt way too long and he held his breath.

"Just get home."

It wasn't a yes but he'd take it. Once home, he'd do whatever it took to make it up to her.

"I love you, Gracie."

"Don't say that to me right now."

"But I do. I know I was an idiot and I swear I'll make it up to you. But you can't stop me from saying it, Gracie. I love you."

She was quiet for a moment then said, "Well, *I* can't say it to you right now. You don't know the night you put me through."

Jesus, she didn't even know the half of it. "You don't have to. I don't deserve to hear it right now." He didn't even deserve *her*. "I'll be home in a few hours and make this right."

Even he didn't buy that last sentence. How the *fuck* was he going to make this right?

*

The two aspirins Sal had taken just before boarding the plane did nothing to defuse his headache. He sipped the ice water the flight attendant brought him. It wasn't just the hangover that made his head throb. Everything he'd woken to was a huge contributing factor.

If he had known Melissa was even going to be in Vegas he would've never come. First chance he got he'd be telling Jason off for not telling him she'd be there. He let his head fall back on his seat and gulped hard. He could only hope what happened last night didn't come back to haunt him. He remembered Jason's words and the saying, "What happens in Vegas, stays in Vegas." It was now something he'd be banking on. But with Melissa, you just never knew.

Blurry bits and pieces had begun to come to him about the night before. Like the two guys fighting just before he'd walked out of the bar. As much as he wanted to believe Melissa had snuck in his room that morning and somehow set up the whole thing up, there were two vivid moments that for some reason kept flashing in his mind. And although they were tiny bits they were very significant. One was of Melissa pulling his zipper down and another of her kissing his lips while she lay next to him.

Sal banged the handrail with his fist. The lady in the seat next to him shifted away from him. He apologized quickly. She just shook her head and continued reading her magazine.

Alex looked at Sal funny the second he walked up to him at the airport. "What's wrong with you?"

Sal's head no longer throbbed but the pain still lingered. "I've got a damn headache."

Alex smirked. "The party was that good, uh?"

"This is why I don't like to drink," Sal said.

Walking out into the bright sun didn't help either.

Alex clapped him on the back. "You gotta learn to pace yourself, man. So how was it?"

Sal had given some thought about telling Alex. He wasn't going to because he knew Alex would be mad but he needed his take on how best to handle this. Honesty seemed completely out of the question, but he dreaded Grace finding out some other way, too.

He flung his duffle bag in the back of Alex's truck. "I messed up."

Alex stared at him across the bed of the truck. He didn't say anything then his brows pinched. "Whatcha do?"

The more he thought about it the more the reality of just how badly he'd messed up sunk in. He rested one arm against the truck and ran his other hand through his hair. "God, Alex. I fucked up bad."

Alex crossed his arms in front of him. "Well, you're not in jail so how bad can it be?"

Giving it one last thought before finally saying it out loud he let it out. "I slept with Melissa."

Alex was stunned into silence for a moment then he finally spoke up. "Ga Damn it, Sal. Why the hell did you do that?"

"I don't even remember it happening! I was so wasted. But she was there in my room this morning." Sal shook his head disgusted with himself. He'd keep the part about not having found any used condoms anywhere to himself. Alex was already worked up enough. "Should I tell Grace?"

"*Are you crazy?*"

"What if —"

"Sal you'll crush her."

Leave it to Alex to make him feel even worse. "Don't you think it'll be worse if she finds out later somehow?"

"How?"

"I don't know. But Melissa isn't exactly predictable. She was pissed this morning when I blew her off, telling her it was a mistake and asked her to keep it to herself." Alex's scowl was still as fierce as when Sal first laid the news on him. "What if she calls or shows up at the restaurant again and mentions it?"

They both got in the truck. "I still say you're better off taking your chances that Melissa won't do anything stupid. Did she agree to keep it to herself?"

"She did say she wouldn't tell my *little girlfriend*."

"There you go. Gracie doesn't need to know. Trust me."

The ride to the restaurant was a somber one with A-lex shaking his head every now and again. When they got to the restaurant Grace was busy in the kitchen.

"Don't do it, Sal." Alex warned, as he passed him. "I'm telling you."

Sal followed him to the back, all the while thinking about the dreadful possibility of losing Grace if she ever found out. She turned and her eyes met his. There was that smile he loved so much. Damn. He'd only been away from her for a day and it felt like an eternity. He had to make sure she never found out. There was no way he'd survive her walking out of his life now.

Even though she smiled, he saw the apprehension and he couldn't blame her. He'd been a total ass.

"So you had a good time?"

His gut cramped up. "It was good." He wanted to

add that he missed her more than he had imagined he would, but it just didn't feel right at the moment. Not after just saying Vegas was good. Instead, he kissed her but he noticed she didn't kiss him back with her usual enthusiasm. The texts last night were obviously still on her mind. "C'mon let's go talk."

He took her by the hand to the back room. Alex was in there. He gave Sal a warning look and smiled at Gracie. "Good to have him back?"

She smiled but didn't respond otherwise.

Alex sensed Sal's need to be alone with her and stepped out, closing the door behind him. Sal wrapped his arms around her waist, pulling her close. "I feel so stupid about those texts. I can't apologize enough, but I can promise you this. It won't happen again." He'd already decided he'd never drink that way again—no matter what. Part of the reason why he'd handled it so badly, was because he never *had* drunk that way. Not even in college.

Her eyes were uncertain. "I was so worried. I didn't know what to think. I was up half the night, wondering why you would say that and what you could be doing."

Feeling his gut wrench with guilt, he hugged her. Honesty was usually the best way to go no matter how hard it was, but there was no way he would risk not only losing her but hurting her in any way. "I don't know, Grace. Maybe one of the idiots I was with sent them." That was another possibility he'd considered. "It got pretty bad and we all had *way* too much to drink. I've never drunk to the point of completely forgetting what happened." And he prayed she'd never find out the other thing he'd done and couldn't remember.

She leaned against his chest and he felt her take a deep breath. "I'm just glad you're home and it was nothing. I *did* consider that maybe someone else had gotten a hold of your phone. I just couldn't believe you would say that. It was such an ugly feeling to read it."

Sal could only imagine. The very thought of her with someone else sickened him. "I'll make it up to you. I promise."

Grace smiled. "Just having you back is enough. But I don't think I'd ever be comfortable with you going to another bachelor party." she smirked. "I don't think you can handle them."

"You got it." He'd agree to anything at this point, as long as she forgave him. "I didn't even want to go to this one but I'd already promised. Never again. From here on, I don't do bachelor parties." He kissed her this time feeling the Gracie kisses he'd come to need. When she stopped to catch her breath he stared at her, feeling bittersweet about being forgiven so easily, but unable to hold back he whispered, "I love you, Gracie."

She smiled, as usual her eyes were getting misty. "I love you, too."

*

Two weeks after the horrific night Grace had spent, wondering who the hell was keeping Sal so *busy* in Vegas and why the world he would text her that, she'd finally shaken off the insecurity that he was keeping something from her.

They still hadn't made love but he'd told her he wanted her first time to be special. She nearly melted in his arms when he explained how it felt like this was a first for him too. Since he'd never been in love before, this would be extra special for him also.

This was it. She'd gulped when he told her he scheduled them both off for the entire weekend. He said he was taking her away and she was his for the whole weekend.

After staring at him speechless, she finally asked him where to? But he said it was a surprise. Now the butterflies in her belly were going wild as she packed an overnight bag. He'd be there to pick her up before noon.

Rose sat on the bed next to her bag, watching her pack. Grace had asked Sal about Vincent coming out for the summer but he said he hadn't heard anything about it. It relieved her a little but it hadn't been a definite no. Now Rose was the one that seemed worried. "What's wrong?"

"This thing with you and Sal is getting serious."

"And?"

"Well, what if he asked you to marry him? I'll be stuck here by myself."

The thought had actually crossed her mind, especially because it was getting harder and harder to leave Sal's house every night. Once she slept with him, she knew it'd be just a matter of time before she started staying with him, more and more. "I'd never leave you."

"But you can't take me with you. That wouldn't be very romantic."

Grace laughed. "It's *way* too early to start worrying about me leaving, Rose. But I promise if it ever comes down to that, I'll figure something out."

"I'll get a job and go live with Taylor and Joey, if I have to."

"You're not getting a job, silly. And I'm not going

anywhere, so don't worry."

Her phone buzzed, making the butterflies she'd felt all morning go wild again.

I'm here. R U ready? >=)

She smiled and texted him back that she'd be down in a minute, hugged and kissed Rosie with a reassuring smile and took a deep breath as she walked out her bedroom door.

CHAPTER 23

The nightmare in Vegas had left Sal no choice than to stall for time. There was no way he was putting Grace in danger of getting any disease he might've picked up from Melissa. He'd always been careful, something he'd even harped about to his brothers for years before they both settled down. But the fact was, he hadn't been able to find a condom anywhere in the room. He'd nearly flipped the bed over trying to find one and nothing.

He didn't want to contact Melissa for anything. Not even that. He got tested the first chance he had after he got back. He wanted everything checked. The results came back fairly quickly, and thankfully he was clean, but he still needed time to prepare what he wanted to do for Grace. So here, it was two weeks later and finally it was going to happen.

The moment he saw she carried a good-sized tote when she walked around the corner of her building he jumped out of the car. He rushed over and took it from her, kissing her, the anticipation already multiplying.

"So can you tell me where we're going now?"

"Nope. You'll see when we get there."

He smiled at her confused expression when she saw they were headed back to his place. "We're stopping at your house first?"

"Something like that."

She peered at him. "What are you up to?"

"You'll see."

They arrived at his house and he saw her trying to figure it out. He took her hand and he covered her eyes with his other. "Okay, close your eyes. Make sure you don't peek."

"What are you doing?" Her laugh was a nervous one and he was sure she probably expected to end up in the bedroom.

Instead, he headed to the backyard. When they were under the patio, he took a deep breath and prayed this wouldn't backfire on him. He was sure she'd love it but there was still that tiny possibility it might depress her. The *last* thing he'd want to do today. "Ready?"

She nodded, her smile widening. He removed his hand and she glanced around at his recreation of a campsite. His heart drummed when he saw the smile slowly dissolve. She stood there, taking everything in. The tent in the grassy area of his yard with a portable fire pit just outside and table set up with everything you'd need to roast marshmallows. The inflatable rowboat in the pool with the makeshift fishing gear. There were no fish in his pool but he'd bought a fishing game. The fishing poles were long plastic rods with big hooks on the end and he'd thrown in all the plastic fish in the water so they could pretend to fish.

Minutes had passed since he'd uncovered her eyes and she still hadn't said anything but her eyes had gotten misty. *Damn it.* "I was uh… actually gonna take you camping but I wanted you to be able to go swimming and I figured it's still too cold to swim in any river or lake this time of year so I improvised."

She finally spoke but still didn't look at him. She stared at the pool. "Isn't the water in the pool cold also?"

He smiled slightly relieved that she didn't sound upset. "It's heated." He walked her over to the picnic basket on the table and opened it. "I got stuff for tortas. You'll be starving after a good swim." Their eyes met and she smiled.

"I can't believe you did all this."

He shrugged. "No biggie." He wouldn't mention the wrestling match he'd had with the tent he borrowed from his parents. It was old school and he'd forgotten what a *bitch* it was put up especially by himself. When they'd been kids it was hard enough to put up and that was between him, his brothers and his dad.

Grace leaned in and kissed him. "Yes it is a biggie. This is *wonderful*. I couldn't ask for anything more."

"Did you see the best part?"

Her eyes pinched and he pointed to the other side of the pool. Her head tilted not quite getting what it was. He'd gone to every damn toy store he could find until he found the biggest stuffed elephant made and placed it by the pool, its butt facing the water.

"You can look at that while you swim—an elephant butt."

She laughed out loud when it finally sunk in, then wrapped her arms around his neck and he wrapped his around her waist. It felt perfect to hold her like this. "What did I do to deserve you, Sal?"

"You have it backwards, Gracie. I don't deserve you." His gut wrenched as the reality of that statement sunk in. He kissed her desperate to push any negative thoughts away. He wanted this day to be perfect. After minutes of kissing her deeply, he felt a little better he pulled away and leaned his forehead against hers. "You wanna go get into your bathing suit? The water should be warm enough now."

She nodded her head with those twinkling excited eyes that he loved so much now.

Once in their bathing suits, Sal jumped in the deep end of the pool and encouraged Grace to do the same. "The water's perfect." She stood at the edge, looking very apprehensive. "C'mon, baby. I'll catch you."

She pinched her nose with her fingers and jumped in. Sal's arms were all over her the moment she hit the water. Just the touch of her excited every part of his body. His lips were on hers as soon as her head popped out of the water. He had to pace himself. He wanted to be the one that showed her confidence in her swimming. "Relax, babe. You'll be fine, just go with it. I'm right here. I'd never let anything happen to you."

After a while, she was swimming back and forth from one end of the pool to the other. Sal cornered her and she wrapped her legs around him. This wasn't happening in the pool. He had something better prepared so he forced himself to pull away. "You wanna fish?"

Grace smiled, but her eyes smoldered. "Is that what you call it?"

Sal had to laugh. "What!"

Grace laughed too, but undid the hold her legs had around his waist. "Yeah, let's fish."

They climbed up on the raft, but not before falling a few times and Grace falling in his arms all slippery wet. Sal was in heaven.

When they finally both sat in the raft trying to fish for the fake fish, Sal loved how Grace concentrated. He didn't even try. He just watched her and how hard she tried to get the fish. "I got it!"

His eyes were on her the entire time she pulled up the plastic fish, then kissed him in the excitement.

"You hungry, Gracie?" he asked, barely able to take his lips away.

"Yes!"

They got out and Sal walked over to the picnic basket after drying off to get the *toleras* for the *tortas*.

"I can make them," Grace offered.

"Nope. I'm making them. You just get comfortable."

Sal had made plenty of cold *tortas* in his time. He put everything together and walked out with a platter to where Grace was lounging by the tent. She smirked. "I peeked in. It looks comfortable. That's not what we used when I went camping."

Sal had to laugh. "Okay, so I can't sleep on the ground and the inflatable mattress almost rivals the mattress in my room, but still, we'll be in a tent, outside. Let's not get too nitpicky."

Gracie laughed. "Oh no, you didn't just say that with a straight face."

Sal laughed and set the tray down. They ate in silence and he watched Gracie, enjoying his food for once, instead of the other way around. "This is good," she said, covering her mouth.

"That's just the water talking. Everything is delicious when you've been swimming."

"No! This is *really* good." She leaned in and kissed him. "You're making this day so perfect... I love you, babe."

That was the first time she'd called him that, and it felt damn good. "I love you, too. And I wanted this to be perfect for you... for *us*."

After they ate, they laid on the oversized lounge chair again, making out. "So what are your plans once you graduate?" Sal knew she was graduating in a few weeks and her mother was no doubt doing nothing for her. He had a few plans up his sleeve.

Grace ran her fingers up and down his bare chest. "I have it all mapped out. Save up for two years, I'm hoping by then I'll have enough to lease my own restaurant. Nothing nearly as fancy as Moreno's but my own little place that I can build on, little by little. And certainly not in La Jolla. I'd be lucky if I could afford a place in Chula Vista, maybe Calexico."

Sal lifted his head to face her. "So you're planning on leaving Moreno's high and dry?"

She made a pouty face and shrugged. "Having my own restaurant has always been my dream. Joey and Taylor are already looking for a place to open up a bakery. Joey will do all the baking and Taylor, who's majoring in business management, like you did, is handling the business end. They're living their dream. It's inspiring." She smiled. "And now working for you and your family is even more inspiring, especially knowing how it all started. When you told me your dad started with a taco truck, it really gave me hope that I can do it someday. Maybe I can start with a taco stand or something. Anything is possible, right?"

Sal caressed her hair. He had bigger plans for her, but he wouldn't lay them on her just yet. "Yep, anything is possible." He kissed her forehead. "Ready for some more swimming?"

Grace sat up. "Yes, I'm getting good."

"I told you. There's nothing to it. When the weather heats up we'll go camping for real. Maybe even take a drive to Elephant Butte."

Her eyes lit up. "Rose would love that."

"Yeah, we'll take her. Maybe even make a group thing out of it. I'll talk to my brothers. We haven't done something like that in years. I doubt Alex will want to this summer with the babies being so young, but I'll ta-lk to Angel and my sister, even Romero."

Sal was going to have to keep coming up with ways to excite her, because he couldn't get enough of those bright eyes.

They stood up and jumped in the pool.

*

Roasting marshmallows using metal prongs over Sal's expensive fire pit wasn't quite the same as roasting them over a makeshift fire pit made out of rocks using actual twigs but it still brought back the memories. Sal had thought of everything, even bought salmon steaks to barbecue, and Grace whipped up some roasted pota-toes and a salad.

The entire day had been one thing after another that proved to Grace how wonderfully thoughtful Sal was. He'd done all this for *her*. She glanced around his backyard, wondering how this could be. How did *she* end up *here*, with *him*?

"What are you thinking?" Sal pulled his marshmal-low away from the fire and blew out the small flame that had started on the tip.

Grace held hers in the fire a little longer and stared at it. She liked hers crispy. "How lucky *I* am."

"I've been thinking the same thing all day. How lucky I am."

Grace smiled, feeling like this couldn't get any bet-ter, but she knew they'd be in the tent soon and her stomach was already doing that thing it did, every time she thought about Sal making love to her.

They ate their marshmallows and roasted a few

more before Sal walked to the small refrigerator in the outdoor kitchen and pulled out a bottle of wine. "We'll have *one* glass each," he said, as he walked back toward her with the bottle, two empty wine glasses, and a corkscrew opener. "I want you fully aware of everything that happens once we get in that tent. I want you to remember this night forever."

"I'll remember this entire day forever."

Sal opened the bottle and poured them both half a glass. Grace took the glass he handed her. "Does that mean I get two of these?"

Sal laughed. "No, that *is* a glass of wine. You know that, Ms. Superstar Bartender."

Grace smirked, taking a sip of the wine, hopeful that it would calm her nerves. Sal sat down in the chair next to her and held his glass out. "To good times."

Grace clinked his glass with hers, feeling a blend of excitement and nerves accumulating inside her. "May there be many more."

"Oh, there will be, Gracie. I promise."

He leaned in and kissed her before sipping his wine. Grace sipped her own. When they were done, Sal set both their glasses down and Grace did feel a little calmer. He stood up and held his hand out. "Come on."

She stood, thinking they were headed to the tent but instead, he walked toward the house. "Where are we going? I thought we were sleeping in the tent.

"Oh, we are. But we gotta shower first. You don't wanna go to bed with all that chlorine on your skin. You'll itch in the morning."

Grace swallowed hard. She'd been mentally preparing herself to be in bed with him, but in the shower?

They walked into his bedroom. He'd given her the

grand tour her first night there and she'd immediately fallen in love with his bedroom. Most of the other ones were empty but his was well decorated. Just like the stockroom at the restaurant, his exquisite taste in décor and attention to detail was evident in the furniture he chose and the decorations that adorned his room.

The master bathroom in his bedroom was bigger than Grace's front room and kitchen combined. The shower alone had two shower heads and the marble on the wall must've cost a fortune.

Sal opened the door to the shower and started the water. He turned to Grace who stared at the water. "You can do this alone if you're more comfortable that way or…" his eye fell into that smoldering gaze that always made her knees week and he smiled, "there's enough room for both of us in there."

Since they were both still in their bathing suits, Sal wore only his trunks. Grace walked in the shower taking him with her. Once under the shower Sal took her in his arms, running his hands freely over her wet body like he'd done all day in the pool. He kissed her softly as the water splashed over them.

Grace could feel it building, the same warmth she always felt in the pit of her belly begin to manifest throughout the rest of her body. Her heart sped up when she felt him undo the strings of her bikini top. First the ones on behind her neck and once her breasts were free of her top's hold, she felt him take a deep breath. He brought his hands around and cupped her breasts in them, caressing them softly before pulling his lips away from hers and leaned down bringing one to his mouth.

Her breath caught at the sensation of his tongue on her nipple and she struggled not to pant. She undid the strings around her back taking the top off completely and let it drop on the floor. Taking a step back to support herself against the wall, she flinched at the feel of the cold marble against her back.

"You okay?" Sal asked, pulling away from her breast for a moment.

She nodded but refused to speak afraid he might hear just how aroused she was. He went back to sucking her other breast and his free hands made its way down to her bikini bottom, pulling it down on one side. "Let's get this off," he whispered against her breast. She helped pulling down the other side. Once all the way down her legs, she stepped out of them and he pulled back to look at her, completely naked now.

With her own breathing labored now, she stood trying to control her emotions, as his eyes took her in slowly from top to bottom. "God, you're beautiful." He kissed her this time with even more passion, pressing his erection against her. His hand slid all the way down her stomach and with his knee spread her legs.

Feeling his fingers between her legs made her moan, remembering the night in the Jacuzzi. He pulled away from her and stared in her eyes as his fingers spread her. "Promise me you'll tell me if it hurts," he whispered.

She nodded, her eyes closing as she felt his finger begin to enter. Expecting to feel discomfort, she waited for it but he slipped in and it felt so good she moaned softly, wrapping her arms around his neck. "You okay?"

"Yes." She finally spoke.

He slipped in and out a few times then pulled his hand away and hugged her instead. "God, I can't stand it anymore." He pulled away and reached for the shampoo that sat on the shower rack. He squeezed some in his hand then held it out to for her. Grace held her hand out, palm open, surprised at the interruption. He poured some in her palm. "You drive me crazy, Gracie. Let's just finish showering and get out of here. I want you in my bed."

Gracie couldn't even concentrate on washing her hair, thinking of his last sentence. After rinsing off her conditioner, she opened her eyes and froze. He stood under the other showerhead, rinsing off. He'd taken his trunks off. She'd seen naked men in pictures plenty of time. Joey had a whole calendar of them. But to be this close to one in person took her breath away. It didn't help that his body was right up there with those models in Joey's calendar.

Her eyes went from bottom to top, stopping at some of the most essential places. It wasn't until her eyes made it all the way up to his big chest and the strong shoulders she'd indulged in touching all day that she noticed him watching her—watching him.

"You ready?"

That smile of his always did things to her but now it did more than just speed her heart rate. It burned her up. Boy, was she ready.

CHAPTER 24

Sal had to regain control here. He'd nearly finished in the shower when he'd gone just a little further than he'd ever gone before with her. He stopped for the same reason he he'd stopped the first time, before going there in the Jacuzzi. How in the world would he get through this without disappointing her? He was too damn old to be feeling like a sixteen-year-old ready to explode just because he'd gotten past second base. But he knew this wasn't just any girl. This was *Gracie*. He should've anticipated this, prepared himself more mentally.

After drying off, he took her by the hand back into his room. He headed for the bed. "I thought we were sleeping in the tent tonight."

"We are," he said, pulling her towel away and taking a very deep breath. "But we're making our first stop here."

She shivered and he realized even though she'd squeezed a lot of water out of her thick hair in the bathroom, it was still wet and draped down her naked back. He lifted the plush down blanket. "After you."

Once she slid in, his heart could barely take the sight of Gracie naked in his bed. How many times, since she'd started working at the restaurant, had he dreamt of this? He'd lost count.

He undid his own towel, let it drop and slid in next to her. The moment he got in she wrapped her entire body against his and kissed him with a hunger like she had the day she'd asked him to make love to her. He had to slow this down but he couldn't. His own hands roamed all over her warm body. He loved the feel of her leg wrapped around him. His hand slid up it until it reached her behind as he kissed her frantically. This was madness. He'd been in bed with a woman plenty of times, but he'd never felt this urgency.

He *had* to take it slow with her. He'd never forgive himself if he hurt her. With her leg over his, there was more than enough access to try what he'd tried in the shower again. It was important he prepared her for what would come next. His fingers caressed her and immediately the soft pants that drove him crazy in the shower began.

He slipped a finger in easily enough and concentrated on her face. That was one way to keep from going over the edge. Concentrating on her facial expressions, making sure he stopped the moment he detected *any* discomfort would help keep him under control. As he went in deeper he took the crease between her eyebrows and her closing her eyes as a sign and stopped. "Don't stop," she begged.

"Are you sure?"

She nodded and licked her lips. "I like it."

He groaned, burying his face in her neck but continued. When he was ready to try for another, he brought his face up again to watch her as he did it. Normally he took pleasure in watching the facial expressions as his fingers worked their magic, but this time it was different. His concern outweighed the pleasure. He was actually thankful for it or he might've been a goner by now.

"Still okay?"

Once she accepted three, without any complaint,

and instead seemed to be enjoying it he concentrated on getting her there. He knew he had to now, because the way he was feeling already, it was going to be over embarrassingly fast. As annoying as that was—her first time being over so fast, he was confident that after the first time, his performance would greatly improve. They were in for a *long* night.

He used his thumb to rub the spot that made her arch her back and moan while his fingers continued to do their job of prepping her. Continuing to be very gentle, he was determined to make this as pleasurable for her as possible. He felt her begin to tremble and she moaned a little louder. He kissed her softy, as her trembling heightened to a level that he knew was almost there. His kisses grew deeper at the feel of her accelerated heartbeat against his own pounding chest. She moaned in his mouth and squeezed her leg around him. He pulled away to watch her and slowed his fingers.

Her beautiful breasts rose up and down as she tried to catch her breath but he could see in her face, feel it in his fingers she was still enjoying it. He kissed her forehead. "I love you, Grace."

She smiled, closing her eyes with a look of complete satisfaction—exactly what he was striving for. He watched her for a little longer before leaning over to his nightstand and pulled out a condom. Glancing at Grace, he saw that she watched him. "You're sure about this, right babe? Because I'd totally understand if—"

Grace touched his arm. "I'm sure—completely. And I couldn't have planned today more perfectly than you did. Thank you."

Feeling an ache in his heart and an overwhelming

fear about the possibility of ever losing her, he leaned in and kissed her. "I'd do anything for you, Gracie. *Anything.*"

With the condom on, he lay over her again. Nothing fancy the first time. He just wanted her to get through it as painlessly as possible. Spreading her legs gently, he positioned himself between them. He held both her hands on either side of her face and leaned in to kiss her as he entered her slowly... carefully. He continued to kiss her softly, feeling her breathing accelerate, the deeper he went. "How you doing?"

"Good," She nodded. "I love you so much, Sal."

"I love you more." He saw her wince and he stopped.

"No," she whispered. "Don't stop."

"You sure?"

"We're almost there aren't we?"

Sal tightened his jaw. "Not even halfway, babe."

Her eyes widened. "Don't stop."

He made his way in slowly. Since he was so worried about hurting her, he began to think it wouldn't be over as fast as he'd first thought. He'd imagined this going very slow and gentle, but once all the way in and her initial discomfort gone, he began to accelerate his thrusts.

She reveled in it, lifting her hips for him, wanting him deeper so he complied. "You still okay?" He could barely speak.

"Yes! Oh yes... "

Her longing voice only heightened his arousal and he drove in harder and deeper each time. Hearing her cry out with pleasure, he was only able to go a few more times before the enormity of the fact that he was making love to *Grace* kicked in and it was over. He squeezed her hands grunting as the incredible surge of pleasure pulsated through him.

He collapsed gently on her, feeling her heartbeat against his chest. He kissed her on the temple then her forehead. "My God, Grace. What you do to me. I can't even tell you—"

She touched his cheek with the back of her hand. "You don't have to tell me. I know. I felt it, too."

Sal stared at her feeling the icy terror creep down his spine. After today, he definitely didn't know how he'd ever live without her.

*

Sal made out Melissa's blurry smile as she looked up at him. His arm was draped around her neck. "You got it, babe?"

He tried smiling back but could barely get the words together to respond. "G-got it."

The hotel room opened and they walked in. Something was wrong. This whole situation was wrong but Sal could barely put two coherent thoughts together much less figure out what it was. As soon as the door closed, Melissa's hands were on Sal's pant's zipper.

Sal jerked out of his sleep, the bright sun immediately making him squint. It took him only a second to remember where he was. In a tent, in his backyard with *Grace.*

He had a feeling he'd wake up early, but he thought it would be because of the sun coming up so early. Not because of this. His heart pounded. The dream was the exact memory he had of that night in Vegas only the snippet of memory was a little longer this time. Further proof that he *had* been with her that night. Gulping hard trying not to think about it, he checked his phone for the time. It was only six.

Even with his rude awakening Grace hadn't budged. She still slept soundly on her stomach, her face on her pillow, facing him. He turned to face her, still breathing hard from his dream and studied her delicate features. The beautifully elongated eyes he'd loved staring into last night each time they'd made love. Those lips, he could kiss them forever and never tire of tasting them.

She gasped suddenly. Sal stared at her ready to wake her if she appeared to be having a bad dream. The corner of her lip went up ever so slightly and she let out a very satisfied sigh. He had to wonder if she was dreaming about last night. He'd been so exhausted by the time they knocked out he hadn't even dreamt, at least he didn't remember dreaming anything—until the morning's disturbing dream.

He lay back on his pillow again and brought his phone up to his face. Not wanting any interruptions yesterday, he'd placed his phone on silent the entire day. He figured if anything was important enough, they'd leave a voicemail. The whole day he had only checked his voicemail once and to his annoyance it had been from Melissa. He deleted it without even listening. But he had several texts he hadn't checked.

The first was a picture from Alex of one of the twins, smiling in her sleep. Like his mom had said a few days ago when he'd gone over and saw one of them do the same thing, "probably gas." Still he smiled and saved the picture on his phone.

The next three were from Melissa he turned the phone just slightly so there was no way Grace could see and began highlighting the entire thread to erase it. D-amn phone. He wished there was a faster way to do this.

"Good morning."

He was so startled by Grace's voice, he dropped the phone and it promptly clunked him on the forehead.

"I'm sorry!" Grace giggled.

He picked the phone up, blinking a few times. Grace was already on her elbow leaning in. She kissed him on the forehead and nose. "does it hurt?"

"I'm good," he said, rubbing his forehead then putting his phone aside and taking her in his arms. She yawned. "It's too early—damn sun. You wanna go inside? I have solar shades on my bedroom windows. You'd literally think it's night time unless you peeked out."

She yawned again and he kissed her head. "I could probably fall asleep out here again but if you'd rather go inside, that's fine, too."

"Yeah, let's go." He reached for his boxers on the side of the mattress and handed Grace his t-shirt. She slipped it on then glanced around. Sal stood up. "What are you looking for?"

She grinned. "My underwear."

Sal reached his hand out. "You're not gonna need them. Trust me."

Grace took his hand and stood up. Unfortunately, his t-shirt was long enough to cover everything. They both walked out into the sunlight squinting.

They walked in the house and Grace walked directly to the guest restroom. "I gotta go in here first."

Sal took advantage, speeding up to get to his room. "I'll be in the bedroom."

He went straight to his restroom and closed the door. Before he forgot, he made sure he deleted Melissa's texts. He frowned, pressing the buttons on his phone. He was going to have to figure out how to block her number.

By the time he walked out of the restroom Grace was already in the bed. Sal climbed in next to her ready to go another round... or two. After a few rounds the night before she'd been able to enjoy it more. He kissed her, slipping a hand down her leg, stopping just on the inside of her thigh. "You tired?"

She let her leg fall open, and smiled. "Not *that* tired."

Sal groaned, taking her mouth in his again, as if he'd never kissed her before.

*

The Friday morning after Grace's glorious weekend of *camping* in Sal's backyard she walked out of her room and into the kitchen. For once, she wasn't running late and was looking forward to making herself a nice omelet. She'd been walking on air for weeks now. But this past week had been surreal.

"Grace, I've been meaning to talk to you." Her mother sat at the table, a cup of coffee in front her.

"'Bout what?"

"Frank stopped by the other day and—"

"Mom." Her mom hadn't mentioned him in weeks. "I'm not doing anything with Frank so don't even ask."

"Will you let me finish?"

Grace rolled her eyes, pulling a frying pan out of the cupboard. "Go ahead."

"So he's only had a few slot machines put into the lobby of his hotel. He said he's just getting his feet wet, and already he's seeing a huge return. He's ordering more machines and starting up the remodeling to have the full blown casino up and running, hopefully by this summer."

Her mother paused and Grace turned to her. "And you're telling me this because..." Grace splashed the pan with cooking oil.

"Well, you know me — always thinking."

Calculating was more like it.

"He happened to mention he'd be looking into investing some of his extra capital soon. He said he's going to need a lot more tax write-offs, if this takes off like he thinks it will. So I mentioned your hopes of opening up your own restaurant someday..."

Grace turned to face her. She didn't like where this was going. Her mother grinned before taking a sip of her coffee. "He said he'd be more than happy to help you out with that. Imagine that, Grace. You can get your restaurant going so much sooner than—"

"Forget about it."

"Why? Graciela, don't be a fool. This man is offering to help you out with your dream. All you have to do is be *nice*—"

"It's not happening."

"You're being stubborn. There is nothing wrong with being civil to the man."

Grace shook her head as she diced up onions and green peppers.

"Look." Her mother stood up and leaned against the counter. "He mentioned us going out to visit him and enjoying a few days in his hotel again. We could all go as a family. Your boyfriend doesn't even have to know—"

"You're crazy. I'm *not* doing anything sneaky. Sal would be livid, and to tell the truth, I don't even think I'm ready to run my own restaurant yet. It's a lot of work."

Her mother put down her cup on the counter. "I can help you."

Grace laughed. "Like you helped in Juarez? You hated working in the restaurant."

"I'll work the business end. You can do all the restaurant stuff. Rose can help, too. She mentioned the other day wanting to get a job."

Grace turned to her. "She did?" That bothered her. Was Rose still worrying about Grace leaving her? Grace *had* ended up sleeping over Sal's on Sunday as well. The only reason she'd come home at all on Monday was because of Rose. Otherwise, she might still be there now. Sal certainly wanted her to stay. She remembered Rose's comment about getting a job and moving in with Joey and Taylor.

"Yes, wouldn't it be nice working side by side with your little sister?"

Grace continued making her omelet. It *would* be nice but doing anything with Frank was out of the question. "It'll happen someday. But not with Frank. I'll do it when I'm ready... and on my own." She flipped her omelet a couple of times before flipping it onto her plate.

"He'll be here this weekend." Her mother crossed her arms over her chest.

"What?" Grace stopped at the refrigerator where she held the door open, looking back at her mom.

"I think it's a great opportunity, Grace. Aren't you tired of living in this hell hole? This could be our chance to get out of here. Finally have a *real* life."

If her mother only knew she *could* be out of this place and living in a dream home with Sal. If it were up to him, she'd already be there. The only thing keeping her here now was Rose. "What is he coming for, mom? I told you I'm not doing anything with him anymore."

"You don't have to. Just come home early when you get out of work and talk to him. Throw some ideas around. He knows you're in a relationship now. He's not expecting anything. It's strictly business."

Grace shook her head and picked up her plate and the glass of milk she'd just poured herself. "Nope." She started walking to her bedroom.

"Graciela, think of your sister." Grace slowed d-own, feeling the guilt grenade her mother just threw at her begin to detonate. "You're hardly ever home now. This would be a great way for you two spend more time together."

The grenade went off sending shards of guilt through Grace's already frail conscience. She stopped, not turning around, just taking in her mother's words. She could almost feel her mother's wicked grin pene-trate through her back. She held her head up, shook it, and began walking again. As conniving as her mother had always been, Grace had to hand it to her. She'd succeeded in making her consider it—but only for a second.

CHAPTER 25

After making sure Rose was spending the night over a girlfriend's Grace spent Saturday night at Sal's. She hadn't spent the night at his place since the past Sunday and she was really beginning to hate saying goodbye every night. That wasn't even the main reason. Fear of him dropping her off and Frank's car being parked outside of her building had a lot to do with it. The last thing she wanted was for him to get upset over such a non-issue.

Of course, Sal was more than happy to have her stay with him. He'd been saying things all week like, "I got you your own toothbrush and I cleaned out a space for you in the closet." Leave it to her mother to dampen the euphoria she'd felt all week by laying on the guilt about her being gone so much.

They'd just finished showering, after an incredible morning in bed. Sal walked up behind Grace as she finished combing her hair and wrapped his arms around her. Both had the day off and they were taking a champagne brunch cruise off the marina with Angel, Sarah, Sofia and her fiancé Eric. It was part pleasure and part research. Angel and Sarah were thinking of doing something similar with their restaurant—offer brunch cruises on Sundays. Sal said he'd taken a dinner cruise before, but it was a long time ago and he hadn't been paying attention to any of the details.

"Almost ready?"

Grace nodded. "You think…" Sal stared at her through the mirror. "You think it would be okay if my sister came with us today?"

His expression wasn't a good one and she wondered if he'd expected this to be more a romantic thing. "Let me call Angel and see if he can get her in. He booked this earlier in the week. You should've said s-omething sooner, babe." He pulled his phone out of his holster and kissed her on the cheek before dialing. "Y-our sister's welcome to tag along with us anytime, Grace."

After checking with Angel, then waiting for him to call back, Rose was in. Grace hugged him as soon as he was off the phone. "And we'll have time to pick her up?"

Sal glanced at his watch. "Yeah, there's plenty of time."

Grace kissed him then hurried to her phone. She called Rose instead of texting and explained she needed to hurry and get ready. Rose sounded excited when she heard the word cruise. This would be a first for both of them. Grace made sure to text Rose after she'd hung up and asked her if by any chance Frank was still there. To her relief, he'd only been there a short while last night and left.

They arrived at the marina a bit early and had some time to kill so they spent it in Angel's restaurant. The men went to the back office. Angel wanted to show them specs online about the cruise services he'd looked into. Grace sat at a booth with Sarah, Rose, and Sofia. Sarah had the waiter bring them drinks.

Sofia's expression changed now that the girls were alone, and she suddenly grinned. "So what have you done to my brother, Grace? I've never seen him like this. I even caught him humming the other day in the back room." She laughed.

Grace smiled, feeling a sudden heat. "I've never been happier myself."

"I'm so happy for you two." Sarah smiled. "This is what Sal needed. Everybody's noticed the change in him."

"But I don't want him to change," Grace said quickly.

"For the better, Grace," Sofia assured her. "Trust me. He was getting way too uptight. He nitpicked about the smallest things. He's always been Mr. Do-It-Right-or-Don't-Do-It-All. Which is fine, especially when you're running a business. We need at least one person to be that way. But he was a little too much sometimes. Ever since you've been around he's eased up a lot."

"Most importantly, I think you proved his theory wrong, too," Sarah added, stretching her neck to see if the guys were on their way back yet. "He was driving Angel crazy—adamant about not hiring any cooks with too little experience. He's since hired two for us that I don't think he would've ever considered before you came along and they're doing fine."

Grace couldn't help grinning. "I *thought* one of the guys that was here the day I showed them how to make the new recipes was a little young."

"We're all happy about this, Grace." Sofia reached over and squeezed her arm. "The only one I think is a little jealous is mom. Even though she makes her remarks about Valerie barely being able to put a tuna sandwich together, I think she secretly likes that Alex still comes over so often to eat her food. But with you, she knows you'll give her a run for her money in the kitchen."

Sarah laughed. "I'm not much of a cook either. Thank God we own a restaurant or Angel wouldn't be eating very well either."

They all turned when they heard the laughter and the guys coming from the back office. "You girls ready?" Angel asked.

They slid out of the booth and made their way out of the restaurant.

The cruise was exactly what Grace needed. The food was excellent, and the champagne relaxed Grace when she discovered being out in the ocean made her a little nervous. Most importantly, Rose had a blast and the time they spent together, especially the laughs Rose got at Grace's expense when she admitted the moving boat made her nervous was priceless. Grace hadn't had that much fun with her sister in a while. Sal promised they'd do something similar again soon.

After the cruise, Sal invited the gang over to his place to hang out and maybe barbeque. He called Romero and somehow convinced Alex and Valerie too, along with the babies.

Rose offered to keep an eye on them when they got there so that Alex and Valerie could relax. Everyone sat in the patio, enjoying the nice afternoon. They were all still too full from the brunch to start the barbeque yet. But Grace put together a quick avocado salsa and set it out with chips for everyone to munch on. She was busy making a pitcher of margaritas, using the outdoor kitchen when she noticed Sal had disappeared. She couldn't find the lime squeezer but she knew he had one.

Walking in the sliding back door, she thought she heard the front door close. She waited to see if maybe that was Sal walking back inside from wherever he'd gone but no one walked in. As she dug through the drawers in the kitchen, she heard the front door open and then voices. She looked up to see Romero and Isabel. "Oh, hey you guys."

Romero held a twelve-pack of beer and gave her a strange look. "Where should I put these?"

Grace pointed to the backyard, feeling a little weird that he'd asked *her*. "Either the fridge or Sal has an ice chest out there." She glanced out the window to the backyard. Everyone was out there but him. "I'm not sure where he is." Remembering she heard the front door earlier, she asked, "Did you guys see him out front?"

They exchanged a glance, before shaking their heads, no. Isabel cleared her throat and then suddenly smiled. "Valerie's here?" She hurried to the back door. Romero glanced back at Grace, with that strange expression again before following Isabel out back. *Odd.*

Grace finally found the lime squeezer and headed back toward the patio, when she saw Sofia walk in and Eric rushed behind her toward the front door. He was about to say something but stopped when he saw Grace. Next, Alex walked in and followed them. "Stay here," he said to Grace as he walked by her.

Romero walked in and Alex turned to him, lifting an eyebrow. Romero didn't follow him instead he stood there watching her.

"What's going on?" she asked.

"C'mon out here, Grace," Angel said from the patio. She walked out. A very bad vibe suddenly chilled her. "Where did everyone go? Where's Sal?"

"I think he's on the phone," Angel said. Sarah and Valerie wouldn't even look at her. "How 'bout them margaritas?"

With a sudden urge to go find Sal, she turned to see Romero standing at the door, almost as if to block her. She took a step then heard Sarah, "Stay here, Grace."

"Why? You guys are scaring me. What happened?"

No one said anything then finally Romero spoke. "Sal's got an uninvited guest. Don't worry about it. They're taking care of it."

She froze staring at Romero. "Uninvited guest? Who?"

Romero shook his head. "Doesn't matter. She'll be gone soon."

Grace gripped the lime squeezer, feeling her insides heat. "She?" She took another step toward the door. But Romero didn't move. "Let me through."

"Stay here, Grace," he insisted.

"Let me through!"

"Let her go." She heard Angel say.

Romero frowned but moved. "Go with her, Angel," Sarah urged.

Grace rushed to the front door, feeling her insides ignite. Was it Melissa or someone *else*? She put her h-and on the knob to the front door and took a deep breath before opening it. The first thing she saw was Eric trying to calm a very angry Sofia, off to the side of Sal's front lawn. Alex who stood a few feet away from them turned and his eyes met Grace's. "Where's Sal?"

"Go back inside, sweetheart. He'll be right in."

"No, where is he?" She walked up the front walk-way until she got to the end and was able to see around the garage.

He heart jumped to her throat when she saw Sal talking to Melissa who held his arm. Another girl was with her, trying to pull her away. Melissa stopped talk-ing when she saw Grace. Sal turned to see who Melissa was glaring at. He gave Alex the most exasperated look then turned back to Grace. "I'll be right in, babe."

For a moment, Grace was speechless. She couldn't take her eyes off of Melissa's hand on Sal's arm. "Why is she here?" she finally asked.

"Why are *you* here?" Melissa took a step toward her and Sal stopped her.

"She's his girlfriend, you stupid bitch!" Sofia yelled.

Hit with a bolt of rage fueled by the anger that radiated off Sofia who now stood next to her but was still being held back by Eric, Grace charged at Melissa in a violent craze. Alex grabbed her by the shoulders, stopping her. "C'mon, Gracie. You don't wanna do this," Alex reasoned. "She's drunk and stupid and totally not worth it."

Between Sal and the other girl with Melissa, they managed to get her across the street to their car. They struggled with her as she yelled and screamed things Grace couldn't even make out, but she did hear the last thing she said before they finally got her in the car. "Did he tell you about Vegas?"

She may as well have punched Grace in the stomach, because that's exactly how it felt. The texts that night came back to her in an instant and she could barely breathe. As soon as the car drove away, Sal rushed back across the street. "Let me go, Alex." He did and she rushed to Sal. "What about Vegas?"

Sal shook his head as he approached her in the driveway and tried to take her hand but she pulled it away. "Was she there?"

"Let's go inside."

"No! Was she in Vegas with you? Is that who you were with that night?" She had to fight the urge to slap him. She'd let him answer first.

"No." He spoke calmly. "She was there. She's part of the wedding party. I didn't know she was going to be there." He reached for her hand but she pulled it away again.

Grace took a step back and he stepped forward. "Why didn't you tell me?"

"'Cause I knew you'd be mad. I didn't wanna upset you for nothing." He turned and gave Alex a hard look as if he wanted privacy but they all stood there staring as if they were watching a catastrophic train wreck.

Grace felt the tears coming and it enraged her, she stepped back again but he followed. "Did you spend time with her?"

"No. I was with the guys the whole time and she was with the girls. They sent over drinks one time but we never hung out. She was just trying to get in your head, baby. She probably figured I wouldn't mention it. I should've." He reached for her hand again and this time she let him. She needed to feel his touch—his re-assurance. "I'm sorry."

"Why was she here today?"

"She's drunk. Her friend said if she hadn't driven her here, she was gonna drive herself. She's stupid that way." He squeezed her hand. "Gracie, she means *nothing* to me."

She stared at him, wanting desperately to believe him. He took another step forward and hugged her, kissing the side of her face. "I'm sorry," he whispered.

She finally lifted her arm and hugged him back. "I hate her."

"I do, too."

*

A week later Sal still couldn't get over Melissa showing up at his place. He treasured every moment he got with Grace but he lived with constant fear of the possibility of it all being ripped away by something Melissa might say or do. He considered just confessing and praying Grace would forgive him, but he knew she'd be crushed — he saw the trepidation in her eyes the day Melissa showed up.

The memory of her kissing him that night had gotten longer since then. He now remembered her telling him how much she missed him, but he had no recollection of what his response was only that she kissed him again. He'd tossed and turned even on the nights Grace was lying right there next to him. A few times he even lay there, staring at her wondering what he'd do if he lost her. One thing was for sure he wouldn't go down without a fight. If he had to get down on his knees and beg, he would.

It was early and Grace wouldn't be in until a few more hours. He sat in the back online looking up cars for sale. He hadn't told her yet but he was looking into getting her a car. Joey was dropping her off today, but she'd told him that before, then he found out later that she'd actually taken the bus, because at the last minute Joey's car wouldn't start and she didn't want to call Sal to pick her up. He hated her taking the bus. She was one of, if not *the* most important person in his life now. He wasn't about to keep risking something happening to her.

Alex walked into the back. "What are you doing?"

"Looking up cars."

"For Grace?"

"Yeah."

"'Bout time. I don't see how you've let her take the

bus all this time. It's dangerous."

Sal frowned. "Well, most of the time I make sure she doesn't. But she's stubborn. She says it's not my job to chauffer her everywhere."

"You don't have to tell me about stubborn women."

Sal chuckled and spun his chair around. "Close the door will you? I wanna talk to you."

Alex did and stared at him curiously. "I'm thinking about telling Grace about Vegas."

Alex's face immediately went hard. "Are you *insane*?"

"Don't you think it's just a matter of time, before Melissa does? Wouldn't it soften the blow if she heard it from me and not her? Fuck!" He dropped his head back. "I've tried so hard to remember how I could possibly let that happen. I don't remember shit!"

"Why don't you file a restraining order on her ass? You can keep her away that way."

Sal covered his face with both hands then slid them down slowly. "If she wants Grace to find out, she'll get the message to her one way or another. I'm literally losing sleep over this, Alex. Seriously, what would you do?"

Alex started to auto-answer then stopped and seemed to ponder it a little longer. "I'd play the odds. Melissa already made an ass out of herself. She probably didn't count on all of us being there either. My guess is once she sobered up she felt pretty stupid. She's an attorney, Sal. She can't be doing shit like that. Maybe you can warn her that you'll slap her with a restraining order if she keeps it up. That can't look too good for her and I'm sure that kind of shit shows up if someone ever runs a background check on her. That might make her think twice before doing anything like that again."

Sal thought about it. He hadn't heard a thing from her ever since she showed up. Not even a text. Before that she'd been texting him at least once a day, so the theory about her feeling stupid made sense. Maybe she finally got it. *Nothing* was happening between the two of them ever again. If he filed a restraining order now he might piss her off. "You're right, she can't be doing that shit anymore. If she texts me again I'll tell her I'm filing a restraining order, because I'm not calling her."

"And you're not telling Grace."

Sal nodded in agreement. "No I'm not." He couldn't even imagine having that conversation. "Thanks, man." He turned around and went back to searching for cars.

CHAPTER 26

"You bought me a *car*?" Grace stared at Sal for a moment then glanced back at the black Jetta parked in the restaurant's parking lot.

"It's a write off." Sal shrugged. "I can list it as a delivery car for the restaurant but it's yours."

Grace shook her head. "I can't accept this, Sal."

"Why not?"

She laughed. "What do you mean why not? You bought me a car."

"I'm telling you, the restaurant can use the write-off."

Hearing about write-offs reminded her of Frank and his hotel. Her mom was still pushing the trip. "I can't afford the insurance."

Sal pulled her into his arms. "You won't be paying for it."

"You're crazy. You can't buy me a car *and* expect me to let you pay for the insurance."

"Yes, I can. Remember I said I'd do anything for you?" He kissed her. "I'm not being as selfless as you think. I did this just as much for myself as I did for you. It's for my own piece of mind, Grace. I hate knowing you're on the bus."

Grace pulled away from him and walked over to the car. "I don't even have a license."

"Do you know how to drive?"

She ran her fingers over the side of the car as she walked alongside it. "Yeah, one of my mom's ex-husbands taught me. I passed all the classes I needed to and took all the tests, just not the main driving one." She glanced back at Sal, still unable to believe he'd done this. "By the time I was ready for it they were divorced. Her next husband drove a motorcycle. No way was I testing in that and since I didn't have a car, I never bothered."

"So you go get it with this now."

She turned and leaned against the car. "I can't believe you."

Sal walked up to her and leaned against her. "You're not mad are you?"

"How can I be mad?"

He kissed her softly. "You and your sister can go places on your own now. Shopping—the movies."

She lifted an eyebrow, remembering what Taylor had said about the way Sal had looked at him. Then she remembered his reaction to Frank showing up at the restaurant. She really hoped this car thing had nothing to do with him not wanting her to spend time with Joey and Taylor. "I'll make an appointment with the DMV."

Sal smiled satisfied. "Good."

*

Sal muttered under his breath as he finished up the schedule for the next week. A few days after he'd gifted Grace her car, she brought up going out with her friends. "I've been spending a lot of time with your family and friends and I love it, but I'd also love for us to spend time with Taylor and Joey."

He should've known Grace was too smart to not pick up on him hoping the car would also make her less dependent on Joey and Taylor. He didn't realize he was still muttering until Alex walked in the back. "What's your problem?"

Sal didn't even look at him. "Nothing. I just gotta hurry and get out of here."

"Where you headed?" Alex opened up the cabinet.

Sal turned to face Alex. "To get Grace. We're hanging out with *her* friends tonight."

Alex obviously picked up on the sarcasm because he smirked and waited for the punch line.

"The two guys that used to pick her up before I started taking her home."

Alex's jaw dropped. "She still hangs with them?"

"Well, she's always with me now. But every now and again she'll do something with them, shop—catch a movie."

Alex's faced soured. "And you don't have a problem with that?"

Sal stood up. "They're gay and they're her best friends."

He grabbed his phone off the desk and searched for his keys. "I think I'd *still* have a problem with it. Some of those guys swing both ways."

Sal stopped and squeezed his eyes shut. Damn. He and Alex *did* think alike. He never thought it possible. He hated to admit it, but deep down he *did* worry about that. He'd justified the ridiculous paranoia to him being so crazy about Grace, but he didn't like to think he and Alex thought the same when it came to women. *Geez.*

"Yeah, well I trust Grace. And she's hardly around them anymore anyway. Which is why we're doing this tonight." And if Sal had to be honest with himself a part of him was actually anxious to get to know them—

make sure once and for all that he *didn't* have anything to worry about.

Alex shook his head. He obviously didn't agree with Sal but who cared. Sal knew he could trust Grace. All the way to Grace's apartment, Sal tried to think positive. He was determined to make tonight a good thing. These guys were a part of her life and it wasn't fair for him to ask that she just forget about them.

Both she and Rose came out after he texted her to tell her he was there. They stopped to pick up a twelve pack of beer and some chips. Then they drove to a slightly better neighborhood than Grace's about ten minutes away and he parked his car on the street, making sure he set the alarm.

Grace smirked when he clicked it twice to double check that it was set. "What?"

"It's not La Jolla is it?"

"I didn't say anything." The last thing he wanted was for her to think he was judging. He was just being careful—nothing wrong with that.

Joey greeted them at the door, hugging and kissing Grace. "I finally get to formally meet you, Sal." He held his hand out. "I'm Joey."

Sal shook his hand. "Nice to finally meet you too, Joey."

They walked in. Taylor was in the tiny kitchen, working on something on the counter. "Hey you guys. Just in time. Grace isn't the only one with some bartending skills. Don't worry, Rosie. I made something special for you, too."

"Grace, I told you not to bring anything," Joey scolded as he took the beer from Sal and the chips from Grace.

Sal glanced around the colorful apartment. Admittedly, he'd expected something more flamboyant. But it was tastefully decorated with pictures and paintings of bakeries and coffee shops. As small as the apartment was they'd used every inch of it quite stylishly without making look overcrowded and their furniture matched their polished wood flooring, giving the whole place an aura of elegance.

Taylor came around the small counter separating the kitchen from the front room. He wore camouflage carpenter shorts that had a few strategically placed rips in them. They hung just off his waist and the muscle shirt he wore looked a size too small. The pitcher he held was very big and Sal knew just by the color, the orange slices and different berries floating around just what it was. "You have to try my Sangria. It's the best." He glanced at Rose. "I made pink lemonade for you, sweetie."

Sal noticed how comfortable Rose was and how she made herself at home, immediately, walking into the kitchen to grab a glass.

Taylor poured everyone but Rose a tall glass of Sangria. It was damn good. Sal nodded and gave Taylor the praise he was obviously waiting for. "Good stuff."

"Hors d'oeurves!" Joey called from the kitchen.

He brought a great looking spread of different appetizers. "Wow, that looks delicious." Sal had to admit.

Joey set it down on the coffee table in front of Grace and Sal then put his hand over his mouth. "I gotta tell you, Sal. I don't know how Grace does it. I've been a wreck all day, knowing I'd be cooking for you."

Both Grace and Sal laughed. "Joey, I told you we could just order pizza. You didn't have to do all this," Grace said, reaching for an appetizer.

"Are you kidding me, Grace? And miss showin' off for one of the owners of Moreno's? I don't think so. Wait 'til you see what's for dinner."

"Well, I appreciate it and even though you didn't have to, I'm already impressed." Sal reached over and put a fork through something that looked like a cheese puff. Everyone stared at him as he bit into it. It turned out to be a crab puff and it was delicious. He lifted his other hand and connected the tips of his thumb and forefingers and held it out for Joey as he chewed; once done chewing he wiped his mouth. "God, that's good!"

After going through most of the pitcher of Sangria and munching on all the appetizers, Grace and Joey were getting a little giggly. Since they were both just about done with school, they were reminiscing about some of the things they'd gone through.

"Remember when they teamed you up with Herman The German for that one presentation?" Grace laughed.

"Ah shit. I had to hear about that for weeks." Taylor rolled his eyes, pouring himself another glass.

Joey didn't laugh. He looked pissed. "He asked me, 'What means blackened?' Are you fucking kidding me? What third year culinary student has to ask that?"

"Joey, the poor guy's English was limited," Grace said taking another sip of her drink.

"Was he really German?" Sal asked.

Joey and Grace looked at each other then fell into one another laughing hysterically.

Taylor smirked, shaking his head. "Apparently the guy was short with a bad hair cut and a weird mustache, so these two decided he looked like Hitler. Hence, Herman the German, but he was as Mexican as they are. I hope you know you have a spoiled snob on your hands."

"I am not!" Grace protested.

"She has every right to be a snob!" Joey sat up straight. "She out cooked even the professors. God, I loved it when she showed them a thing or two and left them speechless. But spoiled? Never!" He put his arm around her. "My baby girl has worked so hard to get where she is."

Suddenly both Joey and Grace teared up. "All right that's enough Sangria for both of you," Taylor said.

Sal slipped his hand into Grace's and squeezed it. She pulled out of Joey's embrace and wiped her eyes. "We're so stupid," she said smiling.

"I know. I know." Joey stood up. "Taylor get that stuff away from me—you know what it does to me. And I haven't even finished showing off for Sal."

"You want some water too, Gracie?" Taylor smiled at her sweetly. "Because that's what Joey is getting for the next half hour or so, or at least until he has a full meal."

Gracie smirked at him then glanced back at Sal. "Yeah, I better."

Dinner was impressive—oven roasted sea bass with ginger and lime sauce. It was all very impressive and Joey had the presentation down to an art. Sal was also glad it wasn't anything heavy. After over-helping himself to the appetizers, he couldn't take anything too heavy and he knew Joey would be watching closely as he ate.

They ate in the front room with dinner served on the coffee table. When they were all done, Taylor cleared the table and Joey brought out the cards. Grace leaned against Sal. "I'm so stuffed," she whispered.

"Me too."

"Have you ever played hold 'em, Sal?" Joey asked as he shuffled the cards.

"I've played a little."

Taylor brought out a silver poker chip suitcase and started counting stacks of chips. "Don't get obnoxious, Joey," he warned, as he continued to count.

Joey stared at him while shuffling the cards with one hand. The cards moved through his fingers almost magically. "Whatever do you mean, Taylor?"

Gracie laughed. "You're such a show off."

As expected, Joey was the hands down star player, beating them all several times. Taylor had made another batch of Sangria and Grace was getting giggly again.

Joey passed out another round of cards. "Did Grace tell you about the time we went to Vegas?"

"No, Joey!" Grace laughed, holding her cards in front of her face.

"It's okay, honey." Joey peered over his cards. "Now we know. *Never* mix what Gracie drinks."

Gracie covered her face with the cards and groaned. "Don't tell him!"

"What?" Sal's curiosity had piqued.

"Let's just say." Joey added another three chips to the pot. "We know Gracie's talents are in the kitchen, not on stage singing Pat Benatar."

"Try screeching," Taylor laughed.

Grace fell back onto the sofa laughing. "You encouraged me!"

"I said sing a ballad, sweetie." Joey's eyebrows lifted. "Not 'Hit Me With Your Best Shot.'"

"No, it was 'See me if you're best off!'" Taylor sang loudly. "You'd think she'd sing something she at least knew the words to the chorus."

Gracie buried her face in the cushions of the sofa, l-aughing uncontrollably. Sal had never seen her like this but it was nice to see a different side of her.

"In her defense, Sal." Joey patted Grace's leg. "At that point she wouldn't have known the words to Happy Birthday."

"So why'd you let me get up there?" Grace sat up, wiping tears of laughter away.

"Let you?" Joey stared at her like she was crazy. "I wasn't about to tackle you." He turned to Sal. "Gracie should come with a warning label. 'Alcohol may cause her to believe she can sing.'"

Grace fell into another fit of laughter. She threw her cards in. "I'm out! Joey, I can't believe you told him!" She wiped more tears away.

By the time the night was over, Sal was convinced these two were nothing more than true friends who cared deeply for not only Grace, but Rose as well. He understood now why Grace was so close to them. They were fun to be around and there was no doubt how sincere their feelings for her were.

Joey and Taylor walked them all the way out to Sal's car. "Sal, I have to say something to you," Joey declared once at his car.

"Joey, don't start," Taylor warned.

Joey lifted an eyebrow. "Taylor, she's our girl and I'm just looking out." He turned back to Sal. "I have never seen her so happy." His face fell into the same grimace it had when he'd teared up earlier.

"Here we go," Taylor said, putting his arm around Joey's shoulder.

Grace brought her hand to her mouth. Sal pulled her to him and hugged her.

"I just wanna say," Joey continued, "she means everything to us and we're so glad she's found someone that obviously makes her so happy. Please don't ever hurt my baby girl."

Sal took a deep breath, feeling a jolt of guilt in the pit of his stomach. "She means everything to me, too, Joe." He kissed the top of Grace's head. "I'll do my best to do right by her."

Grace dozed off on the ride home. Sal glanced in the mirror. "You mind spending the night at my place, Rose? There's a bed in one of the extra bedrooms."

"Yeah, that's fine," she smiled.

"This way Grace doesn't have to deal with stairs tonight."

Rose giggled. "Good idea."

Sal smiled and touched Grace's cheek. More memories of his night in Vegas had come to him. The only thing he'd learned from them was that Melissa had been the one that walked him out of the bar. He still hadn't heard a peep from her since she showed up at his place. He could only pray now things stayed that way.

*

Graduating from a small culinary school was nothing like doing so from a big college. The graduating class was less than fifty, but all Grace cared about was that she was finally done.

Sal filmed the entire ceremony, while her mother didn't even try to hide her boredom, yawning obnoxiously several times then shaking her head as if it was near impossible to stay awake. Grace was a little surprised she'd actually showed up, but after the ceremony she found out why.

Sal drove them to the Marina where he surprised Grace with a dinner cruise exclusively for her and their friends and family. Everyone was there including Joey and Taylor. Grace was surprised even Sal's parents made it. It was overwhelming.

Her mother was never one to pass up a free meal or in this case a very elegant dinner cruise. Grace knew Sal had paid for it all. She knew for sure her mother hadn't. She was even more glad her step-dad hadn't been in town for it.

Joey made a heartfelt toast that nearly had Grace in tears, to which she responded with her own toast for him. He *had* after all graduated also. When they finished dinner and everyone got up to enjoy their drinks and the view of the sunset, Grace stood on the deck of the yacht with Sal. He stood behind her, his hands on the rail caging her in. He kissed her neck softly. "I'm so proud of you," he whispered.

She smiled for the first time proud of herself also. "I'm just so glad I'm done."

"The fun starts now, baby."

Grace turned around to face him. "Really? I thought it'd already started."

"Nope. You ain't seen nothing yet." He kissed her softly.

That excited her. "What does that mean?"

"Means I have big plans for you. You'll see. The future looks bright, Grace. And everything in my future, includes you now."

Grace was in heaven. She never thought she could ever be this happy. Leaning her head against his chest, she took a deep breath. She could hardly wait for her future to begin.

CHAPTER 27

Grace had picked up such a rhythm now at the restaurant. Being at work reminded her of being in her grandmother's restaurant's kitchen. It felt like her second home and she'd come to love it.

Sal was meeting with the investors to inform them about the decision he and his family had come to. They would take on another restaurant but only one at a time until they felt they could do more without being overwhelmed.

She glanced up to see a smiling Alex walk out of the office and toward the kitchen. Then he turned to the dining room and something wiped the smile right off. He turned and walked in that direction instead. Curious, Grace walked over to peek. Immediately she knew why Alex had such a change in expression. Melissa stood in the front dining room, talking to him with her hand on her hip.

Grace wiped her hands and threw the towel down. She was done putting up with this bitch's shit. She didn't want to make a scene in the restaurant but she wanted to make sure Melissa knew she wasn't backing down no matter how much she persisted.

As soon as she walked out into the dining area, Melissa smirked. Alex backed up immediately making himself a barrier between her and Melissa.

"Oh I'm sorry if my presence upsets you." Melissa glared at her. "But if I wasn't carrying his baby I wouldn't be here."

Grace's heart nearly stopped and she glanced at Alex who looked as stunned as she felt.

"We had a lot of fun in Vegas, but now he needs to own up to his responsibilities. I'm having his kid." A slow sardonic smile spread across Melissa's face.

Grace felt ready to pass out. She held it in, but barely. "You're lying." She tried taking a step forward, feeling something squeeze her windpipe. But Alex stood firmly between them.

"No I'm not. That's why I'm here to let him know. He won't answer my calls." She turned to Alex who looked ready to pass out himself. "It's not something I want to leave in a voicemail or text you know? But I've been patient long enough. I'm sure you'll let him know how wonderful it feels to be a daddy."

"I don't believe you," Grace said, but she could barely hear her own words over the hum that had begun in her ears.

"He never told you? That surprises me. I always thought Sal would be the come-clean type of guy. Especially since he *did* insist on sending those texts to you that night, practically spelling out what we were doing. You know, just to unload his conscience a little."

Grace wanted nothing more than to slap the smirk off Melissa's face. The rage she'd felt when she first walked out there ready to take Melissa head on, was now replaced with something that rendered it impossible for her to speak. She swallowed hard, angry at the hot tears that blurred her vision, satisfying Melissa. She'd accomplished what she obviously come here to do.

"I'll let Sal know you were here and why," Alex said. His voice sounded almost robotic to Grace, as if he too were having a hard time getting the words out. "You'll hear from him for sure. But for now I think you should go."

Grace turned around and hurried to the back room. She refused to fall apart in front of Melissa. She wouldn't give her the pleasure but she could barely breathe by the time she closed the door behind her. Within seconds, the door opened and she spun around, feeling ready to hyperventilate. "Do you think it's true?" She wiped the tears away but they kept coming.

"I don't know, sweetheart." His phone was already in his hand and he dialed.

"Don't call me that!" She was furious. Furious that she'd been taken in by the entire family and their charm and now she felt her heart ripping apart.

"Sal," Alex said, looking into her eyes as she waited, taking trembling breaths. "Melissa was just here. She said she's pregnant—and she told Gracie it happened in Vegas."

"Is it true? Ask him if it's true!" Grace was beginning to feel hysterical. She'd trusted him completely. Believed every word he said when he explained about the texts that night. When he said he hadn't spent time with her the day she showed up at his place. "Ask him!"

Alex handed her the phone. "He wants to talk to you."

She took the phone. "Tell me it's not true. Tell me you didn't sleep with her." The memory of her begging her grandmother to tell her it wasn't true that her dad was dead assaulted her and she gasped.

"Grace, I'm on my way to the restaurant now. I'll explain—"

"Did you?" A sob escaped her. "Just tell me!"

There was silence then, "Yes, but—"

She shoved the phone at Alex, nearly dropping it.

She couldn't breathe; she gasped, trying to catch her breath. "Are you okay, Grace?" Alex put his hand on her shoulder.

Finally, she felt a slow trickle of air enter her lungs as if it were coming in through a straw. But the pain she felt in her heart was brutal. Not even the deaths of her father and grandmother compared to this. Their losses, while devastating, weren't a betrayal. They hadn't knowingly done something that they knew would tear her heart out.

She grabbed her things out of the cabinet. Alex was talking but she couldn't hear him — didn't want to. All she could think of was running far, far away from the Morenos. All of them. She wanted nothing to do with any of this anymore. Her head was spinning. Somehow, she knew it all along. It was just too good to be true. Things like this just didn't happen to girls like her and here was the agonizing proof. Grace didn't even bother trying to wipe the tears that streamed down her face. It was useless; they wouldn't stop now.

"Where are you going?" Alex asked, still holding the phone to his ear.

"I quit." She threw the keys to the Jetta on the desk as she stalked by him.

"Grace, wait. How are you getting home?"

She didn't answer just walked right by a stunned looking Melanie. "What's wrong?"

Grace pulled her phone out, ignoring everyone that asked the same question as she rushed through the restaurant. Alex ran after her and caught her just outside. "Gracie, please let me take you home."

She tried walking around him. "No, Alex. I just want to get away from here."

He stepped in front of her. "I'll take you. Don't walk."

"I'm not walking." She struggled to catch her breath again and talking was only making it worse. "My friend is picking me up."

"Grace, he fucked up, okay? He was drunk. Doesn't even remember. I *know* he wouldn't willingly hurt you like this. But you guys can get through this."

Yet another agonizing blow to take. Alex knew all along. She thought of how odd everyone had behaved at Sal's house the day Melissa showed up. Were they *all* in on it? She glared at him. "Get through this! He's having a baby with that bitch and..." It really sunk in. Her fairy tale future with the guy she was so hope-lessly in love with was over. Just like that. "I'll never get through this, Alex. *Never.*" She sobbed and tried walking around him and he attempted to stop her. "Let me go. I have a ride. I have to get out of here."

"Then wait for your ride here."

She shook her head. "I'm meeting him up the str-eet."

"I'll go with you and we'll wait together."

She ignored Alex and dialed Joey, a tough feat with as much as her hands shook. She could barely speak when she asked him if he could pick her up. She knew he hadn't understood much of what she said only that she needed to be picked up and he quickly agreed.

"Where's he picking you up?"

"He'll call when he's close and I'll let him know where I am. I need to walk."

They walked silently for a few blocks. Then Alex fi-nally spoke, "Gracie, alcohol is the devil. It fucks up so much shit. I only hope that you can forgive Sal— eventually. You really do mean everything to him."

The fact that Alex knew everything all this time was

utterly humiliating. She wanted nothing more than to be away from him — all of them.

She'd finally managed to stop crying and now she felt a boulder sized lump in her throat again. Her entire life was defined by one devastating event after another that changed everything. This was just another one. She only hoped that like all the other times she'd be able to survive this. Her phone rang and she let Joey know where she was.

Without responding to Alex or even acknowledging that she'd heard anything he said they continued to walk in deafening silence until Joey pulled up next to them.

"Sal's gonna come looking for you, Gracie. You know that," Alex said as she reached for the car door. "I don't want this to be goodbye."

Grace refused to look at him.

He touched her arm but recoiled when she flinched. "Maybe not right away. Take all the time you want but your job will be waiting, no matter how long it takes… I'll miss you."

Unable to hold back the devastating tears she got in the car with Joey, pulled the door shut and locked it, not looking at Alex.

"What happened, sweetie?" Joey asked his voice full of concern as they drove away.

She waited until Alex was out of sight before completely falling apart.

*

Sal banged the steering wheel. He should've told her before. He knew this was going to happen but the pregnancy — that came out of nowhere. Although the thought of there being no condom anywhere in the room had popped the idea in his mind a few times he didn't think he could be that unlucky. Sure, he knew he fucked up, but he didn't think it could it get any worse than it already was.

Traffic was the pits. Of course, he'd have to be clear across town when he got the call. After calling Alex back several times to no answer he'd called the restaurant and was told Alex had stepped outside with Grace. Apparently, he hadn't taken his phone with him. Grace had obviously turned her phone off because his calls were going straight to voicemail. He left one saying he loved her and begged her to give him a chance to explain, but he didn't her call back after that.

It would be a miracle if Grace was still there when he got back. His phone rang. Finally, Alex was returning his calls. "What happened?"

"She's gone, man."

"Home? Did she take the car?"

"No. She left the keys here. Wouldn't even let me give her a ride."

Sal gulped, the dreadfulness of this was sinking in. Grace was *gone*. "You let her take the bus?" He took a quick right nearly sideswiping someone.

"No. She insisted she'd get a ride so I walked with her a few blocks until her friend picked her up. Sal, how you gonna fix this?"

"I dunno. But I have to." He really did. He couldn't lose Grace. He just couldn't.

He hung up with Alex and raced to Grace's apartment building. He still didn't know which one she lived in so he knocked on the first one he came to on the third floor. That much he knew. The older lady that answered either really didn't know what apartment Grace lived or wasn't willing to part with the information. He quickly knocked on the next one. No one answered. After banging on a few more doors, he finally got a man who pointed him to Grace's apartment. Her mother answered in a robe. It was after noon and she looked like she'd just woke up. "Is Grace home?"

Her smile turned into confusion. "I thought she was working?"

"She was but she left."

She shook her head, saying she hadn't come home but invited him in. Sal declined and took off in a sprint. He'd try Joey and Taylor's next. He cursed himself as he rushed down the stairs. He should've gone there first. One of them had obviously picked her up and she probably figured he'd come looking for her here so she must've gone there instead.

At first no one answered the door at Taylor and Joey's either. But he heard voices inside. "Gracie, please just let me explain it's all I want. Then I'll go away I promise."

The door flung open and a red eyed Joey stood before him, leaning against the door. "I'd like to hear your explanation before you put her through any more. You have no idea what you've done to her." His face screwed up and he took a deep trembling breath. "This is killing her and *that* kills me. Do you understand?"

If this was the only way he'd get a chance to explain then he had no choice. "Listen to me, Joey. I don't remember anything about that night. I didn't spend any time with her the evening all us guys went out. I got totally wasted and somehow she ended up in my room the next morning. But I don't remember anything about it. She told me that we'd been together and that I'd texted Grace the night before. I didn't even remember that. But I swear to you I would never do anything to risk losing Grace."

Joey nearly fell when the door was yanked open further and Grace stepped up. Sal felt the life sucked out of him when he saw her devastated face and how bloodshot her eyes were. "But you did and now she's pregnant."

"Baby, I'm sorry. I'll do whatever I have to —"

"There's nothing you can do! You said you loved me and I believed you!"

"I *do* love you!"

"Stop!" She started toward him, arms flailing but Joey held her back. "Don't ever say that to me again! I hate you!"

Taylor came out from behind the door and helped Joey hold her back. "You should go now, Sal," he said, pulling Grace inside.

"Grace please —"

"No, *you* please, Sal! Please leave and never come back because I want nothing to do with you ever again!" She collapsed onto Taylor's chest and he held her.

Joey cried openly now, too, smoothing her hair, then turned to Sal, eyes as broken as his own heart felt. "You need to go."

He closed the door leaving Sal standing there frozen, feeling a sense of utter hopelessness come over him. He hated himself for what he was putting Grace through, as if she hadn't had enough heartache in her life already.

His whole life nothing had ever been impossible. Hearing anyone even use the phrase, *That's impossible*, made him angry. There was nothing that would ever stand in the way of his dreams and goals. Where there was a will, there was a way. Now he'd finally hit an unforgiving wall of impossible. Aside from hoping Grace could somehow find it in her heart to forgive him, there was no way around this. He'd lost her and the reality nearly strangled the life out of him.

He left there feeling like his entire world as he'd so perfectly molded it, had just come to an explosive end. He never thought he'd feel like this, but without Grace, nothing mattered. He saw no joy in anything he accomplished from here on. How could one person have such a huge effect on another one's life? The nightmare that haunted him for weeks now was a reality.

His phone rang as he drove still feeling the haze of overwhelming hurt and doom—Sofie. Great. He'd be hearing it from everyone soon enough. Let the tongue-lashing begin. He deserved every bit of it. He clicked the earpiece and answered.

"Tell me it's not true, Sal. Tell me you didn't actually sleep with that *bitch*."

Sal took a deep unbearable breath. "I wish I could, Sofie."

"*Why*? Why would you do that? How *could* you?" She sounded ready to cry.

Shit. As if he didn't already feel like the biggest dick on the planet. He explained again, the story sounding lamer every time he told it. Being drunk was no excuse, but it was the only one he had.

"Have you ever considered maybe *nothing* happened?" Her voice went from devastated to suspicious.

"Sof, she's pregnant. *Something* happened."

"No. That doesn't mean anything. Even if something did happen, it may not be yours. I hate to say it, but women can be evil and I saw it n her eyes the day she insulted Grace; this bitch is as evil as they come. I wouldn't trust a word she says."

Sal sighed, feeling dead inside. "I dunno, Sof. I'll have to look into it all. I wasn't planning on just taking her word. But the fact remains she woke up in my room that morning."

Sofia was quiet for a moment. "Have you talked to Grace?"

"Yeah." The image of her distraught face and her words came at him again. *I hate you!* "It's over. She wants nothing to do with me anymore."

"Well, you can't give up."

"I don't think there's any way to fix this."

"Where there's a will there's a way, Sal. Aren't you the one always saying that?"

"I know but—"

"No, no buts. I'm calling Romero."

"For what?" The last thing he wanted was for the whole world to be in on his stupidity. But who was he kidding? With Melissa pregnant with his kid, everyone would know soon enough.

"This doesn't end here, Sal. Melissa doesn't get to win this easily. I have serious doubts about this whole thing. And I'm sorry, but if it turns out that she really is pregnant and this *is* your baby, I'll love it just as much as I'll love my nieces but I will never accept *her* as part of my family."

Sal knew that much already. Even if his brothers would somehow find a way to tolerate Melissa, if necessary, Sofie wasn't about to be that gracious. In fact after seeing her reaction to Melissa showing up at his house, it'd be best to keep those two out of the same room, especially now.

After hanging up with Sofia he did what he dreaded most, but knew he had to. He called Melissa.

CHAPTER 28

Melissa answered on the first ring. Sal pulled into the parking lot of the restaurant and parked.

"I had hoped to give you the news first but you left me no choice. You're not mad are you?"

Sal leaned his elbow against the door and rested his head on his hand, feeling completely drained. "Mad doesn't even begin to explain what I'm feeling right now, Melissa."

"It's not like I planned this."

Sal rolled his eyes. "I want proof before I accept any responsibility whatsoever."

"How dare you!"

"Don't act surprised. You know damn well I'd be stupid to just take your word for it. In fact I question the validity of the pregnancy all together."

"You really think I would make something like this up?"

"Yes. I really do." Sal wasn't about to fall for her feigned hurt act. She'd just cost him the one thing he knew with all certainty he could never replace. There was no room for compassion here—none at all.

"I have proof."

"And that would be?" He waited, eyes squeezed shut.

"I'll show you the pregnancy test. I've taken three now and they're all positive."

He was almost relieved. "Not good enough. Unless you take it in front of me, I wouldn't put it past you to have had a pregnant friend take it for you. If not, I'm sure anything can be faked these days."

Her forced laugh was a loud one. "Your arrogance is beyond belief. That I would do such a thing just to land the great Sal Moreno, obviously *the* most eligible bachelor in La Jolla is ridiculous. Though I wouldn't mind us having a civil relationship for the sake of our child. I'm not asking you to marry me, Sal. But don't forget what I do for a living okay? I know my rights."

"Even having my kid, you wouldn't *land* me. Besides I'm not an eligible bachelor remember? I have a girlfriend." He wasn't about to give the satisfaction of knowing she'd accomplished what she so aggressively set out to do. "And I don't need to be an attorney to know I have rights, too." He opened the door to his car. The dull headache he'd begun to feel the moment he got Alex's phone call alerting him of Melissa's visit and announcement had now grown into a full blown migraine.

"She's still clinging to you even though she knows you cheated on her? How pathetic."

That brought him to an enraged abrupt stop, taking a deep breath he tried to remain as calm as possible. "There's nothing more pathetic than a girl who jumps in bed with a guy who's rejected her repeatedly. You knew the only way I'd ever fuck you again was if I was totally wasted. I'm only glad I don't remember any of it." He took a deep breath trying to calm himself before he walked in the restaurant. "Just so you know, nothing short of a notarized written note from your doctor will convince me you're pregnant."

Sal massaged his temple as he walked in the back door of the restaurant. She was quiet for a moment probably letting his insult simmer.

Silence. And even though that silence brought with it an ounce of hope that maybe she *was* lying, it still didn't fix the fact that Grace now knew Sal had betrayed her in the worst way. The torment he'd seen in her eyes today would be forever imprinted in his head. The very torment he now carried in his heart and would probably be carrying for a very long time, if not forever.

"I've already made an appointment to see my doctor. I'll just wait until then and bring you the note. After that we can get on with how we're going to handle this. I know you're angry now but I do hope you're going to want to be part of our lives, Sal."

"First things first, Melissa. And the note alone is not gonna cut it. Even it *were* notarized I'd still have to run it by someone to make sure it's authentic." Sal hated sounding like such a dick but Melissa may have single handedly ruined any chance of complete happiness he may ever have. The last thing he wanted to discuss was any kind of relationship with her. "I gotta go. Let me know when you get the note."

He expected the mood from the other employees to be somewhat somber but he didn't expect the cold shoulder and downright haughtiness from some of Grace's closer friends. If it were for any other reason he might be irritated by it but he was just as pissed at himself as they were. He'd never forgive himself for the pain he'd caused Grace. If the pain of knowing he'd lost her was this excruciating for him, he could only imagine what she must be feeling, knowing he'd done this.

Sofia was on the phone in the back room when he walked in. "Perfect. Oh, he just walked in. Let me make sure." She looked at Sal. "You stayed at the Hard Rock

Café that night in Vegas right?"

Sal nodded. He knew Sofia was adamant about this but it surprised him that she was already on the phone with someone about it.

"Yeah, it was the Hard Rock. Okay. Thanks."

She hung up and smiled big at Sal. "Romero said he might be able to get the tapes from the casino that night you were there. He said casinos hold on to their surveillance tapes for months or in some cases, years. Normally we'd need a court order to get a hold of them but," she winked, "good ole Romero has connections."

As much as Sal appreciated the effort, it was too hard to get past the hopelessness of the situation. "S-of," he said, plopping down in the chair, as the memory of Melissa unzipping his pants came flying at him like a slap across the face. "She was in my room that morning. Her damn panties were on the floor. Romero is better off looking into whether or not she's lying about being pregnant. That's probably the only thing we can hope for at this point, because even if she's not, Grace won't be forgetting and much less forgiving the fact that I cheated on her." He shook his head disgusted with himself. "And with Melissa of all people."

Sofia shook her head also. "And you call women naïve? You don't think that psycho bitch would have it in her to plant her stink ass panties in your hotel room? I put nothing past her." She opened the cabinet and pulled out her purse. "Now that you're here I can leave."

She stopped when her eyes met Sal's. He must have looked as miserable as he felt because her hard expression changed immediately to commiseration. Sal let his head hang back and closed his eyes. He opened his eyes when he felt her lips on his forehead. "It's gonna be okay, Sal. Something tells me Grace will somehow find it in her heart to forgive you." Before he could retort she added. "If, in fact, there is anything to forgive." She straightened up and pulled her purse over her shoulder. "And if it does turn out Melissa made this whole thing up, that sorry bitch is gonna have a lot answer to."

If it wasn't for his heart feeling the weight of the world crushing it, Sal might've laughed. His brothers and sister were always so ready to kick some ass. If only that could fix everything, his siblings would rule the world.

Once left alone, the dread really sunk in. He leaned his face into his clasped hands like a man praying for a miracle as visions of Gracie's anguished expression assaulted him. He'd done that to her. And if *he* could never forgive himself, how could he ever expect *her* to? It was over.

*

It took a few minutes after opening her eyes for Grace to realize she was in Joey and Taylor's bed. But it took less than a few seconds to remember why. She closed her eyes again, wishing to God she hadn't remembered.

Joey lay next to her fully clothed. He hadn't even taken off his shoes. The poor guy must've fallen asleep trying to console her. He'd cried almost as much as she had. She scooted off the bed slowly, careful not to wake him. It was still light out. She remembered Taylor giving her a pill to take to calm her. He said it was harmless but might make her drowsy. Well, it sure had knocked her out. She wondered now if he'd slipped

Joey one, too.

She'd just stepped out of the restroom when Taylor and Rose walked in the front door. As soon as Rose saw her she rushed to Grace and hugged her hard. The emotion overtook Grace and once again she was crying. "I'll stop talking to Vincent if you want. Once you're over Sal I don't want anything to remind you of him and make you sad."

Grace took a deep breath, shaking her head and struggled to get the words out. She cleared her throat. "No, you don't have to." She tried pulling away but Rose wouldn't let go.

"Grace." It was only then that Grace realized Rose was crying, too. "I hate that you're so sad. When Taylor told me how much you were hurting it ripped my heart out."

Immediately Grace went into big sister mode. She smoothed Rose's hair and sucked it up. "I'm gonna be fine, Rose. I promise."

Up until that moment she had no idea how she'd get through this. She'd felt like her entire world had come crashing down on her. Now she realized, just like in the past she had to get through this. Not just for herself but for Rose. She couldn't let even this get in the way of her dream of moving her and Rose out.

"I hate him for doing this to you. I'd never seen you so happy and now…"

Grace fought the knot that began to form in her throat now that she refused to cry. "He's not the only man in the world." It hurt to even say the words, because she knew without a doubt she'd never love another man like she did Sal. "I'll get over him."

She glanced up at Taylor whose smile didn't even begin to hide the sorrow in his eyes. Though he hadn't wept for her like Joey did, she'd felt the emotion in his touch when she'd sobbed so hopelessly in his arms. She took another long and determined breath. Just like she had when she was younger she'd save her sobbing from here on for the shower or when she knew none of them were around. Just because Sal had shredded her heart didn't mean they all had to suffer with her.

"That's enough, Rose." She pulled away gently then wiped the tears from Rose's face. "This is just another turning point in my life. One I wanna move on from as quickly as possible. We're not going to stand around and cry about this for weeks or even days. Okay?" She gulped hard, trying to focus on something—anything else. "I need to find a job." She turned to Taylor. "That's what I'll pour my energy into from here on."

He nodded just as Joey walked in the front room from the hallway still looking very somber. "We're moving on, Joey," Taylor informed him with a look. "Gracie is gonna focus on getting a job."

Joey seemed confused at first but when Taylor gave him another warning look he nodded. Grace could see he couldn't even muster up a smile but silently agreed.

"Rose brought you a change of clothes, Grace," Taylor said, pulling out a frying pan from the cabinet. "In case you wanna shower and get out of those clothes. I'm gonna make us dinner." He turned to Joey. "I bought stuff so you could make something for dessert. I think we can all use a good dose of chocolate tonight."

Rose handed Grace the small bag of clothes. None of them mentioned it but it had just dawned on Grace that she was still wearing the polo with the restaurant's logo on it. She gulped, trying not to think about how she'd never step foot in that restaurant again. In fact if she hadn't just promised she was moving on, she'd suggest they all take a drive to the beach and burn the damn polo in a bonfire.

With a small smile she took the clothes. "Thanks, I think I will take a shower if you don't mind."

"Not at all," Joey said. "There's a brand new loofah under the sink, if you wanna use it."

He snuck in a quick hug as she walked by him before Taylor called him off. "Joey."

He pulled his arms away quickly. "Okay, okay."

Grace smiled but hurried to the restroom, locking the door and turning on the shower as quickly as possible. She was only in there for a minute before she buried her face in one of the towels, praying it would muffle her crying. How in the world would she ever survive this? The deafening pain she felt when Sal confirmed he had slept with Melissa was back and she could barely catch her breath again.

Get over him? Move on? *Impossible.*

*

A week later Sal dropped by his parent's house for lunch. His dad said he wanted to talk to him. He hadn't heard a thing from Melissa since the day he called her and he was still numb from the damage she'd caused to his life. He'd hardly slept or eaten that entire week and he wondered if maybe Alex had told his parents. Just the other day Alex sympathetically let Sal know he looked like shit.

To his surprise Alex was at his parent's when he got there, looking just as unaware as Sal was about why they'd been asked to come over. Then his dad dropped an unexpected and unpleasant surprise on them both.

Their uncle had asked him for a favor and he had agreed. Their cousin Vincent would be staying with his parents over the summer and he'd be working at the restaurant.

Both Sal and Alex had protested that Vincent couldn't be trusted, to which their dad informed them he'd already warned their uncle. "First sign of trouble, he's gone."

That conversation had been a few days ago. Now Sal sat in the back office, adding Vincent to the payroll and the schedule. He'd be there today and even though Sal wasn't looking forward to it, they could use the extra help. Alex was still only coming in part-time. He had school and the babies were a handful.

Something this simple Sal usually got done within minutes but he'd been at it for over a half hour now. His mind constantly wandered off into thoughts of Grace and how his heart ached to be with her. A few days ago he'd lost the ability to even listen to her voicemail message once she changed her number. She'd completely cut him off now.

He'd tried once again out of sheer desperation stopping by Joey and Taylor's to beg Grace for forgiveness but she hadn't even come to the door. Taylor had stepped outside to let him know it was best if he just stayed away. Grace had made her decision and it was final. He said if Sal really cared about her he'd make it easier on her by not coming around anymore.

As an adult, Sal couldn't even remember going through motions of crying but the pain he'd been feeling all week and hearing Taylor so grimly inform him of Grace's decision, had finally done him in. Of course he'd waited until he was home alone, and ever since he'd been dead inside.

The knocking pulled him out of his painful thoughts. He'd spaced out again. Vincent stood by the door. "Hey, Sal. Here I am. Reporting for duty."

Sal had already decided he was just going to have to make the best of this. He stood up and shook his hand. "Welcome aboard."

Sofia walked in behind him. "I already set him straight on the ride over here. He's gonna behave. Although," she turned and gave Vincent a look. "I don't know how much he heard of it, since his attention was mostly on his phone the whole time. That's gotta be a girl right? Your girlfriend?"

"Not yet," Vincent smirked.

Sal remembered Grace telling him about her sister and Vincent texting all the time now. He had a sudden suspicion about Vince's motivation to come stay with his parents. Sal eyed him. "What does that mean?"

"Means not yet, but I'm working on it."

Sofia pulled two aprons out of the cabinet and tossed one at Vincent. "That's gonna be a little hard now that you'll be here all summer, won't it?"

Another sly smirk swept across Vincent's lips. "Not really. She lives out this way."

Sal stared at him now. "You're not talking about Rose are you?" His tone was a reflection of how he'd felt all week.

"Relax," Vincent laughed. "She won't even be around for a while." He worked on getting the apron on then rolled his eyes. "Just when I finally get the okay to come out here, her mother and sister decide to take a trip to Laughlin and take her with them."

Sal had stopped looking at him for a second to check his phone that buzzed on his desk but just the mention of Rose's sister and then Laughlin made him freeze. He brought his attention back to Vincent. "Laughlin?"

"Yeah, and she doesn't even know how long they're going to be out there."

Trying not to be too obvious, Sal sat down slowly on the chair and glanced back down at his phone nonchalantly, his racing heart didn't make easy. "Is it a vacation?"

He gulped, picking up a pen on the desk, trying to rid the image of the guy with the roses outside of the restaurant and the disappointment on his face when Sal informed him he couldn't see Grace anymore.

"I think she said it was kind of a spur of the moment thing." Vincent paused before adding, "I heard about you and Grace breaking up. I'm sorry to hear it, man."

Nothing could hide the pain Sal felt just hearing her name. He couldn't even think of any other way to respond to that other than nodding. Sofia must've sensed the need to change the subject because she jumped in. "All right, Vinnie. Ready to be trained?"

Vincent smiled. "Ready when you are."

"Let's go then." She gestured to the door and Vincent walked out.

Sofia turned, giving Sal a small smile before walking out. He could only hope this was the worst pain he'd ever had to endure in his life because he couldn't think of anything more excruciating. Somehow he thought time would make things better, but it only seemed to get worse with each passing day. Knowing she'd gone to Laughlin, no doubt her mother's idea, now topped that agony with a blinding rage.

CHAPTER 29

After fighting the grief for days it began to take a physical toll on Grace. Days of nonstop job searching on little to no sleep and even less food finally did her in. The few times Joey and Rose persuaded her to eat she'd been violently ill. Then her body let her know it was done trying to keep up on so little rest and nourishment. She crashed down with the worst flu she could remember having.

She cried for days beside herself, assuring Rose and her two best friends that it had nothing to do with Sal. It was the frustration of not being able to fend off the illness that rendered her completely exhausted and helpless. She was dehydrated from throwing up and her fever raged because of it. It was a vicious cycle the more she tried to eat and take liquids in to hydrate herself the more she threw up.

Without insurance she couldn't even see a doctor, unless she was willing to pay through the nose. Technically her insurance from Moreno's was still active and she was sure Alex wouldn't have a problem with her using it but she refused to have any kind of connection with that family ever again.

Finally an entire miserable week later of being so sick, Rose mentioned to Joey and Taylor about her mom's insistence of taking a vacation to Laughlin. She even told them how it would be free.

Joey who was convinced that her illness had been brought on by the heartache over Sal and was also terribly worried about her, said a vacation was exactly what Grace needed. Rose and Taylor agreed. Her mother needed nothing more than for Rose to point this out and she got the ball rolling.

Even though her mom had been disappointed when she heard about Grace and Sal's breakup it was almost as if she expected it. For once Grace had seen in her mom what only a lifetime of experience could teach you. Everyone else had been so sure she and Sal were right for each other. Even Grace had finally began to believe it with every ounce of her being. Yet her mom had shrugged it off as it she'd known all along it was only a matter of time. Grace had no place in a man like Sal's life.

"*Mija,*" she'd said as she cheerfully helped Grace pack. "This is going to be good for you. We'll go out there, eat at nice restaurants, gamble a little, do some swimming. Frank even said he'll take us to the river and we could rent some jet skis. You and Rose will have a blast. By the time we get back you'll be ready to move on." Then she winked. "And if we play our cards right, maybe ready to start looking for a place to lease for your new restaurant. Frank is *very* interested in investing in something out here in California. This is gonna be perfect. You'll see."

Her mother seemed almost giddy about the fact that Ruben would be working and not able to go with them. Grace had sat on her bed, feeling the hollow inside her deepen. Not even her dream of having her own restaurant was enough to snap her out of it. But she'd taken the trip anyway. She needed to get out of her room, needed to feel normal again. If only it didn't feel like an impossibility. She'd *never* be normal again.

The answer to the age old question, was it better to

have loved and lost than never loved at all, if anyone asked Grace, was a resounding no! Even as beautiful as her time with Sal had been, and as happy as she'd been with him, she truly wished now she'd never been lifted so high. The drop was so profoundly bottomless, the climb back up would be brutal, if at all possible.

She tried her best to at least appear to be having a good time in Laughlin but she got the feeling Rose wasn't buying it. Though she had moments where she thought she might be relapsing into her fits of nausea and even thought she felt a little feverish, she was able to function better than that first horrendous week after breaking up with Sal.

Her mother tried relentlessly to get her and Frank alone. She was determined to arrange a business partnership between the two of them. Grace had only agreed to be out there for a few days. By her third day her mother succeeded in getting her alone with Frank.

To her surprise, Frank had been more than modest when describing his hotel. It was far fancier than he'd made it out to be. He had even reserved private huts by the pool for them for the entire week. Not that Grace planned on staying out there that long.

When he stepped into their hut that evening to say hello and ask if they needed anything, Grace's mother invited him in to join them. As soon as he took a seat next to Grace, her mother excused herself and Rose, saying they needed to go grab a few things from their room. Grace started to get up to go with them but her mother immediately rebuffed the idea saying she should stay and keep Frank company until they got back.

Frank ordered them both drinks. "Your mother tells me you're looking for a possible partner to help you get your restaurant going." He crossed his leg over his knee and sat back. "Did she mention I'm looking for projects to invest in? I think a restaurant would be a great investment."

Grace sat up straight. "My ultimate dream is to have my own restaurant. But I'm not sure if I'm up for it right now." That was putting it lightly. Just getting out of bed without falling apart was a struggle for her right now.

"Oh, I think you have it in you and your mom says your talent in the kitchen is something you were born with. A gift like that shouldn't be wasted."

Their drinks arrived. He'd taken the liberty to order her their signature specialty drink. Carrot cake martini. Grace had never been into the milky drinks but she wouldn't insult him by refusing it. She reached for it off the waiter's tray with a smile. The smell alone caused something in her stomach to stir .

"Your mom also told me about your falling out with your boyfriend. I'm sorry you're hurt, but I can't say I'm sorry to hear it, for personal reasons."

Thoughts of Sal weren't just painful, they literally sucked the air out of her. She closed her eyes desperate to will away the emotion even the mention of him brought her, then took a sip of the drink. Cinnamon overpowered the drink. The entire blend of milky sweetness, cinnamon and alcohol, along with the sudden heartache that stabbed at her made her stomach turn and she nearly gagged. Pulling her legs over the side of the ottoman, she stood up in a panic.

Frank sat on the edge of his seat. "Are you okay?"

She nodded, holding her hand over her mouth, unable to speak. *Shit*. It was happening again. Unable to even look at the drink anymore, she set it down on the small table next to the ottoman. "I'll be back."

Her stomach roiled and she barely made it to the ladies' room, before throwing up her entire lunch. Rose rushed in as Grace finished rinsing her face in one of the sinks.

"Grace, I thought you were better." She walked up to her, placing her hand on Grace's back.

"I am. It was just the drink that Frank gave me. I've never liked those kinds of drinks and it didn't sit well with my stomach." She clutched her clammy hands together before Rose could see how they still shook. Rose's troubled eyed tugged at her heart. She hated for her to be so worried. "I'm fine. I promise." She smiled, ignoring another wave a nausea. "Lets go sit in the Jacuzzi."

Finally, Rose's expression softened a bit. "You sure?"

"Yep."

One way or another Grace was going to have to snap out of this. It had gone on long enough and she hated what it was doing to Rose. Nothing could be done about the way things had turned out, but she had to find the strength to push past this.

Instead of letting yet another excruciating facet in her life define it, she had to turn it around and somehow make it the new beginning. There was no such thing as the perfect life and she'd been a fool to think she could have it all. But she would certainly make the most of what she *could* have.

"Let's ask Frank and mom if they want to join us." Rose's scandalized expression made her laugh. "It was a little rude of me to run away and be sick when he was trying to impress me with their signature drink." She shrugged, taking a deep breath. "Least I can do is offer to spend a little time with the man. He *is* footing the bill for this entire vacation, Rose."

Grace smiled big, trying to convince not only Rose but herself that she'd be okay sitting in a Jacuzzi and not thinking about the first time she'd ever sat in one... in Sal's backyard.

*

Sal stared into Melissa's eyes as the image of her smiling face, lying on the pillow next to his went in and out of focus. "You're not Grace."

The smile vanished. "Is that her name?"

Sal thought he nodded but he couldn't be sure. His entire body felt numb.

Her hand caressed his face. "It's better this way, Sal. It wasn't meant to be. Remember that."

The ceiling fan above his bed came slowly into focus. The memory that had come to Sal in his sleep wasn't a new one, but the last part was new. He blinked a few times, making sure he was wide awake. Some of the times before when he'd thought he'd woken he'd gone right back into the dream but it didn't get longer. It only repeated itself.

The last part new of this dream didn't feel like it was an element of the memory. It almost felt as if it was his self consciousness trying to force him to just accept it. Why would Melissa say that?

He showered and dressed, the dream on his mind the entire time. That night in Vegas would forever haunt him. He'd most likely never recover from it.

The text came just as Sal pulled up to the restaurant. He stared at it with mixed emotions.

I lost the baby. It happened yesterday, so there's no need now for me to try to prove anything to you. It's done. I hope you're happy. I know your pathetic girlfriend will be.

Of course even after all the trouble Melissa had caused she'd have the nerve to try and make him feel guilty, then top it off with an insult. He still wasn't sure he believed she was ever pregnant but at least now this part of his nightmare was over.

He walked through the motions of opening up the restaurant in the same mechanical way he'd done everything since Grace had left. As much as he wanted to believe that somehow things would go back to the way they once were before she walked into his life, that he could go back to be being fired up about expanding his family's business, deep inside he knew it just couldn't. There would forever be a void in his life. A huge part of him was gone now.

Sofia rushed in the kitchen where Sal made his final walk-through before opening the front doors. "Romero is on his way. He said he has some stuff on Melissa. He hasn't had any luck with the surveillance tapes but—"

"She's not pregnant anymore, Sof."

Sofia's usual big eyes got even bigger. "She's not?"

"She lost it yesterday."

His sister's expression went blank before turning into disgust. "I doubt she was ever pregnant."

"Well, it doesn't matter now. Does it?" He walked past her and out of the kitchen.

Sofia followed him. "Yes, it does. Because if we can prove she never was then maybe we can prove nothing even happened that night. Think about it. If she'd lie about something this big then—"

"Sweetheart, I appreciate what your trying to do here. But I'm almost certain something *did* happen. I may not remember all the details but I remember being in bed with her." He stopped to unlock the front door and turned back to her. "It's not all clear but the parts I remember are pretty damning."

She glared at him arms crossed, then looked over his shoulder with a smirk. Sal turned to see Romero standing on the outside of the glass door, grinning.

"It's open," Sofia said.

Romero pushed the door open and walked in. "You have my burrito ready?"

"No," Sofia said, a hopeful smile spreading across her face. "But we'll get it started for you. First I want the scoop."

Sal began walking back towards the bar area, less enthused about what possible information Romero had. It's not that he didn't wish more than any of them that this whole situation could somehow be remedied but neither of them had heard or seen Grace the day she found out. Nothing short of a miracle would fix this. The facts still were, he'd been in bed with Melissa and one of the most vivid memories were of her unzipping his pants. It didn't get any worse than that.

"All right," Romero started. "So this Melissa bitch is a real whack job and is full of shit about a couple of things."

"I knew it!" Sofia almost jumped.

"According to all her medical insurance records she hasn't even made an appointment to see a doctor for *any* reason in months."

Romero finally had Sal's attention. "And this information is as of when?"

"I ran that report last night."

"So yesterday, she wasn't in the hospital at all?" Sal felt his insides heat. All this time he'd been so guilt ridden, he hadn't actually allowed himself to seriously consider that Melissa might actually have faked the pregnancy. If she had, she'd done it for one reason and one reason alone.

"Nah, that report is in real time. Why? Did she say she was?"

Both Romero and Sofia stared at him as he nodded but said nothing, still taking in what Romero had just dropped on him.

"If she'd been in the hospital yesterday it would've showed up. Besides I've been tracking a few of her credit cards. The girl is a shopper. She was at the courthouse most of yesterday, bought lunch there and a shit load of coffee all day. Then she headed to the mall and dropped some serious loot on clothes and shoes. Which brings me to the next thing she's full of shit about." Romero took a seat at the bar.

"Hold that thought," Sofia said then yelled Romero's order for the usual breakfast burrito he always had. "Okay. Go on." She stood across from him on the other side of the bar ready to hang on to his every word again.

Romero smirked, his eyes going from Sofia's to Sal's. "She ended her day at DJ's for a few drinks. I can't see what kind of drinks she bought but she was only there for an hour and she dropped over fifty bucks. Unless she was drinking some expensive ass non-alcoholic drinks this pregnant woman got a pretty significant buzz last night."

"I told you! I bet you anything nothing happened that night." Sofia leaned in and lowered her voice. "Let's be real here. If you were really that wasted that you don't even remember anything how likely is it that you'd actually be able to … you know, perform?"

Melissa's words the morning after, suddenly slammed into Sal. *You were amazing.* Sofia had a point. How amazing could he have been? Even the few times in the past that he remembered being a little loaded it had somewhat impaired his *performance*. Not that he hadn't finished the job but it'd been far from amazing. As pushy as Melissa had been he just never thought that she, that *anyone* would go to these lengths. Maybe his sister was on to something. "What's going on with those surveillance tapes?" Allowing an infinitesimal bit of hope creep in, Sal would now be hanging on Romero's every word, too.

Romero frowned, shaking his head. "I've struck out twice now but I have one more guy looking into it. He's a little more expensive but I think he's worth it. The problem is," he paused when the server brought out his burrito and placed it in front of him. "Thanks, man."

Sofia poured him a soda.

"You see, without a court order," he continued. "The only way to get a copy of the tape is by breaking into their computer system. These casinos have top notch security. Not only that, they change their security codes all the time. This guy I have looking into it now actually got in, but halfway through searching it knocked him out and the security code was reset. The good thing is this guy is a fucking freak when it comes to his work. He's taking this as a personal challenge. He won't stop now until he gets it."

"I'll pay whatever it takes." The wheels were spinning in Sal's head now. Was it really possible that Melissa had planned the whole damn thing? The panties on the floor came to mind. They were the first thing he saw when he sat up that morning and that was when he was still in a complete hung over daze. How could Melissa have missed them right there in the middle of the room? Then something else came to him. He turned to Sofia. "Do we even serve a drink called Liquid Cocaine?"

Romero nearly spit out the food he was eating. Sal watched him grab for a napkin and wipe his mouth. "What?"

Romero glanced at Sofia, seemed as if he was about to say something, then shook his head. "I've never heard of the drink. But it sounds lethal. Is that what you were drinking that night?"

"Yeah, and they were being sent over by Melissa and the group of girls she was with—the bachelorette party. "

"Oh my God, Sal!" Sofia said completely exasperated. "She totally had this planned. How did you not see it?"

"Sof, she was in my room the next morning and I didn't remember a damn thing." He did feel pretty stupid now. "What was I supposed to think? I was in such a panic about the whole thing I never stopped to consider she'd go through all that trouble."

"I told you she was evil." She picked up her phone and started typing something.

"What are you doing?" Sal asked.

"Googling Liquid Cocaine. That doesn't even sound legal."

Romero chuckled again.

Sal's irritation levels had spiked. "What the hell is so funny?"

"I'll tell you later," Romero said. "Anyway, out of curiosity I did check out why she made quite a few visits to see a quack a few months ago. This chick is on some heavy meds. I'm surprised she was drinking at all.

Most of the shit she's on you *do not* mix with alcohol."

Sal stared at him. "What kind of meds?"

"Xanax and lithium for starters." Romero shrugged. "I didn't read through her whole file; it's a fucking book. Those are the two main whacko meds I remember but there's more. The other ones just didn't jump out at me like those two."

"Well, that explains a lot." Sofia said, putting her phone down. "And the drink is legal but just a couple are supposed to knock you on your behind. How many did you have?"

He told them about losing count and the fact that the lethal concoctions came after a parade of tequila shots.

"Dude, I've been wasted plenty of times and let me tell you," Romero laughed. "there is no way anything happened that night. You'd have to be a super hero to get any kind of rise. Even a big fat blue pill wouldn't have helped with getting a wood after all you drank."

Sal shot him a look and glanced at Sofia. She laughed. "It's okay Sal, I'm twenty-one now, remember. If my ears didn't even bleed back when I was your baby sister and you and the other two thought they would if I was exposed to this kind of talk, they certainly won't now."

Sal didn't say all he normally would about her still being his baby sister, only because now his adrenaline was pumping through him so fast he could hardly think straight.

He hadn't asked Vincent anything about Grace or Rose since his mention of them being in Laughlin. Why torture himself? But in light of that morning's revelations, he could hardly wait for him to start his shift today.

CHAPTER 30

On their way to see the fifth restaurant/home for sale Grace tried not to think about how lightheaded she'd begun to feel.

"Luckily this area has a lot of these restaurants with living quarters. So many of the families that come over the border are used to that. In Mexico, there are tons of families who make a living out of cooking and serving in their own kitchen. If their food is a hit, they usually start building onto their own homes and expanding it into a more restaurant like atmosphere." The real estate agent that was showing them around talked non stop. "Unfortunately, on *this* side of the border, there are regulations that need to be followed. So a lot of these restaurant slash homes are not permitted and you'd need a miracle worker and a ton of money to get them up to code. I won't even bother showing you those."

Grace leaned against Rose. She was as tall as Grace now so they were shoulder to shoulder in the back seat of the agent's car. Their mom sat in the front with the agent.

"Are you okay?"

Grace nodded but didn't lift her head from Rose's shoulder. "I think I might be getting a little car sick. After this one, we should call it a day."

Rose stroked Grace's hair. "Okay."

As much as Grace had been playing the part of being back to normal now, she still wasn't feeling it. But for the sake of everyone not worrying about her anymore she'd told them all she was. She even agreed to partnering up with Frank to get her restaurant going. It was her mother's idea to find one where they could live as well. Her mother had always hated that tiny apartment of theirs.

Most importantly, Grace suspected that once settled in to their new place her mom was giving Ruben the boot. That was the only ray of light she'd come across in the sea of black she'd been swimming in these days.

After walking through another restaurant with a couple of rooms in the back and a tiny bathroom that doubled as a shower, they called it a day. The agent drove them back to his office where they all jumped into Frank's Cadillac — another thing that under normal circumstances Grace would have never agreed to. Since Frank had bought himself a sportier, more extravagant car, he'd offered to lend them his Cadillac until the restaurant was up and running and they could afford to purchase their own car.

Of course her mother had jumped on it the instant he offered it, explaining later when they were alone that he was only looking out for them because he was a good man. Grace wasn't naïve. No man would be willing to offer so much in exchange for nothing. She'd seen the way he looked at her when she extended her invitation of him and her mother to join them in the Jacuzzi. There was a definite expectation of something more than just shared profits of her restaurant.

The only reason she'd given in without much of a fight is because that was one thing even her mother had to know. There was *no way* that anyone would be persuading Grace to open up her heart to *anyone* for a very long time, if ever.

On top of everything that was happening now in

her life she had yet another thing to worry about. Since Vincent's texts were the one thing that kept Rose so distracted she hardly noticed that Grace was far from being well, Grace had insisted she didn't have to cut him off on her account. Now that he was in a much closer proximity, Rose had begun to ask about the possibility of her hanging out with him. It was funny that Rose didn't bother to ask her mother. That woman had zero parental instincts. She'd say yes to Rose in a heartbeat, no questions asked, if it meant getting Rose out of her hair. But Grace was worried enough for the both of them. Sal had stressed about Rose keeping her distance from Vincent.

Grace lay on her bed now, fighting an incredible fatigue again while Rose pled her case. "Have you ever known me to be a bad judge of character? None of my friends are bad. I would never hang out with anyone I thought might be trouble."

Grace's eyelids were so heavy now she could barely keep them open, and the last few nights she'd finally slept like a rock. She rolled to her side in an effort to stay awake. "Rosie you have to understand—"

"He's under strict warning, Grace, that if he screws up even *once*, they send him back home. He really *really* wants to be here all summer. Do you honestly think he'd risk being sent home?"

Frustrated that she didn't have the energy to give Rose a good argument she was afraid she was losing this battle. "Where would you hang out?"

Rose smiled and sat down next to Grace, then her smile suddenly vanished. "You're still not feeling well are you?" Rose stroked Grace's hair again.

"No, I am. I'm just feeling a little tired." She sat up, unwilling to let Rose see just how lifeless she really felt.

"So where would you hang out?"

The smile crept back onto Rose's face. "Well, if they even let him drive all the way out here—he's gonna ask today. But nowhere far. Outside in the playground area or I can make us sandwiches and we can have a picnic where the barbeques are at. It doesn't matter."

Her little sister's eyes sparkled, reminding her of how she once felt so excited to just be around Sal. Rose was too young to be feeling this. It scared Grace to death. What she was going through, she didn't wish on even her worst enemy, but especially not Rose. She reached over and took her hand. "Rosie, you know y-ou're too young for a boyfriend right? You said he was just a friend. Promise me that that's all this is going to be. He's going back at the end of summer. I don't want you to be heartbroken when he leaves."

Rose smiled and hugged her. "Don't worry. We're just friends. I promise."

Grace prayed she wasn't making a mistake agreeing to this. When Rose pulled away, Grace looked at her very seriously. "If I get wind that it's become anything more than just a friendship, I'm gonna have to put a end to it, okay? I don't want you to be angry with me. I'd only be doing it for your own good."

Rose nodded, grinning way too big for Grace's liking, then hugged her again in a near squeal, before jumping off the bed to grab her phone from the desk. Yeah, a teenage girl got *that* excited about being able to hang out with a boy who was just a *friend*.

The bad feeling she'd had in her stomach through-out the entire conversation just got worse. As if she needed this added to her plate right now. Grace made herself comfortable in her bed, lying back down again, and dozed off within minutes.

Romero was still there when Vincent arrived. Sal had agreed to let Vincent drive the Jetta to and from work. He walked out into the bar area still tying his busboy a-pron on. "Hey, Vince."

Vincent looked up at all of them and smiled.

"Is Rose still in Laughlin?" Sal asked, getting right to it.

"Nah, they got back a few days ago, but she's been busy packing for uh…" He glanced away from Sal, fin-ishing tying on his apron and walked over to them. "You think maybe it's okay for me to drive out tonight and see her for a couple hours after my shift?"

Sal barely heard the second part of Vincent's resp-onse. He was still hung up on the first part. "You mean unpacking, right?" Sal eyed him until Vince's eyes met his again.

"Um yeah," Vince nodded. "Something like that. I guess."

"Well, which is it? Packing or unpacking?" Sal pus-hed.

Vince shrugged. "I dunno. Unpacking I guess. Point is, she was busy. So you think I can go?"

"You and Grace's sister, uh?" Romero asked, crum-pling his napkin and throwing it on his now empty plate then burped. "She's straight jail bait, man." Ro-mero shook his head. "I couldn't believe it when Grace said she was only fifteen."

Vince's face screwed up. "Jail bait? What the hell does that mean?"

Romero smirked, obviously amused at Vincent's annoyance. "Means you're gonna have your hands full, fighting off older guys who might mistake her for an eighteen-year-old."

Sal saw Vincent's eyes light up but not in a good w-ay — one thing about his young cousin that had always reminded him of his brothers. "No I won't. 'Cause she's not like that."

Romero lifted his hands in the air, still smirking. "You wanted to know what I meant. I was just explaining."

Sal decided to play into Vincent's already ruffled f-eathers to try and get more out of him. "Romero is right. She did already get asked to that prom by an older boy." Sal smirked adding, "I dunno you really think she was busy for days *unpacking*? That's kind of odd. Isn't it? You sure maybe her prom date wasn't keeping her busy?"

The second Vincent turned to him, Sal saw it. Bin-go — he hit just the right nerve. "She was packing, o-kay? I wasn't supposed to say anything but they're moving."

The smug feeling from having Vincent fall right into his trap, was replaced with an icy panic down Sal's spine. "Moving where?"

"They're not sure yet. That's another thing that's kept her busy, *Sal*." If Sal wasn't so suddenly uptight he might of laughed at his cousin's irritation over his insinuation about Rose. "They've been busy looking for a new place, too. But all we do is text so she can't write it all down." He stopped a slow grin appearing across his lips and lifted an eyebrow. "If I see her tonight. I'll finally get to talk to her. I can get the whole scoop for you."

Normally Sal would've said *hell no* to his less than trustworthy, barely-old-enough-to-drive cousin about driving all the way to Chula Vista. But the morning's eye-opener had changed his outlook on more than a few things. "Sure you can go see Rose, Vin." Vincent's grin got even bigger. "But I have a few conditions."

His cousin's grin turned into a suspicious stare. "What kind of conditions?"

"Well, for starters the obvious. Rose is only fifteen and a very sweet girl. *Do not* let me hear that you've gotten her into any trouble or that you've disrespected her in any way." Sal saw Vincent's eyes roll up and he frowned. "I'm serious, Vin. I swear to God, I get even one complaint about you, and your ass will be back in La Puente so fast you won't even know what happened."

"I'm not gonna get her in any trouble." He turned and glared at Romero who was smirking again. "And like I said, she's not like that, so you can count on me not disrespecting her either."

Romero stood up off his bar stool with a chuckle. "I'm out of here. I'll call you if I hear anything."

Sal nodded. "Yeah, keep me posted."

Romero smiled at Vincent. "Listen to your cousin, Vin. A girl like that can be trouble."

"A girl like what?" Sal could see Vincent wasn't playing anymore. Romero had purposely pushed too far. "You don't know shit—"

"All right, all right!" Sal interceded as Romero laughed, walking away. It was one thing to rile Vincent up, he didn't want him so mad he wouldn't be willing to agree to the rest of Sal's *conditions*. "He's just messing with you, Vin. You're right he doesn't know anything about her. She's a *very* nice girl." He turned to Romero who was already halfway to the door but still laughing and looking back at them. "Get out of here, ass. And don't forget to call me as soon you know anything."

Sal waited for Romero to walk out before turning back to a still very irritated looking Vincent. Sofia had gone into the back room but was on her way out again holding her purse. "I'll be back to close, Sal. I gotta drop off Eric at the airport."

"Where's he going?"

"Conference in New York." She mussed Vincent's hair as she walked by him. "You be good you hear?"

Vincent rolled his eyes again but his glower brought on by Romero's remarks was now replaced with a smirk. "I'm always good." He looked back at Sal once Sofia had left. "So what other conditions are there?"

"I need a favor," Sal gave Vincent a very serious stare. "And I don't want you mentioning any of this to Rose."

Vincent's eyebrows pinched and Sal had a feeling his cousin might not be too keen about this. He almost felt bad that he'd have to use Vincent's obvious longing to see Rose as leverage. But he had no choice. "Have a seat Vince." He pointed at the barstool. "We need to talk."

*

In a deep fog, Grace felt suddenly unable to breathe and she sat up, realizing she was choking on her own saliva. She hacked uncontrollably, trying to catch her breathe in between, tasting the horrific acidic spew that attacked her throat. This was the second time this week it happened. Waking up because she was choking was decidedly the worst way to wake up *ever*.

She made it out of her room and into the restroom

where she placed her hand under the faucet and brought it to her mouth. After a few drinks she felt slightly better. The coughing subsided slowly as she wiped her face down with a towel. Just as she walked back into her room it dawned on her that Rose wasn't in bed with her. Starting to panic she remembered she'd fallen asleep in the day. She glanced at the small digital clock on her nightstand and saw it was only seven in the evening.

With her breathing finally back to normal she picked up her phone and saw she had two texts. One from Joey and one from Rose. She read the one from Joey first.

Hey, sweetie. I talked to Rose and she told me you're taking a nap… in the day...AGAIN. You're not fooling anyone. You're still not well. Call me when you wake up!

Graces eyes were still leaking from her cough attack, and her throat burned, but she still had to smile. She clicked over to her next text, from Rose.

Vince is here! =) We're downstairs in the bbq area and we're not going anywhere I promise so don't worry. He could only stay until 7:30. I'll be up when he leaves. Thanks again sissy! Love you!

Grace frowned. That text was a little too syrupy for someone who was just spending time with a *friend*. And to think, he'd be here all summer. As if she didn't have enough on her mind to deal with already. She walked over and peeked out the window. She had a perfect view of them sitting on one of the picnic tables with their feet on the bench, talking. Grace wondered if Rose had done that on purpose—sit in plain view of their bedroom window so that Grace could see they were doing nothing wrong.

She watched them until Vincent laughed, his smile

reminding her so much of Sal it nearly choked her. Clearing her throat, she walked away from the window and decided she'd call Joey.

Before she could, there was a soft tap at her door then it opened and her mom stuck her head in. "Oh good, you're awake, *mija*."

Grace waited as her mother stepped all the way in closing the door behind her without responding. The word *mija* from her mother's lips was never a good thing.

"Ever since we got back from Laughlin, unless we're out looking at real estate, you've done nothing but mope around and sleep. You need to get out. It does you no good to be locked up in here." She sat down next to Grace on the bed and put her hand on her knee. "There is a new place that just opened up, over by the marina. It's supposed to be really neat. My friend said it's all Mardi Gras style. What do you say we go there this Friday night? You can invite Joey and Taylor."

Grace began to shake her head. She just wasn't ready for going out yet—wasn't sure she'd ever be. "I don't really feel like doing anything like that."

Her mother frowned. "Now Grace I'm not taking no for an answer. Besides." She cleared her throat. "Frank is going to be here this weekend—"

"No mom." Grace turned to her with a scowl. She knew it. Her mother's concern about her wellbeing should've been her second clue after the word *mija*. "I'm not doing anything—"

"Graciela." Her mom squeezed Grace's knee. "He is our business partner now. He's putting a lot of money into this restaurant not to mention our new home. The least we can do is show a little gratitude." She stood up as if there was nothing more to discuss. "We were his guest when we went out to Laughlin now he'll be ours."

"He's staying here?" Her mother was beyond ridiculous.

"No. Don't be silly. But he'll be in town and I agreed we'd entertain him while he was here." Her mother stopped at the door before walking out. "This really will do you some good, Grace."

She walked out closing the door. Grace took a deep breath and made that call to Joey. No way was she spending the evening on a double date with her mom, Ruben and Frank. This might actually work to convince Joey she *was* feeling better, even though she wasn't. "You don't have any plans for Friday night do you?"

"No. Why?"

"Perfect. We're going to Mardi Gras."

CHAPTER 31

This was the first night since Grace was gone that Sal had sat out in his backyard. He hadn't wanted to enjoy the view without her. He sat staring out into the city lights and the ocean, feeling a deep emptiness.

His heart literally ached. Finally he understood how powerful depression could be. All those times he'd read about people who felt such despair that nothing, not any amount of money, fame, success could lift them out of it, he never understood it. Now he did, because at that moment, staring out into the distance not really focusing on anything in particular, the anguish weighed heavier than he'd ever felt it.

Everything, especially around the restaurant reminded him of Gracie, but nothing was a more painful reminder of her than his backyard. She loved it out here—could spend every minute at his house outside. Memories of the times they'd made love on the very lounge chair he sat on now, strangled his heart, forcing him to gulp back the tightness he'd begun to feel in his throat.

His phone ringing on the patio table pulled him momentarily out of his world of pain. He stood, breathing deeply. The name on his caller ID rattled him. It was Vincent and he had no idea what to expect.

"Hey, Vin. What's up?"

"She didn't say a whole lot, Sal. Only that Grace has been sick." He was quiet for a moment and Sal waited for more as the image of Grace sick only intensified the pain in his heart. "She hadn't told me before but she did tonight. I know why you guys broke up." Again there was silence and Sal braced himself to hear about Grace hating him. "That's pretty fucked up, Sal. Rose said she'd never seen Grace so broken up. Not even when her grandma died. I thought you really liked Grace, man."

"I did. I do." Sal sat down resting his elbow on his knee and squeezed his temple. He hadn't thought he could feel any worse. But hearing this nearly did him in. "I didn't do it intentionally."

"What? How do you not—"

"Look it's a long story. I don't have time right now. Did she say anything about Laughlin?"

Sal had told Vince not to probe too much but ever since he'd mentioned Laughlin, it killed him to think her mom might still be trying to set her up with the casino owner. He'd given Vince strict instructions to find out anything about *that* specifically. The more info Vince got him the more generous Sal would be with the use of the car. He didn't even feel rotten about bribing the kid. The past few weeks had been torturous not hearing anything about Grace. At this point he'd do anything for even the tiniest bit of information about her, especially about this.

"All she said is that it was a vacation Grace needed. They did the usual vacation stuff, swam, went to the lake, rented jet skis. She didn't say anything about the casino guy until…"

"Until what?"

"Sal, I feel like a jerk telling you, because she specifically asked me not to say anything to you about Grace."

Normally Sal would agree that prying like this was

wrong. But nothing had been normal in Sal's life since Grace had walked into it. His entire world had shifted and it would never be the same again. He stood up, feeling his patience thinning. The thought of Grace with the casino owner burned him up. "You wanna be able to use that car again, outside of to and from work?"

He heard Vince sigh. "This isn't right." There was a muffed sound then Vince spoke again. "She texted me on the way home. And yes I waited until I was home to read it." He sighed again, cutting deeper into Sal's patience. "I guess that guy's coming out this weekend and Grace is going out with him Friday night. She said Grace felt guilty about leaving her home alone since her mom and step-dad are also going so she actually suggested Rose and I do something Friday night."

A slow heat started up inside him and Sal welcomed it. The past few weeks had been nothing but agonizing pain mixed with guilt. Hearing that Grace was going out with this guy this soon after their break up, at least lessened some of that guilt. Even if Grace thought she was only *entertaining* him having a few drinks and dinner with him for her mom's sake, Sal saw the way the guy looked at her the night he came by to pick her up. He was expecting more. And now that she was free for the taking and more vulnerable than ever he wondered if she'd give in.

"Did she say where?" His words were as coarse as they felt coming out.

"No, but she did say Grace said it was a business date, so you don't have to get all pissed about it."

Sal didn't even know why he was asking. What was he going to do—show up enraged and demand to know why the girl whose heart he trampled on was on a date?

Still, she was *his* not too long ago and as far as his heart was concerned she still was damn it. The truth was even though the choppy memories he had of his night with Melissa gave every indication that he *had* slept with her, there was still no proof of it.

Hearing about Grace from such a close source after not hearing anything about her for weeks had rekindled that feeling inside him. That feeling Taylor had snuffed the day he'd gone back to their apartment again, willing to beg for her forgiveness. *Walk away*, Taylor had said. *Let her be.* As if it were really that simple.

"Anything else?" Sal paced back and forth on his patio, feeling more determined by the second.

"That's it. So you think I can use the car Friday night to hang out with Rose?"

Sal pinched the rim of his nose, closing his eyes. "What do you plan on doing Vin? I know you don't expect me to be okay with you going over and hanging out at her apartment when no one else is there."

"Nah, man. I keep telling you. She's not like that. We can go grab something to eat, then maybe catch a show. Which brings me to my next request."

Sal still didn't open his eyes. "What's that?"

"Can I get an advance on my pay?"

A chuckle escaped Sal, even though his lips could barely form a smile. "Yeah, but our deal still stands."

Vince exhaled heavily. "You better never tell her I told you any of this. Rose would be so pissed if she knew. It's just not right."

Sal walked into his house. "Save that conscience of yours for when you're alone with Rose and you get any funny ideas, Vince. You're gonna need it if you wanna stay in La Jolla for the summer."

This time it was Vincent who chuckled. "Trust me. After seeing her tonight, I ain't doing shit to risk getting sent home."

Sal knew that last sentence was meant to give him reassurance that Vincent wasn't going to step over any boundaries with Rose, but it did just the opposite.

*

Friday morning Sal got the call. It had been two days since Romero had any news for him—two days since Vince had told him about Grace's date tonight. He was just about to start his car and head to the restaurant when he saw Melissa's name on his caller ID. He almost let it go to voicemail but something made him want to talk to her. Maybe it was the desperation of any revelation that might possibly shed some hope on his situation with Grace. Whatever it was, not only did he answer, he decided he'd play nice.

"Good morning, Melissa."

She didn't speak for a moment. His civil voice obviously took her by surprise. "Good morning, Salvador."

If she'd made any attempt to conceal her slurred speech, it was a very poor one because she butchered his name. Sal wondered if she was drunk this early as she'd often been in the past when she left him messages or if it had anything to do with the heavy meds Romero had mentioned she was on. "Are you okay?"

"Of course I'm okay." The slurring was less prominent, until she spoke again. "Why wouldn't I be okay?"

"Just asking," he said, careful not to sound condescending. "To what do I owe the pleasure?"

She giggled then hiccupped and Sal deduced that it

must be liquor making her slur, but this early on a weekday morning? She *did* have a job. "I was just thinking about you... about *us*. I just never understood why it didn't work out for us. We were perfect for each other." She stopped and he heard her sniffle. "Can you just tell me what I did wrong?" On that last question her voice had been reduced to a high pitched whine.

If there was ever a moment to try to get the truth about that night in Vegas it was now and Sal sat up straight. "Sure I can tell you but first I'd like you to tell me something if that's okay."

She sniffled again then her voice was a near squeak. "What?"

"That night in Vegas is still foggy for me. I really wish I could remember more of it. Can you refresh my mind about exactly what happened? How did we end up in my room together?"

More sniffling and Sal held his breath wondering if she'd be honest. "You'll probably never remember, you were so drunk."

Sal feigned a weak laugh. "I know, I was feeling it for days after. That's why I was surprised I was able to text Grace that night but even more surprised when you said I'd been amazing the next morning."

Silence.

Sal gave it a few more seconds before speaking again. "Melissa?"

"It's your turn to answer my question, Sal." She was doing a better job of hiding the slurring, or maybe that last comment had sobered her up.

Sal squeezed the steering wheel, feeling a rage in him like none he'd ever felt, but he was too close to blow this. Had she really played him and concocted the whole thing? He had to stay calm—had to keep her talking. "I think maybe it was bad timing for us." It was a struggle to not speak through his teeth and he gulped big chunks of air to try and stay focused. "Maybe we can try again another time."

"What about Grace? Why wasn't the timing wrong for you and her?"

He recognized that venom in her voice. It was the same one from when she'd shown up at his place. He had to calm her down too if he was going to get anything more out of her. "Oh, it was. Things didn't work out for us either. It's this whole expanding the business thing. It has me real tied up right now. But tell me, Melissa. That night in Vegas... was I really that amazing or were you just saying that to make me feel good?"

The silence was like thunder. It took everything in him to not yell into the phone what he wanted to yell at the top of his lungs now. His life had been torn apart by what had happened in Vegas and now here was near proof that *nothing* had happened.

"It's okay, Melissa. You can tell me the truth. Maybe I could make it up to you."

"Really?" He could almost picture her smiling.

"Yeah, really. Just be honest."

"Well, I actually don't remember either, but since you'd always been amazing before I just thought—"

"Nothing happened. Did it Melissa?"

More silence followed by a nervous laugh was her response. Before she could say anything he added what he'd held in for a better part of their conversation. "You made the whole thing up didn't you?" His words were harsher with every breath he took. "You made me think I slept with you, so I'd break things off with Grace and when I didn't you made the pregnancy thing up too, didn't you?"

"You're crazy!" Her attempt to sound offended fell flat.

"No *you're* the crazy one." His heart nearly slammed through his chest as the reality of it really set in and he was yelling now. "Anyone that would go to these lengths has got to be a fucking crazy as shit mental case! And that's what you are!"

The line clicked and for the first time in all the times he'd talked to her over the phone she actually hung up first. He sat there trying to catch his breath, the rage burning through him at how stupid he'd been to fall for her shit. Not even what should have been delight at knowing he hadn't actually betrayed Grace did anything to calm him. Out of nowhere he heard a growl and he realized it had come from deep inside him.

Images of Grace's agonized face and thoughts of all the pain she'd gone through and for what? For *nothing*. Deep inside he'd known it all along. He could never do anything to hurt Grace. Not even in a drunken stupor. But even now this wasn't proof and that's what he'd need if he even had a prayer of Grace believing him because he knew Melissa sure as hell would never admit the truth.

After taking a few minutes to calm himself he did the only thing he could think of—called Romero.

*

Between her mother, Rose, then Joey and Taylor, Grace had been talked into letting her hair down and dressing up for her night out. She now sat nursing her drink in the bar area with all of them except Rose at The Voodoo Lounge, the *neat* nightclub her mother had told her about, in a tight little black dress and three inch heels.

Taylor and Joey had done a number on her hair and makeup and though she'd argued she was overdone, they'd been right. She fit right in with all the other sexy-as-hell, single women at the bar who were there to find a man. Only in her case that was the last thing on her mind. And though she might look the part she certainly wasn't feeling it.

Frank had yet to arrive and Grace hoped he'd be a no show. Of course her mother had made sure the chair next to Grace was the only one available for when he did arrive.

She took tiny sips, careful not to stir up any bad vibes in her stomach like she had earlier and had to rush to the ladies' room, but it'd turned out to be a false alarm. As the music around her blared and the flashing lights bounced all over the walls, Grace was still trying to get over the annoying fact that she was at her first night club with her mom and Ruben.

Doing a double take she turned to see Frank walking toward their table. It was almost as he'd had a makeover as well. Instead of the usual drab colored suits he wore he was in black jeans with a dark long sleeved, firm fitting cotton shirt. He'd cut his hair to shorter, much more stylish 'do. It was amazing how a few changes could make someone look so different. He even looked younger.

As he got closer, Grace noticed he carried two red roses. He handed her one as he reached her then gave the other to her mom. "You look fantastic, Grace," he said, taking the seat next to her. Even his cologne was alluring although he wore a bit too much.

"Thank you," she said softly then introduced him to

Taylor and Joey. They shook his hand. Joey bobbed his
eyebrows at Grace when Frank turned away to say
hello to Ruben.

She smiled but he *had* to know any interest in a romantic relationship with anybody would be the fur-
thest thing from her mind for a long, *long* time.

Frank leaned into her and whispered. "I hope the
rose didn't make you uncomfortable. I just couldn't
help myself when the guy outside selling them hit me
up."

"No, not at all," she said bringing it to her nose, and
smelled it with a smile. "That was sweet of you."

The waitress came by to take their orders though
Grace's drink was still nearly full. While Frank was distracted putting in his order in, Taylor leaned into her
and whispered in her ear. "Don't look now but there's
this girl who's been looking at you all night over by the
rail to my left. It's almost as if she'd trying to get your
attention. At first, I thought she might be looking at me
or Joey but her eyebrows nearly hit the ceiling when
Frank arrived and sat next to you. She's still looking
now, so be casual about it."

Grace nodded, smiling as if he'd just said something funny. She stirred her drink, glancing in the opposite direction Taylor said, then casually brought her
eyes back to the area Taylor meant. Her heart sank and
she felt her chest constrict when she saw her. Sofia
smiled and waved. The last thing she needed was a
reminder of that family. Immediately she felt the tension in her throat, but she smiled and waved back.

When she saw Sofia start toward her Grace stood
up alarmed that Sofia would come over and talk about
something that might upset her in front of Joey and
Taylor. She was trying so hard to convince them that

she was better now, but just seeing Sofia was added proof that nothing could be further from the truth. "I'll be back." She touched Taylor's shoulder as she stood up. "I know her."

Knowing that as soon as Joey saw Sofia, he'd remember her as Sal's sister, she smiled big at him to squash any possible indication of what she was really feeling. She met Sofia halfway and they hugged but Grace pulled away quickly afraid anything longer might make for a more emotional reunion.

"Hey! Oh my Gosh you look *hot!*" Sofia smiled, looking Grace up and down.

"You do, too. As usual." Grace tried to match her smile but simply couldn't. The tightness in her chest was a living thing. "What are you doing here?

"Eric is out of town for a few days, so," she turned back to the two girls standing nearby, "I decided to take a girls' night out. Something I so rarely do. They've been going on and on about this place since it opened." She glanced over to Grace's table. "What about you? New man in your life already?"

The very thought of a new man in her life *ever* was such a joke. But why let Sal and his family in on how pathetic she was? He'd obviously had no issues delving into new waters the moment he'd had one night away from her. Now that they'd been apart for this long, he was probably meticulously planning his future with Melissa and their child. Grace shrugged. "New friend."

Thankfully Sofia didn't ask more about Frank or bring up Sal. Instead she reiterated how good Grace looked then almost brought her to tears when she told her how much she was missed at the restaurant. Sofia must've seen the hurt in her eyes because she hugged her again this time holding onto her longer, making the tears that had gathered in Grace's eyes stream down her cheeks.

"She's not pregnant, Grace," Sofia whispered in her ear.

Grace froze, for a moment unable to breathe.

Sofia pulled away. "I don't know if that changes anything for you but—"

"It doesn't."

Grace would never get past the fact that the moment Sal had been away from her, his supposed love for her hadn't been enough to fight off temptation. And that temptation would always be there, especially for a man like him. Women would always throw themselves at him. Her heart would never survive that kind of betrayal again.

Sofia stared at her, the sadness in her eyes as deep as what Grace felt in her heart. She wiped the tears away and shook her head. "It doesn't, Sof." She forced a very weak smile which made no sense at all because the warm tears still slid down her cheeks. "It was good to see you again. I gotta get back." She motioned to her table. "They're waiting for me."

She turned around, taking a very deep breath and wiped her eyes gently, mindful of all the makeup she wore. Joey and Taylor both noticed as soon as she sat down but she waved them away with a smile, taking her compact out of her purse to assess the damage— not as bad as she thought. Once she cleaned it up she did her best to smile at Joey and Taylor who were both looking at her very concerned. "Who wants to dance?"

Frank was immediately on his feet. "Let's go."

Even as she stood and felt Frank's hand slide into hers, the tightness in her chest nearly suffocated her. "C'mon let's all go."

Ruben and her mother didn't budge. She knew this wasn't their kind of music but Joey sprung out of his chair, looking very relieved that Grace had snapped out of it so quickly. And here he thought he knew her so well.

CHAPTER 32

Romero's connection still hadn't had any luck with the surveillance tape from the casino. But after Sal let him in on his conversation with Melissa and told him how convinced he was now that nothing had actually happened that night, Romero had an idea.

Since Romero had so many clients who hired him to get proof their spouses were cheating he'd long ago acquired ways for tracking text messages and emails. If Melissa had texted or emailed even one person to tell them about what she'd done Sal would have his proof. Romero said he'd get on it ASAP, but he still had his guy trying to track down video of that night at the casino.

Sal had been at the restaurant reading through his emails when Alex walked into the back office where he sat. "Any news from Romero yet?"

"Nothing new," he said, without looking away from the computer screen.

Sal had filled him in on the theories about the possibility that nothing may have happened. Alex was as optimistic about that fixing things as Sofia was.

"Have you heard from Melissa?"

Before he said anything to Alex or Sofia he wanted to have some kind of proof. He knew Alex and Sofia would be all about him going straight to Grace with the news, but he needed more. He didn't want to open up any more wounds, before he knew he could back up his story with something solid. Still he thought Alex would be a little less gung-ho about it than Sofia so he spun around in his chair to face him as Alex stood there, pulling a restaurant polo over his head.

"She called me yesterday morning."

"For what?"

"She was drunk but I almost got her to admit nothing happened between me and her in Vegas."

Alex's eyes opened wide. "What do you mean almost?"

Sofia walked in and Sal bit his tongue but it was too late. Alex pushed on. "Did she actually say nothing happened?"

Sofia's eyebrows pinched. "Who?"

"Melissa," Alex smiled, the excitement in his eyes said it all he *was* going to be gung-ho. "She called Sal and almost admitted nothing happened in Vegas."

Sofia's eyes immediately lit up. "You're kidding me. What did she say? Have you called Grace?"

Damn it. This was exactly what he'd hoped to avoid. "No. She didn't say it exactly but her reaction to my questioning pretty much said it all. She went quiet and when I all out accused her of making the whole thing up she hung up on me. She's never been one to walk away or end a conversation with me. She's always done just the opposite."

"I knew it. I knew it!" Sofia held her hand up and high fived Alex then held her hand up for Sal. "So you called Grace?"

Sal didn't even raise his hand. "No."

"What?" This was exactly what he expected from Sofia. She brought her hand down looking almost disgusted. "Why not?"

"Because I still have no proof. Grace isn't gonna buy this shit. If the tables were turned I'm not sure I would either."

"But you have to at least tell her there is a very high probability, Sal. What if you wait too long and she... you know moves on?"

Sal noticed Sofia's level of a excitement take a sudden nose dive with that last question. "I'm working on it Sof. Romero's doing some more digging for me. I'm hoping he'll have something for me soon."

"Grace won't be moving on, Sof," Alex said with a frown. "You didn't see her the day Melissa told her about Vegas."

Sal's heart ached at the thought. Her agonized expression at Joey's and Taylor's when she told him she hated him would forever haunt him.

"You wanna bet?"

His thoughts were still so consumed in the memories of that horrible day that Sofia's words barely registered, but he glanced at her as she pulled her phone out of her purse. "Does this look like someone who's not moving on?"

Both Sal and Alex waited as Sofia's fingers tapped and glided over her touch screen phone then flipped it around for Sal to see the picture on the screen. He reached over slowly, staring at the picture of an almost unrecognizable Grace on the screen.

"That was last night at the Voodoo lounge. She was there with someone and he seemed very smitten from where I was standing."

Slapped with the overpowering feelings of raw jealously, Sal pulled his eyes from Sofia's phone to look at her. "What do you mean?"

Alex took the phone from Sal. "Oh damn, this is Gracie?"

"Slide over to the next picture and you'll see what I

mean."

Alex slid his finger over the screen and Sal saw his expression immediately go hard. "What the fuck? Who's the guy?"

Sal grabbed the phone out of Alex's hands. In the picture Grace was on the dance floor, smiling at a guy who had his arm around her waist. A guy he didn't recognize as the older guy with the roses who'd come to pick her up that night. Sal's insides were ablaze. "Did you talk to her?"

"Yeah. I asked her if she'd moved on already and she didn't say yes but she didn't deny it either, Sal. She said he was a friend but she looked spectacular. Like she's ready to move on. Why else would she be at a nightclub all done up with another guy?"

Sal stared at the picture of Grace and the other guy, feeling ready to explode. Business date his ass. "What do you want me to do, Sof?" His gruff voice did nothing to hide what he was feeling and he didn't even care anymore. He was done playing the part of the in-control brother. Seeing Grace in the arms of another man made him feel things he didn't even know he was capable of feeling. "I don't even have her number anymore and she won't see me. She begged me to stay away from her."

Julie stuck her head in the door. "They need one of you out here to sign for a delivery."

Sofia frowned, shaking her head, but turned toward the door. "I got it."

Even though he didn't care about being in-control anymore Sal still tried to collect himself. He needed to gather his thoughts. He swiped Sofia's phone again and the next photo made him suck in a breath. It was of Grace and the guy walking off the dance floor holding hands. She was looking down but the guy gazed at her with an undeniable look of desire in his eyes. He tried swiping again but it was the last picture on her phone.

"Fuck!" He tossed the phone as if he held it any longer it would burn a hole through his hand. Either that or he'd be buying Sofia a new phone since he had a very strong urge to fling it across the room.

Alex picked it up. "Dude. Valerie begged me once to stay away from her. I was stupid enough to do it for over a year." Alex stared down at the phone, frowning. "Yep. This is what happens. Damn she looks different."

"Hot is what she looked like," Sofia said, walking back into the room. "I told her about Melissa not being pregnant."

Sal felt the hair on the back of his neck stand as he turned and stared at his sister. "And what did she s-ay?"

Sofia chewed the corner of her lip. "Obviously she's still hurt, but I really don't think you should wait on this, Sal. That guy she was with last night was totally into her and I gotta tell you." Sofia turned and opened the cabinet, giving her back to Sal. "She seemed sad for a moment there when I brought up Melissa but she got over it fairly quickly. This could be her rebound guy you know. Even if she is just using him to help her get over you, he certainly didn't look like he'd mind being used and abused by the suddenly hot Gracie."

His jaw hurt from how hard he'd been clenching it the entire time Sofia spoke. If Sofia's phone had still been in his hands it'd be in a million pieces now for as tight as he was gripping the arm of the chair. "But she said he's just a friend."

Sofia turned to him making a face. "Yeah, you think she'd actually tell me if she was doing anything else with him?" She pulled her apron around her. "Though her behavior around him last night sure made it look like she is."

Unable to sit anymore, Sal stood up, nearly sputtering his words. "What was she doing?" He wasn't even sure why he was asking. Just the thought crushed heavy into his chest like a freight train. Did he really want to know?

Sofia smirked. "Not much more than what you saw in those pictures." She patted Sal's arm. "She just looked like she was having a good time with him. That's all. But it made me nervous, Sal. If he can make her forget about you even if it is only for an evening, that could be how it starts."

"She's right, man," Alex added, still looking down at Sofia's phone. "This would make me nervous as shit. Hell, I ain't you and I'm nervous for you. You gotta move, Sal. Before this guy does."

As tempted as Sal was to look at the photos again he resisted grabbing the phone from Alex. Even another glance at the asshole with her in the pictures and he was certain Sofia's phone would go flying across the room. Instead he pulled his own phone out of his holster.

"You calling her?" Sofia's bright eyes were hopeful.

"No, I don't have her number, Sof." But they were right. He had to do something. "I'm calling Romero." He walked past her and out the door with the phone at his ear. "I'll be outside."

He needed air—needed to breathe. If he stood in that room any longer thinking about Grace and the guy she'd been with things were going to start flying in every direction. For the first time Sal understood now how Alex's temper could torpedo in an instant. He flexed his empty hand as he walked out the back door then paced, waiting for Romero to answer. When the call went to voicemail he hung up and dialed Vincent. He answered on the first ring. "Hey Sal."

"Did Rose say anything else about this *business* date Grace was on last night?" The more he thought about it the hotter he got. He pulled on his collar and loosened his tie. His next call would be to cancel the meeting he had scheduled with the same investing group he'd b-een in the middle of negotiating with when Alex had called to tell him about Melissa showing up at the restaurant and dropping the bomb on Grace.

He didn't care that day that he'd blown them off the moment he realized what had happened and he didn't care now.

Vincent exhaled loudly, an indication that Rose had said something. "Out with it. Vin. Is she seeing this guy?"

God that pissed him off. Sure she was under the impression he'd betrayed her but it hadn't even been a month. He couldn't even begin to think about seeing anyone else and she was out dancing with this fucker? And from what Sofia said, enjoying it?

"She didn't say much about it last night," Vincent said. "But this morning she texted me to say they're going house hunting all day today. The guy she went out with last night I guess is buying the house with them."

Sal stopped his pacing, his eyebrows shooting up. "They're buying a house together?"

"I guess. She said he was going because he'd be part owner."

Sal could barely bring himself to ask the next question but he had to know. Speaking through his teeth he barely got the words out. "Is he moving in with her?"

"Whoa. I don't know about that. I can ask her if you want. But dude aren't you having a kid with—"

"No I'm not!" His voice a near roar now and there was little he could do about it. "Ask her and call me back."

"I'll text her then forward you whatever she responds. I'm not supposed to be using my mom's minutes. But Sal... "

"What Vincent?" Sal's patience was completely shot now.

"I was just gonna say, it may take a while because I can't just ask her you know? It'll be too suspicious. I'll have to work my way to the question."

"I'll be waiting."

After hanging up with Vincent Sal paced for a few more minutes outside. He knew there was no way Grace could be sleeping with this guy, but what other incentive would he have to buy her and her family a fucking house? He tried making sense of it. The guy owned a casino in Laughlin. Why would he be looking into moving in with Grace in California?

Once he felt calm enough at least to speak without growling he called and cancelled his meeting. There was no way he'd be able to concentrate on anything now.

He tried Romero again. This time he answered.

"You got anything yet?"

"I was just going through some of her email. But fuck she has a lot. I was able to filter out the ones that were just business. All the court crap."

Sal ran his fingers through his hair. "Doesn't she have a personal email?"

"Yeah, problem is, she uses that one for all her court shit too. But I'm getting hot. I found a couple between

Melissa and her cousin—I guess your friend's wife."

Sal winced remembering how he'd skipped out on Jason's wedding. After everything that happened he didn't even want to be in the same room with Melissa and since she was a bridesmaid she would be there for sure. He'd lied through his teeth, telling Jason he was sick as a dog but he knew Jason had still been disappointed. He hadn't talked to him since. "Kat?"

"Katherine? That's what the email says."

"Yeah, that's her."

"So I'm sifting through this shit and your name has come up but only to ask if you'd be in Vegas. The report for the text messaging just came through; I was getting ready to switch over to that. Maybe I'll have better luck there. It's huge though. I can only imagine the amount of garbage I'm gonna have to go through."

"Dude, you gotta find something. I need this *now*."

Romero promised he'd do his best and Sal hung up with him, the frustration weighing even heavier. Then he noticed he had a text—from Vincent.

He took a deep breath before reading it. The first part was Vincent's text to Rose where he cleverly asked her if she was blowing him off and if she really needed to go with her sister and her new *boyfriend* to look for *their* new place.

Her first response, although she didn't comment on the boyfriend inference or the "their place" comment, was somewhat reassuring. She said Grace didn't like to spend that much time with him alone so she'd asked her to come with them. Sal stared at the rest of the text conversation feeling sick to his stomach.

Vince: *?? Why would she go out with someone she doesn't like being alone with?*

Rose: *It's complicated. All I can say is he's going to a* *big part of our lives now.*

Vince: *Really? So it's getting serious?*

Rose: *Something like that. We're here I'll ttyl!*

Rose: *Oh and remember don't you dare say anything to Sal!*

The last part of the text was from Vince addressed to Sal.

You better never tell Grace I forwarded you this. I already feel like I'm going straight to hell. Can't tell you how many times I've assured her I would never pass on any info to you man! This is some bullshit! >=(

Sal stood there still staring at the text, his heart pounding in his chest. *He's going to be a big part of our lives now.* What the hell did that mean?

CHAPTER 33

There was just too much excitement going on this w-eekend — that's what Grace kept telling everyone — and herself. From her Friday night out to her long day Saturday with Frank. Though she didn't admit that seeing Sofia had been the most detrimental to her already fragile state. It only confirmed what she already knew. That she was nowhere near even beginning to get over Sal.

Her tiresome day of house hunting Saturday had also taken its toll. The heat wasn't helping matters either. It was no wonder why she kept having dizzy spells. Somehow she couldn't convince anyone that she was fine. She'd just been a little winded yesterday when her head spun after getting out of Frank's car and she had to hold on to the door for a few minutes before she could walk. She'd seen the fear in Rose's face and no amount of reassuring could persuade her not to worry.

Frank had been there the entire weekend. Her mom had everything to do with that. She'd invited him back over on Sunday. Grace had been lying in bed still when her mother walked in to tell her.

"I was with him Friday night, and most of the day yesterday." Grace argued. "I'm sorry I'm not spending today with him, too, mom. He's gonna get the wrong idea. This is a business partnership and nothing more."

"I know this and so does he, Grace. We're just being hospitable."

"Well I think he's beginning to get the wrong idea."

She regretted now that Friday night she hadn't protested when Frank slipped his hand into hers several times. It just didn't seem like a big deal walking off and on the dance floor. "You can be hospitable for the both of us today. I'm going over to Joey and Taylor's." She sat up and immediately felt lightheaded. *Shit.*

She glanced over to where Rose sat on a bean bag in the corner of her room glad she was too engrossed in her texting to notice Grace needed a moment to focus while the room finally stood still for her.

Her mother was busy still rambling about why Grace should reconsider staying and hanging out with Frank for a least a little while but she didn't want to hear it anymore. She stood up slowly and carefully, hoping Rose wouldn't notice anything.

Seeing her mother cross her arms in a huff as she walked past her did nothing to slow her down. She was done with this conversation. The only good thing that had come of this weekend was that they finally narrowed their choices down to two restaurant/homes that both Grace and her mother agreed were acceptable. Both were in Chula Vista which meant Rose wouldn't have to change schools.

The agreement with Frank had been that he'd help Grace and her mom get the restaurant going but eventually, once the restaurant took off, she and her mother would buy him out, leaving them the sole owners. Her mother still insisted that there were no ulterior motives and that Frank was doing this out of the kindness of his heart and a few years of extra profit brought in by the restaurant was incentive enough.

The fact that he was supposed to go back to Laughlin yesterday morning and he'd hung around a few extra days when talk of them spending the day together

Saturday had come up, and now he'd happily agreed to coming over to spend yet another day with her instead of going back to check on his casino said it all. Besides Grace wasn't blind. She'd seen from their very first night out, the way he'd looked at her. His gazes were becoming increasingly uncomfortable. And she wasn't the only one who'd noticed it either. Taylor was very keen about noticing *everything.* Just like he'd noticed Sofia watching her at the nightclub, he also noticed and even asked if she thought it was wise to partner up with a man who was obviously interested in doing more than just business with her.

It got her thinking and it was one of the reasons why she was getting the heck out of there before Frank arrived. But not the only reason. She had something else she needed to finally face. Something that had crossed her mind a few times in the last week but she hadn't allowed herself to seriously consider.

If it weren't for the fact that she knew Rose would more than jump at the chance to be able to spend time with Vincent, Grace would almost feel guilty about suggesting she make plans with him again. He was actually coming in handy, not only to keep Rose company Friday night but today as well. Normally she'd balk at her little sister spending so much time with him but she needed to talk to Joey and Taylor without Rose there and she knew her sister would tag along rather than stay home with her mother and Ruben to entertain Frank. So Grace agreed to let her go to the beach with him today but only for a few hours until she took care of what she needed to.

An hour later, despite her mother's protests, Grace and Rose walked out at the same time. Vince had texted Rose that he was just around the corner. She felt guilty when she saw Frank pull up and park behind his own Cadillac. The very vehicle she'd be using to flee his company today.

"Oh God. I should've left sooner."

Rose glanced at Frank who'd already gotten out of his car and was on his way to meet them. "What are y-ou gonna tell him?"

"That I have errands to run," Grace whispered as he got closer. "I'm *not* staying and hanging out with him again. Mom's nuts."

Suddenly she regretted that in her haste to rush out before Frank arrived she'd neglected to eat anything because a wave of lightheadedness swept over her a-gain just as he reached them.

"Going somewhere?" he asked.

Trying hard to ignore the fact that the dizzy spell she was experiencing was one of the worse she had to date, she smiled. "Yeah, I have a few errands I need to run today. I'll be gone all day but my mom and Ruben are up there waiting for you."

Vince pulled up in the Jetta, reawakening the pain of her heartache but she was still relieved to see him because Rose immediately waved goodbye to them and walked away. As soon as she turned her back Grace reached out for Frank's arm, needing the sup-port before she fell. "You okay?"

He brought his arms around her as Grace leaned against him, willing the spell to go away. What the hell was wrong with her?

"Maybe you shouldn't be driving like this."

Grace looked up at him, his face close enough she could smell the mouthwash on his breath, then glanced over to where Rose now sat in the front seat of the jetta and both she and Vincent were looking their way. She managed a smile before they drove away. "No I'm okay." The spell was already passing, but she did need to get out of there. Now more than ever. "I'll be fine. I just skipped breakfast but I'll grab something."

"You sure?" Frank searched her eyes, his hand still firmly on her elbow.

"Yes, I'm sure." She smiled, fishing the keys out of her purse. "I'll be fine as soon as I grab a bite." His eyes still seemed unconvinced. "It's the first thing I'll do. I promise."

Okay so she lied when she said it would be the first thing she would do, but it was for good reason. Some things were more important at the moment. She waved as she drove away feeling that familiar tightness in her throat. She didn't think it possible and she prayed that she was wrong. Her health hadn't been an issue in years. Unbelievably life could be getting even more complicated for her now.

Of course it would be Grace's luck that there'd be three other people waiting to use the blood pressure machine at the pharmacy. A sad indication of her n-eighborhood's status level. Like her, most probably didn't have insurance and had to rely on the free re-sources available to them.

She walked around through the vitamin aisles. For weeks she'd suspected her dizzy spells were a sure sign that her anemia was back. She'd suffered from it when she was younger but it had gotten better and sin-ce she'd read that it was curable with good diet and i-ron supplements, she made sure she ate well and took her pills. Unfortunately, she stopped worrying too mu-ch about it and began neglecting taking the iron sup-plements after a few years of zero symptoms.

Shock she was told, was also something that could

bring on the sudden drop in blood pressure, something she so often had when her anemia was at its worst. Nothing could have shocked her more than finding out about Sal and Melissa. She was certain that's what had started it all, and now she'd hardly had an appetite since the break up. And the last thing on her mind lately had been to take iron supplements, in fact she'd run out years ago and with no symptoms she hadn't bothered replacing them.

After grabbing a generic brand of iron pills she walked back to where there was only one person waiting for the machine now.

When it was her turn she sat down and even though she'd done this many times before she was nervous. The instructions on the machine said to push the stop button if she began to feel dizzy or faint. Grace remembered once becoming so lightheaded while taking the test she'd hit the stop button in a panic. She *already* felt dizzy and she hadn't even hit the start button. But she had to know the severity — had to know if she was going to have to bite the bullet and use the insurance she was sure Alex hadn't cancelled yet. Her anemia could get bad. And with the frequency of the dizziness she'd been feeling lately, this couldn't be good. She couldn't take a chance of falling into that kind of illness now that she was getting ready to start her own business.

Taking a deep breath she pressed the start button. The machine did its thing and began to squeeze around her arm. Her hand was ready to push the stop button but it happened too fast. An incredible wave of lightheadedness swept over her and before she could react everything went black.

It took Grace a few moments after the two unfamiliar faces staring at her came into focus to realize where she was and what had happened. She sat up quickly from the chair she was slumped in, immediately regretting it as a sudden jolt of nausea and lightheadedness threatened to take her out again.

"Sit back," the older man in a white coat ordered.

How long had she been out that there was a doctor already there?

"You think we should call the paramedics?" the older plain clothed lady said.

"No!" There was no way she could afford a trip to the emergency room. "I'll be fine. My blood pressure is just a little low and—"

"Yeah," The man nodded. "That'll do it. How's your head feeling?"

"My head?" Grace reached up and within a second felt a small bump on her forehead.

"That'll probably turn into a good sized knot for a few days from where you slumped over and your head clunked the machine. That's what got our attention." He motioned toward the pharmacist station and she realized he was a pharmacist not a doctor.

"How long have I been out?"

"Just a couple of minutes. We had just rushed over when you started coming to."

They let her call someone, refusing to let her drive. She called home figuring it would be the fastest since Joey and Taylor were further away. When she was finally able to walk around without feeling like she was going to pass out she grabbed the iron pills and walked down the dreaded aisle where she knew they had the one other thing she needed to buy. She hurried and paid for her things before her mother could arrive and see. But she should've known. Her mother didn't even bother to come. She sent Frank by himself.

"How are you feeling?" he rushed to where she sat waiting, the overly concerned expression making her a little uncomfortable.

"I'm fine, really," she said, grabbing her things and standing up. "I've always had low blood pressure. Using that machine was not a good idea today."

He continued with the concerned questioning most of the way back to her apartment until she changed the subject. "I think my mom and I finally decided on which place we should make an offer on. Did she tell you?"

"Yeah she did. The one on the corner. That's kind of a busy spot. You sure you wouldn't mind living on such a busy corner?"

Grace glanced up at her old building. "Anything is better than this place."

Frank parked and she got out of the car immediately feeling lightheaded as she stood. She'd noticed that's when it was the worst; after sitting for a while and then suddenly standing. Frank was at her side in an instant taking her by the arm then bringing his arm around her shoulder as they walked the rest of the way into her apartment. Not only was it uncomfortable, it was getting annoying. She moved her purse over to her other shoulder as they reached the stairs and was able to casually move his arm off her. "I'm fine Frank. Thanks."

He finally got the hint and let her walk the rest of the way up without him holding her arm. Once inside she explained to everyone about what happened, adding that they need not worry she would be fine. Although she wasn't really feeling hungry she boiled an egg, nibbled a few crackers and forced herself to drink a V8. Then she took her vitamin supplements. She needed to get better. The last thing she wanted was for Rose to see her like this.

After eating she walked to her room and pulled out what she'd purchased at the pharmacy and stared at it. Rose would be home in a few hours. Grace had told her she wanted her home early so she only had short while before she got home. She did what she'd planned on doing at Joey and Taylor's then called them immediately after to explain why she wasn't going over after all. "I'm better now but I wanna get some sleep before Rose gets back so I'll can come over tomorrow. You'll be there right?"

"Yes, but I really wish you'd stop being so stubborn and get your butt to the doctor already."

Grace was silent for a moment. "Grace?"

"Yeah. Don't worry, I'm seriously considering seeing a doctor now."

"Good. You should've gone a long time ago."

"Is Taylor going to be there tomorrow when I come over?"

"Yeah, why?"

Grace shrugged. "I just want you both there."

"I don't think he has plans but even if he does I'm sure if I tell him you want him here, he'll cancel."

Grace had to smile. She was so lucky to have them. "Thank you, Joey. I'll see you then."

*

With his anxiety reaching a new level, Sal needed the distraction Sunday. He was glad Alex suggested he go with him to the gym. He'd been neglecting working out for some time now and working off some stress did him good.

Romero hadn't had much luck with Melissa's texts yet but he said there was still a shit load he needed to go through. The waiting was the worst.

He headed back to his parent's house instead of going home after, with the excuse that he hadn't been over in a while but really he was anxious to talk to Vincent. He was tired of the short texted answers. Sal knew Vince had spent the day with Rose and he'd pushed up the urgency that he find out more about Grace. He wasn't sure how much longer he could hold back before confronting her about what the fuck was going on between her and the casino guy.

It was irrational to think he had any right. He knew this. But he'd never felt such desperation in his life. He had to do something. There was no way in hell he could stand by and watch the love of his life just slip away like this for nothing. All because some psychotic bitch had come up with a way to split them.

He sucked in a hard breath at the thought that Melissa may've pushed Grace into the arms… the bed of another man. Any relief he'd gotten from his workout flew out the window in an instant. A roar snuck up from inside him again as he slammed his fist against the steering wheel. That was it. Proof or not if Vince didn't have any answers for him today he'd be getting them for himself. He wasn't waiting on anyone anymore. Fuck the casino guy — Grace was *his* damn it.

At that very moment reality beat down on him like a mallet. As much as he hated to admit it, he *did* think just like his brothers when it came to women. Still it wasn't just women he argued with himself. This was love. Since he'd never been in love until now, he'd never understood his brothers' crazed thinking when it came to their wives. It was as plain as the rage he tried to mollify now—he got it—no mistake about it. He completely understood now.

With the heated blood racing through his veins he stepped out of his car and walked to his parent's front door with a purpose. Greeting his mother, who was more than happy to see him calmed him some but very little. He followed her, by request of course, to the kitchen. His mother was determined he'd never leave her house unfed.

His mom informed him Vince was in the garage and Sal promised he'd be back in a few to eat, walking out the back door toward the garage. Vince had the radio on and Sal turned it down when he walked in. Vince sat up on the weight bench when he saw Sal.

"You're not supposed to be lifting without someone to spot you," Sal said, but before Vince could respond he added, "did you find out anything else?"

He saw Vince take a deep breath and then frown, making Sal's heart beat even harder.

"According to Rose she's been telling me they're just doing business together and since they're business partners he's going to be around a lot now but…"

Sal waited while Vince seemed to ponder on his next words. His normal patience was gone now. It'd been gone since Grace walked out. "But what, Vince?"

"I don't know. I saw something today and even Rose couldn't explain it."

Sal gulped, waiting.

"I got there today just as the dude picked up Grace.

They were both outside…"

She'd been with him all weekend? Sal could hardly stand it anymore. "I don't have time for this shit, Vince. Just spit it out."

"Well," Vince scratched his head, unbelievably still stalling. "Rose started to say the guy wasn't there for Grace. Grace was supposedly on her way out by herself and he was just visiting her parents but then…" He took another annoying deep breath and looked away from Sal's glaring eyes. "It seemed they were about to kiss until Grace looked up and saw us watching. I drove away after that and Rose just shrugged, saying she didn't know what that had been about. As far as she knew Grace wasn't at all interested in him but we both knew what we saw."

Sal was having a hard time getting any words out. His stomach had bottomed out at the very thought of Grace almost kissing someone else. "What do you mean it almost seemed? What did you see exactly?"

His young cousin frowned apparently uncomfortable about the question but Sal didn't care. He needed to know. "I don't know. I just saw what happens when someone is about to kiss. He put his arms around her and their faces came dangerously close until she looked up and saw us watching."

The visual served only to further the anxiety and rage Sal was already feeling. "Did Rose say *anything* else? I don't care how insignificant."

Vince shook his head. "No. She changed the subject after that, but later when we were at the beach I brought it up casually, asking if she knew where they were moving to. She said she was pretty sure they were staying in Chula Vista. Then I asked if the dude was moving in with them and she said she didn't think so."

This was ridiculous. "How can she not know?"

"Well she'd seemed pretty sure about everything between Grace and that guy but after today... I did notice she was quiet for a while there after we drove away. Like it had surprised her, too. So maybe Grace is keeping something from her." Vincent's face soured suddenly. "Maybe Grace suspects you might be making me pump Rose for info. Damn, I hope she doesn't figure it out."

"She won't." Sal began to walk away then turned back. "So that's it? Nothing else?"

Vincent shook his head. With that, Sal was off on a mission. Grace may think he slept with someone else but the fact remained he hadn't. Whether or not he could prove that now, didn't matter anymore. All that mattered now is that he stop this... *thing* she had going with the casino guy. He had to do something now. Alex's words slammed into him. *Make a move now before this guy does.* Maybe he already had. *Fuck!* He hurried into the kitchen where his mom was just serving something on a plate. "Whatever it is, mom, make it to go."

"What? You're leaving already?"

"I gotta go. There's something I need to do."

His mother looked so disappointed he felt guilty but the urgency he felt now was unrelenting. "I'm sorry, mom. This can't wait."

He thought about calling Romero when he got in his car then decided not to. He was done waiting on everyone else. It was time to take matters into his own hands. Just as he put the phone down in the cup holder it rang—Jason. Not exactly the person Sal wanted to speak at that particular moment but he hadn't talked to him since the day he called to tell him he wouldn't be at the wedding.

In no mood to answer he let it go to voicemail. Jason never left messages unless it was important. Sal would call him later when he was feeling more up to it. For now he had more important things to think about.

He'd only driven half a block when his phone went off notifying him of a voicemail. Frowning, Sal hit the buttons to the prompts for his voicemail and set the phone back down on speaker. A few seconds later the message started but it wasn't Jason that spoke it was Kat.

"Sal this is Katherine. I need to talk to you. It's about Melissa. She's been in the hospital all weekend. She overdosed on her medication. The family thinks it was accidental but I know it wasn't. Jason didn't want me to call you and I know you want nothing to do with her, but I had to. I really need to talk to you. Please call me back as soon as you get the message."

Sal pulled over and sat there even after the call ended, numb from the news. From the moment he heard overdose thoughts of his conversation with her Friday morning came to him. The way he'd gone off on her and worse—he called her a mental case. He rewound the message to make absolute certain he'd heard right. This was the *last* thing he needed right now.

CHAPTER 34

Sal braced himself as he waited for Kat to answer the phone. She did on the second ring. "Sal?"

"Yeah, what's going on?"

"You heard my message right?"

"I did."

"First of all I want you to know, because Jason was upset with me about this. I swear to you I had no idea she was on anti-depressants or that she had any of the issues that we found out about today. Growing up we knew she was a problem child. She ran away a few times but since she was an only child we all thought it was the same old thing every time. Melissa was an attention whore, always had been. And she was a teenager, everyone said it would pass. It did or so we thought but until today my aunt had never said anything about her being on meds. Apparently she's had diagnosed psychological issues since middle school but my aunt and uncle never told anyone.

"Anyway like in the past my aunt was going to keep this to herself too until she broke down this morning because Melissa still hasn't woken up . She couldn't take it anymore and called my mom sobbing. She told us about how they'd found her in her apartment Friday after her work called to tell them she'd never showed up or called and they hadn't got a hold of her. She was out of it when they found her but still semi-conscious. I was totally buying the accidental overdose thing until my aunt said..." Kat's voice gave, and Sal heard her soft cries.

He held the phone tight not sure what to say to her.

Then she spoke again. "My aunt said she repeated the same thing twice before she completely passed out, 'Don't hate me, Sal.' And that's when I knew. Her overdose was no accident." She sniffed but was in more control of her speech now. "Jason didn't want to involve you in this. He refused to call you when I asked him to but he finally gave in and said I could if I wanted to. I know it's a lot to ask but I just think maybe if she heard your voice you know. She's been out for almost three days now and —"

"What hospital?" Sal started the ignition on the car.

Kat seemed surprised but grateful and gave him the information. The entire way to the hospital Sal didn't know what to think. He didn't even want to imagine the possibility of Melissa dying and having to know the last conversation he had with her was probably what threw her over the edge. He knew she was on meds damn it. He should've taken that into consideration before he went off on her.

Kat met him at the entrance. Her face was worn and pale and her pink eyes were an indication of the crying she'd been doing. "Thank you so much for coming."

"Not a problem." He said with a gulp.

"Your timing is perfect. No one knows I asked you to come. And they all just left to grab something to eat. Only Jason knows and he left to get us something to eat, too. I told them all I wanted to stay." They walked quickly down a corridor. "It's better that they don't know. My aunt would make a huge deal if she knew what I suspected."

She stopped before they got to the ICU. "Whatever happens Sal. Jason wanted me to be sure to tell you,

I'm in no way blaming you. She's always had issues I just never knew the extent until now. The only reason I asked you to come was because I thought maybe, just maybe it would help bring her out of this. The doctors said they won't know anything for days."

Sal shook his head. His conversation with Melissa Friday morning was still repeating itself in his head over and over. They walked in and the reality of it struck him when he saw her. She was hooked up to so many tubes and she didn't look anything like the perfectly groomed Melissa he'd always seen.

"Melissa," Kat whispered next to the bed. She touched Melissa's arm. "Sal is here. He wanted to come by and see how you were doing."

Kat looked at him from across the bed and nodded. Sal took the few steps to near Melissa's bedside. "Hey, Melissa." Almost instantly there was a flinch in Melissa's eyelids. Sal looked at Kat. She was wide eyed and brought her hand to her mouth. He was almost afraid to say anything else but Kat's expression pleaded with him.

"I uh… was worried, but I know you're strong." They waited watching anxiously but there was no more movement.

Kat touched her arm again. "I'll give you two some privacy."

Sal had no idea what else to say. All he knew is he wouldn't be in there with her long. He was beginning to think this was a mistake. Maybe him coming today would give Melissa the idea that this kind of thing is what she needed to do to bring him to her.

As soon as Kat walked out he decided he knew what he wanted to say. "Listen. I don't hate you okay? I was mad but I understand now that… you weren't

well. I get it. And I want to make sure you know that.
You should just focus on getting well. Don't worry
about anything else." He squeezed her fingers and for
a moment he thought he felt her move them then nothing. "Goodbye, Melissa." He wanted that to sound as
final as possible. "I know you'll find happiness, but get
well first."

He walked out and an anxious Kat stood outside.
"Did she move again?"

Sal shook his head, wanting nothing more than to
get out of there as soon as possible. After speaking
with Kat for a bit longer he finally said goodbye and
left before Jason got back. He'd wanted to wait for him
and apologize again for not making it to his wedding.
Instead he apologized to Kat and left. He just couldn't
stand being there anymore.

When he got back to the restaurant Sofia was a little
too excited to see him. "Where've you been? We've
been trying to get a hold of you. How come you're not
answering your phone?"

Sal patted the phone on his holster as he walked to
the back room and remembered he'd put it on silent
before walking into the ICU. "I forgot to take my
phone off silent. Why? What's up?"

He walked into the back room. Romero and Alex
both sat at the desk. "Dude!" Romero said when he
saw him. "Where've you been?"

"Why? What's going on?"

"You should have a seat," Sofia who had followed
him to the back room said.

Sal turned to her then back at Alex who shook his
head. A feeling of dread began to come over him but
when he saw Romero smirk he knew it couldn't be
about Grace.

"What is it?"

Sofia pushed the chair next to Romero in front of the computer. "Romero came through. As always. Have a seat."

Sal glanced at her then sat and watched as Romero clicked a couple of icons opening up one that started a video.

"I got more than just proof that you didn't do shit that night. I got proof that *she* did more than we thought."

The video started panning out across certain areas of the bar where they'd hung out. There was a shot of a group of girls then Romero slowed it down and froze on a girl—Melissa. She was doing something with a shot glass, her back was turned away from the other girls as if to shield it.

"So let's go to another angle." Romero typed something in and there was the same shot from a different angle. "You see here?" He stopped it and zoomed in but the picture got blurry. "So we focus this," he said typing more stuff in and suddenly the picture was clear. Romero slowed it down so you could see exactly what she was doing in slow motion.

Sal sat up when he saw what she was doing. She'd opened a capsule and poured a little of what was in it into the shot glass.

"Okay so we know what she's doing right?"

Romero fast forwarded the video until they saw a waitress come by. Sal recognized her as one of the waitresses that was bringing over the drinks the girls sent. At first she seemed to shake her head.

"I didn't even catch this part the first time I saw it. It happens so fast but look here." He slowed down the video and points at Melissa slipping the girl something in under the tray. "If I zoom in you can see it's a fifty but I want you to see what happens next."

Sal watched astonished as the waitress took the shot glass Melissa handed her and placed it on her tray. Romero typed in something so they could see from a different angle as she walked away from Melissa to the bar. She picks up more shots but moves the one Melissa gave her to the side then walks over to where he and the guys are.

"And there you have it." Romero froze the video on the moment she hands Sal the shot glass Melissa obviously paid her to make sure *he* got.

Sal's eyes were glued to the screen remembering how odd he'd began to feel after the shot and how he'd thought the waitress had been flirting with him when she handed him the shot. Even knowing now that Melissa had issues he still couldn't believe she'd do this.

"But wait," Romero pointed a finger in the air with a smirk. "There's more! The bitch wasn't done yet."

Sal turned to him flabbergasted. "What?"

Romero nodded but said nothing grabbing the mouse. "Watch this."

After fast forwarding for a while he slows at another image of Melissa spiking yet another shot then she put something away in her purse, picked up the shot glass and walked out of the camera's view. He typed in something else and a different camera picked up her image. Melissa walked across the bar with the shot glass still in her hand and she went straight to a very wobbly looking Sal and handed it to him.

"I don't remember that at all." He thought hard and remembered being handed shots but not who handed them to him. He assumed it had been Jason or the waitress.

"You're lucky you were so wasted you spilled half that shit or she may've killed you!" Alex fumed.

They watched several more videos of Sal walking through the casino and to his room hanging on Melissa the whole way. There was no video of what actually h-appened in the room. But Sal knew without a doubt nothing had happened, especially not after seeing just how out of it he'd actually been. The only other evi-dence was that she hadn't even spent the night. She walked out of his room twenty minutes after walking him there and didn't return until the following morn-ing.

Her spiking his drink made total sense now. No wonder the memories of that night were so damn choppy.

"Are you calling the police?" Sofia asked. "or are you going straight down there to file the report?"

Sal shook his head still staring at the video Romero had now rewound to the part where she spiked his drink. "I'm not doing either."

Both Sofia and Alex spoke at the same time. "Why not?"

"First of all," he said turning to face their stunned faces. "This tape would never be admissible in court. Romero could even get in trouble for having it."

"Actually there's ways around that," Romero smirked.

Sal was adamant. "Even if there is. I'm not." If this girl nearly took her own life because she thought he hated her, he could only imagine what she'd do if he ruined her. This would get her debarred for sure. Sal took a deep breath and explained briefly about Melissa overdosing and what Kat had told him. "She's unstable but having this evidence against her could be enough to keep her away for good. I don't even wanna have contact with her again but I could pass the word through Jason that if she so much tries to contact me or Grace I'll go to the police."

None of them seemed content with his decision, least of all Sofia. "What about Grace? Are you going to show this to her?"

Oh he certainly planned to. "Yeah," he turned to Romero, "but I need another favor from you."

For some reason what he needed to know now outweighed any worry he'd had in past weeks about clearing his name. Unbelievably something that had actually made him start questioning his desire to have Grace back in his life.

*

The next morning Sal got two calls: the first one was a relief; the other one his worst nightmare. Kat called to thank him again for coming to the hospital and told him Melissa had woken up just hours after he'd left. As much as a relief it was to hear that news he still had one not so pleasant thing to do when it came to Melissa. He asked Kat if he could speak to Jason. First he apologized again for not making it to the wedding.

"Don't worry about it, man. I get it now. I wouldn't have wanted to be there either if I was in your shoes. But you gotta know I would've never pushed for you to go out with her especially a second time if I had known about all this."

"Of course I know that," Sal said. "But believe it or not there's more. Can you put me on speaker because I want Kat to hear this too?"

Sal told them everything. About the Vegas stunt to the fake pregnancy and then dropped the big one about her spiking his drink. "Don't ask me how but I have it on tape. I just want to make sure you guys know that I'm not going to the police with this *yet*. When she's better I need for you two to make sure you tell her that I'm willing to overlook this. Let it go and we all know this is huge." The thought of it was beginning to piss him off again. "But I'm willing to not ruin her career and possibly throw her ass in jail so long as she stays the fuck away from me and my family. I don't want her anywhere near my house, the restaurant, anyone I know and I don't want her contacting me in any way."

After the initial shock of it both Kat, but even more adamantly Jason, agreed they'd make sure Melissa had it straight. And Kat thanked him repeatedly for not going to the police.

Sal sat back in his chair when he got the second call. It couldn't have come at a worse time. Once again he had a meeting that day with the investors. He was just waiting for Alex to get out of class and come relieve him so he could leave and meet with them. But Romero threw a wrench in those plans.

The night before Sal had asked him if he could find out a little bit more than what Vincent was giving him about Grace and this Laughlin guy. He'd remembered a part of the conversation he had with Grace the day they left the hospital when the twins were born. When he asked her why she'd come back to the restaurant even though she was so adamant about not being hired as a bartender she'd said "sometimes necessity makes people do things they might not otherwise."

Without a job, Sal knew Grace must be in a bind.

She'd told him she wasn't attracted to Frank in any way. And she'd told Rose she wasn't interested in him either. So if she was sleeping with the guy now—the thought alone made him squeeze his eyes shut so hard he saw stars. But if she was it was for one reason only—money. Sal knew no matter what he could never respect someone like that. Grace said she wasn't like her mother but... necessity. She sure as hell hadn't wasted any time after they broke up to take a *vacation* in Laughlin.

Sal knew there was no way this guy would be buying her a house and going into business with her if there was nothing else involved. As much as it killed him he had to know.

He answered Romero's call on the first ring. "Hey, man. I don't have much yet except one little, yet very significant, thing that's gonna piss the fuck outta you. But I thought you should know."

Every muscle in Sal's body went taut. "What?"

"Well you said the dude was down here this weekend right? And he drives a newer model, beige Cadillac with Nevada plates?"

"Yeah," Sal's jaw was already working in anticipation.

"I had a job near Chula Vista early this morning. I got here a little too early so I thought I'd drive by her place, you know to check out what might be a good place to get the best angle if I decide to stake it out." He paused for a second before continuing. "The car was there, man. And if I had to guess because it was so early, we're talking just after five, it was there over night."

Sal bolted out of his chair in reaction to that news. The guy was there all fucking weekend and he'd spent the night at her place? He ran his hand roughly through his hair. "And you're sure it was Nevada plates?"

"Yep, I mean it could be a coincidence but—"

"Nah, it's no coincidence that's his car." Sal couldn't believe he could be so wrong about her.

"Yeah, I didn't think so either. So whatta ya want me to do? I could still look into it but I mean... this pretty much says it all."

Sal stopped pacing and shook his head. "No. Don't waste anymore time on her. I don't need to know anything else. But thanks."

The second he hung up Sal picked up the coffee mug on his desk and flung it across the room. Hearing it smash into a million pieces was what he needed at that moment. But it did little to calm him.

Oscar rushed in the room. "You okay in here?"

Sal could barely breath straight much less talk. He nodded and pointed at the door. "Just close the door will you? I need a minute."

Oscar stared at him for a moment without moving.

"Close the fucking door!"

Oscar flinched at Sal's booming voice but reached for the knob and walked out closing the door behind him.

By the time Alex got there Sal had done nothing but obsess about Grace with that guy and even though he'd told himself he'd want nothing to do with her if she was sleeping with him he needed answers or he was going to explode.

Alex stopped and stared at the coffee stain on the wall and then the shards of coffee mug all over the floor. "What the hell? What happened?"

Sal grabbed his keys and phone. "I'll explain later. I gotta go."

He rushed past a still stunned looking Alex and out the door.

CHAPTER 35

After hours of trying to figure out how best to handle Grace's latest *dilemma* she finally had to change the subject. She was so drained from this topic already.

"So Rose is mad at me."

That obviously surprised both Joey and Taylor. "I thought you said you haven't told her."

"No not about this. It's about Vincent."

Joey nodded knowingly. "Ah, what happened?"

"Yesterday after she got home — mind you she spent Friday evening with him and most of the day yesterday — she asks if it would be okay if he picked her up from school instead of taking the school bus. So I told her no. Three days in less than a week is a bit much, don't you guys think?"

Taylor made a face and she knew he would. He, as always, was on Rose's side. God, he loved spoiling her. Before he'd start stating why he didn't agree with Grace, she lifted her hand. "Remember, Taylor. She's only fifteen."

"But if they're just hanging out and if you know you can trust her, and you know you can Grace, then I don't see the issue."

Joey shook his head. Finally someone was on her side. "I think you're forgetting, Taylor, what it's like to be a sixteen-year-old boy. Too much time together could be trouble. Not to mention that his own cousin warned Grace about him." Joey turned back to Grace. "So she's mad at you, sweetie?"

Grace nodded a bit saddened. "I hate for her to be mad at me but I told her it was for her own good. I knew the time would come when she would rebel even against me. I just didn't think it would be after only a couple of times of hanging with him."

"You really think she'll rebel? Like maybe get sneaky?" Joey asked.

Grace hadn't thought that far ahead but the thought was alarming. What if she did? As if she really needed more to worry about.

The knock at the door was loud and severe, making all three of them turn at once. "Grace? You here? I need to talk to you."

Sal's voice was ominous — demanding. Rose was the first thing that came to mind. School had been out for over an hour and she hadn't checked in like she normally would when Grace wasn't home at that time. Grace assumed it was because she was mad at her but with Sal banging at the door she wasn't sure what to think. She jumped from Joey and Taylor's kitchen table where they'd all been sitting the entire time.

Without even thinking she hurried to the door and swung it open, her heart at her throat then feeling the all too familiar rush of emotion at the incredible sight of him. She barely managed to say the words. "What happened? Is Rose okay?"

A strange expression washed over him. "Rose?"

"Isn't that why you're here?" Her heart and mind raced at the same time.

His expression went suddenly hard. "No. I'm here because of that asshole you've been with all weekend."

With the relief of knowing this had nothing to do with Rose, suddenly the anger and hurt that she'd worked so hard to keep sedated over the past month began to emerge. The front she had to put up for everyone else's sake, out of fear of worrying them she could no longer contain. "You have *got* to be kidding me."

Sal didn't back down instead he stood even taller, every word more looming than the last. "Is he here?" Sal eyes searched the small apartment. "I saw his car out front. Are you seeing him now, Grace?"

"That is none of your business."

"Are you? It's been what? A fucking month since we broke up?"

"What I do now is none of your business! Do you understand? You have a lot of gall coming here—"

He took one step forward cupping her face in his hands weakening her resolve just like that and she went speechless, staring into his frightened eyes. "I didn't sleep with her, Grace. I swear to you. She concocted the entire thing. I have proof for you. But I need to know what the *fuck* is going on with you and this guy? Why is he here with you? And why've you've been with him all weekend. Are you..."

His words seemed to catch while Grace tried to make sense of what he'd just said. "You have proof..." She almost allowed herself to believe it but caught herself. "No!" She pulled his hands away from her face. She wouldn't fall back into this. "You said you did. You can't just take that back now." Feeling what she'd known all along she'd feel if she ever had to be around him she could barely speak now. "You need to leave. I told you I want nothing to do with you anymore."

"Just tell me. Is he here?" He looked around again eyeing the hallway to the bedrooms. "Is he fucking hiding?"

"No!"

"Then what's his car doing out front? I *know* I can

prove to you I didn't do a damn thing with Melissa, but you've been with this guy all weekend." The fire in his eyes was ever blazing and she knew she should be mad but he sounded so determined when he said he could prove his innocence it gave her mangled heart an ounce of hope.

"I'm driving his car. He loaned it to me."

Grace could see that only added fuel to his already lit eyes. "What? Why?"

"Because we're going into business together. He's helping me get my restaurant going."

She hadn't thought it possible but the ferocity in his eyes went up a notch and he took a very deep breath. "Really? He loaned you his car and he's getting you a restaurant, too? In exchange for what, Grace? Your business partner nearly kissed you yesterday... or maybe he did. You wanna explain that?"

"Grace," Taylor spoke up. "Maybe you should tell him."

Sal's suddenly alarmed eyes finally pulled away from the glaring hold he had on Grace to look at Taylor. "Tell me what?"

He turned back to Grace and she bit her lip, the words still unbelievable even to her as she thought them, but she forced herself to say them. "I'm pregnant."

The look in Sal's eyes was not what she expected. She knew he'd be surprised and she didn't exactly expect him to be thrilled but she wasn't expecting the devastating expression he wore now. His eyes full of questions, he asked the last thing she would've imagined he'd ever ask. "Whose is it?"

Before she'd even allow the massiveness of what he just said to her manifest, she slapped him so hard it stung her hand.

*

Even with the heat of her hand still stinging his face, two thoughts buzzed in Sal's head loud enough to almost drown out the words Grace now yelled at him. Grace was pregnant — with his baby.

"I said get out!"

Sal snapped out of his daze and reached out for Grace's hand. She pulled back but he reached for it again and held it firmly staring into her tear-filled but angry eyes. "I'm sorry, Gracie. I just... I don't know. You were with this guy all weekend. It made me so crazy." He pulled her to him and thankfully she didn't fight him. "This whole time without you I've been going insane. I don't know what I was thinking. I didn't mean that —"

"What else could you mean?" Even though her words had lost their wrath her eyes bounced from his eyes to his lips but she was still insisting on one thing. "I need you to leave."

Unable to control the incredible urge to taste her lips again, he kissed her softly and though she didn't really participate she didn't push him away. "I think we both know I'm not leaving, especially now. Not without you anyway."

"I can't."

Joey who had jumped from the kitchen table to come to Grace's aid or maybe Sal's when Grace slapped him, but stopped in the middle of the front room when he heard Sal apologize finally spoke. "Grace you should talk." She turned her attention back to Joey. "Whether things between you two work out or not, you still have to talk about some kind of arrangement. You may as well get it over with now. "

Sal knew exactly what was going to happen between them because nothing was keeping him away from her now but he'd keep that to himself for the moment. And the only thing they were getting over with was this damn relationship—business or not—she had with the casino guy. It didn't matter what Joey said if he could convince Grace to leave with him, Sal would bite his tongue.

Grace glanced at Taylor. "But—"

"But nothing," Taylor said. "I'm with Joey. Put your feelings aside for just a moment and think of what's best for this baby. The rest will work itself out."

The baby. Sal had been so strung out with his thoughts of Grace and the other guy it hadn't really registered yet. She was having his baby.

She turned back to Sal who could barely restrain himself from taking her and smothering her in his arms. But he managed to refrain and instead said, "We do have a lot to talk about."

"I'm in Frank's car."

Sal's jaw tightened at the sound of her saying his name. Before he could spit out what he was thinking, Joey once again had the answer to that protest. "Taylor and I can drive it back to your place, or Sal can bring you back later."

"Take it back," was Sal's immediate reaction. If he had it his way he wasn't bringing her back. Not tonight—not ever.

Taylor nodded. "We can do that."

Grace still seemed very apprehensive. She turned and their eyes met again. "I can only talk for a few minutes but then I have to go home and check on

Rose."

She pulled her hands from his and walked back to the kitchen. Both Taylor and Joey watched and if Sal wasn't mistaken, though they weren't blatant about it, they seemed pleased. That only gave him more hope that if he couldn't convince Grace to come back to him maybe he could count on them to help. He knew they wanted nothing more than for their *baby girl* to be happy. He wasn't crazy about hearing Joey refer to her as that the first time but at the moment he loved what it meant. It meant Joey would love nothing more than to make sure Grace was happy and taken care of. Which was exactly what Sal planned on doing.

They were barely to his car when he pulled her to him. She began to protest but he felt her body slowly give into him and he leaned against his car pulling her to him.

"You said you have proof," were the first words out of her mouth.

"I do."

He told her about the video and Melissa and how she'd spiked his drink.

"I went to see her yesterday."

Grace jerked away from him. "You went to see her?"

"In the hospital, Gracie." He pulled her back to him. "She overdosed... on purpose."

Grace's eyes grew wide and got even wider as he filled her in on everything about Melissa and how unstable she was. "When I figured it out finally this past Friday, I really told her off. I called her a mental case. I shouldn't have but I was just so fucking pissed. All the hurt you had to go through for nothing." The enamel on his teeth was going to wear out from all the grinding he'd done ever since this whole nightmare with Melissa started.

Grace seemed to ease up but Sal could still see the apprehension. "Did she send the texts that night?"

"I'm fairly certain. When you see how out of it I was that night you'll know there was no way I could've verbally put two coherent words together. Much less text them."

Grace frowned but didn't say anything at first. Then she looked him in the eye. "I didn't believe her when she first told me." She shook her head her eyes welling up a bit. "I just couldn't believe that you would…"

"And I didn't. You know that now."

She breathed in deeply and nodded. "But when you said you did…" she looked away.

The hurt was still there and he didn't want to, but he hated Melissa for that. He thought of what he felt when Romero informed him Frank's car had been at Grace's all night so he knew what Grace must've felt— remembered the desperation in Grace's voice over the phone when she begged him to tell her he hadn't slept with Melissa and he couldn't. It choked him up just thinking about it and he brought his arms around Grace hugging her tight. "I wish I could take back all your pain. I swear to you I do, baby. But at least it's over now."

She pulled away from him to look at him. "Is it? How can you be sure?"

"Trust me. I took care of it." He looked in her big eyes, feeling suddenly more emotional but in a different way than he had this past month. In a way that nearly took his breath away he brought his hand down and placed it on her belly. "How long have you known?"

She looked down, placed her hand over his and whispered. "Since last night." Her face turned back up and met his eyes. "But I don't want you to think that I..." she hesitated before continuing. "You know that you have to..." She stopped again and shrugged. "After everything that's happened, I don't want this to be the reason that —"

"Are you kidding me? You really think I wouldn't be a part of this? Grace I'd stop at nothing, especially now —" He stopped when it suddenly hit him. The pictures of Grace at the nightclub with that guy looking so different. Her spending the entire weekend with him. He was buying her a fucking house — handed over his brand new luxury car. Every muscle on his body went tense. "Wait, what do you mean everything that's happened?"

"I'm just saying, even before all this happened we weren't together *that* long. I'm sure you weren't thinking that far ahead and certainly not in terms of marriage and I don't expect you to just because —"

"Believe me, Grace. I *was* thinking all those things and more from the moment we came to an agreement. You don't have to worry about any of that. But what I do need to know..." He took a moment to calm himself because he didn't want to ruin things now that she seemed ready to forgive, and move on. As much as he tried his words were strained. "What the hell is going on between you and this guy from Laughlin?"

"It's just business."

"Really because that's not what Sofie said it looked like Friday night and yesterday you almost kissed him." Sal's heart had started up again. This was not how he wanted their first reunion to be like but he couldn't help it.

Grace's brows pinched. "Yeah, you said that earlier. Who told you I almost kissed him?"

Sal almost wished she'd just deny it. This only enraged him further. "Vince made an observation when he picked up your sister. So did you, after they drove away?"

She thought about it for a moment then it seemed to come to her. "Oh that."

"You did?" Sal stood up straight, no longer feeling the ease to just lean against the car anymore.

"No!" Her hand slipping into his had an amazing way of calming him. "I was feeling dizzy. Of course I didn't know it at the time but it's all pregnancy related. The dizzy spells and horrible nausea I've had for weeks have completely drained me and Rose has been really worried. So I'd waited for Rose to walk away before leaning against him for support."

Sal stared at her remembering Vince mentioning she'd been sick. As much as he felt the urge to pick her up and take her home to start taking care of her, one nagging thought still occupied his mind. Even feeling *completely drained* she'd still gone out dancing Friday night—with Frank—looking hotter than ever. But before he could put it aside for now, and focus on her health instead she added, "but we do need to talk about me and Frank."

Me and Frank. Never had three little words had such a nauseating effect on him.

CHAPTER 36

The ride to pick up Rose and bring her back to Sal's with them had been somewhat quiet and a bit uncomfortable. Grace noticed Sal attempted to hide his change in mood after she let him know they did need to talk about her and Frank but the change was significant enough. His eyebrow lifted and stayed firmly that way the entire time.

"She's mad at me you know."

Sal finally glanced at her. He'd been staring straight ahead most of the way. "Who Rose?"

Grace nodded.

"Why?"

"Because of Vincent."

She didn't think he lift that eyebrow any higher but higher it went. "Why? Did he do something?"

"No. It just makes me nervous that they're spending so much time together. She says they're just friends but she's not fooling me. I see it in her eyes. She's falling for him." Grace lifted a shoulder. "She's too young and I worry about how she's going to feel once he leaves. I don't think she's thought that far ahead but I'm afraid she'll be heartbroken. Especially with the distance between them, how likely is it that things could work out for them? It's inevitable that she'll get hurt."

Sal reached his hand over to her and she took it, lacing her fingers through his big strong fingers. God how she'd missed this — missed him.

"Gracie, I know what it's like to want to protect

your loved ones. Growing up, nobody and I mean *no-body* messed with my sister without paying dearly. But there are some things you're going to have to let her experience for herself so she can learn to deal with them. You're not always going to be there to take that bullet for her you know. Her whole life you've been absorbing all the pain for her. The pain of your father and grandmother's passing, even trying to hide the fact that you're not feeling well just so she won't worry." He shook his head.

Grace was surprised he'd picked up on that. If he only knew how sick she'd made herself, trying to hide the fact that she'd been so devastated from his sup-posed betrayal.

"I'm just saying. I get that you don't want to expose her to any kind of danger and you have my word that I'll make sure Vincent doesn't get her into any. Turns out he's not such a bad kid after all and he's been duly warned let me tell you. But if the worst thing that will come from this is her being a little sad when he leaves then I think that's a fairly painless way to start. It's not like it'll come as a shocker. She knows he's leaving at the end of the summer."

She knew he had a point but he didn't just have a sister. He had two brothers and loving parents who he spread his love out for and who in return showered him with that same love. All Grace had was Rose. It was so hard to think of her being hurt.

"I was gonna have Vin pick her up from my place and maybe take her to grab a bite or something so it would give us some privacy but if you don't want to I won't."

Taking a deep breath as they drove up to the front of her apartment building she smiled weakly. "No.

You're right. I can't shelter her forever. And her hanging out with him a few times a week really is harmless."

She texted Rose to ask her to come with her to Sal's place for a while. Knowing Rose would wonder what was going on, she told her she'd explain everything later. At first Rose declined, saying didn't really feel like it. Then Grace texted her that Vincent would be there and Rose texted back immediately.

I'm on my way down.

Grace smiled at Sal after reading it, trying to hide her concern. "She's on her way."

While Grace texted with Rose, Sal texted Vincent to let him know what was going on. Not only did he agree, he was already at Sal's house when they got there. Rose didn't even go in the house, jumping straight into Vincent's car. They were going to eat and Sal spotted Vince some money to take her to a show, too. Apparently he had a long talk in mind.

Sal offered her something to eat or drink but as was the case lately, she had no appetite.

Grace pulled a tea bag out of her purse. "I'll take a cup of hot water."

She'd never been much of a tea drinker but lately it seemed to be the only thing that soothed her stomach. After fixing her mug of tea they walked out into his yard and sat at his patio table. Just being in his house again did things to her. But taking in the view, a view she never thought she'd be seeing again, brought a lump to her throat. She took a sip of her tea trying to swallow it back.

Sal sat close to her and leaned into her kissing her cheek softly. "It's so good to have you back, Grace."

She turned to face him. "It's good to be back."

He took a deep breath and his expression changed a little. "Now tell me about Frank."

Grace glanced away and stared at her mug playing with the teabag string that hung off the side. "He agreed to invest money into a restaurant with me and my mom."

"And lend you his car."

She nodded knowing exactly what he was thinking. "Why?"

"He thinks it's a good investment and he could use the write-off."

"Why else?"

She glanced back at him and sat up straight. She knew what he was getting at and yes maybe Frank had other underlying reasons for being so generous but Sal had to know she wasn't that type of person. The more she'd thought about this the more she had to agree with her mom that it was a great opportunity. "Those are the only reasons he's given."

"You're not still thinking of going through with this are you?"

"Why wouldn't I?"

He cocked his head back. "What do you mean why wouldn't I? You have to know this guy wants more than just to do business with you."

"You don't know that."

"Oh don't I? Tell me something is that why you went on that vacation to Laughlin? To *talk* him into investing in your restaurant?"

Grace didn't appreciate his tone and certainly not the implication. "I went there, Sal, because I was falling apart and I needed to get away. It actually helped. The idea of him helping me with my restaurant was one that had been brought up long before me and you even broke up. And it was never *me* trying to talk *him* into it rather the other way around."

"Was it now?" A glimmer of the blaze she'd seen in his eyes when he showed up at Joey and Taylor's was back. "When were you planning on telling me about it?"

"I wasn't because I had no intentions of taking him up on the offer. I'd already told my mom it was out of the question."

"And why was that, Grace?"

Damn it he had her and the rage in his eye said he knew it, too.

She held her chin up. "I didn't need the job at the time. I had a good one with you and I was only getting my feet wet in a big restaurant like yours. I didn't think I was ready."

The outraged expression turned almost smug. "No other reason? Why hadn't you even mentioned to me that the offer had been put out there?"

Grace tipped her head trying to stay nose to nose with his challenges but she could already tell she was fighting a losing battle. "I didn't think you'd be happy about it."

"You're damn right I wouldn't have been." He leaned in closer his legs practically straddled her chair now and his tone softening just a bit. "Grace, baby, the guy showed up with roses for you, ready to go on a *date* with you. He's driven more than four hours each way several times just to spend time with you." He kissed her forehead then lifted her chin and looked deep into her eyes. "I love you more than anything."

That damn lump suffocated her. "I love you, too."

He pulled her closer to him. "I'm never letting you out of my life now, you know that right?"

Grace gulped nodding softly. "I don't wanna be out of your life."

He smiled and kissed her softly. "Good because it'll never happen again. I'll do whatever it takes and that's a promise." His eyes went hard again. "But if you think for even a second that I'm gonna let that fucker stay in your life you're out of your mind."

Grace tried to conjure up some kind of strength to argue and she didn't even know why. "But—"

"I saw pictures, Grace." His breathing suddenly accelerated.

"What?" She searched his fiery eyes. "Pictures?"

"Sofie took pictures with her phone the night at the night club." The vein on his neck protruded and he seemed to wait for her reaction.

"And?"

"I saw you with him." There was a subtle but undeniable raise in his voice now and she knew any kind of partnership with Frank was officially over. "I saw the way you dressed, the way he touched you and held your hand—the way he looked at you. You still gonna tell me it's just business?"

She stared at him knowing there was nothing she could say at this point that would convince him and she didn't even care. She squeezed his hand. It was so tense and he closed his eyes. "I said partnering up with him was out of the question before me and you broke up because I had a feeling there was more to it than just business."

"Of course there was—"

She put her finger to his lips. "But I've never done anything to even give him the idea that I might be willing. Except for allowing him to hold my hand to and from the dance floor. I don't want you to think anything ever happened. Okay?"

He stared at her breathing hard. "I don't want him around you anymore. Give the car back, too. Give it to your mom. I don't give a shit. I just don't want *you* in it."

"Okay."

She saw his shoulders and chest fall slowly as he exhaled. "But," she said making him tense up again and an eyebrow to lift. "I will have to talk to him to explain it. We *were* getting ready to make an offer on a property. I'll be pulling the rug out from under everybody's feet."

Sal reached down to his waist and pulled his phone out. "Call him."

"No."

"Why not?"

"Because I have to explain to my mom first. She's not going to be happy about this and even though I don't care, I'd still like to tell her before I tell him."

After a few moments of him staring at her he finally spoke. "But you'll do it over the phone right? You don't have to see him to tell him."

Grace smiled, running her fingers through his soft hair. "Unless he's okay with my mom still borrowing his car he's going to have to come pick it up."

Sal frowned at that and for some reason that made Grace chuckle. "Sweetie, I can see your reluctance about me going into business with the man but me being around him for a few minutes while he picks up the car he was nice enough to lend me is not going to kill anyone."

"It'll kill me," he muttered

That made her laugh and she brought her hands to his face. "You'll be just fine." Then she leaned back and picked up his hand placing it on her belly. "Now lets talk about something else." She smiled feeling the tears come as she remembered the dread that kept her up all night last night knowing she'd have to face him again and again with the knowledge that he'd never be hers yet he'd be a permanent fixture in her life. A torment she'd be forced to endure forever. She took a deep breath. It was a miracle how feelings about this had gone from dread to absolute delight. "You're gonna be a daddy."

His eyebrows pinched and seeing the tears in his eyes made her arms instinctively wrap around his neck. Nothing felt better than feeling his arms around her. It's where she belonged and for once in her life she believed it. She *could* have it all.

"My baby momma," he said against her ear.

She pulled away to look at him and he laughed wiping away a tear from the corner of his eye. She wiped the tears from her eyes and had to laugh, too. "What?"

"Well you know that's what you'll be unless you marry me right?"

She stopped laughing and felt the smile dissolve feeling overwhelmed with emotion again and here she thought she already had it all. Then she remembered one very important thing. Rose.

*

As the months went by and Sal didn't get so much as a text from Melissa, he'd begun to believe she'd finally accepted it and he wouldn't have to worry about her ever again. Then it came: the morning of his wedding. Over four months since he and Gracie had reunited. He logged on to check his email and there it was, an email from her in his inbox. He glanced up but Grace was still sound asleep. She'd slept so much since she'd moved in with him and today of all mornings he was letting her sleep as long as she wanted. He almost didn't want to but since this was the morning of his wedding he wanted to make sure Melissa wasn't planning on doing anything to ruin it. So he clicked on it and held his breath until it opened and read:

Hey there. Just wanted to congratulate you on your big day. I won't lie. A part of me still wishes it was me and not her but I get it. You only get one love of your life and apparently she's yours. For a long time I thought you were mine until a ton of therapy helped me realize you were what I pictured my ideal guy was. Perfect in every way, but other than how beautiful you are and ha! How well off. I knew very little about you. And obviously you knew even less about me. But enough of that. I just wanted you to know how grateful I am that you didn't go to the police. I wanted to thank you for that so many times before but Kat and Jason were adamant about me not contacting you even for that. I'm sorry that I caused you so much pain and heartache. Believe it or not, that's what is going to take me the longest to get over, but I'm working on it. I wish nothing but the best for you.

Missy
P.S. I know you're going to be a great daddy. =)

Nothing could describe the enormous relief he felt after reading that. It felt so good all he wanted to do was slip back in bed and hold Grace so he did. He'd come to live for spooning Grace's warm body and holding her close against him.

She exhaled with a smile in her sleep. Okay maybe

there was something he loved more. He kissed her cheek. "I love you," he whispered.

To his surprise she murmured back, "I love you, too."

A little annoyed at himself that he woke her he whispered, "Go back to sleep."

Suddenly she clutched his hand and went tense.

"What's wrong? You okay?" His anxiety levels since he witnessed a few of her dizzy spells had been at an all time high lately.

"I think..." She went stiff again. "There it is again.."

"What?" His heart was now going a mile a minute.

"The baby."

"What about it?"

She spun around and put his hand on her belly. "I felt it move."

Sal concentrated but felt nothing, still it was exciting to see the emotion in her eyes. "I felt it, Sal. On my wedding day. Our baby."

Sal took a deep breath and smiled. "He or she is up early and ready for the day mommy and daddy say *I do*."

"I've said it a million times in my head already," Grace said smiling at him.

Sal kissed her. "This is just a formality for everyone else's sake, Gracie. You've owned my heart since day one."

She wrapped herself around him, Sal's breathing was just beginning to accelerate as he kissed her deeply, when there was a knock at the bedroom door. They both froze. Grace pulled away and made a pouty face, obviously reading the disappointment in his face.

"Come in," she said unwrapping herself from him and sat up.

"Sorry," Rose said chewing her bottom lip. "I was waiting for you guys to wake and I heard you talking so I just thought…"

"What's up?" Grace asked.

"I made the team," Rose said with a smile.

"You did?" Grace got out of bed and rushed over to hug her. "Oh my God I knew you would!"

Since Rose was now living with them and Sal remembered Grace telling him about her mother not willing to pay for her club soccer team all year round, he decided he'd sponsor her. At first Grace said it would be too much but Moreno's sponsored plenty of players, so Sal insisted they could sponsor her too. The only club teams in this area were silver teams or higher and Rose had only ever played on bronze teams. But Grace said that was only because in their area they couldn't afford better coaches or scouts so the only teams they had out there were bronze. She said Rose was a stand out. Rose was nervous about trying out for a silver team. But here she was, smiling big.

"Way to go, Rose. You see your sister was right. You are a superstar. Can't wait to see you play."

After giving them the rundown on everything about her practices, uniforms and games she excused herself to start getting ready. Sal had to laugh. The ceremony wasn't until late that afternoon, but Rose always took hours to do her hair. Today she would be Grace's maid of honor so he supposed this called for an even longer grooming session.

Grace closed the door after Rose walked out and Sal smiled when he saw her lock it. She turned around with a wicked smile.

"What are you up to Mrs. Moreno?"

She smiled even bigger as she climbed onto the bed.

"Ooh I like that."

"I love this," he said wrapping both arms around her and pulling her tightly to him.

"But that reminds me of something scary my mom said before she left."

"What's that?" Sal searched her eyes curiously.

"She said she had a sneaking suspicion both her girls would be Morenos someday."

Sal smiled and kissed her. "You never know."

Rose and Vince had gotten nerve-wrackingly close this summer. And even though the summer was over now and Vince had gone back to La Puente, they were still going back and forth texting nonstop. Her mom could be on to something.

Her mom *had* been right about one thing. Turned out Frank had come in handy. Ruben got a DUI over the summer and his class A license was taken away. With Frank's plans to open a restaurant out here with Grace foiled and Ruben no longer able to drive long hauls; Frank offered them both jobs at his busy casino. Grace's mom wasn't thrilled about having to work but at least she'd be living in a fancy casino now with maid service instead of the run down apartment building so she took the offer and they moved out there.

There was never even a question of where Rose would stay. With three extra bedrooms in Sal's house there was more than enough room and he wouldn't have it any other way.

The look on Grace's face said it all. She was still ap-prehensive about Rose and Vince. "He's not as bad as I made him out to be. Just hung out with the wrong crowd for a while there but he actually has a good head on his shoulders."

Finally Grace gave way to that smile he loved so

much. "I guess anyone related to you has to be pretty awesome."

Sal laughed. "I wouldn't say all that." The Morenos weren't without their loonies. What family wasn't?

"I can hardly believe I'm going to be part of such a big family now."

"You already are, sweetheart." he said moving a strand of hair away from her eyes. Then he brought his hand back down, placing it over the small bump on her belly. "And we're gonna make this family even bigger now."

She closed her eyes. "It's hard to believe I'm not dreaming."

"Open your eyes, Gracie," he whispered against her lips. "We're living the dream. Forever starts today."

She opened her eyes and stared at him. "Forever?"

He smiled nodding before kissing her again. "Forever."

Epilogue

Alex

Sienna ran up to Alex sopping wet and handed him a-nother rock. "Where's your life jacket, baby?"

She ignored the question and skipped away. Back toward the water.

"The life jackets were giving them both rashes un-der their arms so I took them off." Valerie said, walk-ing up to him with Savannah in her arms.

Alex frowned, putting down the fishing pole he w-as trying to untangle. "I don't want them near the wa-ter without them, babe."

"Relax, we're all watching them. No one's letting them out of our sights." She leaned in and kissed him, before grabbing her sunglasses from the beach bag that hung on his chair.

Savannah puckered up so Valerie leaned her in and Alex kissed her, too.

"Daddy fish?"

"Yeah," Alex smiled. "Daddy's gonna catch a big one for us today."

"Your daddy don't know about this," Romero said.

Alex glanced over at Romero who sat under the ta-rp trying to untangle the fishing line on his pole. He'd been at it for over fifteen minutes and it looked worse now than when he started.

Alex shook his head as he reached over and stroked Valerie's belly. "How you feeling?"

"Perfect." She put her sunglasses on. "After the hell I went through when I was pregnant with the girls I'm shocked I haven't had any morning sickness this time."

"Don't be a braggart," Isabel said, sitting up from where she was lying on a towel next to Romero's chair.

"You still feeling nauseous, Izzy?"

Alex glanced at Isabel. She nodded miserably. Her face was as pale as he remembered Valerie's getting when she was pregnant with the twins.

"Try sucking on a lemon, Isabel." Valerie suggested. "That always used to help me."

Romero put his pole down. "Don't get up, babe. I got it. One lemon coming up."

Alex chuckled. Isabel's pale face also reminded him of when she gave Romero the news she was pregnant two months ago. Since both she and Valerie found out they were pregnant almost at the same time they decided to plan a night out with all the couples and announce it together. Alex thought Romero was going to pass out.

"How did Grace hear about this place anyway?" Romero asked, slicing a lemon on the picnic table. "Elephant butt—what the hell's that about anyway?"

Alex shrugged, concentrating again on untangling the damn line on his pole. "Sal said her dad used to bring her here when she was a kid. I think it's cool." Alex glanced up at Valerie who balanced Savannah on her hip. "You sure you should be carrying her?"

"Alex she's not even two. She weighs nothing." She turned toward the shore where Sienna ran past baby Sal who was still taking wobbly steps nearly causing him to tip over, but Grace was there, arms out ready to catch him if he did. "Sienna, honey be gentle with your cousin. He just learned to walk."

Sal grabbed Sienna as she tried to run past him and she squealed when he spun her around.

Alex eyed Sarah and Angel who sat on beach chairs in the water. They were supposed to be on twin patrol but Angel held a Corona, and Sarah held a red cup, no doubt sipping on wine. Sarah lifted her cup to them and smiled.

"You're supposed to be watching my girls. Not drinking."

Sarah put her hand to her ear pretending not to hear. "What was that?" Then took a sip of her cup with a smile.

"That brat," Valerie said. "She knows I'm dying to have a glass of wine."

Alex shook his head. "Not happening."

"I know." Valerie said, putting Savannah down then walking after her as she ran toward Sal and Grace.

He watched as she reached Grace. Alex was surprised Sal agreed to make the trip since Grace was five months pregnant. This family—he shook his head. Next year they'd need an RV; their SUVs weren't going to cut it much longer. The only ones left were Sofie and Angel.

Sofie and Eric were newlyweds and she said they were going to wait, but Sarah and Angel had been trying for over a year now so it was just a matter of time before those two started popping them out.

Romero opened the ice chest, pulling out a beer. "You want one man?"

"Yeah, I'll take one."

Romero handed it to him before sitting down. He took a long cold sip, glancing around at his fast growing family and smiled. Life was good.

Sofia

They were so far away from the shore they could barely make out who was who from where they stood in the lake. Sofia smiled wickedly at Eric whose heart was still pounding against her chest as she kissed him one last time.

"I can't believe we just did that, Sof."

She giggled. "Why? We did this in Hawaii."

"Yeah, but your brothers weren't sitting just couple hundred yards away on the shore."

She laughed even more at his exasperated expression. "We're far enough there's no way they can see what you just did to their little sister."

Eric smirked and glanced back toward the shore. "Not funny. This was your idea as usual."

Sofia wrapped her legs around his waist and her arms round his neck again. "Tell me you didn't enjoy it."

That finally made him smile and he groaned, kissing her. When he was done he pulled back. "So did you decide?"

Sofia rested her cheek on his shoulder. "I don't know. Maybe we should wait until we get back home. I'd hate to ruin the trip for Sarah and Angel."

"You really think it would ruin it?"

She lifted her head up to face him. "When Valerie and Isabel announced they were pregnant at that dinner, they seemed happy enough for them but I'm sure it had to be hard, especially since Grace got pregnant again so quickly after having the baby." Sofia thought about how devastated they'd felt after finally getting pregnant only to have Sarah miscarry. "They've been trying for over a year now. Here we've only been married three months and already I'm knocked up." She shook her head. "No I don't think we should say anything until we get back."

"It's your call, Sof."

She nodded, a little saddened that she knew it was just a matter of time before Sarah and Angel knew even if it wasn't until they got back but she was certain it would touch a nerve. She remembered the last time Sarah thought she might be then when it turned out to be a false alarm she'd cried when she told Sofia but made her promise not to tell Angel. She didn't want him to know how heartbreaking each month that went by and she wasn't was for her.

They made their way back to the shoreline. Sal and Alex were already working on getting one of the tents up. Sofia walked up behind baby Sal who was tugging on one of the corners of the tents and squeezed him kissing his fat little cheek. "Hey little man. You helping daddy?"

He garbled something loud and with conviction. Sofia lifted her eyebrow pretending to understand him. "Really?"

"I still can't get over how much he looks like you, Sal," Eric said.

"You think? I think he looks like Grace."

"Nah," Romero shook his head. "That's all you. Poor little dude."

Sofia walked over to where Valerie and the other women sat at the picnic table They were making *tortas*. Sarah helped Savannah with hers while Valerie tried to calm Sienna who was whining about something.

"What's wrong with her, babe?" Alex asked.

"Nothing she's just getting fussy. This is their usual naptime."

Angel came up from behind Sienna where she stood on the bench next to Valerie and kissed her head. "Naptime, Sienna?"

She put her arms out and he picked her up.

"Oh sure," Valerie said. "She's all smiles for uncle Angel."

Angel walked away with her toward the other guys putting up the tent.

Sofia sat down in the space Sienna had occupied. Rose was lying on the beach with a towel over her face since before she and Eric had gone out into the water. At nearly eighteen, she was just as womanly looking as any of the other women here today. "Grace," Sofia motioned to Rose. "Is she okay?"

Grace glanced back at Rose and nodded "She's just tanning."

Sofia lowered her voice. "Is she finally over... you know?"

Grace shrugged. "She says she is but sometimes she still seems a little down."

"Maybe once he gets out of the Army they can—"

"No," Grace said firmly. "She wants nothing to do with him again—ever."

Sofia wouldn't say it but she remembered Grace saying the very same thing about Sal once upon a time. She glanced back at Rose again. Never say never.

Romero

Seeing Isabel emerge from the ladies' room for once not looking like a ghost made Romero smile. Ever since she'd dropped the news about being pregnant he'd been a wreck. *Him* a dad? Sure Manny and Max were already on board with helping out. Even though they could afford to buy a play set which the baby wouldn't be using for years anyway, those two nuts were already building one from scratch.

Manny had tapped his chest several times already saying it was being built straight from the heart. Even when that hand had a bandaged thumb from where he'd hammered it. Romero chuckled. That probably wouldn't be the last bandage the building of that play set would be producing.

"What are you smiling about?" Isabel said slipping her hand in his as she reached him.

"I was just thinking about the play set Manny and Max are building."

Isabel turned to him. "I thought you told them not to bother. That's a huge job they're taking on."

"Yeah, you try telling those two. Aida said it's just another excuse for Manny to go out and buy more power tools."

Isabel laughed. "Oh well, as long as they're enjoying it."

"You sure you don't wanna find out what we're having?" Romero's eye teased. "Because Manny said if it's a boy they could make it into a real cool looking fire station theme. And if it's a girl he has this whole castle theme he could do instead."

Isabel's eyes teased right back. "Yeah, well what if it's one of each?"

Romero stopped and looked at her, barely able to take another breath. Then she laughed. "I'm kidding!" Romero clutched his chest. "But it's a possibility. Not only that, I wanna have *more than one*. What if we do have one of each eventually? They should keep it neutral."

They'd started walking again and Romero's heart

was still trying to get over her unfunny joke. Then he thought of what she'd just said. More than one. Here he was barely getting used to the idea of having one kid and Izzy was already thinking more?

As they got closer to their campsite and Romero took in everything he had to smile. Damn what a turn his life had taken ever since he met the perfect girl. All those nights of partying and meaningless sex he would've never imagined his life turning into this. He watched as Sal applied sun block on his son and tried unsuccessfully to get him to wear a sun hat. Then he turned to Eric and Sofia who lay on the blanket under the tarp. Eric's hand stroked her belly gently, making Romero raise an eyebrow. Could they be? Nah, they would've said something already. Though he wouldn't put it past those two. They could barely keep their hands off each other.

Alex was showing one of his girls how to reel in the line on the fishing poles while the other one gave Valerie a hard time about putting on her water shoes. Romero still couldn't tell them apart but if he had to guess based on their actions, Sienna was the one fighting the water shoes.

Angel and Sarah were far out in the water doing God knows what. Why did everyone think they were so sneaky when they did stuff like that? There was only one reason you'd go out so far.

"Let's go in the water." Isabel said, tugging at his hand.

"You sure?" Isabel hadn't felt like doing much since they got here. The damn morning sickness really was doing a number on her.

"Yeah, I'm sure," she said with a smile.

Once in the water up to their chests, Romero pulled

her to him and she wrapped her arms around his neck. "So is this kid going to go by Romero, too?" she asked.

"Not if it's a girl."

Isabel tilted her head. "And if it's a boy?"

"How does Romero Romero sound?"

Isabel laughed. "No!"

"Why not? There was a guy in high school named Gaspar Gaspar. It was fucking hilarious."

She eyed him. "And that's what you want your son to be? Fucking hilarious?"

"Oh he's gonna be funny. I guarantee you that."

Her smile softened. "And if it's a girl?"

God that scared him more than anything. How would he ever deal with a little girl? A son he wouldn't have a problem roughing him up and making him tough as nails but a little girl? He'd go fucking nuts if anyone ever messed with her. He glanced back at the shore and watched Alex holding both his girls in his arms now. He supposed if Alex could deal with two at once he could handle one. He'd have to follow Alex's lead. So far he seemed to be doing a pretty good job with the twins and growing up he'd been damn good about looking out for Sof. Yeah, that's what he'd do. Follow Alex's lead.

"Hello?" Isabel said, snapping him out of his thoughts. "I asked you a question. What if it's a girl?"

"She's gonna be perfect." He kissed her softly. "Like her mommy."

Isabel's face flushed. After all these years he could still make her blush. God he loved her.

"I meant her name."

Romero thought about it for a moment. "I like Amanda."

Her face brightened up suddenly. "I've always

liked Amanda."

"Amanda Romero." Romero said, his mind wandering off to a little girl being fawned over by him and his uncles. Ballerina classes, painted flowers in her bedroom like the ones in the twin's room.

Isabel dipped her head in the water as Romero continued to day dream about his little girl. He watched as Isabel smoothed her hair back after coming back up smiling, looking as beautiful as only she could. "I like Romeo," she said.

All his thoughts came to a screeching halt as he took in her words. "Who the fuck is Romeo?"

She laughed. "The name. For a boy. Romeo Romero. Isn't that cool?"

She'd stepped away from him when she dipped her head in the water and he pulled her to him again. "I don't know. I'll have to think about that one."

Then she smiled wickedly and wrapped her legs around his waist. "I'm feeling better now. What do you say we go deeper in?"

Romero kissed her instantly hard, already thinking about just how deep in *her* he wanted to be. "You really are perfect you know?"

Sal

With his son finally out, Sal could now enjoy a few relaxing minutes in front of the fire with his wife.

Valerie peeked into her tent and smiled. "I think Alex might've passed out with them."

"Wasn't he supposed to be putting them to sleep not the other way around?" Sal asked.

"He might be just pretending to sleep until he's sure they're out before making a move." Valerie grabbed a stick and stuck a marshmallow on it.

"Grab me another one please?" Grace said.

"You don't wanna roast marshmallows, Rose?" Sal asked, moving his marshmallow around in the fire.

Rose shook her head, placing her earphones back in her ears as she sat back in her chair. Sal couldn't help still wonder if she blamed him for how things went down with Vincent. Grace assured him she didn't.

All Sal knew is he'd stuck his neck out for Vince last summer when he'd come back for another stint at the restaurant and Vince blew it. Grace had caught them making out in the backyard. While they finally fessed up that yes they were a couple now, Vince assured him that he wouldn't take it past making out. Sal had convinced Grace that it would be okay and they'd just keep a close eye out. Everything was fine all summer. Then just five months later after the summer was over Sal got the call from Vince's dad and shit hit the fan.

The zipper on the tent where Alex had been putting his twins to sleep opened and Alex emerged. "Damn," he said, shaking his head. "Savannah was out almost as soon as I laid her down but Sienna fights it tooth and nail *every* time."

"Tee hee," Romero said, taking a swig of his beer as he sat down next to Isabel in front of the fire. "Now we know which one's gonna give you trouble."

Alex frowned, taking the seat next to Valerie. "No she's not. They're both daddy's little angels. They're never gonna give me trouble."

Sofia laughed, snuggling up against Eric. "Alex, you are *so* in for it."

Alex rolled his eyes and kissed Valerie then licked his lips. "What is that?"

"S'mores," she said, shoving another one in her mouth.

"How many of those have you had?"

She shrugged. "Lost count."

Angel stood up and walked over to the ice chest and grabbed a beer then started pouring some wine into a cup. "Anyone else want a beer?" Sal, Eric and Alex all lifted their hands. "Sofie looks like you're the only girl here besides Sarah that can drink. You want one, too?"

"Uh," Sofia shook her head. "No, I just opened an iced tea." She lifted it for him to see.

After passing the beer around Angel sat down next to Sarah. "This place is a cool park, Grace. We should do this every year, Sal. Make it a family tradition."

"I'm down with that." Sal said.

"Us too," Romero said, his eyes opening wide. "Izzy, next year we'll have our baby with us."

"Yep," Grace smiled. "There will be three more little ones by next summer. It's gonna be a circus."

"That's if Valerie and Alex don't pop out another two-fer," Romero laughed.

Valerie dropped her head back. "Don't even say that. My God."

"Why not?" Alex frowned. "We can handle it."

"Yeah, you're not the one that has to carry them for nine months."

Sal glanced at Sarah and Angel. They were the only ones who didn't seem to be smiling as big as everyone else. "Since this is our first night doing our new family tradition, I propose a toast." Sal lifted his beer. "To family."

"May it only get bigger," Alex added

"And may we always stay this close." Sofia said.

"Love you guys." Angel lifted his beer.

"Salud!" Romero said.

"To family," they all said before finally taking a drink.

The End

Alright you guys, I'm sure you're wondering why Angel didn't get his own POV in the epilogue. Well, that's because he gets his own bonus short story! You guys asked for more Angel and Sarah and what my readers want my readers get. Enjoy!

ONLY EIGHT DAYS
(A Moreno Brothers bonus short story)

CHAPTER 1

An entire ten minutes had passed or maybe more and Sarah still sat staring at the phone. She knew she was being silly for getting choked up about something like this but Angel had to know that hearing about other couples getting pregnant was hard for her. Sure she played it off when Valerie and Isabel announced their pregnancies a few months ago, and she'd cried in private in the restroom when they got home. Even if she didn't say it Angel had to pick up on her change in mood. Didn't he?

How could he drop the news on her like that so nonchalantly? *Oh by the way Sofie's pregnant.* They'd only been married three months and already they had what she wanted *so* bad. She was happy for them. She really was, but she couldn't help the pain in her heart — and yes, the jealousy — from their news.

A tear slid down her cheek. They were all pregnant now. In nine months they'd all have new babies. The pain was becoming excruciating and the worst part is she was sure it was her. Obviously the Moreno's baby making powers were just fine. And it certainly wasn't for lack of trying.

Painfully she and Angel knew they *could* make a baby. Just eight months ago she was delighted to find out she was pregnant, then six weeks into it she lost it. It was the most devastating loss of her life. The doctors told them it was nature's way of saying that baby just wasn't meant to be but they could try again as soon as she got her next period. Sarah was almost afraid to. She didn't know if she could survive a loss like that again. But they had tried again and ever since. Each month that passed and it didn't happen was more painful than the last.

By that afternoon, Angel's announcement to her about Sofia and his total disregard for her feelings when slapping her with the news had her so worked up she needed to vent.

Ever since Sydney married and moved clear across the country to North Carolina, their communication had dwindled down to a phone call every few weeks then it turned into months, with texts and Facebook comments and messages replacing the calls. During the past year he'd reached out to her a bit more often since he'd begun to have marital problems. It didn't look good from what he'd told her. Every time she spoke with him it was worse. He wasn't even sure he was in love with his wife anymore. The last time he called he sounded really distraught.

Sarah was completely open with Angel about Sydney and had been for years since he didn't seem to be bothered by their relationship anymore. She wasn't sure if it was because he finally got that Syd was truly just her friend or because the times she actually spoke with him were so far and few in between it wasn't worth getting worked up for.

Usually it was one of the girls she'd reach out to

whenever she was upset with Angel and needed to talk. But how could she tell any of them, their pregnancies were part of the reason she was feeling so down? And she wasn't about to call her mom on her honeymoon. She'd be gone the whole week. She needed Syd now. She called him but it went to voicemail so she left a message.

When she heard the garage door open that evening she couldn't help feeling angry. She wasn't really angry at Angel as much as she was angry at the world. The past thirteen months since they'd begun this baby making journey had really begun taking its toll on her emotionally.

She was just days away from when she was supposed to get her period and if her mood was any indication it looked like it was going to be right on time... again.

Angel walked in from the garage door that opened into the kitchen. He smiled as soon as he saw her and she had to look away. "What's wrong?"

Oh *now* he was attuned to her feelings. She shook her head and walked away toward the stove where she had rice simmering. He came up from behind her and hugged her, kissing the side of her head. "You not feeling well?"

"I'm fine, Angel."

She felt him go stiff and he turned her around to face him. "All right what is it?"

Before she could answer her phone rang. "Ignore it," he said staring into her eyes.

"No, I have to get it. I'm expecting a call." She walked away from him and grabbed her phone off the counter. "Can you watch that rice for me please?"

She answered her phone, "Hey Sydney." She headed out to the front room and toward the front door already feeling her throat tighten.

"Lynni how are you?"

She'd barely walked out the door when she managed to whisper. "Not good."

"What's wrong?"

"Sofia is pregnant. I just found out today."

Sydney was quiet. That's all she'd had to say and she knew he got it. She'd called him the day after Valerie and Isabel's announcements too and just like then he reminded her that she and Angel hadn't even gone to a fertility expert yet. "For all you know it might be a quick fix."

She had only brought up the possibility of seeking medical help five months after they'd lost the baby and they still weren't pregnant. Angel didn't think it necessary but said he would if she really wanted to. She said she'd give it some more time but hadn't brought it up since. It was almost as if they did it was their first step toward the real possibility of finding out they may never be able to have children. She couldn't even bear the thought.

As she talked to Sydney she walked all the way around their property. It reminded her of how excited they'd been when they purchased it. They'd lived in a duplex for the first year and a half of their marriage. They were too excited about getting the restaurant up and running to think about buying a house. It was only when they decided they were ready to start a family that they went to Valerie to help them find a home. They fell in love with it the moment they saw it.

The excitement of owning their own home began to fade after the first several months of trying to conceive with no success. Even now neither wanted to admit they were worried. It was as if saying it out loud made it more real.

She was in the back patio now and had been on the phone with Syd for almost a half hour when Angel slid the back door open and stuck his head out. "You almost done? This rice has been ready for a while now. What were you gonna do with it?"

Sarah knew that tone. He wasn't happy about her being on the phone with Syd this long. It had been a while that she'd even been on the phone with Syd while Angel was home and it'd never been this long. She tended to cut the calls short when Angel was around but today she just needed to let it out.

Turning her face away from him quickly to hide a tear that escaped she said, "Yeah, I was wrapping it up."

"Hey,"

She blinked her eyes in hopes of making the tears less noticeable before turning to face Angel again.

His eyebrows pinched and he slid the door wider and took a step outside. "You okay?"

She nodded and smiled. "I'll be right in."

Angel stared at her for bit too long before nodding and stepping back in the house.

"I'll call you tomorrow, Syd. Angel is home and waiting for me."

"Okay and listen going to a doctor about this doesn't mean you're admitting anything. All it means is you're getting a little help. Thousands of couples go through this. It's nothing to be ashamed of."

"I'm not ashamed. I'm just scared."

"Don't be. You're both surrounded by people that love you. You'll have a ton of support and family to hold your hands through this, including me."

She took a deep breath feeling emotional all over again. "I love you, Sydney."

She hadn't said that to him in years. Once they were both married it felt a little weird. They'd replaced it with *I miss you*. But at this moment it felt right. She'd needed the comfort he'd brought to her in just those few words.

"I love you too, Lynni."

After hanging up she took a few deep breaths to try and wash the emotions away, before making her way back inside.

*

It'd been years since he had to even think about Sarah and Syd. And even longer since he'd worried about it. She was his wife now. He owned her body and soul just like she owned him. She assured him of this, and it went both ways. So why the fuck was he getting so worked up? To walk into his kitchen and feel that vibe. A vibe he didn't like from Sarah and then have her pull away from him because she had to take this call — a call from Syd. Really?

As if that weren't bad enough she walked out of the house. She'd never done that. Not that she talked to Sydney often these days but if she happened to she did so openly and freely without any reservation about Angel hearing her conversation.

The sliding door opened and Angel leaned against the counter in the kitchen waiting for her to come around the corner. She did but avoided his eyes placing her phone on the counter nearest to her. "What's going on with Syd?"

She shrugged. "He's getting divorced."

That only intensified what he was feeling. "Is that right? For sure? Or is he just thinking about it."

"No. It's a sure thing. He's not even staying with her anymore and he got served with the papers a few days ago."

Sarah walked up to the stove removing the lid from the pot of rice. Angel reached out for her hand and pulled her to him. "Let's try this again. What's wrong?"

She shook her head and said nothing staring at his chest. He lifted her chin and saw her tear filled eyes. Immediately his worries about Syd were gone, replaced by overwhelming concern. "What is it?"

She shook her head again, wiping a tear that escaped down her cheek. Angel wrapped his arms around her waist pulling her even closer, refusing to drop the eye contact. "Look at me, Sarah. You can tell me."

"I'm ashamed to."

Angel's breath caught. He wouldn't let that statement and the fact that she just had a long conversation with Sydney, one she obviously didn't want Angel to hear manifest into something ugly. "Don't be silly. Just tell me."

She leaned in and rested her head against his chest. "I don't want you to think I'm not happy for Sofia and Eric. I really am. It's just that..." She took a deep trembling breath and right then he knew exactly what was wrong.

He'd thought about it when he hung up with her after giving her the news. Maybe he should've waited until he got home to tell her. But Sofia had just told him when Sarah called and it was still so fresh on his mind. He stroked her back. "Listen, I've been meaning to talk to you about that. I wanted to bring it up but since you hadn't in months I was afraid to. What do you say if it doesn't happen this month we go see a doctor?"

She lifted her head away from his chest and stared at him. Her big beautiful green eyes were full of worry. "I've done some research, babe," he said, kissing her forehead. "There's all kinds of reasons why it might not be happening. It could be something really simple."

"I've been looking it up, too. But I'm just so scared. What if they tell us we can't *ever*?"

"Sarah, we already know we can." God he'd never forget how devastated she'd been. He had been too but he hurt more for her than anything. He knew how excited she'd been. Not that he hadn't been but he decided long ago that he could be happy going through life without kids as long as he had Sarah by his side. But since this was so important to her he'd do whatever it took to make her happy. "It already happened once, baby. It'll happen again."

Her eyes went from worried to hopeful. "You think?"

He smiled kissing her. "Yeah, I think."

She smiled, taking a deep breath and leaned against his chest again. "Okay so if it doesn't happen this month, I'll make an appointment."

"Good." He kissed the top of her head. "Now you wanna tell me why you had to go outside to talk to Syd?"

She continued to lean against him. "I didn't want you to hear me tell him I was upset about Sofia's news."

Angel clenched his teeth, taking a deep breath. He had to remind himself that Sarah had always been close to Sydney. So close that sharing something this personal with him was normal. He only hoped that now that he was getting divorced it didn't mean she'd be hearing more from him. Best friend or not, Angel had never truly accepted it, just learned to tolerate it. Sarah had to know this. But he'd let it go for now.

He turned to the pot of white rice on the stove. "So you really making dinner?"

Sarah pulled away glancing at the pot then back at him with a smirk. "Why is that so hard to believe?"

Angel laughed. "I didn't say that. I'm just saying," he glanced around at the otherwise empty stove top. "Are we playing survivor or something? Is rice all we're having?"

She laughed. "No I was going to make some teriyaki chicken."

Angel crinkled his nose. "What do you say we go grab a pizza and some beer. Well, wine for you. " He leaned his forehead against hers. "Might not be too long before you can't have wine anymore ."

That brightened her eyes and she nodded. "Okay."

"Okay," he said kissing her. "I love you."

"I love you, too."

CHAPTER 2

Sal explained the final task needed to close out the books for the month. Ever since the third restaurant had been opened up in La Jolla Shores last year, he'd had his hands full, but he was still insisting he could manage all three restaurants. The back office stuff anyway — things he'd gone to school for all those years. But knowing how busy he and Grace were with the new restaurant and now Grace taking time off to be home more with baby Sal; Sarah had finally convinced him she could take over some of the things he normally did at her and Angel's restaurant. It was a bit more daunting than she'd expected. He always made it look so easy but she was catching on. If only her mind didn't keep wandering.

She was two weeks late now but refused to make any announcements. The initial home pregnancy test had come back positive and even though she'd allowed herself to jump into Angel's arms and cry overjoyed; there was still a very small possibility it could be a false positive, or she could lose it again. Her appointment with her doctor was still a few days away. Secretly she knew she was. She was already feeling all the signs from the first time. They would hold off until she was past that twelve week mark. It was a long time to keep it to themselves but she knew this family. They'd make a huge deal out of it which would only make things worse if something went wrong.

Raul, their newest waiter, walked in the back and

started putting on his apron. Unlike most of the waiters they hired, since he'd worked at several of the trendy marina restaurants he'd needed the least amount of training and he doubled as a bartender when they got real busy on the weekends. He was a little cocky and outspoken and flirted wildly with the other waitresses, not to mention the customers, but Sarah had to admit he was good.

Sal turned to face him. "So how we doing? You catching on?"

Raul brought his eyebrows together with an expression of sheer confidence. "With my eyes closed."

Sarah was glad for the distraction because her phone had buzzed a couple of times since Sal started explaining everything to her and she thought it rude to check her texts so she took advantage now that he chatted with Raul.

Both texts were from Sydney. She clicked on it and read the threaded messages.

Sitting at the airport. Flights delayed and I'm bored as hell.

Then:

How are you feeling?

He'd was the only other person that knew about her positive pregnancy test. She tried to keep it from him but the last time they talked he knew something was up when she stumbled on her answer about why she still hadn't made an appointment to see the fertility specialist. He knew her too well so she decided to just tell him, but made him promise to not mention a word to his parents until she gave him the go ahead.

She was about to text back when Sal stood up. She looked up at him. "Are we done?"

"Yep, that's it. For the monthly stuff. I'll come back

and show you the quarterly stuff next month."

He kissed her head and she thanked him for his patience. He and Raul walked out together into the dining room and she texted Sydney back.

Tokyo again? So far so good. But my appointment isn't for another few days.

Sydney worked as a technical engineer for a giant computer software company whose headquarters was based in Tokyo so they flew him out there at least once a month. When he first hired on he'd actually lived out there for a few months.

She went through some of the stuff she and Sal had just done on the computer while she waited for him to respond.

Angel walked into the back; before she could even say anything he leaned in and kissed her deeply. When he finally came up for air she smiled. "Wow. What was that about?"

He shrugged smiling. "You just do that to me." He glanced behind him. "How you feeling? Any nausea yet?"

"A little earlier, but I'm fine now."

He seemed concerned for a second then the corner of his lip went up, flashing her his beautiful dimple. "You know you are, babe."

"But don't say anything yet. It's too soon."

"Okay, whatever you want." He kissed her again. "You think you're up for a ballgame this weekend? Romero and Isabel are stopping by to have lunch and he has extra tickets to the Padres game this Friday. It's a play off game."

Her phone buzzed and she glanced at it. So did Angel.

"Sure. That sounds like fun."

Her phone buzzed again.

"You gonna get that?" Angel asked, pulling open the bottom drawer of the desk. He started looking for something.

"It's just Sydney. I'll text him back in a little."

Angel looked up at her, his eyebrow raised. She knew he'd noticed the increase in texts from Sydney but he had to understand this was a really hard time for Syd. And they were just texts.

"What's he up to now?"

"He's stuck at the airport and bored."

Angels eyes locked on hers for a second before looking back down into the drawer. "Hmm. Alright so I'll tell Romero we're in."

He began to straighten out and she pulled him to her and kissed him. "Thanks for understanding about me not wanting to say anything yet."

"You know I'll agree with whatever makes you happy."

She waited until he was out of the room before picking up her phone. Sydney would always be a sticky subject for them. She still didn't understand why after all these years Angel could possibly be insecure about this. She hadn't even seen Sydney in over a year. Sighing, she read the text and smiled.

*

He's single now and he has no one but Sarah to entertain him? A married woman whose husband has never made it a secret that their relationship is not one that thrills him? How stupid was this guy?

Romero and Isabel walked in. They came up to Angel and Isabel hugged him. "I thought you said Manny and Max were coming too?"

"They are." Romero said. "They're on their way."

Angel showed them to one of his bigger tables. "I'll go get a waiter."

Isabel took a seat but Romero followed him. Angel didn't need to go too far. Raul was already on his way to their table.

"Izzy just order me the usual. I'll be right there." He turned back to Angel. "So you want them?"

Angel stopped. "Yeah, Sarah says she wants to go."

Romero pulled them out of his pocket and handed him the tickets. He started going on about how great the seats were and he was supposed to go with Alex but the twins were under the weather and neither he nor Valerie wanted to leave them. Angel took a few steps away from the table where Isabel sat, hoping Romero wouldn't hear Raul doing his usual flirting.

"And get this. Manny's friend will be able to get tickets if they go to the World Series."

Just then Raul laughed and so did Isabel. Romero stopped and glanced back at them taking in Raul from top to bottom. He glanced back at Angel. "New waiter?"

"Yeah, just started couple of weeks ago." Angel took a deep breath as Raul started his usual, 'you look so familiar' routine.

The table covered Isabel's swollen belly so there was no way Raul could tell he was flirting with a pregnant woman. And the last time the whole gang had been together, Sarah had had to endure Valerie, Isabel and Grace complain about their pregnancy woes. One of which was Isabel saying she couldn't wear her wedding ring anymore because her fingers kept swelling up.

"So the World Series uh?"

Romero turned back to Angel and Angel could see Raul had already struck a nerve with him. Before Romero could answer Raul continued.

"It must be that sweet smile."

Though Romero had gotten better about his temper, he still annoyed easily especially when it came to his Izzy. "Is this guy for real?" he said, glaring at Raul.

Thankfully Raul walked away from the table just then right past Angel and Romero who stared him down *hard*.

"Relax he does that with everyone." Angel smirked trying to soften the moment but Romero wasn't smiling. "I'll go get your drinks."

Angel hurried back to the bar area where Raul was waiting on Romero and Isabel's drinks. "What's that guy's problem?"

"That was his pregnant wife you were just flirting with, you idiot. Will you stop laying on the flirting shit so thick and just take orders like a normal waiter?" Angel reached for the tray with the two drinks for Romero and Isabel. "I got this, and have Julie take over this table."

"Are you serious?" Raul chuckled.

Angel shot him a look and Raul lifted his hands. "All right. But don't you think that's kind of stupid to go all cave man over something so small. I complimented his wife. He should be flattered."

"Yeah, well he wasn't."

After dropping off the drinks then the tray back at the bar Angel headed to back room lost in thought. He thought about Raul's comment. Was it stupid for Romero to get so worked up so easily? In the middle of that thought he walked into the back room where Sarah was laughing reading her text. Immediately the annoyance he'd felt earlier was back doubled. "What's so funny?"

She seemed startled but attempted to play it off and shook her head. "Sydney."

"Really? What about him?" Angel wasn't so sure what pissed him off more. The fact that Sarah could smile so brightly over something Sydney texted her or that they'd obviously been texting all this time.

"He had sent a text earlier saying it should be illegal for some people to wear flip flops. Then just now he sent a picture he took of the guy's feet he was talking about." She put her hand over her mouth to stifle a laugh. "His toes are all nasty and hairy."

Angel couldn't even force a smile. "How long has he been stuck at the airport?"

"I don't know—couple of hours I think," she said, still smiling.

"And he's been texting you all this time?" Angel opened the back cabinet to put on a baseball cap with the restaurant's logo.

He glanced back at her. The smile was gone. "No he hasn't, Angel. I said he'd sent me that text about the guy's feet earlier. I got caught up with what I was doing I hadn't even responded just now when I got the picture."

"I was just asking a question, Sarah. No need to get all defensive."

"I'm not getting defensive."

Angel put the cap on and hurried to the door. "All right you're not." He stalked out before he blew up. *Fuck!* He was better than this. It *was* stupid to go all cave man on her but he couldn't help it.

Luckily Romero flagged him down as soon as he

saw him. Manny, Aida and Max were sitting with them now.

"I wasn't there," Manny said as Angel walked up to their table was. "But this guy was. Hey, Angel, tell Izzy about the time Romero burned his eyebrow off trying to light that bonfire at the beach. You should've seen him," Manny turned back to Isabel. "And then he wouldn't shave off the other one so he wouldn't look so stupid with only one eyebrow so he walked around for weeks like this." Manny covered one eyebrow with his finger and wheezed in laughter. Aida snorted and Romero rolled his eyes. After a few minutes with those guys, Angel snapped out of his mood — a little.

CHAPTER 3

The doctor had confirmed what they already knew. Sarah was pregnant. With the twelve week mark long behind them now everyone knew and they'd even made it through the not so wonderful part of being pregnant — the first trimester.

It hadn't actually been too bad. The physical symptoms weren't nearly as bad as the raging hormones. Sarah cried at the drop of a pin, and even though it didn't annoy Angel nearly as much as it bothered him, he'd always hated to see her cry, Sarah admitted she was getting on her own nerves.

Understandably even Angel had gotten choked up when they first heard the heartbeat. But weeks later Angel's heart nearly stopped when she suddenly jerked awake in the middle of the night only to tell him she'd felt the baby move. That was just the beginning. A few weeks later the leg cramps in the middle of the night started; the first was the scariest. She yelped in pain nearly stopping his heart again and when he got the light on he saw her leg in the air.

"Cramp!" was the only thing she said. Her agonized expression told him the rest. Luckily, both Isabel and Grace had recently mentioned this. Both Sal and Romero had had to come to their rescue by massaging down the cramped area so Angel jumped on it, attacking that cramped muscle on her leg like it was the enemy. He massaged with conviction glancing back at his poor wife as her expression slowly soothed.

After that he had it down. The moment it hit again he didn't even have to turn on the lights. Though the amount of times it happened decreased once they looked into what was needed to avoid them. As much as Angel had prayed Sarah would finally be pregnant he never imagined it would be so nerve wracking, until things took a completely unexpected turn.

All this time Angel had searched online for things like morning sickness remedies, mood swings and how the hell to fix it. He'd never taken into consideration some of the more pleasant side effect of pregnancies. At first he didn't think much of it. Three nights in a row Sarah had attacked him before he even tried to make a move and then woke the next morning in the mood again.

He sat in the back finishing up the schedules for the next week when Sarah walked into the back room with a wicked smile on her face and her green eyes smoldered.

He couldn't help smiling. "What?"

"We have that call to take remember?" she said, locking the door behind her.

He thought about it for a second as she walked to him. "What call?"

"You know. The one I just told everyone we'd be on for a while."

She straddled him, rubbing him in such a way that had him stirring in his pants at once. "Baby, what are you—"

Her kiss was so frenzied it made his legs weak but other parts went solid immediately. His arms wrapped around her and stroked her back as her hands held his face. Angel hadn't felt this damn excited since they'd found out she was pregnant and he'd been so focused

ELIZABETH REYES

on her well being—both physical and emotional.

Her hands came down to his pants, undoing his button and unzipping him, then she stood just long enough for him to pull them down. For a split second he actually considered objecting, they *were* in the restaurant and employees were just outside the door, but that passed real quick. He hadn't even thought about it until then that Sarah wore a skirt. She rarely wore skirts to work. His eyes opened wide and he looked up at her. "Did you plan this?"

Her only response: a big sexy smile, as she slipped her panties off from under her skirt, making his heart beat even more wildly. She made her way on to his lap again, staring deep into his eyes as she sat down slowly and he slipped right in.

Wrapping her arms around his neck she began to ride him. Angel tried but couldn't help groaning.

"Shhh," she said, but even that was strained. Her own breathing was labored now.

They kissed, their rhythm, long ago perfected though right now, Sarah couldn't seem to get enough; sucking his tongue, then his lips, as she began riding him faster and harder. She lifted her feet off the floor and he went even deeper. Sarah moaned, pulling away from his lips and burying her face in neck as she began to pant and he felt her unmistakable trembling.

Angel brought his hands down to her legs and squeezed her soft thighs just as her panting got a little louder. He felt her squeeze around him and the oh so familiar wet signs that she was just about there when she licked his neck and he was a goner.

He squeezed his eyes shut as he pushed up into her as deep as he could and felt her nails dig into his shoulders. They sat there for a few moment, breathing hard without saying anything before Angel reached for the apron he'd taken off earlier and thrown onto the other chair.

Sarah finally pulled away from his neck and faced him. He smirked. "What's gotten into you lately?" Then added quickly. "Not that I'm complaining."

She shrugged and if he wasn't mistaken his pregnant wife who was still straddling him in broad daylight in the back room of their restaurant, where their employees were just on the other side of a wall, and this was all her idea — was blushing. He had to laugh and he kissed her. "You're amazing. Whatever it is. I just want you to know I'm loving it. And if this has something to do with you being pregnant and somehow makes life easier for you. I'm willing to take one for the team every time the mood strikes." He leaned his forehead against hers. "I mean that."

She giggled, kissing him back. Once she left the room he looked up, *increased sexual drive during pregnancy*. Bingo. He was right. First thing he looked for was how long it lasts. It was about time one of these pregnancy side effects went his way and he was going to make the most of it. He couldn't believe some idiot husbands were actually complaining about it in some of the discussion boards. Angel was already shifting in his pants just thinking about what he was in for that night. He smiled when he read one woman mention it only intensified as her due date got closer.

*

Of the five babies all due that same year, baby Vivianna had been the first to arrive. She was a chubby little thing with a ton of hair just like her mommy. Grace named her after the mother she'd never met. Sal couldn't be happier about his little princess and Sarah loved going over to hold the newborn. She could hardly wait to hold her own.

Next came Amanda Romero. Unlike Vivianna, Amanda was born with virtually no hair and Manny told everyone that listened that just like her daddy, *Mandy* would probably be bald as an egg for the whole first year of her life.

Surprisingly since Isabel had to have a C-section and had limited physical capabilities for the first week Romero became Super Dad. The man once terrified-of-even-holding a baby was now doing it all. Even with her sisters and mom offering to help he insisted he could do it, telling everyone "I got this." And he certainly proved he did.

Then came baby Alex. Even though he'd weighed more at birth than both twins put together Valerie was so relieved she didn't have to deal with another set of twins. And the twins were eager to help out with everything that had to be done with their little brother. Well, everything except change his "stinky *diapuh.*"

Sofia and Sarah were the only two left still waiting but Sofia was due first. She had less than two weeks to go while Sarah was only in her thirty-third week. Unlike Sofia, who knew she was having a girl, Sarah and Angel wanted to be surprised. Though she was dying to know she wanted to wait until that beautiful moment in the delivery room she'd dreamt of so often when they told her what she'd had and she finally got to hold her baby.

Though her pregnancy thus far had gone pretty smoothly they'd had a few instances where Sarah had panicked because it'd been too long since she last felt the baby move. She'd called the doctor who advised her to drink something really cold and lie on her side. She didn't think it would actually work but she did as she was told and several minutes later after feeling the baby jolt she felt incredibly guilty that she'd woken him or her that way.

Angel didn't want her working full shifts at the restaurant anymore. He preferred to know she was home resting and staying safe. He wasn't thrilled about her driving around too much anymore either. Even a fender bender might do her some harm and he said there was no sense in taking chances. So Sarah wasn't going very far on her own these days.

That morning she'd gone to her mom's for breakfast and now she was going to put a few hours in at the restaurant and then head home early. She was beginning to feel more and more tired now that she was getting bigger and it was starting to affect how comfortable she could get at night to sleep.

She'd just stepped out of her car in the parking lot when she heard him. "Lynni!"

Her heart leaped as she turned and saw Sydney step out of a cab. They rushed to each other and hugged. He picked her up off the ground, laughing. "God, this is perfect timing."

They moved out of the way to let a car that had pulled into the parking lot go by. Raul waved as he drove by but looked at her a little weird. She turned back to Sydney. Her once-chubby childhood friend had grown into a rugged, handsome man. He'd let his hair grow out a little and he had a five o'clock shadow but not like he'd forgotten to shave. It was too clean like he was wearing it that way on purpose and it suited him. "What are you doing here? How come you didn't tell me you'd be coming?"

"I wasn't," he said looking her up and down. "I just had a stop here between flights and I took a chance. I actually gotta get back; my flight leaves in less than an hour. I knew it was a long shot that I might actually catch you here, but I'm so glad I did. Wow." He rubbed her belly. "Look at you, Lynn. You're absolutely stunning."

She smiled, placing her hand over his and pulled it to the side of her belly. "Feel."

His eyes opened wide as the baby tapped the side. "He or she's been very active this morning."

Sydney's bright smile softened a bit. "I still can't believe you're going to be a mommy soon."

"I know." She slipped her hand in his. "Can you come in and have something to eat?"

"No, sweetie. I gotta go. This," he gestured back to the waiting cab, "is crazy! I did this on a whim. Hopped in a cab and kept my fingers crossed that I might find you here. So when we pulled up and I saw you getting out of the car I nearly jumped out before it even stopped."

Sarah laughed then pouted. "So you really have to go now?"

He pouted too and nodded. "But I'll be sure to make it a point to come out just to see you—hang out for a few days. Maybe after the baby is born. It's ridiculous that we've let this much time go by without visiting each other."

"It is." She agreed. "You have to come back when the baby is born."

"I will. I promise." He looked at his watch and frowned. "I gotta go. I'm so glad I got to see you." He hugged her again holding her for a bit and she took in the smell of him. It brought back so many memories. He pulled away and smiled. "I've missed you."

"I miss you too."

He kissed her hand then rubbed her belly again. "I love you, Sydney." The words just came out. She hadn't realized how much she missed him until she saw him.

"I love you, too." He promised he'd be back soon before saying his final goodbye and walking back to the cab. She watched and waved as it drove away, memories of running with him and their long ago lengthy chats on the phone danced in her head. Years of her life that seemed at times now gone, almost as if they never were. She walked through the parking lot lost in thought.

It happened so fast, she never even saw the concrete parking block she tripped on, before she could even try to break her fall, she hit the ground on her side *hard*.

CHAPTER 4
A.S.A.P

It had been a while since Angel worked the bar. He'd been so preoccupied the last couple of weeks with baby stuff he'd messed up on the schedule and three bartenders were off today so he was helping out. Raul had walked in minutes ago and was in the back getting suited up. He could have him work the bar today and when Sarah got there he'd have her take orders though she wouldn't be carrying any of them out.

It was actually good every now and again to get away from the back room. Lately he'd been glued to his computer looking through catalogs of all the stuff he wanted to shower his baby with. The backyard play set Alex got for the twins was awesome and Sarah had laughed when she caught him on the website that had them custom made. She said what he should be looking into was starting up a college fund for the baby. School was expensive and the sooner they got started the better. That was true but those websites were boring.

Raul came out from the back but stopped when David, one of the other waiters stopped him to tell him something and they both laughed loudly. "Hey when you're done messing around I'm gonna need you in the bar today."

Raul walked away from David with a smile. "Sure thing boss. Did someone call in?"

"Nah it was my fault actually. I messed up. I scheduled too many people off at once. I gotta double check next week's, make sure I didn't do the same thing. So I'll need you to bartend today but not until Sarah gets here. I'll have her take over your section."

"Isn't she here already?" Raul asked.

"No," Angel wiped down the bar. "She was having breakfast with her mom this morning."

"She was out in the parking lot when I drove in. I thought she'd be in here by now. Unless," Raul smirked, "that guy whose arms she flew into stole her a-way."

Angel turned and peered at Raul not sure if he was serious. He had the stupidest sense of humor some-times. But apparently he was serious. "What are you talking about?"

"Some guy who got out of a cab and hugged your wife, man. He picked her up off the ground he hugged her so hard." Raul pulled out the paper pad out of his apron's front pocket and stuck a pen behind his ear. "I don't know maybe he's family. Does she have a brother?"

"No, she doesn't."

Raul shrugged. "She's probably still out there." He walked away to his first table of the day.

That was strange. Who would be visiting Sarah in a cab? Then it hit him. Something began to warm his in-sides just as he saw her walk in. He fully expected to see Sydney walk in behind her but she was alone. He met her by the hallway leading to the back room. As soon as their eyes met he knew something was wrong. "You okay?"

She nodded but looked away quickly and kept walking to the back.

"You sure?"

"Yeah, yeah, I'm fine. I'm just a little tired," she said, sitting down with her hand over her belly.

"You should go home then, babe. I don't want you working if you're not up to it." Then he remembered. "Who was out there with you?"

She seemed dazed and it unnerved him. "Huh?"

"Raul, he said he saw you out there. A guy in a cab hugged you." He raised his eyebrow. "Picked you up?"

It was the strangest thing, she was looking at him and listening but it was as if she were a million miles away. She told him about Sydney swinging by between flights and how he couldn't stay. If it hadn't been for his concern over the way she was acting he might've been a little more ticked about the fact that Sydney had been so moved to see her he actually picked her up. Raul hadn't been exaggerating since Sarah didn't deny it. Instead he stared at her trying to figure out what this strange demeanor was about.

Angel got down on his knee in front of her and rubbed her belly. "Are you sure you're okay, baby? You're scaring me."

Finally she looked at him and not through him like when she first arrived and smiled rubbing his hand on her belly. "I'm fine. But I think I will go home. I didn't get very much sleep last night."

"All right." He stood up and held his hand out. "I'll walk you out."

Even after he knew she was home and safe in bed he couldn't shake that feeling that something was wrong. Then he got the call.

Sarah was crying. "Please don't be mad at me?"

His heart began to race. "About what?"

She sputtered out the rest so fast and he got most of it even in between the whimpering. She'd fallen just outside the restaurant but didn't want to alarm him for nothing. His heart had immediately spiked the moment he heard her say she fell, but the last part nearly made him stop breathing. "I'm not feeling any kind of discomfort or anything but I had some pinkish discharge and my mom says I should go to the hospital just to play it safe."

She hadn't even finished saying it and he was already rushing through the restaurant with his keys in his hands. He called Sal who told him not to worry he'd take care of the restaurant for him. Memories of when Sarah had miscarried the first time slammed into him and he choked back the lump that was already forming in his throat.

*

It was pink not red. Sarah kept telling herself. Not like when she lost the first baby. And she wasn't cramping or feeling any kind of discomfort. After checking everything, all of her and the baby's vitals were fine but the fact that they wanted to keep her overnight for observation still made her very nervous. Were they not telling her something?

Sarah smiled trying to be brave and squeezed Angel's hand. Everybody else that had come by, her mother, his parents, even Alex and Valerie had left hours earlier. Angel wanted to stay as late as possible but it was almost midnight and he looked so tired. "You should go home, honey. Get some rest." His eyes were as anxious as she felt. "And try not to worry; the doctors said they're just being cautious."

He leaned in and kissed her. "No way, baby. I'm not leaving. I won't get any sleep anyway. Not without you there by my side."

She smiled. "But you have to. You'll need to be rested so you can take me home tomorrow."

He gestured to the recliner behind him. "I'll rest right here. I'm *not* leaving you."

As expected she had a hard time falling asleep. After a few hours Angel had knocked out on the recliner. The nurse came in to check her vitals. "So there really is no other reason why they're keeping me, right?"

The nurse smiled reassuringly. "The fact that you spotted on the day you fell could very well be coincidental, but since it did happen on the same day, the doctor just didn't want to take any chances." The nurse touched her arm lightly and winked. "You're fine."

After the nurse walked out Sarah grabbed her phone and texted Syd. When she'd first fallen she had the absurd thought that it was God's way of punishing her for loving Sydney. Maybe it was wrong. Maybe she shouldn't feel for him what she did. But now she realized that was silly. She loved him like she's always loved him — like the very best friend anyone could ever ask for.

She explained to him what happened and assured him that she was fine then ended the text with a goodnight and again she told him she loved him. Then she finally fell asleep.

She woke up about five in the morning feeling strange. Angel wasn't on the recliner but his keys and jacket were there; he must've stepped out. Something was wrong. They'd dimmed the lights in her room but even with the darkened room she could see something when she pulled up the blankets. She reached for the lights and thought she might faint when she realized she was bleeding. Swallowing hard and trying to hold it together she rang for the nurse. Within seconds the nurse was there.

"I'm bleeding!"

The nurse quickly assessed Sarah's condition then called the nurses' station and Sarah heard the most frightening words she'd ever heard. "Get the doctor here ASAP, looks like Moreno is going to deliver."

"Deliver? I'm only thirty three-weeks!"

"I don't know honey. Something's happened and this baby is coming now."

Sarah was already in tears. "Where's my husband? I need him here."

"You just relax, we'll get him for you."

The doctor was there within minutes. After examining her he confirmed what the nurse had said that she would have to deliver. He explained that the most common damage a fall or any kind of trauma that occurs during pregnancy causes is tearing of the placenta. It's what had concerned him and why he'd kept her. Apparently he made the right call.

Angel rushed in just as the doctor explained what would happen next. At this stage of her pregnancy he strongly recommended no pain medicines for the delivery. "It'll make the baby sluggish. Any chance of survival, we'll need this baby as alert as can be. You'll have to do this on your own."

"Then don't give me anything!" Sarah cried.

Angel held her hand tight, his face as terrified as she felt even though she could see he attempted to keep it together.

"Okay." The doctor nodded. "Lets get started."

CHAPTER 5
Eight days

Four hours later, after agonizingly having to endure seeing Sarah in so much pain, she delivered a tiny baby boy. She'd cried when they whisked him away so fast she never even got a chance to see him. Angel's heart ached for her and as much as he wanted to go investigate—find out just how his baby was doing—he couldn't tear himself from her side. She was so incredibly sad and he wanted nothing more than to comfort her. He knew she had to be replaying the same words in her head that he had ever since he heard them. *Any chance of survival.*

He'd hardly slept the entire night; he'd been tossing and turning, worried that something like this would happen. After hours of crying Sarah had finally fallen asleep. As tired as he was Angel refused to leave the hospital until Sarah left with him. The nurse said she would be setting something up for him to sleep in. In the meantime he was finally able to go into the NICU and got the first glimpse of his son.

After walking by several other tiny babies hooked up to all kinds of tubes looking dreadfully sick he almost smiled when he saw the incubator with the Moreno label. He didn't look much smaller than what his nieces looked like when they were born but he did have a million tubes hooked to him.

The labels said he was three pounds thirteen ounces. That wasn't that bad. He'd read some of the others who were only one or two pounds. Here his son was almost four. Something beeped and a nurse came over and opened the incubator. Immediately alarmed he asked the nurse. "What's wrong with him?"

"Bradycardias," she said, massaging the baby's chest with her fingers.

She could have been speaking German and he wouldn't have understood less. "What is that?"

"Heart is too slow," she clarified.

Angels eyes widened.

"Normal for a preemie," she added quickly. "I stimulated his heart. See." She pointed at the monitor as if Angel knew what any of the numbers meant. "Already better."

Angel stared at the baby and could hardly believe he was his. It felt surreal. He and Sarah had made this little guy. He wished she could be there with him but in a way he was glad she wasn't. The baby's appearance would probably make her sad. He did look positively fragile.

It wasn't until he walked into the waiting room and was immediately surrounded by his family that he let out everything he'd felt that night the knot in his throat, finally gave and he wept in his mother's arms as she stroked his head and his back. "Cry, *mijo*. Let it out. It's okay. It's okay."

His brothers assured him they had everything under control at the restaurant—told him not to worry about anything. After letting them know Sarah probably wouldn't be up to any visitors until maybe that evening they left. Angel visited his son again. Then went back to the room. Sarah was awake.

"I wanna see him," were the first words out of her mouth when she saw Angel.

"You can't, babe."

The doctors had described Sarah's postpartum bleeding as "on the heavy side." They were monitoring her closely to make sure it didn't crossover to hemorrhaging. That was common when there is damage to the placenta which in Sarah's case they were almost certain that's what had happened. They wanted her to stay in bed for at least a day before attempting to walk.

"Maybe tomorrow."

"Did you see him?"

God he hated to see her so sad. "I did. He's beautiful." He sat on the side of her bed and pulled out his phone showing her the pictures he'd taken of their baby. "Look he's not as small as some of the other babies in there. He's almost four pounds. The nurse said the only thing they're watching him closely for is his heart slowing down." He knew that would scare her and he saw it in her eyes. "But she said that's normal for preemies."

Sarah held his phone staring at the small screen her hand over her mouth and her eyes welled up again.

"She also said unlike some of the other babies in there that will probably be here for months, we might just be looking a few weeks."

She finally pulled her eyes away from the phone to look at him. He didn't think it possible but he saw her spirit fall even further. "Weeks?"

"Baby he's too little. He needs to gain weight and be able to eat, breath and stay warm on his own before we can take him home. But other than that he's healthy." He kissed her softly. "Have you thought of a name?"

"I have to see him first."

Angel smiled. "All right then for now he's just our

baby."

She took a deep breathe and leaned against him chest. Angel always thought he'd want a big family, especially since Sarah was an only child but after the ordeal they'd gone through he wasn't sure he could go through something like this again.

*

Angel had warned her about their baby's appearance. So she braced herself as she was wheeled into the NICU. Her heart nearly broke for all the other tiny babies in there who looked so shriveled and barely human. Some looked like just breathing hurt. When she reached the incubator labeled Moreno she was overwhelmed with emotion. Angel was right. He wasn't nearly as small as some of the other babies and except for being so little and all the tubes on him he looked almost normal. He slept soundly.

The nurse walked by and smiled. "No bradys for almost five hours."

Sarah looked at her having no clue what that meant.

"It's what they call it when his heart slows down," Angel translated.

Sarah glanced at him then back at her baby. He was perfect and she teared up. "My little angel." She turned back to Angel wiping her tears away with a smile. "It's perfect. He's an angel and at the same time he can take his daddy's name."

"Really? Are you sure?"

She nodded, her spirits rising. She always considered naming their first born son after Angel, and now that there was a baby Sal and baby Alex why not keep with tradition? "Baby Angel," she said staring at her son. Her son—she could hardly believe it—she had a son.

Leaving the hospital empty handed was harder than she imagined; the first few nights they'd driven back to the hospital in need of being near him again.

Baby Angel was progressing superbly. He was gaining weight on schedule and had begun to drink from a bottle. The first time they got to hold him had been emotional for everyone. It was the most beautiful feeling to finally hold him in her arms. Then there was a setback. They'd begun the countdown. With his weight nearing five pounds and him eating on his own the doctors said as soon as he went ten days without any bradycardias he could go home. The most he'd gone was an entire twenty-four hours and then he had one and the clock had to be started again. It was heartbreaking but Sarah was still thankful that he was healthy in every other way.

Angel was excited that unlike all his nephews and nieces whose eyes were immediately piercing dark brown, his sons eyes were very gray, almost blue, a sign the doctor said that they may very well end up being green like Sarah's. He said he'd always loved her eyes and that it'd be awesome to see such a huge part of Sarah in his son every time he looked into his eyes.

After going another full ten hours without a brady the machine went off again. Both Sarah and Angel knew how to stimulate his chest now to get the heartbeat to speed up and she did holding back the tears.

She sat there now hours later holding him. It was so unfair. Just a few days ago Sofia had given birth to a perfectly healthy baby girl and was already home with her. Sarah fought the feelings of bitterness and reminded herself it was miracle her baby was doing so well. Some of the other babies were not faring as well and had a ton of issues. One had even passed a few days ago. Sarah couldn't even imagine the anguish those parents must've gone through and instantly felt guilty. She kissed her baby's forehead and was slightly startled with Angel's voice. "Have you talked to Sydney lately?"

She looked up at him and shook her head. She'd never tell Angel but she was convinced now after texting Syd the night before she woke up bleeding in the hospital that God was punishing her. It wasn't right to love two men. Even though she loved them both in such different ways. She knew it would hurt Angel if he ever heard her say she did—knew how much it bothered him years ago. That's why she'd stopped doing it. Why had she started up now? She had no idea. But she wouldn't chance it anymore. She hadn't even told Syd she'd had the baby though she was sure he knew because her mother had probably already told his parents.

"Maybe you should call him."

She looked up at him confused. "Why?"

"I don't know. Might take your mind off things."

She smiled but if he knew what she thought had brought all this on he wouldn't be suggesting such a thing. She lifted a shoulder. "I'll call him when I get a chance."

As bad as she felt about cutting off Syd's calls these last couple of days, and only responding to his texts, there was so much more at stake now. The baby clasped his tiny little hand around her finger making her even more emotional. There was no way she was jinxing this.

*

As much as Angel hated knowing that Sydney had his own way of making Sarah happy, he hated seeing her sad even more. Their bond was something he'd never understand and probably never really be comfortable with but he'd do anything to see her happy. He almost hated telling her Sofia had had her baby. And he knew when Sofia had come by to visit them and see baby Angel before she went home with her baby just a day after delivering, had to be heart wrenching.

If talking or texting Sydney made her feel a little better or even distracted her for just a little while, Angel was more than willing to deal with it. But she was so obsessed with counting down the hours and the days the baby went without bradys for even Syd. So when Sydney finally showed up at the hospital days later Angel was strangely relieved to see him. "Hey, man. Thanks for coming."

Sydney shook his hand and slapped him on the shoulder. "You kidding me? I'm dying to meet little Angel. I hear he's almost ready to go."

"Yeah, he's gone five days now without his heart rate slowing down. If he can go five more, he's out of here."

Sarah was even more of mess now. Every day that went by she worried it would happen again and they'd have to start the countdown all over again. Though she'd also confessed that she was a little afraid of being home alone with him but the day they could take him home would be the happiest of her life. Just that morning she sort of snapped at him when he saw her massaging the baby's chest and he happened to comment that she didn't need to do that unless his heartbeat slowed. "It's not hurting him if I do. And there's nothing wrong with making sure he stays stimulated."

It wasn't necessarily a snap but he'd certainly heard the attitude. He knew she was just on edge and he wanted nothing more than to find a way to help her relax.

He walked Syd through the motions of scrubbing down before entering the NICU. Since little Angel was breathing on his own and feeding regularly on his own he no longer had as many tubes on him. Except for the wires monitoring his breathing he was almost wire free.

Isabel was holding the baby when they walked in. Romero knelt down next to her smiling as the baby squeezed his fingers. To say Sarah was surprised to see Sydney when they walked in was an understatement. Angel didn't now what to make of it. At first she looked almost horrified then she brought her hands to her face and finally she did what he was hoping Sydney's presence would do, she smiled.

"Hey, Lynni."

She glanced at Angel a little hesitantly but Angel smiled and she hugged him. Romero gave Angel a look. Angel didn't expect Romero to understand although he was sure if Romero was in his position he just might do the same. Sarah's happiness came before anything to him. Even if it meant him having to endure seeing her happy to see another man. So be it. He knew what he and Sarah had and he was done feeling insecure about Syd. He knew now no matter how long he and Sarah were married he'd never like her relationship with Syd, but he could deal with it—for Sarah.

Syd was only able to stay for the day and left the next afternoon. Not that Angel was too broken up about it, especially after that first night he said he was beat and was going to bed and Sarah stayed up chatting with Sydney for another hour. Angel didn't even know why he'd gone to bed. It's not as if he slept a wink until he had her safely in his arms.

Three days later the baby had gone eight full days without a brady. The morning after day eight Angel's heart dropped when his phone rang and he saw it was the hospital. They'd just finished having breakfast and were getting ready to head out to the hospital again as was their regular routine now.

Sarah stared at him, looking as terrified as he felt. The cheery voice on the other end confused him. "Are you ready to come pick up a little boy who's asking about his mommy and daddy?"

"What?" he glanced at Sarah who hung on his every word. "I don't understand. It hasn't been—"

"Oh well, the doctor was just here and after a thorough exam he was so impressed he signed off on letting him go home a couple of days early." The emotion overtook him. It felt like they'd waited an eternity for this.

The tears flooded his eyes and Sarah grabbed at his shirt. "What is it? What's wrong?"

"Nothing's wrong. Sarah... we get to bring him home today."

Her hands flew to her mouth and just like that she was crying, too. "Really?"

Angel let the hospital know they were on their way and hung up. He was done holding it in. "Really." He hugged her, picking her up and spinning her around, burying his face in her neck.

The second her feet hit the floor she was moving. "Let's go!"

CHAPTER 6
Welcome home

Sarah at in the back seat gazing at her beautiful baby boy, snug in his car seat. He was perfect. She could hardly believe he was coming home.

Angel was still muttering up front in the driver seat. "Does every one have to drive like idiots damn it?

Sarah giggled, caressing her baby's cheek. "Too many whippersnappers for you, honey?"

She watched as her usual lead-foot husband who drove like an old man now, glared out the window at the car passing them up. "The speed limit is fifty-five, asshole!"

It made her smile and stared down at her little angel. *Yeah, precious cargo will do that to you.*

Unsurprisingly, her mother, his parents and Sals's cars were there. A giant wooden stork holding a bundle was staked into his front yard. And a banner hung in front of his garage:

Welcome home baby Angel! We've been waiting for you!

Suddenly she was feeling emotional again. Their parents, Sal and Grace, holding their kids came out to meet them.

Angel's mom already had a ton of food in the kitchen. "We won't be here all day," she promised. "but everyone will be stopping by at some point today so I just wanted to make sure you had enough for all of them."

All day long people came through to welcome little

Angel home. By the time the day was over they were exhausted. They lay in bed staring at their baby in between them.

"Do we really have to put him in his crib?" Sarah asked kissing the baby's nose.

"Sal said we don't wanna start bad habits. They messed up with little man. He is still sleeping with them. But I think this guy's first night home we can make an exception."

A year and a half later

A slap to the face woke Angel. "Hey man!"

His eighteen month old son was trying to climb his face, giggling.

"Why does he always slap my face to wake me?" He turned to little Angel and flipped him over, tickling him. His son laughed uncontrollably as Angel continued to push him down every time he tried to get up. At eighteen months, even for a preemie, he already outweighed Sofia's baby girl; he wasn't walking yet, which Valerie told them she should be happy about.

"My God, little Alex started running the moment he learned to walk and there was no stopping him. He's been more of a handful then dealing with two baby girls!"

Handful or not Angel couldn't help but get excited every time he saw him pull himself up to stand holding on to some thing. They'd both learned long ago not to compare him to other babies. He was a preemie and though physically he hardly looked the part anymore he was still technically a little behind but the doctors assured them just like his weight he'd catch up and the signs were all there. He'd be walking any day now.

And he had no fear. Unlike Sofia's little Samantha who cried the moment she so much as stumbled. Little Angel could fall and tumble and he'd get right back up with a grunt and even a laugh sometimes.

"Morning, baby," Sarah said.

Little Angel stopped laughing for a second and turned to Sarah. She pulled him to her kissing his chubby little cheek. Angel watched as his son stared at Sarah with his big green eyes, reaching for her nose. Every one said he looked just like him only with Sarah's eyes. All Angel saw when he looked at his son was Sarah's eyes.

He thought back to the day he was born. How terrified they'd been about losing him. For a while there, both he and Sarah had been hesitant to even consider the thought of another baby. Neither had even talked about it, though at times he knew it made her sad to think that because of their fear little Angel might be an only child, Angel just couldn't imagine going through all that again.

They both laughed a few months ago when Valerie exhaustedly announced she was pregnant *again*. Then just a few weeks later Sarah missed her period. It was the last thing they were thinking about and since they'd had such a hard time getting pregnant the first time Sarah hadn't even bothered with birth control after having Angel.

Now they were going to find out if it was a boy or a girl. This time they wanted to know. Would they be getting bunk beds or fixing the other room to be fit for a princess?

Sarah poured herself coffee when her phone went off — a text.

Angel walked up from behind her with little Angel

in his arms and kissed her temple. Little Angel reached out and grabbed her face with his little hands. She leaned in so he could give her a big sloppy kiss on the forehead.

"Who's that, Syd?" Angel glanced at her phone. "Tell him the Cardinals are going down!"

"Ouww!" Little Angel mimicked his daddy.

"Yeah, tell 'em, son. Chargers are gonna beat their ass. They're going down!"

"Ouuww!"

Sarah laughed texting Sydney back. "I'll let him know," she said giggling.

Ever since they had the baby Syd started coming around more. He and Angel had sort of bonded during football season last year. Angel had even texted Syd a few times. Of course it was only when Syd's team was down or lost to say, "In your face!" or some other cruder remark. They weren't exactly tight and they probably never would be but this was a start and he knew it made Sarah happy.

After the ordeal they'd gone through with her first delivery, both of them couldn't really care less about the new baby's gender. All they wanted was healthy and no drama. Angel had admitted to wanting a little girl next but agreed with Sarah that healthy was first priority.

Their ride home from the doctor visit was a quiet one. The baby was sound asleep in the back seat. Angel reached for Sarah's hand. "What are you thinking about?"

Sarah rested her head against the back of her seat and turned to him. "How blessed I am."

"How blessed *we* are."

She smiled. "Growing up I could only imagine what it was like to have any siblings. Valerie said the same thing the other day and now we're both part of this huge family that seems to be growing by the minute. I can hardly believe I'll soon have two little boys to chase after."

"Is that gonna be it? Are we done after this?"

Sarah lifted her head away from the seat and turned her body toward him. "I thought you said you wanted a little princess."

"I already have one." He smiled.

Sarah smiled. "So you wouldn't wanna try for a girl?"

Since they were at a train crossing. Angel turned to her squeezing her hand. "Sweetheart, don't get me wrong. I love my son. Hell I'd give my life for him. And that other little guy on the way I already love him, too. But make no mistake about it. The day I married you my life was complete. Anything else now is just icing. Whatever makes you happy, baby. That's all I want."

Sarah smiled the tears filling her eyes and she kissed his hand. "I love you."

"I love you, too, baby."

More than she'd ever know.

Acknowledgments

First of all I'd like to thank all my *wonderful* readers from the bottom of my heart. As an author who just wanted to get her stories out there to be read, the response to my series has far exceeded even my wildest expectations. You all have made my dream of being able to do what I love for a living possible. I only hope that you continue to enjoy all of my upcoming stories. And for those of you wondering if this is the end of the Morenos, having read Sal's story I'm sure you know the answer to that. ;) 2012 will be an exciting year!

As always I have to thank my family. My husband Mark and my two teens Marky and Megan who have now become accustomed to seeing mom on many days in her pajamas the entire day in front of the computer. I thank you for your patience, understanding and trust that while it may look at times like I'm just facebooking, emailing or tweeting this is all part of my *job*!

I would also like to thank my critique partner, Tammara Webber who at this point I don't know what I'd do without. Your input, praise and highly constructive criticism are invaluable tools that I've now come to rely on. I struck gold meeting you and I look forward to continuing to work with you in all my as well as your future projects. =)

My newest beta reader Judy DeVries who began simply as a reader who enjoyed my books and has helped me enormously in finding discrepancies galore! LOL I've been so blessed to meet some of the sweetest people so willing to help during this journey of mine and Judy is just one of the newest! <3

To my editor Stephanie Lott aka Bibliophile. Thank

you so much for the time and effort you put into editing and making my work look as perfect as possible. Your eagle eyes have caught some things that even after my stories have gone through several other pairs of eyes were not caught. The pelican. Oy vey! I'm extremely grateful that you have such a keen eye and look forward to a continued professional relationship.

—

Read the rest of the books in the series:

Forever Mine – Angel and Sarah's story.
Always Been Mine – Alex and Valerie's story.
Sweet Sofie – Sofia and Eric's story.
Romero – Romero and Isabel's story.
My latest and first in my new series 5th Street **Noah** is now available as well.

What's next?

The answer to this and any questions regarding my upcoming projects can be found on my website www.ElizabethReyes.com as well as my FB fan page http://www.facebook.com/TheMorenoBrothers You can also follow me on Twitter @AuthorElizabeth Also be sure to follow The Moreno Brothers blog tour going on all through January 2012 where the "cast" of The Moreno Brothers series are already scheduled to make a few appearances. There will also be giveaways and lots of hints about upcoming projects! Visit my website for a schedule of all stops.

18817962R00262

Made in the USA
Lexington, KY
25 November 2012